Rebellion Reborn
The Metis Files: Book Three
Brian S. Leon

Rebellion Reborn
The Metis Files™: Book 3
Red Adept Publishing, LLC
104 Bugenfield Court
Garner, NC 27529
http://RedAdeptPublishing.com/

First Print Edition: July 2018

Cover Art by Streetlight Graphics

This is a work of fiction. Names, characters, places, and incidents either are the product of the author's imagination or are used fictitiously, and any resemblance to locales, events, business establishments, or actual persons—living or dead—is entirely coincidental.

To Sheryl A. K. Leon (1943-2018)

Mom, you always believed I was better looking than Duma,
wiser than Athena, stronger than Ab and more reliable than
Diomedes. Mostly you just believed I could do anything.
You will be missed, but I will see you at the gates.

Angel of the Night
Fear not the night.
Fear that which walks the night.
And I am that which walks the night.
But only evil need fear me...
and gentle souls sleep safe in their beds...
because I walk the night.
—Lt. Col. David Grossman

Chapter 1
Gretna, Louisiana, outside New Orleans, March 10, 1919

In the quiet stillness of the early morning, rats began gnawing at the back door of a small corner row house that also served as a neighborhood grocery—one of several in the largely immigrant neighborhood. Dozens of the foul rodents, some still wet from swimming in the Mississippi River just a few hundred yards away, gave off steam in the cool late-winter air as they gathered. Whatever unseen force drew them also drove them to chew just as fervently. The fusty creatures all worked as a single writhing entity, and within thirty minutes, the rodents managed to quietly bite the lower panel of the flimsy wooden door free, providing an entryway—though not for the rats. Once they ate through the wood, the mass of stinking, steaming vermin disappeared back into the night as silently as it had assembled.

A large humanoid figure—more shadow than substance—emerged from the darkness along the fence around the tiny back yard, dragging a long-handled axe over the dirt and sparse grass behind it. The shifting form silently swept up the rickety pair of stairs to the rear door and cautiously, almost reverently, placed the axe down quietly next to the door while it stooped toward the small hole created by the rats.

Silently, the figure peered through the gap left by the missing panel. It gazed into the darkened kitchen beyond for some time, listening and watching for signs of movement within. Then the figure tentatively reached a bony, clawed hand toward the door. Its long, slender fingers moved over the opening as if testing the hole before it extended an emaciated hand through the breach and, more importantly, across the tiny home's threshold. Nothing stopped it.

The figure snaked one arm inside, followed by the other. The limbs bent severely at the elbows so they would fit. The spectral figure forced its head through the small opening, then a series of sounds like muffled pops came from its torso as the creature's unnatural bulk decreased like a wadded-up newspaper. The being crawled through the hole almost like a snake, arms twisted at impossible angles to support its weight as it pulled itself through. Once inside, the figure gathered itself back to its height of nearly seven feet, rolling its head and shrugging its stooped shoulders back into position with a series of soft cracks. Then it began an aberrant convulsive stretching and twisting along its long limbs to reset the dislocated joints. Limbs reformed and functional, it reached back through the opening and retrieved the axe set just outside the door. The being's wraithlike blackness enveloped the small room like a void. Only the very edge of the recently sharpened axe-head glinted in the darkness.

The entity had emerged into a simple, spartan kitchen with a single cupboard, a large sink, and a cast-iron wood-burning stove along the wall to the right, opposite a small dining table flanked by two plain chairs. The tiny room's only other feature was a lone doorway leading to the bedroom—the small home's only other room. A clock ticked, and a muffled snore came from somewhere beyond the doorway, causing the figure to hesitate. As the soft noises continued uninterrupted, the figure silently swept through the doorway.

The bedroom was as austere as the kitchen, just large enough for a bed, a small chest of drawers, two trunks, and a rickety rocking chair at the foot of the bed. The only light came through a gap in the curtains covering a small window set high along the nearest wall and overlooking the alleyway behind the house.

In the center of the room, three people slept soundly on the iron-tester bed. A woman with an infant nestled in her left arm lay next to a man who was the source of the snoring. Mosquito netting, currently pulled back out of use, hung from the bar across the head of the bed frame.

As the dark figure's scrutiny swept from the sleeping forms and back across the room, it noticed a large crucifix on a mantel along the far wall, next to the ticking clock. Paintings depicting not only the Crucifixion but also the Virgin Mary and a praying Sister of Mercy adorned the otherwise-bare wooden walls. The figure recoiled slightly at the collective images then refocused its attention on the small family in the bed.

Standing over the woman, the monstrosity silently drew the axe overhead as far as the ceiling would allow then swung down, viciously striking the sleeping infant on the right side of her head at the neck, killing her instantly. In a continuous fluid motion, the shadowy form brought the blunt edge of the axe across to strike the woman low on the left side of her head near her ear, crushing her skull and knocking her unconscious.

The brutal blows jarred the man awake. Rousing himself, the small man saw the dark figure standing over his wife and child. He froze, blinking hard, trying to make sense of what stood across from him as abject fear gripped him.

Before the man could utter more than a sound, the shadowy figure grabbed him by the face, its skeletal fingers digging into the thin flesh of his scalp, and shoved him off the bed and back against a wall. The man, still mostly in shock, weakly and clumsily attempted to swing his fists in defense of his family, but he failed to connect as the shadowy figure somehow, impossibly, instantaneously closed the distance between them. The man tried feebly to defend himself while the creature toyed with him, batting him around like a ragdoll for a few moments. Finally, like a cat tiring of playing with its prey, it brought the butt of the axe-head down on the man's head, fracturing his skull and rendering him unconscious, though not dead. The tormented man's limp body flopped across the bed.

The continuing commotion within the small space startled the woman back to semiconsciousness. Barely lucid, she had no idea what she was seeing or even what had transpired. Terrified by what she *thought* was standing over her husband's body, she tried to scream, but the sound stuck in her throat. She watched as the shadowy image moved from the opposite side of the bed directly in front of her before she could blink. It reached an emaciated, clawed hand for her, and she froze, consumed by fear, unable to move or even utter a sound as it grabbed her head in a viselike grip and began to squeeze until her world went black.

The next morning, neighbors found the family lying on the bed in pools of their own blood. The unconscious father had collapsed over the dead body of his daughter, while the nearly comatose mother mumbled incoherently, saying her daughter's name—Mary—repeatedly. They found a bloody axe outside the kitchen door, which somehow had a small lower panel removed.

Chapter 2

I arrived at New Orleans Union Station from Chicago on the Number 8 train, the Panama Limited, on Saturday, March fifteenth, at nine in the morning. Though cool, the morning was a pleasant change from the frigid late-winter winds along Lake Michigan and far better than the winters I'd spent overseas working for Army Intelligence during the Great War.

I hadn't been to New Orleans since just after the turn of the new century, when I was chasing the rumor of an apparent murder committed by a being calling itself Comte Jacques Saint Germain, but I always liked the city. As I had during my previous visit, I wished I'd come under better circumstances. Such was my life as the immortal protector of humanity for the past three thousand years.

Exiting the station onto South Rampart Street, I could feel the slow and comfortable Southern vibe the city gave off. Just three blocks to the east, I could see the monument at Lee Circle. I still remembered when it was Tivoli Circle, before they'd dedicated it as a monument to General Robert E. Lee.

Some things in the South die hard.

Standing on the corner of Rampart and Howard, I set down my leather satchel to check the file folder I had been given by the Pinkerton field office in Chicago. I was supposed to meet Francis Deringer, a junior apprentice in the local offices, here—or rather, he was supposed to meet me.

I'd been with the Pinkertons for only a few months, but as usual, Athena—my patron and the source of my strength and immortality—pulled the strings to get me where she believed I would best serve human interests.

Despite the fact I was reasonably new to the agency, they gave me the position of special investigator and the rank of senior agent. As a one-time goddess of tactics and warfare, Athena wielded significant influence, and her organization, the Metis Foundation, had serious political pull. From what I knew of the reason I was standing in New Orleans, the locals, as usual, had no idea what plagued their city. Frankly, even though I was a week too late to celebrate it, as far as I was concerned, the whole situation was made even worse by the fact that Mardi Gras had been cancelled again this year due to the Great War.

"Uh, Mr. Ark-en-ox? The-o-filly Arkenox?" asked an unsure, slightly squeaky voice with an unmistakable Brooklyn accent.

"Ah, it's pronounced Toe-feel Ar-sen-know, but yes, that'd be me." I replied, facing the voice. "I take it you are Francis?" The name I was currently using was one I'd used the last time I lived here almost twenty years ago. It was very Acadian, or "Cajun," as the locals said. Only a very few beings knew me by my true identity, Diomedes Tydides, onetime warlord and King of Argos. But that was more than thirty lifetimes ago.

Dressed in slacks and a worn tweed sack coat over a matching waistcoat, he stood there, wringing a cap in his hands. Nothing about the kid suggested he was anything other than human—and an uptight one at that. While people could certainly cause all kinds of trouble, mortal humans were a comfort compared to what I was used to dealing with.

"Yes, sir. Sorry, sir, lemme grab your bag for you. The automobile is this way," the kid said in his thick accent, grabbing my bag and heading toward a shiny dark-green 1917 Anderson 6-40 Combination Roadster parked just up Rampart.

"Well, Mr. Deringer, it is painfully obvious that you are *not* from these parts," I said, easily falling back into my practiced Southern drawl.

"No... no, sir. I'm from Brooklyn. They just assigned me down here for me, um, my apprenticeship," the boy replied sheepishly while working to convert the car from its roadster form into a more comfortable five-seater by unfolding the rear seat.

"Ah, well, no matter," I replied, climbing into the back of the vehicle. "*Allons-y!*"

"Pardon?" he replied.

"Forgive me. It means 'let us go' in the local vernacular," I said.

"Right away, Mr. Arceneaux," he said, drawing out the name, recalling how to pronounce it properly.

The kid turned the car around on the narrow street, headed us down Howard Avenue toward Lee Circle, and veered around the monument onto Saint Charles Avenue then up toward City Hall and Lafayette Square.

"Where are we headed first, Francis?" I asked, not really caring.

"The main office. It's only a block from City Hall since we was contracted by the city to help keep an eye on the growth of the local Mafia." Taking in the sights as we drove, I found it hard to miss the significant changes taking place in the city.

We pulled into a broad alleyway next to a three-story redbrick building adorned with the ubiquitous iron lace along the porches lining the front façade for which the local architecture was known. Everything in this part of town appeared to have been built recently or was currently under construction.

"The whole third floor's ours," Francis said, beaming as he clambered out of the roadster and grabbed for my bag. "We enter around the back. Front entrance is for payin' stiffs." His enthusiasm made me grin as I followed him around the building to a set of rickety stairs.

"I was under the impression that this office dealt specifically with City Hall and Mayor Behrman rather than the public," I said in response to Francis's comment about "paying stiffs."

"This office, yeah, but they still ask us to use the back entrance to come and go," he replied. "Plus, it's safer some times. Not so public, if you get my meaning. We got a public office down in the French Quarter."

"Indeed. Safer, you say?" I asked, eyeing the dubious stairway.

Francis ignored me and began climbing without concern. We made it to the top of the poorest excuse for a wooden fire escape I had ever seen to a windowless door on the top floor. It was the only entrance onto the unstable structure. Francis dropped my bag on the narrow landing—shaking the entire structure—and removed his cap. Scratching at his head, he mumbled to himself. Finally, he nodded then knocked three times. He waited then knocked once more before trying the knob. The door opened outward, seriously decreasing the space on the tiny landing. The whole thing was clearly defensive in design. Inside the door, two men flanked the entryway, holding shotguns.

I followed Francis into a large dark office area occupied by two desks manned by a young blonde and a middle-aged brunette clacking away on typewriters. Heavy smoke from cigars and cigarettes filled the space, instantly making my eyes water and my lungs burn. There were four doors off the room—two directly behind the desks and one to either side. I couldn't identify any other entrances to *this* office.

The blond typist glanced up and smiled brightly at Francis as we walked in. Both of the secretaries were somewhat less than lookers, but they were probably great typists—especially the older brunette. The kid smiled back at the blonde, dropped my suitcase—again—and adjusted his cap as he approached her.

Francis sat on the edge of the woman's desk, and I stood in awkward silence for several seconds while Francis desperately tried to make time with the woman. Finally, bored by the whole scene, I cleared my throat—trying not to cough up a lung from the smoke—and earned a brief, reproachful scowl from the brunette. She *definitely* ran things around here.

"Excuse me, miss, but in which office might I find the agent in charge here?" I gave her my smoothest Southern accent, laying on the charm, figuring if I made friends with her, it might make my stay in New Orleans easier.

"Are you Arceneaux?" she asked while continuing her typing.

"I am he," I said, "but you may call me Theophile."

She gave me a quick once-over then went back to typing. I knew I wasn't bad looking, dressed in a new light-gray Norfolk jacket, matching slacks, and a bowler, but I insisted on wearing a full beard and mustache, which given the current time of the Red Scare, wasn't very popular. I guess I came across as too Eastern European or like a dockworker. That was what I told myself, anyway. *Whatever. I'm not here to socialize.*

"Agent Carson will be with you as soon as he arrives this morning," she said then glared at me. "You may wait here, Agent Arceneaux." She stressed my last name as she said it, clearly establishing any relationship we might have had as a working one and making it known that my presence was unwanted. *She couldn't have been clearer if she were made of glass.*

I took a seat in one of only two wooden chairs in the room. While I waited, I wondered if telling her I was a veteran of the Great War would earn me any points. American patriotism was high, based on our recent victory over the Kaiser. That information was likely in my file, though, so that was doubtful. Then I wondered, mostly maliciously, what her reaction would be if she knew I was over three millennia old and that my being here meant something truly horrible was going on in the Crescent City.

The idea made me smile, but then it caused me to refocus my attention, too. I sighed, coughing slightly. Nasty situations were my bread and butter. *And it's lunchtime once again.*

Chapter 3

Not even ten minutes later, two men came through the door—one in a serious huff while the other trailed behind with a constipated expression on his face. The man in the lead was taller than me, but leaner, with sandy-brown hair and a huge bushy mustache waxed into curls at the ends. His bright-blue eyes were ablaze even in the dark, smoky room, and he puffed a cigar as he tore through the room, tossing his derby onto one of the desks. He resembled a train steaming out of the station. The tension in the office became palpable.

The man following him wasn't much smaller, though he was much darker—Italian maybe—but he was clearly cowed by the other. He stopped at the blonde's desk, smiled wistfully at the secretary, then spoke quietly to Francis, who promptly darted out of the office with a nod and tip of his cap to the blonde. The brunette secretary stood, handed the uptight man a stack of papers, then pointed at me. The man's reaction was far from hospitable. I was beginning to resign myself to being *persona non grata* around the office when I decided that the brunette had big teeth. That made me feel slightly better for some reason.

"Agent Arceneaux?" he asked, clutching the papers to his chest like a professor carrying too much and clearly exasperated by having yet another thing to worry about.

"Call me Theophile," I replied, getting to my feet and extending my hand.

"Toe-feel? So that's how it's pronounced," he began without taking my hand. "We all assumed it was 'The-o-philly,' but then none of us are locals. Follow me."

He headed into one of the two offices behind the secretaries' desks, and I followed. The door remained open behind us. Inside the office, he dropped the stack of papers on his desk and took off his jacket, revealing a Beretta Glisenti model 1915 in a shoulder holster.

With a huge sigh, he turned to face me. "Toe-feel, was it?" He eyed me like he was about to begin a diatribe of some kind, then he abruptly stopped and stared at all the papers on his desk. "You want some coffee or something to drink?"

"No thank you," I said, noting the placard on his desk. "Agent Dioguardi, is it?"

"Um, yes, but..."

I pointed at the nameplate.

"Ah, yes. Johnny Dioguardi," he said, finally extending his hand. "Welcome to New Orleans. Well, welcome home, anyway."

I shook his hand.

"It has been a while," I replied. "Too long, in point of fact. I hear tell you boys have an issue down here."

"An issue?" His face scrunched up in confusion for a moment before he regained his composure. "Oh, yes, the murders..."

The guy clearly was a bit addlebrained. I wondered if it was normal or because of a current situation.

All of a sudden, a bellow erupted from the office next door, rattling the walls and windows. Dioguardi started then went rigid, closing his eyes and breathing deeply. Somebody was screaming at someone or something. My guess was the human train. I also guessed he was Agent in Charge Carson. I could see why Dioguardi was jumpy. It took him a few seconds to recompose himself after the outburst.

"Penelope," Dioguardi said politely through the open door to the blond secretary outside his office, "would you please get me a bicarbonate?" He sat back down heavily, thumping his chest and belching softly.

"Tell me about the murders," I said, trying to get him to refocus.

"The murders, yes." He reached into a drawer behind the desk and threw a fat folder across it at me.

The first piece of paper in the file was a typed document with New Orleans Police Evidence numbers across the top and stamped copiously with "Copy" in big red letters across it.

Hell, March 13, 1919

Editor of the Times-Picayune, New Orleans:

Esteemed Mortal:

They have never caught me, and they never will. They have never seen me, for I am invisible, even as the ether that surrounds your earth. I am not a human being, but a spirit and a fell demon from the hottest hell. I am what you Orleanians and your foolish police call the axeman.

When I see fit, I shall come and claim other victims. I alone know whom they shall be. I shall leave no clue except my bloody axe, be-smeared with blood and brains of he whom I have sent below to keep me company.

If you wish, you may tell the police to be careful not to rile me. Of course, I am a reasonable spirit. I take no offense at the way they have conducted their investigations in the past. In fact, they have been so ut-terly stupid as to not only amuse me, but His Satanic Majesty, Francis Josef, etc. But tell them to beware. Let them not try to discover what I am, for it were better that they were never born than to incur the wrath of the axeman. I don't think there is any need of such a warning, for I feel sure the police will always dodge me, as they have in the past. They are wise and know how to keep away from all harm.

Undoubtedly, you Orleanians think of me as a most horrible mur-derer, which I am, but I could be much worse if I wanted to. If I wished, I could pay a visit to your city every night. At will, I could slay thou-

sands of your best citizens, for I am in close relationship with the Angel of Death.

Now, to be exact, at 12:15 o'clock (earthly time) on next Tuesday night, I am going to pass over New Orleans. In my infinite mercy, I am going to make a little proposition to you people. Here it is:

I am very fond of jazz music, and I swear by all the devils in the nether regions that every person shall be spared in whose house a jazz band is in full swing at the time I have just mentioned. If everyone has a jazz band going, well, then, so much the better for the people. One thing is certain, and that is some of those persons who do not jazz it on Tuesday night (if there be any) will get the axe.

Well, as I am cold and crave the warmth of my native Tartarus, and as it is about time that I have left your homely earth, I will cease my discourse. Hoping that thou wilt publish this, that it may go well with thee, I have been, am, and will be the worst spirit that ever existed either in fact or realm of fancy.

The Axeman

A cold shiver shot down my spine, and I stared at Dioguardi once I'd finished.

"Yep. The *Times Picayune* got that yesterday, and the police have asked them not to publish it until tomorrow. The whole damn town is already on edge. And I mean everyone—the war, the Spanish flu, the Mob... and now this. We were brought down here to deal with the growing Mob threat, not this stuff."

"So why are the Pinkertons involved with this at all?" I asked.

"Well, so far, most of the attacks seem to have been directed at Italian grocers all around the city, and a group of police detectives thinks it's Mafia related. The mayor wants us to make sure it's not some kinda turf war developing. On the other hand, a lot of the hoodoo locals think it's actually supernatural. We're all a bunch of New York gang guys. We don't know how to deal with the local superstitions and stuff—voodoo and all that rigmarole. Home office sent us you because hopefully, *you* can give us some insight into the local perspective."

I sat quietly for a minute. The axe murder thing in the letter didn't bother me as much as the "fell demon from Tartarus" part did. *And what the hell is the whole Satanic Majesty Francis Josef about?* Either the writer was a certifiable loony or something had, in fact, escaped Tartarus and was playing Lizzy Borden with the locals. I assumed the latter, because Athena wouldn't have arranged for me to come otherwise. *Just peachy.*

Still, I needed to know what types of nonhuman creatures might be causing trouble, and the simplest source of that information would be the one human who had been in control of the city's underworld for the past few decades. If that didn't pan out, I would be forced to wander, uninvited, into all the "hoo-doo" that Dioguardi mentioned.

"I take it 'Millionaire Charlie' Matranga is still the capo here?" I asked, alluding to the man who had been the head of the Matranga crime family since the 1880s.

"Yes," he replied, "We haven't been able to identify any other active families here, so the Matrangas are it, but they are building."

"He still got his place over in the District?"

"District?" Dioguardi asked with a confused expression. "Oh, you mean Storyville. Well, the Department of the Navy officially closed Storyville a few years ago, but he still runs his place there, yeah. Why?"

"I think maybe I should go have a chat with him." I got up from my chair, hat in hand.

"We've already checked that angle pretty thoroughly. Believe me, it's a dead end. The Mob has nothing to do with it."

"Did you talk with him directly?" I asked, heading for the door.

"Of course not. We talked to our usual informants. You can't just walk right in to Matranga's place—" He tried to move out from around his desk to intercept me, but I had already cleared his office door.

I might have heard him say "wait" and "stop" before I walked out the door, but I could have just been imagining things.

Chapter 4

Storyville, or what apparently used to be called Storyville, lay just northwest of the French Quarter on the other side of Rampart Street. I remembered when, in an attempt to control the vice, the area had been designated as the city's official red-light district. Locals just referred to it as "the District," and many still considered it the unofficial home of jazz, though that distinction probably belonged to Congo Plaza a few blocks farther over.

While brothels and gambling halls had always been found throughout the city and its outlying areas, when Carlo Matranga set up his base of operations in the area, the District officially became the red-light district. His saloon was on the corner of Villere and Conti in the northwest corner of Storyville. It was early, but if I was lucky, he would be there. If I was really lucky, I might hear some of the musicians warming up for the nightly entertainment.

Matranga's place was only about fifteen or so blocks from the Pinkerton office near City Hall, so I decided to hoof it and enjoy the walk through the area that had become the city's rapidly growing downtown.

I hadn't been back in years, but I'd spent a few decades there just prior to the turn of the century and the few decades before that, back in the mid-eighteenth century. Most recently, I'd spent time east of the city, on the other side of Lake Pontchartrain, near the Honey Island Swamp. I'd worked for years to keep a growing feud between a newly established coven of Moroi vampires bent on usurping control of the region from the long-established Keitre Clan of werewolves from spilling into the human world. They'd reached a sort of détente, and I'd moved on once things calmed down. Besides, the area was too small and growing too fast for someone who didn't appear to age to stick around.

I wished I could say the smells and sights were wonderful, but in truth, the District never was the nicest part of town, and like much of New Orleans, it was falling into ruin. While there were still a few of the Creole-style mansions along Basin Street, they housed the higher-end brothels and clubs. Most of the cheaply built cribs and wooden structures hadn't fared as well over the years. I did, however, come across a few talented kids sitting on a corner, practicing to become the next Kid Ory or Jelly Roll Morton.

The streets of the District were hardly clean, but along with the moldy smell of dampness and the acrid odors of alcohol and urine, I could make out the scent of food—mostly onions, peppers, and meat—cooking for lunch. That smell took me back to earlier times. *I need to stop by Antoine's or Commander's Palace before I leave. Hell, maybe I'll stop by both of them, or the new place everyone's talking about—Galatoire's.*

I made it to the whitewashed two-story wooden structure at the corner of Villere and Conti that served as Matranga's headquarters. Its ratty white front had a single large window and an open doorway on the lower façade below a dilapidated wooden balcony. A wizened, barefooted black woman in a tattered checkered apron with a scarf around her head swept the covered front walk. She paid no attention to me as I approached. A sign over the door read Old World Social Club, the same as it had thirty years ago.

I walked in and allowed my eyes to adjust to the darkened interior. The room was open, with a simple dark wooden staircase to the second floor along the wall to my left and a well-worn wooden bar along the entire length of the rear of the building up to the stairs. The rest of the room was taken up by four large round tables. The place stank like old alcohol and tobacco smoke. A squat beefy guy stood behind the bar, poring over a stack of papers, apparently taking inventory.

"We not open yet," the guy said, his Italian accent unmistakable.

"I want to see Carlo," I said.

"Who?" he asked, glancing up at me a little too quickly to convince me he really didn't know who I was talking about.

"Your boss. Carlo 'Millionaire Charlie' Matranga, head of the Stuppagghieri here in New Orleans since he closed down the Provenzanos and killed Hennessy back in ninety," I replied, taking off my hat as I noted the layout of the space.

The guy stopped and set his paperwork down on the bar, giving me a hard once-over, as if trying to determine if I was a threat or just some wacko. I walked over to the bar in front of him, making direct eye contact. He wasn't tall, maybe five foot eight, but he was built like a bull. His forearms were massive, and his bald head rested on an equally thick neck. His right ear was cauliflowered, and he bore scar tissue around both eyes. His nose had clearly been broken more than once. Everything about him suggested boxer, and based on the scarring along his thick knuckles, maybe even bare-knuckle brawler.

"Who the hell you think you is, comin' in here an' makin' demands and accusations?" the bartender asked. "*Vaffanculo*." He tried to dismiss me with a violent wave of his hand.

"Now that's not very nice," I said, placing my derby on the counter. "What if I won't fuck off?"

"You don't leave this minute, you gonna get hurt. *Capisce*?"

"I do indeed. Do you?" I asked in return. "I said I simply want to speak with Carlo."

I didn't really expect much else, but call me an optimist. Silly me.

In a sudden blur of practiced movement, the bartender reached under the bar, pulled out a baseball bat, and tried to poke me in the chest with it. I caught the bat well before it made contact and stopped his action abruptly.

Thanks to Athena, the bartender was discovering how much faster and stronger I was than a normal human. But the bartender was a normal human being—granted one with a nasty disposition and a hair-trigger temper—but a human nonetheless, and I had to restrain myself quickly. I was sworn to protect humanity, not hurt it—even if they deserved it. And I had no doubt this guy probably deserved a good beating, probably worse.

I jerked the bat away from him. I couldn't tell if his surprised reaction was due to my catching the bat or pulling it from his hand. Either way, I snapped it in half and dropped both pieces onto the bar.

"Now let's try this again," I said in a smooth, even voice, wiping my hands as if they were dusty. "I have asked nicely to see Carlo. I can ask... less nicely... if I have to. You would rather have me ask nicely. Trust me."

The bartender's hand slowly moved toward the edge of the bar, attempting to make the movement nonchalant. I let him make his move, assuming he was going to press a buzzer to alert whoever was in the back that there was trouble up front.

Within a few seconds, a door flew open upstairs from the balcony above and behind me, and I could hear the rapid footsteps of three people. I shifted slightly so I could see both the bartender and the movement behind me. From almost directly overhead, a man aimed a shotgun over the balcony railing straight down at me. Two more men came down the stairs. One held another bat, and the other had a revolver.

"What's the problem, Frank?" asked the man with the revolver.

"This *jabone* here..." the bartender replied.

The man with the revolver looked confused. I was standing quietly at the bar, but there *was* a broken bat on the bar. When the two men reached the bottom of the stairs, the man with the bat circled around cautiously to stand a few yards behind me, probably to avoid the shotgun if it went off. The man with the revolver stayed at the bottom of the stairs. I faced him then took a few steps toward him, one hand still on the bar, the other relaxed down at my side.

"I simply want to see Carlo Matranga," I said. "That's all."

"We don't care who you wanna see, and I'm gonna tell you this just once: leave. Now," the man with the revolver said.

The gunman was just a bit taller than the bartender but much leaner. He had a narrow weasel-like face with a pencil-thin mustache and dark eyes. I could tell he knew how to use the gun. He was very calm with it and didn't wave it around like a lot of amateurs would. Behind me, the guy with the bat was a bit shorter than the bartender and built similarly, though he wasn't as thick. Probably another boxer, but definitely muscle. I didn't look up to see the shotgunner, but I knew exactly where he was, and the constant shuffling of his feet suggested he was nervous. Even the bartender took a few steps back and away from the potential blast area.

"I come peacefully," I said.

The moment I made the statement, the gunman tipped his head at the guy with the bat then toward me without ever taking his eyes off me. The hitter swung the bat low at my knees. Clearly, these guys didn't see me as a major threat and just wanted to injure, scare, and send me on my way—limping but alive. I moved so fast toward the man with the revolver that the bat just whiffed through the air. I grabbed a piece of the broken bat off the bar and hurled it straight up toward the shotgunner, unconcerned about aiming it well since he was already nervous.

I closed to within inches of the gunman and grabbed him by his throat. The broken piece of bat went sailing upward, past the shotgunner leaning over the balcony, causing him to jerk backward even though it passed nowhere near him. He fired into the ceiling, debris fell on the bar, and the bartender ducked. Then the broken piece of bat I'd tossed hit the floor, causing the other muscleman to flinch backward as well.

I kept the gunman upright, pressed close to his face, and squarely met his gaze. I could tell he was caught off guard only slightly by what had just transpired when our eyes locked. I could feel him tense ever so slightly just before he tried to raise his gun, but again, I caught his arm at the wrist with my free hand before he could move an inch.

"Wha... what are you..." the gunman asked, struggling to speak because of my grip on his throat.

"Just a concerned citizen hoping to find a way to stop all these axe murders," I said. "Used to be nothing happened in this town without Carlo knowing about it, and I'm betting he knows something about this mess, human or otherwise. I'll bet you even carry silver bullets for that pistol of yours, don't you?"

"We ain't got nothin' to do with them murders," the gunman replied defiantly.

I smiled. "I'm sure, but I want to know what Carlo knows about them anyway."

"Then I suggest we talk in my office," said a deep voice from upstairs. "Let him pass before you guys destroy the place."

Suddenly, the entire atmosphere around me relaxed, and I released my grip on the gunman's throat. He wheezed and sucked in air. I gave him a long, hard stare and sneered before I moved away from him, though. It was a bit of a pissing contest, but I had to let him know that we both knew I was better than him. It would keep him in check in the future. I backed off slowly, straightened my coat, grabbed my hat off the bar, dusted the ceiling debris off it, and headed up the stairs.

Chapter 5

Carlo was just like I remembered him, except much older. His thick hair had turned silver, as had his mustache, which he wore thinner than he had the last time I'd seen him. His face was gaunt and his skin sallow. He leaned hard on a cane and moved slowly, but I could still see the juggernaut in his eyes—the man who had taken over the city and waged war against anyone who challenged him, including the police.

This floor had five doors, and Matranga stood outside the only open one. I guessed the others led to rooms used for *nongambling* activities. I followed Matranga into his office, which was little more than a tiny windowless storeroom lit by a single smoky oil lamp. A closed ledger book lay in the middle of an ancient stained and worn desk that stood alongside numerous crates of liquor.

Carlo carefully slid around the desk and sat down heavily in an old chair. There was no place for me to sit, so I just stood in front of him. He clearly wasn't used to entertaining guests in his office, but I could see stains all over the rough pine floors. Blood or booze. Probably a bit of both.

"So, you want to know what I know about the Axeman?" he asked, rolling his hand a bit.

I nodded.

"Why should I tell you anything?"

"This is your city, no?" I replied. "I'm simply trying to help."

"Who *are* you?" He emphasized the word as if to question my capabilities in this endeavor.

"I'm with the Pinkertons," I said matter-of-factly.

"Bah. Who are you really?" He stared at me coldly. "You are not one of the filthy *kukuthi* or *lugat* that defile the city."

I was surprised by his using terms Albanians used for vampires, but then I realized he must be an Arbëreshë Sicilian—an ethnic group from Albania that settled in Sicily.

"I am human," I replied, smiling.

"Maybe, but not simply." He glared at me harder, his bushy gray eyebrows hooding his dark eyes below his creased forehead.

He was clearly an intelligent man, which explained why he'd been able to maintain control for the past forty years. I smiled briefly back at him, acknowledging his statement and, at the same time, letting him know I did not intend to discuss it further.

"What can you tell me about the Axeman?" I asked.

"These murders have not been done by anyone in my employ or within *mi Familia*," he said, sitting back a bit farther in his chair. "Honestly, I don't know *what* is behind the attacks, but I think maybe the Obeah priestess and her followers might be right."

"Oh, and what do they think it is?" I asked, slightly surprised.

"A spirit or maybe even a demon." He made a quick and loose sign of a cross over his chest as he said it. "Two of the groceries that have been hit are mine, and my men have been searching for the *figlio di puttana* for weeks. They have found nothing, just like the police. It's bad enough those damn vampires are pushin' in again and all that Obeah crap we gotta deal with, but now..." He flipped one hand in an absent gesture and shook his head in disgust.

Unfortunately, that was exactly the response I had expected but hoped I wouldn't hear. An axe murder was definitely one major way of sending a serious message to rival gangs. It was brutal and merciless. But if the murderer was human, the Matranga Family was either behind it or knew who was—unless it was a truly random nut. *If only.*

"If you hear anything, or if your men find anything, let me know," I said. "If it's what the others think it is, then you should keep your men away from it. You can reach me through the Pinkerton office next to City Hall. Name's Arceneaux. For now, I suggest you plan a jazz party for Tuesday night."

Matranga eyed me sideways as the crease on his forehead deepened, clearly not understanding my jazz party comment, then he let out a defiant chuff. I left, enduring the stares of Matranga's men, especially the gunman, as I descended the stairs. None of them moved as I walked out.

I strolled back into the midday sunshine and back to the Pinkerton office to get my bag and settle in before I went knocking on the doors of every Vodou practitioner in the city and surrounding areas. And while I would much rather have cut the heads off the local vampire inhabitants than talk to them, I at least had to determine guilt before I did anything to rekindle a war with the parasites.

Wandering into the local occult scene would be the trickier task. I had no idea who sat atop the local Obeah and Vodou community these days. Before and after the War Between the States, I'd known Marie Laveau and her daughter, Marie Laveau II, the self-proclaimed Voodoo Queens of New Orleans. The original Laveau was a witcher—a witch or wizard who learned to use magic rather than being born with the innate ability. And she'd been fairly weak at it, too. She'd provided simple charms and cures, which served to inspire fear and respect, especially among the servants around the city. In reality, what she'd lacked in magical abilities, she made up for with a massive network of informants around the region, giving her the *illusion* of supernaturally knowing all sorts of private information.

In truth, she'd been a benefactor to many of the unfortunate and poor within the city, and I couldn't think of a single evil deed attributed to her or her daughter. At times, they might have been dishonest and conniving but never intentionally malicious. The Hermetic

Order of the Golden Dawn, the group that governed and policed magic use among humans, had allowed Laveau and her daughter to practice without interference, mostly because they viewed them as harmless and doing more good than harm. The mother had such a wide following that her influence kept other practitioners with less-than-decent intentions at bay.

In their absence, Vodou and Obeah had run rampant throughout the region, and much of it focused on the blacker side of things. It was still so scattered and regionalized, however, that the Golden Dawn merely kept a watchful eye on it. I couldn't rely on their help because I didn't get along with them so well, either. They were always so insular, dogmatic, and slow to act. Not to mention elitist—witchers were not deemed worthy of joining the Golden Dawn. I was going to have to navigate the local occult scene entirely on my own.

Chapter 6

I got back to the office and realized I didn't know the secret club-house knock to enter, so I just decided to risk it and walk in. The door was locked, but I just twisted the knob so hard the mechanism came apart in my hand. When the door swung open just a hair, I heard all kinds of scrambling on the other side.

"Uh, it's just me—Agent Arceneaux," I said in a calm but loud voice, hoping to avoid a hail of bullets. "I forgot the special knock, and the doorknob broke off in my hand. I can slide my badge through the door if you want."

I reached into the chest pocket of my coat, pulled out my Pinkerton credentials, and held them in one hand. The scrambling on the other side of the door stopped, and everything was oddly quiet for several very long moments.

"Come on, guys. It's just me, I swear. Don't shoot."

Finally, the door swung open just enough for someone to peer through. It was Francis, staring out with wide eyes through the narrow opening between the door and the jamb. The jerks had made the kid check because they were too afraid.

"Hey, Francis, it's me," I said, relieved.

The tense expression on his face relaxed at once, and he exhaled heavily as he let the door swing open the rest of the way. I handed him the broken knob and mussed up his hair as I walked by. I gave the two armed door watchers a hard, disdainful glare and slowly shook my head as I walked past.

The heavy footfalls of someone walking with purpose echoed through the office as Agent in Charge Carson steamed toward me like a locomotive. His face was contorted into a mask of irritation and rage. *This guy is going to die of a heart attack before he hits fifty, guaranteed.* Everyone in the room went rigid, clearly bracing for the coming torrent. I was unconcerned, which only served to ratchet up Carson's intensity.

He strode up to me in front of the secretaries' desks, plucked the chewed cigar from his mouth, and placed his face inches from mine. I met his forceful stare unflinchingly, though my eyes almost started watering from his foul cigar breath. I found it hard to take any man who waxed his mustache seriously, so that didn't help my usual distaste for being told what to do. That might have been left over from when I was a king, or it was possibly just a character flaw. Either way, it was a good few seconds before I actually began paying attention to Carson's ranting.

"...tell me you walked right into Matranga's place in the District and had a little chat with him? You know how much work we've had to do to establish our network of informants in his group? That kind of cockamamie crap could jeopardize everything we've worked for, not to mention the safety of my people here—and our informants. Dioguardi told me he told you that Matranga's connection to these fuckin' murders was a damned dead end, and you went down there anyway? You can't possibly be that stupid, can you? Home Office said you were the best, really knew your stuff, but you ain't here half a damn day, and you've already fucked up."

Carson's face was past red and heading toward a bizarre shade of purple. The veins on his forehead and neck stood out like cords, and he began spitting as he screamed. He also gestured wildly with his smoldering cigar.

"Sir—" I said.

"Shut up! Don't you interrupt me when I'm talking to you..."

I tuned him out once more for another few seconds.

"...payin' attention to me when I'm talking to you?" I finally heard him ask.

"Oh... of course I am, sir," I replied, caught off guard.

"So what have you got to say for yourself, Arceneaux? Well?" he asked, the backs of his hands resting on his hips.

"Ah, well, sir, you know, I just thought it might be wise to see if Matranga himself really did know anything about these murders, assuming that he would know about all the goings-on in the city. I didn't think informants would know just what he knew or didn't know regarding these murders, you know? I thought it best to find out right from the horse's mouth, sir. You know?" I was deliberately trying to be annoying. It worked, too, because the waxed curl at the left side of Carson's mustache started twitching as he glared at me.

"I swear to God, if you've fucked up any of the groundwork we've laid or cause this office—and especially me—one more single solitary problem, no matter how insignificant, I will end you, son. You understand me? I swear I'll see to it that you never work in this business again! You got me?"

"I do indeed, sir," I said, searching over his shoulder for a clock on the wall or anything that could tell me the time.

I could have apologized just to keep things civil and make some attempt at respect, but I had bigger fish to fry, and once I was done here, I would likely never see these people again. Besides, calling me "son" hadn't endeared him any further to me. I was three thousand years older than this guy. I just had the appearance of someone in my late thirties.

Carson stuck the cigar back into the corner of his mouth and chugged off.

"And someone teach this idiot our identification knocks—and fix. That. Door!" he bellowed as he charged into his office, then he slammed his door, rattling the glass inserts around the office walls.

The tension in the room released like gas from a balloon, and everyone just stared at me. Not finding the clock, I searched the room for Francis. He was hiding next to a bank of filing cabinets.

"Ah, Francis, there you are," I said. "I need to know where you put my luggage. I would also like to check in to whatever accommodations the agency has prepared for me."

Everyone continued to gawk at me, especially Francis. However, the stares had become looks of disbelief, probably because I was unfazed by Carson's tirade. I waited calmly for Francis to begin moving. "On the jump, kid," I finally said, motioning toward the door.

We made it down to the car and to the Hotel De Soto on Poydras Street, just two blocks north of City Hall, without a word uttered between us. The area along the city's growing downtown corridor had been nothing but swamp more than a hundred years ago, infested by newly arrived French vampires fighting for control. Then, it'd been known as the Faubourg Saint Marie, and Poydras had been little more than a canal. Times were changing faster than ever in my long life.

The De Soto was opulent, but its previous incarnation, Hotel New Denechaud, had been considered by many to be the finest hotel in the country. I'd never had the opportunity to stay at Hotel New Denechaud, built in 1907, but the De Soto's splendor was over the top. Its brightly lit grand lobby was festooned with huge crystal chandeliers, lavish furniture, and other ornate finishings—including a harpist. Though electric lights were nothing new in 1919, the hotel, built more than a decade earlier, was one of the first hotels to have been built with them. I was impressed that the Pinkertons would put me up in such a lavish place.

Francis hadn't said a word on the short drive over or during check-in, though he seemed to consider then think better of it on several occasions. Finally, as I headed to the elevators—the first hydraulic elevators in New Orleans—Francis spoke.

"Uh, Mr. Arceneaux," he said, carefully pronouncing the name, "mind if I ask you something?"

"Of course, Francis. Ask away."

"Did you really confront Matranga at his place? I mean, directly?" he asked sheepishly.

"Yes."

The kid's Adam's apple bobbed as he gulped audibly. "I been told we only observe and report. We never interact with the main elements of the Black Hand here in New Orleans. Not just for safety, but so they don't realize we're watchin' 'em. We're only supposed to talk with our informants, and only in a secure location, following special, um... whatcha call... ah, protocols," he said, practically vomiting it all out in one breath.

"Is there a question in there somewhere?"

"Well, I'm just an apprentice, so I'm tryin' to learn the ropes—"

"Ah, I see," I said. "If that's what we're taught as fledgling detectives, then why would I do something so manifestly opposite? The simple answer is this: sometimes you go with your gut. Understand?"

"No, not at all. Especially when the boss screams at you for doin' it," he replied, astonished.

"Well, you'll get it one day," I said, clapping him on the shoulder just as the elevator doors opened.

The operator, largely ornamental in the hydraulic cars, nodded me in. I grabbed the brim of my bowler, nodded at Francis, and stepped inside.

Chapter 7

After a short rest, I headed back out into the brisk evening air and straight for the French Quarter—or what the locals called "the Quarters." I was hoping to find food and locate someone in the local Vodou community that could help me. The people telling fortunes, reading palms, and selling trinkets and supposed potions around the French Quarter were largely charlatans, but with luck, I would find one with a legitimate connection to the practice. True believers would never whore themselves or their beliefs out to tourists and gawkers.

I walked past a few self-proclaimed Vodou practitioners selling gris-gris, charms, and other items—all supposedly for protection—on the sidewalk between Jackson Square and Saint Louis Cathedral as people filed into the cathedral for Saturday-evening mass. Neither the items nor the people selling them had even the slightest aura of magic about them. In fact, I hadn't seen as much as a single mote of energy from the various street vendors—until I noticed a young black woman trying to pass quickly and unnoticed into the cathedral from Pirates Alley alongside the church. Her aura suggested she had significant magical capabilities, whether she knew it or not. I followed the crowd in, located the woman, and sat several pews behind her.

Saint Louis Cathedral had been completely restored inside after a bombing in 1909, the Hurricane of 1915, and the foundation collapse in 1916. It'd been reopened for almost two years, though I hadn't been inside it for almost two decades. They had apparently decided not to update it much during the restoration.

The sanctuary was crowded, and worry and fear were evident on many of the faces as the priest led Mass. The young woman sat through about ten minutes of the service, shifting nervously in the pew the entire time. Just after the priest finished the Penitential Rites, the woman moved quietly to a large votive candle–covered altar along the left side of the sanctuary in front of the pews and beneath a statue of Saint Mary. She knelt, lit a candle, and bowed her head in prayer for ten long minutes. Then she crossed herself, got up, and quickly walked toward the main doors to leave. I followed at a distance.

Once outside, she ducked back down Pirates Alley, headed toward Royal Street, and turned right. She made her way quickly up Royal, working her way into a quieter area just outside the French Quarter until she got to Barracks Street, then headed left. Foot traffic was all but nonexistent, so I had to follow at a greater distance than I would have liked. By the time I rounded the corner, she was gone.

Barracks was lined with slightly better-kept but typical Creole townhouse-type architecture common throughout the French Quarter. The brick facades were a mix of Greek revival, Art Nouveau, Art Deco, Renaissance Colonial, and even Gothic architecture, but they all featured balconies with the ubiquitous iron-lace railings, along with arched passageways and arcades surrounding an inner courtyard below. The woman likely worked as a maid, cook, or nanny in one of the nicer homes along the street.

I took off my hat and brushed my hair back out of frustration before continuing down Barracks Street, just in case I might spot her or catch a glimpse of her aura again. I'd made it about halfway down the street when I sensed I was no longer alone. It wasn't a malevolent feeling so much as a gut feeling that suggested the presence of others. I stopped in the middle of the street and took in my surroundings.

A young black man holding an axe handle emerged from the shadows behind me, while another stepped out of an archway across the street next to the young woman. Her magical aura pulsed slightly brighter as the sun began to disappear behind buildings.

"Hang on, fellows," I said holding my hands up to show I was unarmed. "No need for trouble here." I knew they wouldn't attack a white man willy-nilly, but I needed them to know I really did mean them no harm. The Civil War may have ended, but this was still the Deep South. "I simply wanted to talk with the young woman." I gestured toward her. "I am a special investigator for the Pinkerton National Detective Agency, and I was hoping she might be able to help me."

I slowly reached into my coat and withdrew my badge, holding my free hand up while trying to maintain eye contact with the young woman. The young man behind me circled around then leaned in a bit to get a better view of my badge in the failing light. No one else moved or said anything.

"Miss, are you a priestess?" I asked.

She started a bit, and both men gave her furtive glances. "If you are, I can really use your help. I need *real* help, not from those fakes back at the Square," I said, pointing back toward Jackson Square. "I swear I mean you no harm. Your friends can stay with you."

The three just glanced back and forth at each other.

"It's about the Axeman..." I said.

They all froze.

"I ain't no priestess," the young woman said after a long moment, her voice quavering.

"Oh, please forgive me, but you have a very strong aura of magical ability about you. I mistakenly assumed—"

"My momma, she a priestess," she said, interrupting me with a bit more force and confidence.

"Ah, well, I can tell you will follow in her footsteps someday," I replied, bowing my head slightly. "May I request an audience with your mother, then? As I say, I very much would like her help with my investigation."

"You say you with dem de-tectives?" she asked. "'Cause you don't look... right."

She could probably sense my connection with Athena but had no idea what it was or what to make of its mark on me. I smiled. She was going to be a very powerful witch.

"You ain't one a them vampahyuhs, and you ain't no lou-garou, neither..." Intrigued, she took a few steps into the street toward me, continuing to study me. The young man closest to her tried to grab her arm as she stepped closer to me, but she shook him off. He reluctantly fell in step right behind her.

"I am a Guardian," I said, bowing slightly at the waist without breaking eye contact. "A protector of humanity and Athena's Champion here on Earth. You would know my benefactor as Lady Oya. And I need your help to defeat the evil that stalks this city."

She eyed me cautiously for several long minutes, walking back and forth in front of me before finally taking several more steps toward me. Her aura pulsed brightly in a myriad of colors while tendrils of it cautiously reached toward me as if trying to gauge me.

"You really think you can kill that ting?" she asked skeptically.

"If I know what it is and can prepare properly, I do indeed," I replied. "That is why I require you, or actually your mother's, help."

She nodded as I spoke. A few thoughtful moments later, she spoke again. "I'll talk to her and get you a audience," she said confidently. "She'll send someone for you when she ready."

"Thank you," I replied. "I'm staying—"

"You who you say, she find you. If you lyin', she know that too." Then she walked back into the archway behind her.

The men followed, though one kept watch until the carriageway door was closed and latched.

Walking back toward the French Quarter, I was mulling over what my next move should be when a smell hit me. It wasn't exactly appetizing in the strictest sense, but the aromas of the meats in the butcher's market and the French Market just a few blocks farther down and closer to the river reminded me how hungry I was. I decided to head back toward Canal Street to find some food.

As I walked past the decaying facades of what used to be a vibrant part of town, past the Café Du Monde and the Morning Call coffee halls, the smell of Creole cooking assaulted my nose, sending my stomach into spasms. At the corner of Madison and Decatur, right where Madame Begue's breakfast house used to be, was a big sign for Tujague's. The last time I was in New Orleans, the restaurant owned by Guillame Tujague was farther up the block, and it was famous for its shrimp remoulade. It used to be a lunch spot for all the dockworkers across the street, but the simple food was always excellent. Shrimp remoulade sounded good to me.

Once inside, I could see the place still had the same feel of Madame Begue's, but the new owners had kept Guillame's recipes going. I ordered the remoulade and brisket that made the place famous. I feasted then lingered over the dinner, reminiscing to myself about time spent here and ruminating about the current decaying state of the Vieux Carre.

Through one of the large windows at the front of the restaurant, I noticed a man standing across the street, watching me. He was dressed in simple trousers held up by suspenders over a white shirt with the sleeves rolled up, wearing a newsboy hat. He ducked his head and moved smoothly down the street and out of sight. *Too* smoothly. His movement suggested he was not human. Not anymore, anyway. Languid but deliberate, he moved like one of the local Moroi—parasites that consumed energy rather than blood, like their

Strigoi brethren. While they still retained most of the human form and could die of old age—after maybe a few hundred years—the Moroi were still just another pest feeding off humanity.

I paid my bill and walked outside, glancing both ways along the street, then I headed toward Jackson Square at a slow, unhurried pace, pretending to enjoy a leisurely stroll. Given the current state of the French Quarter, I seriously doubted anyone would enjoy a slow walk through the area anymore. Sauntering would allow me to notice anyone following me, and the slow pace might just annoy an inhuman creature into exposing themselves or acting rashly.

I milked it for all it was worth, taking a good fifteen minutes to walk the few blocks down Decatur to Jackson Square then another twenty to take an unhurried stroll around the park—apparently the only part of the French Quarter still resembling its former splendor.

At nearly ten in the evening, a few vendors were still trying to hawk their wares and trinkets on the promenade between the park and Saint Louis Cathedral. And one old organ-grinder had nodded off while leaning on his street organ. Thankfully, the raucous machine was silent. No other patrons were on the street, but I could hear noise from beyond the cathedral coming from Royal and Bourbon Streets. I walked back through the park toward the river, hoping the isolation would reveal my shadow.

As I approached the park's gate on Decatur, the figure I'd seen outside Tujague's stood straight across from me on the other side of the street. He might have been in his early twenties, and he had dark hair and smooth skin like fine porcelain, made even more unnatural by the moonlight. He nodded when I noticed him, tipped his cap slightly in acknowledgment, and grinned at me in a way that just pissed me off even more.

Moroi were preternaturally fast, some faster than me, which made them ridiculously quick by human standards. Still, when it came to hand-to-hand combat with supernatural or nonhuman creatures, I had long ago learned that they tended to be used to dealing with normal, slow humans.

I bolted toward the vampire, mostly intending to send a message, not kill him. In the blink of an eye it took me to close the distance, he didn't move. As I closed, I swung with all the force of my momentum and every ounce of strength I had, but the bastard simply reached up and caught my fist before I could connect. His shit-eating grin widened at his achievement, and without missing a beat, I shifted to Plan B. I rammed the crown of my head right into his nose with a satisfying crunch of both teeth and bone. It hurt like hell and caused me to stagger back slightly, but the blow, clearly unexpected after the creature caught my fist, knocked him straight on his keister.

I reached up to rub my head and found a part of a tooth embedded just above my hairline. I pulled it free and wiped a bit of blood from my forehead before throwing the tooth fragment at the stunned vampire. He was nursing his face with both hands, as if trying to hold something from leaking out. I could see the pale-pink liquid that passed for Moroi blood leaking between his fingers.

In my burst across the street, my bowler had come off, so I retrieved it, dusted it off, and returned it to my head somewhat painfully. I faced my shadow, who wasn't quite so smug anymore, then pulled a handkerchief from my pocket and tossed it down to him.

"So why are you following me?" I asked, removing my bowler to run my hand over my head again. My hair was wet with blood, but I wasn't going to let him know that.

"Doleac's orders," he said through his hands and my handkerchief.

The only movement along the street came from the coffee shops back to our left, Jax Brewery far to our right, and from the dockworkers along the river on the other side of the levee behind us. No one would be concerned with us.

I grabbed his arm and hauled him back to his feet. His eyes had turned a solid black rather than the white with black irises and pupils they normally showed when trying to blend in. It meant he was likely using his energy to repair his injuries. I had half a mind to pop him again.

"Why does the head of the Dulac Coven want me followed here? We agreed you guys would stay on the North Shore after that whole war with the Keitre Clan." I couldn't help but think I should have killed Doleac rather than broker a truce, but it would have started an even larger war that humans could not have avoided.

"He assumes you're here checking into the murders, and I was supposed to watch and make sure none of our interests within the city were threatened," he said, wiping at his nose. "He also said that if we crossed paths directly to assure you that we have nothing to do with it."

He reached out with the handkerchief as if to hand it back to me, but as I reached for it, he threw it to the ground. He grinned at me, revealing broken teeth under a nose that, while crooked, should have looked much worse. He was healing fast, which meant he was using up a lot of energy, and that meant he would need to feed. Soon. And I didn't like any creature using humans as a food source.

"Tell Doleac if he has nothing to do with this, then the Dulac Coven is of no interest to me and I will honor the amity we struck. If I find otherwise…" I tried to give him my most intense glare.

My vampire shadow spit a gobbet of pinkish goo on the ground at my feet then began walking away.

"Oh, and if you leave a single person with so much as an achy feeling tonight, I will hunt you down and chop off every protruding part of your anatomy and feed them to the alligators."

I ran my hand under my hat again. *Damn scalp wounds bleed profusely. And it hurts, too.*

Chapter 8

I spent all of Sunday with Francis, visiting the different locations of the previous attacks attributed to the Axeman and going over the scant information the police had managed to collect and assemble into their pathetic reports. That afternoon, we were going to a coroner's jury at the Cortimiglia house—the site of the most recent attack. I read aloud as Francis drove us around town, just in case he could add anything not in the reports.

"According to these files, to date, a total of five attacks across the city have been attributed to the so-called Axeman. The first attack occurred on May twenty-second of last year, and the most recent, the attack at the Cortimiglia residence and grocery, took place just a few days ago across the river in Gretna," I said, flipping pages. "All told, nine people have been attacked, and five have been killed, including an infant, whose parents are still hospitalized and the father on the brink of death. Several people have been arrested for a few of the attacks—one of whom is currently awaiting trial. That attack involved a hatchet and, when combined with the bizarre and obtuse testimony of one of the victims before she died, landed the case in the Axeman file as well."

I stopped for a second to see if Francis had anything he wanted to add, but he was more focused on avoiding the mule-drawn carts and the surprises they left in the middle of the street.

"From what I can tell, the incidents occurred anywhere from a few days apart to several months apart, and only two attacks occurred on the same day of the week—a Monday," I continued. "Four of the attacks occurred at the residential storefronts of neighbor-hood grocers, and six of the victims were Italian. Some locations were entered through open windows, while others had only a single small, low door panel carved out somehow. The attacks took place across the city and its surrounding communities."

"That's what it says in the file," Francis said as he swerved the Anderson around a particularly large pile of donkey crap. "The only thing that connects 'em all is they all had been bashed in the head with either hatchets or axes—though some also had other wounds from other, um... implements."

"So it seems. Apparently, the first two victims attributed to the Axeman also had their throats slit by a straight razor almost to the point of decapitation," I replied. "Interestingly, all of the weapons used were left behind, and most were owned by the victims. And even though almost all locations were ransacked, nothing of value was ever reported stolen."

"Yep, and the only descriptions they got from survivors and vic-tims before they passed all say something about a 'large, dark figure.' Spooky as shit if you ask me."

The attacks followed no pattern I could identify, but according to the police reports, the attack last August on Joe Romano had truly begun the Axeman chaos, driven in part by comments made by a re-tired detective linking these attacks to older ones from 1911. Ten-sions were higher given the recent attacks on the Cortimiglia family, and I had no doubt that they would ascend into a full-blown hysteria once the majority of citizens read the letter in the newspaper from the purported killer. I perused the files on the 1911 attacks just to be safe.

"What do you make of this stuff about these attacks in 1911?" I didn't see a connection, but maybe the kid had some unofficial scut-tlebutt.

"Ah, most of us think that's all garbage from the police," he replied. "It's like the police link to the Mafia, too. The police clearly want the Mob outta New Orleans, and since it's mostly a bunch of Guineas that are getting whacked, they just shoved it off on 'em."

Like the kid said, I was pretty sure Matranga was not lying to me about Mafia involvement. I was also reasonably certain it was not the work of any of the local Paranthropoi—those creatures or beings that lived in the shadows alongside humans.

The one overriding theme culminated with the letter, and all of it pointed to someone or some*thing* that simply wanted to instill fear into the hearts of the citizenry. *It had succeeded.* And that had all the hallmarks of the work of a Protogenoi, a being not of our world. *And exactly like a fell demon from Tartarus.*

I recalled all of my encounters with demons, including my most recent run-in with the unholy Knight Furcas in Cornwall about eighty years ago. Without exception, they thrived on fear and carnage, ultimately driving people to lose hope. Their determination of success was bizarre by human standards: They would count a victory at a single soul losing faith or doubting their beliefs after a campaign of a thousand years. If vampires were parasites, then demons would be what science had recently begun calling a "virus." They were infectious and aimed simply to spread their seeds of doubt and despair by any means—especially fear.

Francis and I drove all over the city, visiting the attack sites, but I found nothing useful beyond a few potential future targets for the Axeman out in the Lower Ninth District. In the neighborhoods where the attacks had occurred, no one would even speak with us for fear of somehow inviting the same fate.

The only thing I could tell from cursory examinations of the sites was that the thresholds—the buildup of protective energy that surrounds a home—around all of the homes involved were weak or even nonexistent. Normally, the strength of a threshold increased over time as the homes were lived in and families went about their daily routines. New homes had no thresholds, and older homes usually had solid ones. Homes that had been in the same family for generations were virtual fortresses. This buildup of energy acted as a barrier to most supernatural creatures and even some natural ones as well. Some mundane people could even sense it. People may call a home "cheery" or perhaps "forbidding," depending on whether the energy was overwhelmingly positive or negative. Many supernatural creatures could cross such barriers only with open invitations. That included demons, or even angels for that matter.

Demons in particular didn't need much of an opening for an invitation, though. Use of a spirit board, séances, seemingly harmless spiritual games, almost anything that acted as a medium to span an otherwise-uncrossable barrier.

I noted that three of the homes we visited were located on the backside of neighborhood grocery stores, which by their very nature left a wide-open threshold. The Cortimiglias' home was a grocery *and* relatively new construction. The only odd location was an apartment building in disrepair, likely with a high turnover of residents. All of my searching did give me one idea: if the attacker did indeed intend to instill fear, then I might just be able to draw it to me.

Before we headed across the river to Gretna for the coroner's jury, I had Francis drop by the *Times Picayune* so I could have them insert a note onto the editorial page for tomorrow's edition. *Maybe an invitation is just what the bastard needs.*

Francis and I eventually arrived at the Cortimiglias' home, surrounded by gawkers and reporters, and I pushed my way through the crowd to the yard around back, where the members of the jury stood around talking. The Pinkertons had arranged for me to be there, but I could tell that Sheriff Merrero, one of his deputies, Police Superintendent Mooney, and the coroner were less than thrilled by my presence. The coroner was a small, effete man named JB Fernandez, *Doctor* Fernandez, in point of fact.

Merrero pointed out the details of the scene as it had been found when his men arrived on the morning of the tenth. "Under the steps leading to the kitchen, my men discovered an axe with clumps of hair belonging to the mother, Rose Cortimiglia," he said, quickly asserting his authority. "Entrance into the home was afforded through a small panel somehow removed from the lower part of the door leading into the kitchen. It's unclear if the assailant simply reached through and unlocked the door or if he somehow crawled through the opening."

We all followed Merrero inside the small residence at the back of the store. "The place was ransacked, but my people couldn't find a single fingerprint—even on the most polished furniture," he said like a bored tour guide. "Based on recent gouges in the floor and dust patterns, almost every piece of furniture had been moved as if someone were searching for something."

We walked through the tiny house and into the small bedroom. It was like walking into a slaughterhouse. The walls and draperies were still covered with blood, as was the bed. The smell was overpowering. "My men found a small bone fragment stuck to one of the pillows amid some dried blood and material—"

"I determined that it was brain matter from the little girl," Fernandez said with detached professionalism that likely came along with his gruesome job. He had a smug expression on his face. "I would say, based on the evidence, that the woman and child were attacked there"—he gestured to the left side of the bed—"but Charles Cortimiglia fought with his assailant before being subdued and ended up back on the bed as well." By the time he finished, most of the guests were horrified by the sight and description, and they were eager to leave the cloying room behind.

As the group filed out, I noticed something sticking out from beneath the mattress. Against my instincts to walk over and lift the mattress, I got the attention of one of the deputies and surreptitiously nodded at the protrusion. It took the poor pale fellow a second to catch on, but once he realized what I was showing him, he actually discovered a total of 129 dollars stuffed beneath the mattresses, along with a small pearl-handled .38 revolver under one of the pillows—all of which had been missed during the previous investigation of the house. Both Merrero and Fernandez left the house without saying a word about the discovery.

Back out in the yard, Merrero resumed his dissertation without missing a beat. "No footprints could be found in the yard because onlookers and gawkers had trampled the ground out here so badly that nothing useful remained. We were able to determine that several boards had been stacked against the fence at one side, however, and a neighbor swore to us that this was recent and not something that had been there long."

"Clearly a case of revenge," Fernandez said. "Cortimiglia had made enemies of previous partners and other grocers, and one of them did this." The friends and neighbors gathered around to watch the proceedings all shook their heads and murmured unhappily at the statement.

"I disagree, Doctor," Police Superintendent Mooney said. "This is obviously the work of a madman. Some sort of Jack the Ripper–type lunatic, and this was just the latest of his attacks beginning back in 1911."

I had to suppress the urge to laugh at his statement. Back in the horror of the bedroom, I had noticed but kept silent about the arrangement of a crucifix and three pictures depicting Christian scenes. While they all gave the impression of having been knocked randomly into disarray, the pictures were actually all placed face-down and inverted on the floor under the spot on the wall where they'd likely hung. The crucifix on the mantel was also inverted.

Jack the Ripper–like mad man, my eye.

On the ferry back across the river and all the way back to the hotel, I was preoccupied with the implications of what all the evidence was really suggesting. A couple of times, Francis had to shout just to get my attention, and I could see the concern on his face.

"What happened back at that house, Mr. Arceneaux?" he asked me as he pulled up in front of the hotel.

"Good people were attacked, and a little girl was killed," I replied without inflection.

"Well, do you think it's revenge or the work of some lunatic, like Mooney says?" His concern sounded genuine and not just professional.

"Worse," I said, getting out of the car.

"Worse?" Francis recoiled slightly before sitting up on the back of the car seat to continue talking to me. "What could be worse than a lunatic hacking people up?"

"A fell demon from Tartarus," I replied quietly then walked into the hotel.

Before I made it to the door, Francis was standing right beside me, an expression halfway between panic and apprehension on his face.

"Mr. Arceneaux, you can't be serious. You don't really believe it was a demon, right? Just some evil person touched in the head, right?"

"You don't believe in demons?" I asked, continuing inside with the kid on my heels.

The grand lobby of the hotel was an odd place to have a conversation about demons, but anyone who overheard either wouldn't believe it, or they already believed it.

"Demons? As in angels and demons and all that?" Francis asked.

"Yes," I replied, stopping to meet his gaze.

"Well... no. But Mr. Arceneaux—"

"Not believing in demons is kind of like not believing in gravity, Francis. If it makes you feel better, fine, but that doesn't make them any less real. Whatever you do, Francis, you make sure you're someplace playing jazz at midnight tomorrow night."

I headed for the elevators, leaving a stunned Francis motionless in the middle of the lobby.

While I stood waiting in front of the polished-brass doors of the lifts, I noticed a young black man approach me in the reflection. He was small but stout and dressed like a country bumpkin trying to give the impression of a swell. His pants were way too short and revealed his naked ankles. A smoky wisp of a creature followed him like a shadow and kept entering his body and winding its way out again through his nose and mouth. I was pretty sure it was a type of Loa, an intermediary spirit common in Vodou. This one was harmless, doing little more than guide the man.

"'Scuse me, sir, but I overheard you talkin' wit' that boy a minute ago, over yonder." He pointed back toward the front entrance. "Is you Mr. Arceneaux?"

"Yes, Theophile Arceneaux. How may I be of service?"

He shook his head. "Naw, sir, I comes to bring you to see Eulalie Fazande. You met her daughter, Euprosine, in the Quarters yestadee."

"Excellent," I replied. "I shall follow your lead." I waved him on with a flourish of my hand.

Chapter 9

I followed the messenger to Canal Street, where a donkey-drawn cart sat illuminated by the glowing lights of the businesses along the street and the gas lamps at the corners. A young black man waited impatiently at the reins. As we approached the cart, the Loa streamed from my escort to the driver out to the donkey and back.

It was nearly ten on a Sunday night, so no one except a couple of beat cops and a few other people were out. The few locals we did see were moving purposefully and with haste, as if afraid of being out. My guess was the letter published in the newspaper had sent most good citizens over the edge. Even my two companions acted anxious.

We rode all the way up Canal, through Greenwood Cemetery, and up to Metairie Road. We followed that west for some time. The city faded away almost the minute we passed through the well-manicured land of the New Orleans Country Club, and the landscape became entirely rural as we passed the stone mausoleums in Metairie Cemetery. We turned down several dirt roads, where the area's natural swampland became pristine, and the incessant sounds of the insects and frogs drowned out the clip-clop of the donkey's hooves on the packed ground of our path.

It was another hour before I noticed an orange hue above an area of swamp grass in front of us and smelled wood smoke and other things burning. Closer to the fire, the sounds of nature gave way to people chanting and singing, though I could make out no other instruments save drums. The Loa suddenly left us and fled into the tall grass surrounding a large clearing backed by cypress trees and swamp.

In the center of the clearing, fifty or so people were gathered around a massive bonfire, all dressed in pure white. Some of the women gyrated around the fire in a bizarre dance, made even more grotesque by the play of firelight off their white clothing. Several shirtless men stood stock-still on the edge of the fire, only the whites of their wide-open eyes showing as they spasmed from time to time in the intense heat. Another half dozen men sat around the ring of firelight, pounding on drums of various sizes, keeping time while most of the crowd chanted incoherently. Off to the right of the bonfire was a smaller fire being tended by three women—two of whom were significantly smaller than the third. All three emitted an aura so robust that their magical energy absolutely permeated *everyone* in the clearing.

Belief was a powerful thing that could generate a unique force and even give rise to entities and beings. Few humans could use that power directly, and it often corrupted the ones who could. It also acted as a beacon, attracting Old Ones from their native realms. It sustained them in the Earthly realm, and as a result, they got to play deity. Some of these beings cultivated believers and worshipers in order to generate such power to sustain themselves. Many others were benign, and some even tried to help—my benefactor Athena among them. Other would-be gods used their power to create havoc or manipulate humans. That I could not abide. I needed to speak with the priestess before I passed judgment on the intentions of this group, though.

There were no Old Ones, strong or weak, around the fire, but upon my arrival, I noticed several more wispy forms duck off into the swamp among the cypress trees. Given the nature of this gathering, I assumed they were Loa being drawn to the ceremony.

As I approached, the largest of the three women tending the smaller fire noticed me and immediately held out her arm. Everything stopped—the drumming, the chanting, and the dancing. The sudden silence was almost deafening.

The large woman screeched something in a heavily accented foreign language that I didn't understand, everyone shouted a single syllable in response, and they all focused on me. I was out of place. The woman screamed again, and the dancing and chanting resumed.

The smallest of the women from the trio approached me. She was dressed in white with a red sash around her waist and wore a simple but large white turban-like headdress. As she approached, I recognized Euprosine. She didn't smile but rather presented a serious demeanor.

"Good evening," I said, trying to be friendly.

"The Mambo want to speak with you," she said.

I followed her back to the other two women. All three were dressed similarly, but the largest—and oldest—wore a headdress decorated with feathers and small bones. Her face was painted white in the countenance of a skull. From my understanding of Vodou, that was unusual.

I took off my hat and bowed my head slightly to show her respect as she eyed me. Without saying a word, she circled me twice, stopped in front of me, and flicked a bundle of feathers and smoking grass at me three times. Something like a smile played at the corners of her mouth and also showed in her eyes, though it never fully developed. Again, she screamed something in the same unfamiliar language, and the crowd responded by becoming louder while the beat of the drums increased.

"So you is for the Lady Oya here on Earth," she said, finally smiling. "Amen!" Her shout elicited a similar cheer from the gathering. "You the one gon' help us get rid of dis demon!"

"I am here to find out what is behind these killings, yes," I said. "If it is indeed a demon, I will send it back to hell, where it belongs. But I may need your help."

The Mambo glared at me for a long time. The crowd remained silent, and the only sound was an occasional popping from the fire.

"Are these murders and attacks truly being committed by a demon?" I asked, beginning to grow impatient.

"The Loa tell me that the case, yes," she replied. "Not just any demon, but one of the Irin—Ramiel hisself."

Her words were like a hammer blow to my stomach.

"Ramiel? Are you sure?" I asked. *One of the two hundred Watchers that rebelled?* I had been under the impression they were imprisoned in Tartarus. And not the Tartarus of the myths from my youth—which exists but only in the native realm of the Old Ones—but rather the one that place was named after. My mind raced. That would mean that this Axeman wasn't just a demon. It was one of the highest of their order, imprisoned for thousands of years in a place designed to make even the most loathsome and foul creatures imaginable uncomfortable. "But the archangel Uriel guards the gates of Tartarus, along with thousands of Tartaruchi," I finally said. "How in the name of hell would something have gotten *out* of Tartarus and past *them*? The Loa have *seen* this creature?"

"Yes, and they say it weak, but gettin' stronger with the fear it create by attackin' people," she replied. "Baron Samedi talk to the spirits of those killed by the axeman, and they say it true. They were killed by a Irin."

This literally is a nightmare come to life.

"Do the Loa know where he's going to attack tomorrow night?" I asked.

"They say 'no' when I ask, but them afraid, too," the Mambo replied. "They say that's the purpose—to create fear so it can become stronger. They say it don' need to kill if all them peoples scared it gon' to."

"Do the Loa know where this Irin is right now?" I asked.

"No, and they won' go search him neither," she replied, her tone adamant.

"How can I send this thing back to hell if I can't find it?" I asked out of frustration, without really expecting an answer. My mind reeled, and my heart pounded to the beat of the drums.

"You find it," she said. "If you don', it find you... the Loa have big mouths. Tell everyt'ing in the spirit worl' Lady Oya's Warrior is here to protect the humans." She laughed hard as she said it then went back to her work around the fire.

I stood in stunned silence, unable to determine what my next step should be. The din of the crowd began to rise again, but I barely noticed. Finally, Euprosine approached me, holding something in her outstretched hand. Her presence startled me, and I jumped slightly at her touch. She smiled at me and opened her hand, offering me what she held there. It reminded me of a tiny broom. I was confused.

"For you. For protection. It keep bad juju away."

I took the small bundle of thick bristly hair tied together with a piece of red thread. "Thank you."

"Keep it with you at all time," she said then joined her mother.

All this way for a bundle of hair and a bunch of gossipy snitch spirits.

I didn't get back to the hotel until nearly dawn. The fellows on the donkey cart brought me back to the end of Canal Street, where I had to wait until the streetcar started running again. I was tired, but worse, I was frustrated. This beast, possibly a Watcher escaped from Tartarus, had threatened to attack and kill again tonight at 12:15. Knowing the when just wasn't good enough without the where. I had to hope that gossipy spirits and my little invitation in today's paper would provoke him enough to show up. *Assuming a fallen angel reads the paper anyway.*

I got back to my room, had some food brought up, then went to sleep. I needed to get some rest, because it was going to be a long night.

Chapter 10

I woke to an insistent knocking on the door. The clock on the chest of drawers showed half past two. The light streaming in through the mostly closed curtains told me it was afternoon.

Yawning, I dragged myself out of bed and pulled on a robe over my pants and undershirt. I must have been taking too long to answer, because the knocking got more insistent.

"I'm coming. I'm coming," I shouted in irritation between yawns.

Francis stood in the hall with an expression of absolute panic on his face.

"Oh... come on in, kid," I said, slightly surprised to see him, especially so anxious. "Let me clean up while you tell me what's got you so hot and bothered."

"It's the boss, Mr. Arceneaux," Francis began. "He's flipped his lid since you ain't showed up at the office this morning. Wants to know what you found out so far and what the plan is for stopping the attack tonight. I lied and tol' him you was on to somethin'."

"Well, that's not exactly a lie, Francis," I replied from the bathroom. "I am on to something, but frankly, Carson won't like what I have to say."

"So?"

"So I'm not going to tell him," I said plainly.

"Well, then there's this..." He threw an open newspaper onto the bed.

It was the editorial section of today's *Times Picayune*. I almost smiled. Apparently, my invitation *had* made it into the paper. Of course, no one but me knew I'd written the letter inviting the Axeman to come and attack me tonight and that I would leave the door open for him because I wasn't scared of him. I'd given the address as one of the grocery stores I'd noticed yesterday in the Lower Ninth Ward. That reminded me to make sure the actual residents stayed well clear tonight.

I picked the paper up to read my letter and was flabbergasted to notice at least three other such letters expressing the same sentiment with similar invitations.

Damn. Some Southerners are really hard to spook.

I glanced back at Francis, and he could tell what I'd read exasperated me. I headed back into the bathroom and stared at my reflection in the mirror for a long few minutes until Francis broke the silence.

"Mr. Arceneaux, they brought you down here to do somethin' about these murders, and Agent Carson is screamin' about things bein' all sixes and sevens since you showed—"

"Kid, I didn't say I wasn't going to do anything. I just said I'm not going to tell Carson what it is I'm going to do. As for things being all screwed up, I know exactly what I'm doing." I walked out of the bathroom smiling and winked at the kid in an attempt to relieve his anxiety a bit.

He smiled and instantly seemed to grow a bit taller. "Can I help?" he asked, suddenly enthusiastic.

"Yeah, head back to the office and tell Carson I'll be there by half past three and to have all his agents there. I'll go over my plan then."

"You got it, Mr. Arceneaux." The kid shot out of the room in a flash.

I knew what *I* was going to do, but I still had to come up with a plan to keep all the agents busy and hopefully safe. And I had to come up with an idea they would buy into.

Getting dressed in my room, I came up with a plan that was far from my best, but time was short. The only thing I could think to do was to send agents and police to as many neighborhood groceries as we could cover, with the exception of the one in the Ninth Ward. I especially needed them to cover the addresses of the other letter writers in the newspaper. And I needed them to do so very publicly. Several apocryphal accounts over the past few weeks suggested that the Axeman had been scared off before anything occurred when witnesses happened upon the scene. *Maybe they would buy that as the reasoning behind my plan.*

While I seriously doubted most of the accounts, they made some sense within the context of what I knew: a demon bent on instilling fear into a population could best achieve this surreptitiously and after the fact through rumor and innuendo. Wholesale slaughter to cover up such actions would create a situation so incredulous that people, as a whole, would have problems believing something supernatural was involved. On the other hand, sneaky, hard-to-explain attacks set the imagination to running wild, and fear galloped right along with it.

Meanwhile, I would wait—alone—at the grocery in the Lower Ninth Ward and hope the attacker took me up on my invitation. I wasn't sure if that would make me lucky or unlucky.

Walking to the Pinkerton office, I racked my brain for a better idea. My whole life, I'd been known for my tactical prowess and thoroughness, and now this. I was going to have to do the best I could and eat serious crow if I failed to stop the Axeman from killing again tonight.

I had covered two of the three blocks to the office when I got that creepy feeling I got in my gut when I was being followed. I was so tired of people and creatures popping up that I finally stopped at the corner of Poydras and Saint Charles and overtly scanned the area. Foot traffic wasn't heavy, but there were enough people to provide cover for someone who wanted to blend in. Most of the pedestrians were businessmen, bankers, lawyers, and the like, all well dressed.

A few people stood out. However, only one met my gaze—an older man with snow-white hair and a full beard that would have made Saint Nick jealous. He was leaning on a long staff, and unlike Santa Claus, this man was well built. His movements in no way showed the age I would normally associate with the color of his hair. Next to him stood a young man with the musculature of someone who had worked in a rock quarry his entire life. He was tall—easily three or four inches taller than my six feet—and had dark hair and piercing blue eyes.

The young man carried a massive leather sack over his shoulder. The two men were completely human, without any hint of a magical aura about them. The older man had the bearing of a grandfather dressed in simple but outdated clothes. The young man was dressed similarly. They were both clean, but their breeches and mid-thigh-length coats were worn and very much out of fashion. They could have passed for panhandlers, except they were too clean and fit.

The older man simply bowed his head, while the younger one just glowered at me. Neither one was the Watcher, but whoever they were, I didn't have the time to deal with them, so I moved on. Neither man followed me.

I spent the next few hours laying out my brilliant and elegant plan for the evening, nearly causing Agent in Charge Carson to have a stroke. There was much bellowing about harebrained ideas, my questionable heritage, my intelligence, and a few other things, but in the end, even Carson agreed that it was the best idea, though he'd also suggested he'd thought of it himself. *I really was slipping if that was the case.*

He invited me to head back to Chicago first thing in the morning, where he intended to inform the Home Office of my ineptitude and insubordination. Meanwhile, every Pinkerton agent in New Orleans would pair up and take a neighborhood grocery attached to a home that was not playing jazz—and especially the homes of people who'd been crazy enough to write a letter to the editor of the *Times Picayune*. Carson had already gotten a list of home grocery stores from Police Superintendent Mooney, whose men would also be patrolling those locations. I managed to convince them to leave the homes and stores, including the one listed in the editorial pages, between Saint Claude Avenue and Claiborne in the Lower Ninth Ward to me.

Immediately after the briefing, Francis approached me quietly, making sure no one was watching him. "Mr. Arceneaux, would you mind if I tag along with you?"

"Don't take this the wrong way, but you really don't want to be where I am tonight, trust me," I said then took one last glance at the map that showed the grocery stores.

"Please, Mr. Arceneaux, I swear I won't get in the way. Plus, I'm pretty handy with a gun."

"Don't hitch your wagon to me, kid. It won't do your career any good. But do me a favor, will ya? Keep this on you tonight," I said, handing him the little brush-like bundle of gris-gris Euprosine had given me. He took it with a confused expression, and I left the building.

I walked back down the fire escape and around the building, only to find the two men I'd seen earlier, sitting on a bench across the street, just outside Lafayette Square. I crossed the street and walked right up to them. The older man was reading from an ancient book while the younger one rubbed at a shiny piece of curved metal. The young man's work drew my attention, and as I watched, I realized he was polishing a poleyn—an archaic piece of armor that covered the knee.

The older man closed his book calmly, crossed himself, then kissed the book on its cover before handing it to the younger one. He put down the poleyn, opened a small leather satchel he wore across his shoulder and chest, kissed the book, then placed it into the bag. Up close, I noticed why their coats were so out of date—they were arming coats, the heavy padded garments worn underneath medieval chainmail or plate armor. These anachronisms combined with the book they treated reverently had to make them *Pugnus Dei*. Demon hunters, Soldiers of Christ, and the wrath of God on Earth.

I'd fought alongside Pugnus Dei several times, but not since the Crusades. They were devout men of implacable faith and honor. Though they specialized in demons, they fought anything on Earth that attempted to affect human free will. They would never do harm to a person—never. But when they went into battle, they fought as if the Archangels themselves stood with them. I'd witnessed two brother knights of the Order lay waste to hundreds of lesser demonic creatures with little more than a word. And while there were only a dozen of them at any given time—all named for the twelve disciples—in my experience, they always fought in pairs at least.

Every time I'd encountered them, they fought only out of need rather than desire. While our interests were occasionally somewhat aligned, the brothers of Pugnus Dei viewed me as possessed and heathen. However, I was still human, and they would not attack a human.

"Brothers," I said quietly and respectfully, not sure about their interest in me yet.

The older man rose to his feet. "Diomedes Tydides, hero of Troy and Guardian in service to Athena. It is God's will that at last we meet," he said in a pleasant enough tone with a very heavy French accent.

He held out his hand, and I took it. The grip of his heavily calloused hand was solid and firm.

"I am Justicar Brother Peter," he said, "And this is my novice, Coadjutor Frederick." He motioned to the young man next to him.

His rank of justicar told me he was one of their warriors. His title of Brother Peter, named for the disciple Christ said would be the rock of his church, suggested he was the leader of the order. The young man was likely his squire, training to be his replacement.

"Ah, forgive me. I assumed you both to be brothers," I said, "I have always seen you fight in pairs."

"True, but we don't always travel that way. We often find each other, as we are led by his will. In fact, it is his will that led us to cross your path. I am sure of it."

I knew enough to know that God exists. The one time I'd encountered Jesus, the incredible power he emanated blinded me for several hours. That was the only time Athena's gift was not able to protect me from the true nature of what I saw. Although I preferred to be more hands-on with the problems and issues of my world, I could support Jesus's message of beneficence and love to all people. That was why I could get behind Pugnus Dei, who were literally God's Fist. I didn't believe in God's providence, but it was a hell of a coincidence that a demon hunter—the very head of the Order—showed up just as I identified the problem.

"Perhaps, but if you've come to help me track down and kill whatever it is that calls itself the Axeman, then our purposes are aligned, and it is an honor to work with the Order again."

"Do you have a plan for achieving said goal?" the young man asked, his eyebrow raised.

"Well, only in the loosest sense of the word," I replied, a bit embarrassed. "Assuming the demon reads the local newspaper anyway."

I explained to them what I knew of the Axeman. I also told them that I would consider it a victory if we could just keep an attack from happening and that my plan mostly consisted of trying to provoke the Axeman into attacking me at a home connected to a grocery store.

Neither man acted surprised when I mentioned Eulalie Fazande's claim that the creature could be a Watcher escaped from Tartarus. Brother Peter just nodded as if I'd confirmed something he already knew.

"Well then, I suggest we head over to the area you mentioned and take in the environment so that we may know our surroundings come quarter past twelve," Brother Peter said, a wry grin on his face. "Just in case the perpetrator takes you up on your invitation."

Frederick hefted the massive leather sack off the ground, creating a slight metallic rattle, and we headed off toward my hotel so I could grab my gear. It took me about ten minutes to gather the small bag that contained my cuirass, my greaves and shin guards, and my swords and knives. It also held two Colt 1911s and several boxes of ammunition.

Before we left the hotel, I stopped to tell the desk clerk that some people would be coming to ask for me. I told him to show them to my room and provide them with every convenience and to charge anything they wanted to me. If the Axeman showed and I destroyed their grocery store and home in the process, it was the least I could do.

As we walked across the French Quarter and down to the riverfront toward the Lower Ninth Ward, Brother Peter explained what he knew of the Watchers imprisoned in Tartarus.

"The Watchers, or Iyrin, were originally believed to be beings we call angels sent down to watch over and protect humanity, but some of them became corrupted by jealousy, lust, and doubt," Peter said. "Some say Satan himself twisted their minds, while others say that spending so much time with humans and their emotions caused their breakdown. Either way, two hundred of them rebelled, and some even interbred with human women, giving rise not only to the

Nephilim, as legend states, but several other tainted races of quasi-human Parans—creatures like vampires among them. Some believe these fallen angels also taught humanity how to harness and manipulate energy into what we today call magic or sorcery."

"No offense, Justicar, but I've heard all this before," I replied.

"Did you know that the two hundred led by Samyaza and nineteen others, including Ramiel, were eventually captured by the Archangels and remaining loyal Watchers themselves and imprisoned in Tartarus, where it is said their imprisonment serves only to corrupt and twist them further—"

"Yes..." I said, interrupting him, hoping he would reveal something I didn't know or that might actually be helpful in killing this thing.

"Ah, but did you know that part of the punishment of imprisonment in Tartarus includes permanent exile from heaven," he said, holding up a finger.

"Wait," I replied, stopping in the middle of the street. "That I didn't know. But that would mean that *in theory*, we could actually *kill* this thing, not just send it back to its home realm."

"I do believe he understands now, Fredrick," Peter said, clapping me on the back as the pair continued walking.

That was actually a comforting idea. If—and it was a gigantic *if*—we could kill it, then we would never have to deal with it again. Of course, we were still talking about a corrupted being of incredible power, with its origins in a world we humans could never understand.

The problem was that most of what we believed was conjecture, because no one had seen the Watchers since their imprisonment hundreds of thousands of years ago. *I'm lucky like that.*

When we finally got to the small grocery store I had listed in the newspaper, I told Brother Peter and Frederick to get the lay of the land around the surrounding community while I tried to evict the residents temporarily. It was already getting dark, and many homes were crowded with people beginning to gather for the evening, undoubtedly ready to "jazz it up" past midnight. Other homes were dark and all but abandoned. There were no houses where residents were going about their lives normally.

Good.

I walked around the back of the store, along an alley, and into the small yard leading to the residential side of the structure. No sounds came from the home, but I could see the flickering orange glow of an oil lamp through the only window on this side of the building. I climbed the stoop to the door and knocked. I could hear shuffling inside and a chair scraping across the floor, but no one answered the door. I waited several minutes and had raised my hand to knock once again when the door flew open. I was staring straight down the barrel of a shotgun held by a diminutive older man in an undershirt and slacks with suspenders hanging around his waist.

My first reaction was to take the gun away from him, but I stopped myself. Instead, I backed down the stoop to the yard then introduced myself.

"Ah, excuse me," I said, slowly and deliberately opening my coat before pulling my Pinkerton badge from my jacket pocket with the thumb and forefinger of my right hand. "My name is Theophile Arceneaux, special agent with the Pinkerton Detective Agency, and I mean you no harm, I assure you."

"Pinkertons, you say?" The old man lowered the gun just enough to see past it. His accent was unmistakably old New Orleans—not quite French and definitely not Southern or Cajun. It was unique to New Orleans.

"Yes, sir, Pinkertons. And I have a proposition for you."

He eyeballed me over the top of the shotgun, and I could see the distrust on his face slowly changing to curiosity as his eyes opened a bit wider, and thick eyebrows climbed higher on his forehead. "I'm listenin'," he said.

"I require the use of your home tonight as part of our investigation into these Axeman murders."

"Yeah?" His eyes suddenly widened, and both eyebrows rose high on his forehead. More importantly, he lowered the shotgun and took his finger off the trigger.

"Yes, sir," I said, relieved. "In fact, in exchange for its use tonight, and to keep you and yours safe, the Pinkertons have reserved a room for you and your family at the Hotel De Soto on Poydras Street under my name."

"Hotel De Soto, you say?" he asked, his earlier interested expression yielding to hooded, skeptical eyes. "What are you intendin' to do to my home and store?"

"Nothing sir, nothing at all," I replied, lying through my teeth. "I will simply sit here in the dark, waiting to see if anyone shows up due to the lack of jazz music playing, as the Axeman threatened in the newspaper. If he doesn't show by quarter past midnight, I will depart, leaving your home exactly as you left it. And in truth, I doubt he will show."

"And if he shows?" The man cocked his head slightly to one side, raising the shotgun just a bit, though he kept his finger off the trigger.

"I shall endeavor to apprehend him."

"Just you, all by your lonesome?" he asked with a dry, raspy laugh that started him coughing.

"Yes, sir. The police and us Pinkertons are stretched pretty thin tonight, as you might imagine. However, there will be roving police foot patrols throughout this neighborhood from an hour before until an hour after midnight just in case."

"But you'll be in here all by yourself?" he asked again, scrunching up his wrinkled face even more.

"Yes, sir, as I said, just me inside," I said.

"That Axeman'll kill you by yourself." His tone expressed concern and doubt.

"Perhaps, but better me than you, wouldn't you say?"

"I reckon," he replied, snorting. "I got to buy my own food and drinks at the hotel?"

"No, sir, you can order anything you want, and it will all be charged to the room in my name. All you need to do is head over there right now. I understand they will have their own jazz party tonight, as well, and you and your family are welcome to attend that at no cost to you, either."

"And you'll stay back here in my home and not set foot in the store?" he said, his eyes once again reduced to slits within the folds of skin under his eyebrows.

"I will not leave your kitchen table until we are sure the threat is past, and then I will leave and close the door behind me, I swear." Trying my best to sound earnest, I fought my growing impatience.

"Pinkertons..." he said, staring hard at me. His comment was more a statement than a question, as if he were trying to convince himself.

"Yes, sir." I held out my badge again. "You can take a better look at my badge if you'd like."

"Nah. Hotel De Soto and I ain't gotta pay a thing, no matter what I want?" He shifted the shotgun to one hand and let it dangle, as if forgetting he held the weapon.

"Exactly, but you need to leave immediately so that I can get set up."

"All right, but I ain't got no family. It's just me. My daughter moved all the way over to Biloxi over in Miss'ssippi. Wife's been dead for years."

Despite his verbal agreement, it took the man a few more minutes of hemming and hawing before he finally headed out. As soon as he was gone, Justicar Brother Peter and Frederick snuck around to the door to check in with me. I was laying out my gear and pulling on my armor.

Brother Peter would wait around back, down the alley a bit, while Frederick would wait up the street around front, and they would close ranks as quickly as they could when—and if—the Axeman showed himself. Once we agreed on our plan of attack, which was basically just *attack*, they retreated out of sight.

I rechecked my cuirass to make sure it was secure, rolled up my sleeves, and pulled on my greaves. After strapping on my shin guards, I secured my swords in their scabbards on my back, like I always did. As an added measure, I shrugged into a double shoulder holster for my Colt 1911s—one under each arm—then sat and waited at the kitchen table with a deck of cards and my pocket watch.

The closer to midnight it got, the more dismayed I became. Maybe the Axeman had no intention of attacking someone who was clearly unafraid. On the other hand, if he wanted to instill fear into the locals, what better way to do that than attacking someone who had challenged him publicly in the newspaper? Still, mine hadn't been the only invitation to the Axeman. *I hoped the Loa's reputation for having big mouths was true.*

Chapter 11

I wasn't surprised by the faint noise that came from the backyard. All manner of sounds had come from the back of the house for the past hour or so—most likely caused by an assortment of nocturnal mammals. This time, however, I glanced at my watch. It was ten minutes past midnight, and I tensed involuntarily. I quietly set down the deck of cards I was playing solitaire with and focused solely on listening.

My seat at the table, while adjacent to the open door onto the yard, was behind the wall, so I couldn't see much at all. That was the price I paid so that the Axeman wouldn't see me waiting. The small wedge of the yard I could see was dark and heavily shadowed, so focusing on seeing movement was useless.

As the minutes ticked by on my pocket watch—each taking longer than the last—nothing more than a slight rustling arose from outside. Finally, as my watch clicked at quarter past, a shadow grew over the threshold of the open door.

The instant the shadow broke the threshold, a thunderous shout echoed from the yard beyond, accompanied by a light so bright that I recoiled and had to shield my eyes. Partially blinded, I pulled my swords and tried to clear the table to get to the door.

"Foul creature, you do not belong in this world," Brother Peter bellowed, his voice as clear as a church bell and nearly as loud as a cannon. "In the Holy Name of Christ the Redeemer, I will return you to your hell!"

I tossed the table and almost made it out the door, still unable to see much beyond bright lights and dark shadows. Then something struck me across the chest with the force of a train. It caught me completely unaware, throwing me the length of the small house, through a lath-and-plaster wall, and out through the wall at the front of the house. I landed hard on the small dirt area that led into the storefront. If I hadn't been wearing my cuirass, I would've been dead. As it was, I lay there, trying to catch my breath and gather my wits. In my blotchy vision, I saw a large dark, blurry form come *over* the house, followed by some sort of light-colored blur, while another lighter-colored blur approached from across the street. All three blurs took off down the street toward the river.

I tried to focus and shake the buzzing from my head as I got to my feet. I wasn't doing really well, and someone grabbed my shoulder to help steady me. The figure at my side confused me, sending me back to my days in the First Crusade in Jerusalem. I shook my head again, but the figure remained, then I realized he was also talking to me. The bulky figure wore a full white cassock with a small red crucifix in the center. A hood was pulled over his head, hiding his face, but his hands were mailed in chain, and plate armor with a sword hung at his side. *Another one of the brothers.*

I shook my head to acknowledge the help and indicate that I was okay, and the figure promptly took off down the street in the same direction the blurs had gone. As soon as I was able, I began jogging in that direction, too. By the next block, I was doing better and started to move as fast as I could, trying to follow the blurs and the Crusader. I could hear jazz music coming from practically every direction around me, but I could also hear the sounds of metal striking metal. Occasionally, flashes lit up the sky like lightning above the low buildings in front of me.

I cleared one block and immediately saw more brilliant flashes of light coming from a small park. As I closed the distance, I could see two figures cloaked in painfully brilliant white light on either side of a monstrous black form. Both of the white forms appeared to have sprouted enormous white wings that enveloped them, deflecting blows from the dark thing in the middle in a lightshow that was nearly impossible to view without squinting. With countless appendages, the massive black form in the center struck out as fast as it could move, creating a blur of movement bathed in the brilliant light. Every attack by either side was brushed aside with ease, the frenetic battle a complete standstill. As fast as the creature moved, the two glowing winged figures countered just as quickly.

I moved closer and noticed Frederick kneeling at the edge of the park, praying. I assumed one of the winged figures was Brother Peter, but the other, who I was sure was the person that had helped me, I did not know.

I pulled my swords and began to move into the park. When I got close to Frederick, he reached out and grabbed my pants leg to stop me.

"Let them wear it down," he said, screaming over the din of the battle. "The taint of fighting such a creature could kill you."

While I knew that a demon, or even an angel among other things, seen in true form, could destroy the mind of a normal mortal, I was far from normal. Among the gifts Athena granted me was the ability to see things in their true forms and a sort of psychic shield to protect my mind from what I saw. As I watched the dark form in the middle defend and attack, I could feel the greasy, thick psychic energy it exuded. The sensations were the visual equivalent of smelling rotting flesh mixed with sewage and sickness. In the midst of the blackness of the form, I caught glimpses of a face. Surprisingly, it was almost beautiful at times and grotesque at others. The more I watched, the queasier I became—like being stuck on a boat in rough seas. It might have been because I wasn't in there swinging, though.

I pulled myself away from Frederick's grasp and slowly worked my way into the blinding maelstrom. The energy was unreal. As soon as I pulled away, Frederick screamed again and pointed to the far side of the park. Movement in the darkness across the park from me caught my eye. Frederick wasn't screaming at me but at whatever was moving. His shouts distracted one of the Justicars just enough that one of the countless black appendages was able to strike him cleanly in the chest, sending him tumbling across the park like a tattered ragdoll. The ethereal wings and the light surrounding him suddenly disappeared.

The second winged figure, swinging a bardiche that glowed as though connected directly to the sun, screamed and began to move even faster, pressing the attack. Frederick rushed in from behind me, carrying a glowing battle-axe in one hand and a small buckler shield in the other.

"Stand fast, novice." Brother Peter's voice boomed from the winged figure still fighting. The voice was calm, even, and completely out of place given its source. "Creature, you cannot win," Brother Peter said matter-of-factly, almost as if its demise was a foregone conclusion. "Even if you were to best me, God will protect his children."

Suddenly, the dark form's attention shifted toward the movement at the far side of the park. I tried to see what it was through the visual chaos and thought, for the briefest moment, that it resembled Francis Deringer. I changed my direction and moved as fast as I could toward the creature's new target. I reached him just as several inky appendages merged to form a single massive cudgel, arcing down at him from above. I threw both swords up over my head in a cross and caught the blow, but it drove me to one knee without relenting. I could feel the seething hatred and violence pouring off the creature as it tried to force me to break. I held fast with every ounce of strength I had, but I knew I wouldn't be able to hold out long.

Abruptly, the creature emitted a piercing howl, and the pressure let up just enough that I could direct the massive cudgel-like appendage to the side with an impact that shook the ground. I spun around and brought my left sword down on the limb with every remaining ounce of strength I had, severing it cleanly. Again, the creature shrieked in rage and agony, then shrank to something small and birdlike before it flew away with preternatural speed. I had no desire to give chase and involuntarily fell to my knees, shaking from exhaustion.

The park and the night were dark again. The only sounds came in the form of jazz music from various houses around us. The figure I'd rushed to save was Francis, whose now-prone form lay staring into oblivion with eyes impossibly wide and a mouth agape and edged with drool and spittle as if screaming. His hands and arms were drawn up around his chest into unmoving claws, trapping a small pistol in the rigid fingers of one hand. The little bundle of gris-gris that was supposed to protect him lay on the ground next to him. He wasn't dead, but he was far from alive. His mind had been destroyed by the incomprehensible creature he'd had the misfortune of witnessing. He would never recover, stuck in a perpetual nightmare.

Staring down at the kid's form, I felt more anger than sorrow as I resolved to end his suffering before he had to endure it a moment longer. I picked up the gris-gris and drew my sword, but a hand caught me, staying my blade before I could strike. It was Brother Peter, bardiche in his other hand, helmet tucked under his arm. His coif was pushed back on his neck, revealing a worn but compassionate face. He simply shook his head.

"I know you knew him, but we will deal with this young man. You withstood the full brunt of the creature's hatred in order to defend him, Diomedes. You did the noblest thing one human can do for another."

"Lot of good it did," I said, trying to stand up.

"But you did not know his body was lost before you moved to protect him. His soul remains intact, though it is currently in torment. Frederick and I can free it and send it on its way to be with our Father in peace. Let us do that for him... for you."

It sounded good, and I wished I could believe that the kid's soul would go on to a better place—call it heaven, nirvana, or whatever. All I knew was that no one deserved to continue living in the state Francis was currently in. I couldn't bring myself to stand, so I just fell back, landing heavily on my butt. Frederick helped me back to my feet, walked me over to a bench, then returned to Brother Peter at Francis's side. They knelt over him for some time, praying, until they finally laid a cloth over his head then did the same with their fallen comrade.

I remained in New Orleans for a few months, but no other attacks occurred while I was there. Eventually, I had to attend to other matters, and the attacks resumed later that summer. By the time I was able to return, the attacks had stopped again, but not before two more people were seriously injured and one was killed. That was the last I heard of the Axeman.

Chapter 12
San Diego, California, April 2012

It was very late, I was in a foul mood, and I stank. While complete-ly functional, my shoulder still hurt from being dislocated a few months back, and deep-dropping three-pound squid jigs a thousand feet for four-foot-long Humboldt squid hadn't helped. But the year had started out odd, with the big squid hanging around in droves into the spring, so that was what we did. Clients usually liked the idea of catching the squid until they had to reel up over three hundred yards of line attached to sixty pounds of dead weight. Then I got the distinct pleasure of getting inked and squirted by what amounted to an angry fire hose. And I got to reel up the lines once my clients tired of the novelty. And we did it at night. In the cold.

I finally got myself home, pulled my truck into the garage at my house in the Roseville area of Point Loma, and began the final task of putting my gear away. Then I got that damned annoying feeling that I wasn't alone anymore. I had a heavy rod-and-reel outfit in each hand when I went to see what might be trying to sneak up on me. I didn't see anything at first, so I walked out of my garage to check up the street, thinking maybe it was just exhaustion. Again, no cars moved along the street, no people were walking past, and I didn't even hear any dogs barking. In fact, there was no noise at all, so I began walking back in to finish putting away my rods. That was when something in my brain raised an alarm.

I spun around just in time to see two freakish, long-limbed forms rush me from the bushes to my left. Without thinking, I swung the heavy two-speed reel on its rod in my right hand like a club, hitting the first creature squarely enough to feel bone crack. The force sent whatever it was flying backward into the creature behind it with a wet thud. The fiberglass-and-graphite rod designed to lift five-hundred-pound fish shattered, and the massive four-pound aluminum reel flew into pieces as I connected with the figure. I dropped the mangled rod and spun the one in my left hand so that I could grab it like a two-handed club with the heavy reel as the head.

As I stood just inside the garage, something scrabbled across the asphalt shingles on the roof above me, and I glanced up just in time to see another figure peek over the soffit at me. I swung at the figure above me, but it moved too fast. I spun the rod so that its machined-aluminum butt faced out like the tip of a spear and focused my attention on the two forms on the ground in front of me.

The creature I'd struck still lay limply on top of the one it'd collided with, which began climbing out from underneath, clearly dazed. Without hesitation, I impaled the creature repeatedly as it tried to pull itself free from its prone comrade. A warm, dark, fetid liquid exploded from the wounds like water from a water balloon. In the moonlight, the goo was shiny black, and I could see the creatures were vaguely humanoid in shape, but their limbs were disturbingly twisted and misshapen. The instant my sleep-deprived brain registered that the creatures were Strigoi, I was hit from behind hard enough to cause me to fall over the pair of bodies in front of me.

I tried to roll, but the vampire on my back grabbed my head while it clawed and scratched through the heavy cold-weather fishing garb on my torso. I reached behind me with my right hand and tried to grasp the creature, which stopped it temporarily from tearing at my jacket as it attempted to fend me off. I managed to snag some part of it and pulled with all my strength, trying to get it off me. Apparently, its hold was strong enough that all I succeeded in doing was ripping off a limb. The maimed creature let out a guttural howl and leapt off my shoulders and into the middle of the yard in front of me, then it took off in a freakish lope that reminded me of a lizard trying to run.

The two vampires at my feet were far from dead, but both were wounded so badly that they wouldn't be a real threat anytime soon, so I took the opportunity to thoroughly thrash them to a pulp, shattering bones and finally severing their heads with a pair of garden shears from my garage. *Ah, the middle of the night in the suburbs.*

Before dawn, I dragged an old fifty-five-gallon oil drum from under a tarp in my garage. I shoved aside the dead Strigoi already in there from a previous attack then stuffed the newly ruined corpses in around it. After replacing the top, I threw up from the smell. Then I hosed the dark, sticky blood off my driveway and dumped all my wrecked fishing gear into a trash can. I managed to climb into the shower just as the sun was coming up.

This damn blood feud with the Liuntika Strigoi is going to kill me if I'm not careful. This latest attempt was the third since I'd received their warning back in December. I'd trespassed on their territory in the pursuit of a legendary half-Blud Fae, half-succubus Cambion pain in the ass who framed me for killing some royal Fae muckety-mucks. I'd been lucky so far because all the attackers had been the most feral of their kind—mindless and erratic. But they were little more than fodder to soften me up.

I felt like Liver-Eating Johnson being chased by Crow Indians. The only difference was Johnson had eventually made peace with the Crow. I didn't see that happening with me and vampires. *Ever.* And I had to call someone at the Metis Foundation to come pick up that drum before the smell got worse.

Chapter 13

My ringing phone finally woke me up, and when I squinted at the clock next to my bed and realized that it was well past one in the afternoon, I was ticked. Not sure why. I just was. I stormed through my house to find my chirping cell phone, ready to rip whoever it was a new one. It stopped ringing before I could find it, severely increasing my irritation.

After I pulled all the cushions off my couch and chair but just before I began throwing the furniture itself, the phone began ringing again. I managed to track the sound back to the pile of squid-ink-stained, ammonia-scented clothes left on my bathroom floor. Again, the phone stopped ringing before I could retrieve it from the acrid mound. I pulled the phone free from the pocket of my stinking fishing pants, only to discover the screen was shattered—probably from last night's extracurricular activities on my lawn. It didn't function at all, so I had no idea who had called and no way to click through the shattered glass of the touchscreen to get to any messages. Just as I was about to throw the useless chunk of crap through my bathroom wall, it rang again, and I could just make out the edge of the green Answer tab at the bottom of the mostly black spiderwebbed screen.

"What?" I roared without concern for who it might be.

"The Metis Foundation requests an immediate meeting," someone replied in a curt tone after a few seconds of silence.

The voice was feminine but flat and even, apparently unshaken by my gruff greeting. It had to be the elf who worked for Athena at her offices in San Diego.

"Brey, is that you?" I asked, switching to a friendlier, albeit sarcastic demeanor.

She hated it when I shortened her name. I shouldn't say hated so much as *was irritated by*, but since elves had no real human emotions, it was the only way I knew to get a rise out of her. And getting anything close to an emotional response from an elf, especially Athena's right hand, Breygivila, was worth the effort and an endless source of amusement for me.

"Please be as expedient as is *humanly* possible," she replied without missing a beat.

"Sarcasm?" I said. "Really? From you? I'm flattered."

"No such sentiment was intended," she said flatly. "I merely chose to express the importance of your immediate presence in terms that even *you* would understand."

The sad part was she really didn't mean it as an insult. She was just stating what she perceived as simple fact.

"Got it," I replied. "So anytime this afternoon, then?"

"I apologize, but I believed I was being clear enough. Perhaps I should have just said, 'Please come now.'"

My plan to annoy her was backfiring. I was the one quickly getting annoyed.

"Fine. See you soon, Brey." Unable to see the End Call button, I just threw the phone against the wall to hang up. It made me feel better anyway.

Despite Brey's insistence, I took my time getting ready. I'd worked with Athena long enough to know that if it really was that urgent, my benefactor would have just showed up in my bedroom.

I hated the drive down to the Metis Foundation's offices in the East Village. I had to fight traffic and one-way streets, but no matter how many times I made the dreaded trip, the Foundation's anachronistic office always lightened my mood a bit. The building on the corner of Thirteenth and Island was out of place for a modern downtown. It reminded me of me.

The large Victorian-style mansion, with its fine gingerbread woodwork and almost garish period paint scheme, stood out like a sore thumb among the brick, concrete, glass, and steel of the surrounding neighborhood with an ultramodern baseball stadium in the background. I liked it, despite the fact that parking was always a bitch. As usual, I just blocked the cars in the small lot next to the house with my truck then walked in.

As much as I liked the building from the outside, the inside freaked me out. It was all glass and steel with minor wooden features stuck here and there to soften the industrial feel. That was what designers would've said anyway. In reality, the wood helped alleviate some of the unease of the handful of Fae employees surrounded by all the metal.

I wasn't surprised to see yet another new receptionist behind the massive wood, glass, and metal desk just inside the main door. I *was* surprised that it was a young man, though. I was dressed in jeans and a long-sleeved T-shirt under a fleece jacket—San Diego springtime garb—and completely out of place among the suits and ties. I always was, but most of the people who worked here knew me and expected nothing less.

The new guy had his hair pulled back in a tight ponytail, a heavy black beard, and clothes that were entirely too tight. Clearly uncertain what to do with me, he peered at me through heavy-rimmed black glasses that I wasn't entirely sure were prescription. He probably thought I was a maintenance worker or lost. As I headed for the stairs up to Athena's private office, he said, in an officious, nasally voice, "May I help you?"

From this angle, I could see his hair was actually pulled back into some kind of knot, and hints of tattoos peeked out from under his shirtsleeves at his wrists. This kid wouldn't last the month. Most of the receptionists didn't. Something about the vibe of the place eventually chased them off.

"I'm here to fix the plumbing," I said, hiking up my jeans then wiping my nose with the back of my hand. I added a snort for effect.

The young man actually checked his appointment book to verify my story, but before he could tell me he had no such appointment scheduled, his phone rang. He held up a hand with a single finger extended, asking me to wait one second while he attended to more important business. The moment he answered, his entire demeanor deflated, and his face became pale—or paler.

"Uh, go on up," he said sheepishly.

"You mean up them there stairs right'chere?" I asked then walked up.

The door opened before I reached the top, and I walked in to Athena's private offices, where Brey sat at a large wooden desk—just about the only wood among all the glass, which wasn't *really* glass. On this side of the not-really-glass walls, they appeared transparent, like windows, but from the outside, the walls were opaque. In reality, the walls were either magically or in some other preternatural way alive. Looking through them always gave me the heebie-jeebies because I knew they only appeared to be clear. In truth, they projected what was beyond to complete the illusion. And they did that because that was what Athena wanted them to do at the moment.

"Well, good morning, Ms. Brey..." I said, sitting on the corner of her desk.

"It is afternoon, actually," she said, continuing her work. "And I am not a miss, missus, mistress, maid, maiden, lass, or any other human term for a female since I am decidedly not human, female or otherwise, Diomedes Tydides."

"No kidding?" I replied, acting stunned. "All this time, here I just thought you were just an attractive woman with some freakish traits, you know, like pointed ears and solid green eyes. And I just assumed you had a personality-ectomy, but not being human *would* explain a lot. Especially why you never hit on me."

She finally glared at me blankly.

"You have long known I am an elf, Diomedes, so I do not understand your previous statement. I failed to find a punch line, so I can only assume it was not an attempt at humor, but rather sarcasm. Pitiable, if I may say so."

"Pitiable?" I said, standing up in mock indignation. "What's pitiable is that you wouldn't know funny if it fell on your desk and wiggled."

Just then, the only other door in the room opened. Feeling Athena's presence, I shut up. She said nothing, but I knew I was being summoned.

"C'mon, Brey, lighten up." I winked at her as I walked into Athena's office. "Oh, and can you get me a new phone? Mine somehow got broken."

Chapter 14

As usual, Athena was standing behind her desk, dressed in a custom-tailored suit that somehow drew attention away from her figure but did little actually to hide it. This one was tan. She wore her fiery-red hair in a tight braid, and the creases around her blue eyes revealed a weariness I wasn't used to seeing in her.

I knew she'd been desperately working with several countries, including the U.S. State Department, in a desperate effort to calm escalating problems in Syria that may or may not have been exacerbated by the Cambion Fae who'd tried to frame me. I was convinced that if he'd actually influenced anyone, it was simply to push Assad and others farther along the trajectories they were already on.

Thankfully, affairs of state hadn't been my concern for more than three thousand years. Plus, strictly human concerns fell outside my scope of operation. As a result, when Athena met with me, it was usually to reveal some sort of fresh hell that I needed to fix. I couldn't *wait* to find out what *this* was about.

I plopped down in one of the two chairs across from Athena's desk, spread my hands, and tilted my head.

"Have you heard of Taylon Jones?" she asked in a toneless voice.

"No. Should I have?"

"He's a young African-American man from Tohatchapee, Florida, who recently killed another man in Connecticut with an axe then ate his brain and eyes."

"Yikes." I feigned retching and contorted my face in disgust. "Sounds like he might be a bit on the crazy side. What's that have to do with me? And if you mention my dad, we're going to have issues."

Athena knew I had problems with cannibalism stemming from my father's death. She had originally offered him the chance to be a Guardian but rescinded the offer upon finding him eating the brain of a fallen enemy. My father was a hero, but he'd chosen to die in the most dishonorable way.

She squinted at me for just a second, her blue eyes sparking, then relaxed, as if offended that I would even suggest such a thing. "According to his female cousin, the man kept calling her 'Athena,' and in the transcripts of his statement, he refers to any number of my kind known from your birth era while mumbling nonsensically."

"Okay, still sounds more loony than anything else." I threw my feet up on the edge of her table and interlaced my fingers over my chest in an attempt to appear disinterested. In truth, I knew Athena would never waste my time.

"Maybe, but it has been brought to my attention that, among other things, he keeps mumbling, 'He is coming... God's wrath is finally coming.' In addition, I have information that this man was associated with a group calling themselves the Sons of Belial."

"And that's bad?" I asked, unfamiliar with the group. "Sounds like he was brainwashed by some doomsday cult."

Athena sat and laid her hands on the desk casually. "You may not be far from the truth, but supposedly, this group's main goal is to free what they see as the source of man's knowledge and wisdom—the Watchers imprisoned in Tartarus."

My mind raced back almost a hundred years to New Orleans, and I suddenly sat bolt upright in the chair. "Are you kidding me?"

All I could think about was the greasy, disgusting feeling of the creature I'd encountered in New Orleans back in 1919 and the anger

I'd felt after completely losing track of it. I also owed it one for a kid named Francis.

Athena's voice buzzed in my head like a growing alarm bell, impossible to ignore. "You will meet with Agent Wright in New York then go to Bridgeport, where you will meet with two brothers of the Holy Order," she said, her voice returning to a normal external sound as soon as I focused on her.

She stared hard at me for a few silent seconds, and my anger continued to rise. If this really had anything to do with the Watcher in New Orleans, then the last thing I wanted was for Agent Sarah Wright to be anywhere near it. I understood completely about having knights of Pugnus Dei come along. There were no better demon hunters on Earth. But as tough and capable as Sarah was, I saw no reason to expose her to such a pervasive and insidious evil.

Before I could voice my protest, Athena stopped me with a wave of her hand. "Agent Wright is going because she can give you access under the auspices of Homeland Security to a potential cannibalistic murderer while he's in police custody and because she can help you maintain your objective self so you do not think with your blades." She said the last part with enough force to make me feel as though I'd just been punched in the side of the head.

I wasn't about to say anything else after that. I just glowered and rubbed at my temples with my thumb and fingers.

"Fine," I said, indignant, then stormed out. I practically stomped past Brey, whose only response was to hold out a new phone as I passed. I snatched it without saying a word and charged down the stairs.

At the bottom of the stairs, I nearly ran over the receptionist, who was cleaning up the broken remains of a massive ceramic vase that had somehow shattered. The kid was visibly upset, mumbling about how the four-foot-tall piece had just flown into pieces.

Once I got outside and back into my truck, I pulled out my phone and dialed Sarah's number. Talk about conflicted. On one hand, I was excited to talk to her. We had recently decided to try to take our relationship forward, though slowly, and I'd just been handed an unexpected excuse to see her. On the other, I really, really, *really* didn't want her anywhere near this issue if an escaped Watcher was even remotely involved.

She answered on the fourth ring.

"Agent Wright—" she said.

"Sarah, it's me," I said, my voice a little husky from the adrenaline.

"Steve... oh, hi," she said, her voice instantly softening. "I didn't expect to hear from you until this weekend."

Her tone didn't help my nerves at all, and I had to stop to clear my throat twice before I could finally talk.

We had managed to go on a few dates over the last few weeks, though both of us were a bit afraid of the complications our relationship might produce, especially when one of us was a thirty-two-hundred-year-old troubleshooter for a *mythical* goddess. The Liuntika Strigoi blood feud further increased my trepidation. I could easily imagine them going after her to get to me, and I would not let that happen.

"Hi. So... how are you?" I asked finally.

"Busy, but good. How's your shoulder?"

"Getting there. It's mostly just sore when I overuse it now," I said, relieved by the banal conversation.

"That's great!" Her exclamation was genuine, and it made me smile, which only served to remind me further why I wanted her nowhere near the Watcher.

"I suppose the Metis Foundation has contacted you already?" I asked sheepishly.

"Why, yes. I just got an e-mail a minute ago with a request from my department head to escort several Metis Foundation specialists to question a murder suspect in Bridgeport, Connecticut," she said with only a hint of surprise in her voice and almost no sarcasm. *Almost.*

"Yeah. Listen, I know you want to help, but if I ask, would you back off this thing? After we talk to the guy, I mean."

"What? Back off what thing?" she replied, suddenly defensive.

"Nothing, nothing, just forget it," I said, trying to backtrack quickly. "The guy is probably just totally nuts. That's all."

"Probably? I'm just perusing the attached files that came with the request," she said with a snort. "There is little doubt this guy is bonkers. It says he ate the victim's eyeball and said it tasted like an oyster! *Ewww!* And you want to talk to this guy?"

"Yeah, just need to check. Circumstances are kinda odd," I said, trying to keep her curiosity from becoming further aroused.

"Good luck with that," she replied, laughing. "I hope the other guys coming with us are highly trained psychiatrists with serious meds."

"Funny," I said, trying to force a laugh. "Speaking of which, the other guys are members of a rather special ancient brotherhood—very conservative and very religious, but they are usually good guys. They don't always like me, but there's a mutual respect."

"Oh, yeah?" she said, her tone heavy with interest. "We can talk more when you get to New York. Apparently, I get in at seven tonight. Listen, I better go if I'm going to wrap up what I've been working on in time to leave today."

"Great, I'll call you when I get there."

Chapter 15

I arrived in New York's Central Park via the Telluric Pathways at just past eight. It was dark and cold, and there wasn't a single sign of anyone or any*thing* moving. The whole journey via my usual trail through the Ways took me less than fifteen minutes.

The temperature was in the low sixties back in San Diego, and it had to be fifteen degrees colder in New York. *I really need to pay better attention to where I'm headed before I jump through the Ways.*

I pulled my fleece jacket tighter around me then headed out of the park along Central Park East toward Fifth Avenue. I had all my usual gear in a big duffle thrown over my shoulder, but I was armed with one of my Dvergar knives and a single Sig Sauer P226 Navy in a holster under my left arm.

I wasn't expecting too much trouble, not even from the stinking vampires I assumed would lose track of me for at least a day when I travelled by the Ways. If I stuck around for very long, they would ascertain my whereabouts pretty quickly through informants and familiars. With luck, Sarah and I would visit the wacko tomorrow, and I would be home by tomorrow night.

Once I got to Fifth Avenue, I pulled out my cell phone and switched it back on so that I could call Sarah. Once my phone regained its signal, I got three shrill beeps indicating I had new messages—text messages, no less. They were from Sarah. She wanted to meet at a noodle shop in Greenwich Village near NYU. The cab ride from the Upper East Side took me more than thirty minutes, but at least the cab was warm. I called Sarah to let her know I was on the way. I didn't text.

The noodle shop was little more than a glass-and-steel hole in the wall along a street filled with restaurants. Sarah was sitting at the table closest to the window, so she saw me first. As usual when she was working, she was dressed in a way that made people notice her but not pay too much attention. She was wearing a black pantsuit and very little makeup, with her dark hair pulled back into a loose ponytail. As always, her piercing gray eyes caught me, though. They were pale and almost silvery, and it felt like they could see right through me when she looked at me. When she saw me, they lit up. My heart beat faster, and my hands began to sweat a bit as I walked over to her.

She stood, and I leaned in, kissed her on the cheek, then sat down, hoping I wasn't too awkward.

"So," she said seriously but with the slightest hint of a grin playing at the corner of her mouth, "why would you want me to stay out of this cannibalistic murder thing?"

I got the feeling she was fishing for a specific answer. What I wanted to say was "to keep you safe," which was probably what she wanted me to say, but it felt odd. She was a grown woman, an agent with Homeland Security, and a former member of the FBI's antiterrorism Fly Team. Not to mention the fact that she'd helped me raid a witch's lair and take her out in a supernatural shootout. Sarah was capable, to say the least.

"Well, there may be some connection to demons here—" I said, staring down at the stainless-steel tabletop.

"You mean *demon* like that guy that just tried to frame you *demon*?" Her eyebrows shot high on her forehead, and her eyes grew wide.

"Not exactly. Succubi and incubi are fairly weak demonoids, technically the offspring of a particular fallen angel. They are beholden only to themselves, and they don't seek followers, so they never get very powerful. On a scale of one to ten, they're a four at best. If our information is correct, what I'm talking about is more of an eleven or twelve," I said with a noncommittal shrug. The expression on Sarah's face made me realize that while she knew what I did, she really didn't understand the true scope of the creatures out there. Her brow knitted, her mouth opened slightly, and she began rubbing her hands together. She was horrified. "Uh, well, an eleven might be a bit of an exaggeration. Maybe a nine. Definitely a nine," I said, lying to calm her down. I avoided making eye contact with her as I said it.

"Don't lie to me about this stuff, Diomedes," she said quietly through a clenched jaw, leaning toward me, her hands flat on the table, and her gray eyes flashed silver. That she'd called me by my real name further underlined her agitation. "Look at me," she said forcefully.

I didn't. Then she reached across the table and grabbed my hand.

"Look at me," she said again. "I know who and what you are, but I need you to be honest with me about this stuff. I mean, magic and fairies are one thing, but now you're telling me that demons, like biblical demons from hell, really might be out there, too."

Her eyes were wide but full of compassion. She was right, and I was being childish.

"No *might* about it. Demons exist, but they aren't exactly what you think."

"Well, explain it to me." She sat back slightly, still holding my hand tightly.

"What people call demons vary depending on their upbringing and what they are told is evil. In my day, the term simply meant 'a powerful spirit' and in no way implied morality. The various religions, on the other hand, interpret them as debased spirits or evil creatures capable of possessing a person. Humans just lump things like that into a catch-all category. The truth is that there are very few things that I call demon, and the ones I do are fallen angels, for a lack of a better word, and their offspring."

"Fallen angels, like in the Bible?" she asked, as if struggling to make sense of what I was telling her.

"A bit, yeah. At some point in the past, way before my time, a group of Protogenoi beings was supposedly sent to Earth to watch over humans but not interfere. Some of them broke their covenant and began interacting with us. Some fell in love with various humans, some taught us things like magic and possibly even the use of fire, while others taught us things like greed and jealousy. A war began between those that wanted to interact and those that believed they should stay uninvolved. Some myths call this the War Between the Angels."

"Wait, so that stuff is not just stories they tell in Sunday school?"

"Well, not any normal Sunday school, but it is in the apocryphal books of the Bible. At any rate, two hundred of the worst of the rebellious angels—called the Watchers—were caught and placed into a prison called Tartarus. Other beings were banished to Earth for helping them, and while technically ageless, they are *mortal*. These are the lesser demons like succubi and such. The offspring of the Watchers and humans produced other demons of various strength. It's likely that Lilith, the first and most powerful of all Strigoi vampires, was one of these. Her sister Na'amah is the primordial succubus. The thing is that because of what happened, those banished to Earth resent humans and delight in causing trouble for us. Tartarus supposedly was designed to torment those imprisoned there. My concern for you is that the normal human psyche cannot survive around the worst of these creatures. Believe me when I say I've seen the results firsthand."

Sarah looked like a kid who'd just found out Santa Claus wasn't real and was trying to make sense of all the Christmases past. "So then, what kind of demon do you think is involved here?"

"*May* be involved... *May* be involved," I said, holding up my free hand in an attempt to defuse the situation a bit.

"Okay, what kind do you think *may* be involved here?" She rolled her eyes.

That was what I liked about Sarah. Even when thrown off her game, she got right back in again. It made me smile.

"Potentially one of the Watchers, maybe even one of the twenty leaders of the Watchers themselves." I shrugged like it was no big thing.

At first, Sarah had no response. Her mouth opened slightly, as if she were about to say something, but then it closed again. Finally, she said, "So you're saying the worst of the worst kind of demons is involved in this?"

"*May* be involved. *May* be—"

"Fine, *may* be involved in this." She waved her hand dismissively, rolling her eyes again as she exhaled audibly.

"Possibly, yes. And that's why I want you as far away from this as possible."

She let my hand go, sat back heavily in her chair, and crossed her arms. "I, uh, I think I'm okay with that," she said after a moment. "What about you, um, your psyche?" She circled her finger around next to her head for effect.

"Well, I'm not exactly normal."

"No kidding," she said, snorting.

The rest of the evening was filled with small talk about her cases and my fishing trips, until Sarah got a call that required her to return to the local DHS offices. I just found a hotel and tried to go to sleep.

Chapter 16

Though the original crime had occurred in Bridgeport, we actually had to go to Middleton because the Whiting Forensic Division of Connecticut Valley Hospital there was the only high-security psychiatric facility around.

"According to the report, police arrested Jones in Florida and extradited him for trial for the murder of Jesus Ramirez," Sarah said, going over the parts of the file she'd memorized, while I perused the printed copy she'd given me. "Apparently, on December twentieth, Jones was sleeping on the porch of a vacant house in Bridgeport when Ramirez found him and opened the house for him to get him out of the cold. According to statements from Michelle Rask—Jones's cousin—that was when he claims voices told him to kill the man and eat his brain, which he did in nearby Lakeview Cemetery while he drank sake. Eventually, he confessed to Rask then took a bus to Florida, where police caught up with him. According to interviews conducted over the last several days at Whiting, Jones referred to his cousin as Athena and referred to any number of other Greek 'gods' and other mythical creatures during his ramblings."

"Goody," I replied. "I have the best job in the whole world." *This is going to be fun. A heavy-duty psychiatric facility for the criminally insane and a possibly possessed cannibalistic murderer—what could be better?*

We pulled up to the Connecticut Valley Hospital complex and followed the signs around to the forensic division. I had visions of the creepy buildings in every spooky horror movie that involved crazy murderers and insane asylums, and I wasn't disappointed. The redbrick buildings that housed the forensic division sat among taller, statelier buildings with gabled roofs, cupolas, and towers. The psychiatric ward gave every impression of a prison, with two squat, flat-topped buildings connected by a covered walkway. One building was two stories, while the other was an odd combination of three- and four-story wings with a large brick smokestack to one side. I could easily picture Jack Nicholson running around inside with axe in hand, screaming "Here's Johnny!"

Heavy bars and metal grates blocked the view of the few windows along the building's facade. Two armed men and a chain-link gateway topped with concertina wire guarded the lone entrance. The Strixes and the wastelands that lined the shores of the River Styx were more inviting.

We parked in a large lot next to the lowest building and walked back around to the entrance. Sarah showed her government ID and badge, and I handed over my Metis Foundation credentials. One guard opened the gate and led us to the main entrance doors. He stared up at a video camera overhead, the door buzzed, then the lock popped open. We entered, and the guard returned to his post at the gate in the fence. The inside of the facility was stark white, except the floor, which was a grayish mottled tile. The temperature was only slightly warmer inside the building. The smell was acrid and sweet, like industrial cleaners, though not awful.

We entered a narrow foyer with only one large window in the wall to one side and a single forbidding door with a small six-inch port window about five feet off the ground at the other end of the hall. The big window was two-inch-thick Plexiglas with a small slot cut into the bottom to pass things through and a perforated metal disk that hid a microphone embedded at face height. An older African-American woman with a pleasant demeanor sat behind the bulletproof aperture and waited for us to do something.

Again, we played the ID game, and after we'd filled out several forms and waited a good thirty minutes, a heavyset man with a blond crew cut, wearing white scrubs, finally came through the Portal to Hell to get us. From there, the big man in white guided us into another room with a series of small green metal lockers along one wall, a table, and an old coffee-and-soda machine with a faded-out display. An ancient television was bolted to the wall in one corner on a platform just below the ceiling. It was an old-fashioned box TV that probably only got fuzzy images of daytime talk shows—if it even worked at all—though it was off at the moment. Two men sat quietly at the table. Neither had the aura of anything other than human, but physically, one of them looked like a piece of chewed gum. The other seemed to be an accountant.

The accountant was short, maybe five and half feet tall, balding, with thick horn-rimmed glasses and a tweed suit that had somehow survived from the fifties—right down to its suede elbow patches. The piece of chewed gum was easily my height and wore some sort of black, formless narrow coat. His hands showed evidence of serious burns, with at least three different colors of flesh ranging from an angry red to pinkish, and he was missing parts of two fingers. Most striking, however, was the row of scars that travelled from the top of his bald head down the left side of his face and jaw and disappeared beneath the high-necked collar of his jacket. Most of his left ear was missing, and his left eye was milky white. His remaining eye was a piercing green.

Each man wore a bright-crimson crucifix on his left breast. Though the accountant's was rimmed with some sort of dark, dull metal, the piece of chewed gum's cross was edged by a bright coppery-colored metal.

They ignored Sarah and focused entirely on me. Even without the crucifixes, I would have known they were Pugnus Dei. The scarred one didn't surprise me, but the accountant caught me off guard. *I guess God can use anyone he wants.*

I nodded in deference. "Brothers."

The accountant stood and offered me his hand in greeting, while Chewed Gum remained seated, eyeballing me.

"Ah, Diomedes Tydides, I presume," the little man said with a strong but slightly high-pitched voice.

"Please call me Steve Dore. Steve," I replied. "It blends in better."

"Very well, Mr. Dore, I am Lector Brother Ezekiel, and this is Exorcist Brother Enoch," he said, first placing his hand on his chest before sweeping it toward Chewed Gum.

I was surprised. I had only ever met Justicars, who were knights. I hadn't even known their order consisted of any other rankings.

"Ahem," Sarah said from behind me, clearly annoyed. "Since you big tough men seem to have forgotten me, my name is Agent Sarah Wright of the Department of Homeland Security, and I'm your ticket to seeing Mr. Jones today."

"Ah, so sorry, Miss... um, sorry, Agent Wright," Ezekiel said, stammering. "I apologize for being so rude. Thank you very much for assisting us in this matter."

Brother Enoch and I just glared at each other while Sarah and Ezekiel spoke.

"What now?" I asked after a moment, breaking eye contact to glance around the room, because I was bored of the pissing contest.

"We wait," Enoch said in a cracked and raspy voice that was as rough as his appearance.

"Uh, yes," Ezekiel said. "We were told that the director would come get us once they have Mr. Jones secure in the observation room. Oh, they told us that for those going in to speak with him directly, you must leave all loose items in one of these lockers—including and especially weapons."

"Oh, okay." I took off my jacket and began undoing my holster.

"Agent Wright," Ezekiel said to Sarah, "you and I will remain in an adjacent room, observing along with the director and Mr. Jones's court-appointed representative. You may keep your weapon if you're carrying one." He smiled and leaned in as he told her the last part as if it were a private joke.

Just as I placed my gun, holster, and knife in one of the lockers, Ezekiel spoke up again. "Oh, Mr. Dore, shoelaces and belt, as well," he said officiously.

"No shoelaces," I replied, undoing my belt and rolling my eyes. "I'm wearing deck shoes."

As I put my belt into the locker, three mousy men—two in white coats and one in a dated and worn brown suit—came in and introduced themselves. The men in white were the director of the facility, a Dr. Frank Dukes, and the attending psychologist, Dr. Philip Skinner. The other was Jones's attorney, Mr. Cowen. All were understandably surprised by Enoch's appearance. The two members of Pugnus Dei simply introduced themselves as Ezekiel and Enoch. Sarah did most of the talking, since technically this was a DHS issue, while the rest of us stood around. That was when I noticed that Enoch was wearing a floor-length cassock, not a jacket.

After a few moments of rules and regulations, Dr. Dukes led us down a hall lined with video cameras covering every angle of the passage. Despite being painted bright white, the corridor gave off the impression of being dark and depressing. We went through two key card–accessed security checkpoints before we finally came to two windowless metal doors at the beginning of another hallway. Dr. Dukes motioned for Brother Enoch and myself to enter through the one on the left.

Inside, fluorescent lights recessed into the ceiling lit the stark room in painfully white light. Two men dressed in heavily padded white suits covering them from ankle to ear and helmets with clear face shields stood near the door. The only furniture in the room was three metal chairs around a small metal table, all bolted to the floor. Video cameras behind heavy metal cages sat in each corner near the ceiling, and a large mirror—obviously one-way glass—lined one entire wall. A well-built, somewhat-heavyset black man with short dreadlocks sat in the single chair, wrapped in a straitjacket and chained at the waist to the chair. A plastic mask covered the lower half of his face. I could see immediately that he was possessed. The spirit's form almost totally enveloped him. In fact, little of Taylon Jones remained.

As Enoch and I entered, a metallic voice echoed through the room via intercom. "Please be seated, gentlemen, and let's begin."

As we sat, Enoch glanced at me. He clearly knew the man was possessed as well.

"Mr. Jones..." the weathered exorcist said in a cracked but eerily serene voice. He placed both hands on the table in front of him and closed his eyes. With his hands outstretched, I could see just how badly his hands were scarred. As he sat silently, energy began to emanate from inside him, enveloping his body like armor. The glow was pure blue-white light, though not intense. After a few more seconds, the brightest areas manifested in his chest and head, but it covered him from head to toe.

Across the small table, Taylon began thrashing violently and emitting horrific noises. His feet—the only part of him not bound—kicked out at everything. His eyes rolled back in his head, foam began seeping through the holes in his mask, and he began screeching in some guttural, harsh language. Enoch's eyes sprang open, and he remained stoic. His lips spread into what might have been a grin, but his scars made it lopsided and somewhat scary. The wider he smiled, the more the thick skin on his face pulled at his milky eye, giving him an almost-crazed appearance.

The two heavily padded orderlies immediately ran over and grabbed Taylon by the shoulders in an attempt to hold him down.

Brother Enoch held up a battered hand, waving them off as he got up and walked around the table to stand next to Taylon. The closer Enoch got to him, the more the thrashing became a concerted effort to pull away from him, and Taylon began shouting wildly at the exorcist, though what he was saying was beyond me.

"Perhaps we should give Mr. Jones another small sedative and wait a few more minutes," the metallic intercom voice said. "This type of violent behavior has been his norm since we got him. Though the gibberish is new."

I turned back to the mirror and shook my head slowly twice.

"Very well, but, Mr. Enoch, please keep your distance from him," the tinny voice replied. "And if he doesn't settle down, we'll have to cut this short. We cannot allow him to hurt himself."

Ignoring the order, Enoch put his hands on Taylon's shoulders, and the restrained man went rigid, stopped speaking, and began howling. The white flecks of spittle and drool coming through the mask became crimson with blood.

The exorcist bent down and began whispering into Taylon's ear. I couldn't hear a word of what he said, but Taylon began shrieking and thrashing again. He kicked so violently several times that something I assumed was his leg snapped like a two-by-four cracking. Another vicious kick hit the table so hard that the metal leg bent, canting the tabletop at an odd angle, but the violent behavior didn't slow.

"Mr. Enoch, please step back from the patient immediately," the intercom voice said. The two orderlies, oddly, stayed where they were, either unwilling or afraid to move.

What came next was frightening to witness: the temperature in the room began to drop significantly, and our breath became visible. Once again, the exorcist whispered into Taylon's ear, and this time, the hideous faceless form that enveloped the possessed man began to writhe and twist, causing Taylon to struggle even more. The demonic spirit was resisting being ripped free from its host, but it was failing.

The more it fought, the more Taylon jerked and bayed. The image of the demonic entity fighting exorcism juxtaposed over the violently flailing body was surreal. Finally, the entity, which had become little more than a squirming mass of formless greasy energy, tore free from Taylon and tried to bolt for one of the shocked orderlies.

"No," Brother Enoch said, stopping the mass as if it were at the end of a leash. "Go, there," Enoch said calmly and clearly, pointing to the one-way glass partition—a mirror—and I understood his plan. Mirrors could act as portals to different dimensions, and we could safely banish the demon if we could get him to enter it then break it.

As the mass of energy shot past me into the mirror, I stood and yanked the chair next to me free from its bolts on the floor.

"Sarah, move! Now!" I screamed then smashed the chair into the bulletproof glass. The heavy impact of the steel chair combined with my strength put the seat through a gaping hole in the mirror and all but destroyed the glass, though its protective coating kept it from completely shattering. In the darkened room on the other side of the ruined mirror, the only figure I could see through the breach was Ezekiel, fastidiously writing in a book while seated at a table. He brushed chunks of glass off his ledger with one arm and kept writing. I doubted anyone but the two members of Pugnus Dei and I had witnessed anything more than a man thrashing violently followed by me throwing a chair through mirrored glass. It was probably better that way.

Several long seconds passed before Dukes and Skinner began pounding on the door into our room. By that time, Taylon's form was quiet, his breathing ragged. His head lolled back, and his legs were splayed out in front of him. A bone protruded through one of his pants legs, and blood and urine were puddling on the floor beneath him. Taylon's once-white straitjacket was covered with foamy bloody drool. Enoch calmly walked over and leaned against the door, arms nonchalantly crossed over his chest. The energy he had emitted was gone, and I saw no sign of possession in the bedraggled Jones.

I quickly poked my head through the hole in the shattered mirror and found Sarah shielding the poor attorney on the floor. Both were covered in chunks of safety glass, dazed but otherwise okay. The orderlies were completely dumbfounded, and none of the hospital staff on hand knew quite what to do.

Once I was sure everyone was okay, I walked over to Taylon. I had questions I needed answers to now that he was *theoretically* back in control of himself, and I had only seconds before they took him away.

"Taylon, what happened to you? Where did you find the Sons of Belial?" I asked in a quiet, soothing tone. The only answer I got was a moan as his head flopped over to gaze at me with bloodshot eyes. With the doctors pounding on the door, I didn't have time for patience. "Taylon," I growled through clenched teeth, shaking him slightly, "where did this happen to you, dammit? Did the Sons of Belial do this?" He nodded almost imperceptibly but still said nothing. His breathing was heavy and irregular.

The two doctors in the hall began screaming at us, but I paid them no attention. I didn't even know what Enoch was doing to keep them at bay at this point.

"The Sons of Belial did this to you—where? I need to know," I said, pleading, hoping his mind wasn't too damaged to remember.

"Co... kite... us... but not... the only... one. Many ..." he said just before the doctors managed to shove the door open and storm past Enoch, who then calmly walked over to stand behind Taylon.

Cocytus—one of the five rivers of Hades. Great, this guy really is gone. But if he really wasn't the only one they'd done this to, then I had to figure out why, and fast.

No one said anything as we all stared at each other and the doctors panted like dogs to catch their breath. Finally, after a good minute, Brother Ezekiel spoke up in a cheerful tone from the observation room.

"Well, I guess we're done here," he said, beaming at us through the hole in the mirror.

Dr. Dukes just scowled at us with his mouth agape and his jowls reddening. Then the incoherent, overlapping shouting began from both doctors and Taylon's lawyer. Over the screaming protests, I could see Taylon trying to say something again, but I couldn't make out what until Enoch leaned down and patted his shoulder gently.

"You are welcome, son, but you should be thanking God, not me," he said in a reassuring tone, then he faced the still-uncomprehending and motionless orderlies. "This man needs medical attention, right away."

"What did you say to him?" Dukes shouted over the others.

"Actually, I said nothing to Mr. Jones at all," Brother Enoch replied dismissively.

"We all saw you say something to him. We probably have it on video..." Dukes waved at the cameras.

Two additional armed security guards showed up, and one of the orderlies ran down the hall, presumably to get help for Jones.

"You," Dr. Dukes said, pointing at me. "What were you just asking him? What did he say?"

I ignored him as I forearmed the broken mirror until the whole thing came loose from its frame. On the other side, Sarah and the attorney were a little dazed, though Sarah a little less so. The lawyer's protests, directed at no one in particular, were loud but feeble and incoherent. The chair I'd thrown was imbedded in the wall at the back of the observation room. Ezekiel gathered his ledger and pens into his briefcase and stood in the hall, waiting for us to leave.

Sarah scowled at me but said nothing as she tended to the shaken attorney. She didn't need to say anything—I knew she wanted to know what had just happened. The attorney was having a hard time gathering himself, though.

"I promise you I said nothing to Mr. Jones," Brother Enoch said to Dukes as the orderly showed up with two medical attendants wheeling a stretcher.

Unsure of what *they* should be doing, the two armed guards helped secure the now-passive Taylon to the gurney. As the orderlies, attendants, and guards began to wheel Taylon out, Dr. Dukes grabbed one of the guards.

"You stay with me until we sort this out," Dukes told the man, his voice trembling and unsure as he tried to regain some composure. "Okay, I want all of you back in the waiting area until I can figure out what to do next."

Brothers Enoch and Ezekiel walked calmly down the hall in front of us as I helped Sarah with the shaken attorney. We followed the two doctors and the guard back to the waiting room with the lockers. Outside the door, Dukes told the guard to keep us inside until his return.

"What exactly did you say to Jones?" Sarah asked Brother Enoch.

"As I told Dr. Dukes, I said absolutely nothing to Mr. Jones," he replied.

"We all saw you say something just before he went ballistic and Mr. Dore, there, pulled the chair up and went all berserk," the attorney managed to say.

"I told the sifter demon possessing Mr. Jones to leave immediately," Brother Enoch said matter-of-factly. "And then I sent it to the only safe place."

"The mirror," I said, "and then I smashed it to trap it." I had no idea what a sifter demon was.

Brother Enoch motioned at me in support of what I'd said. A glimmer of understanding flashed across Sarah's face. The attorney, on the other hand, went ashen, and his jowls sagged as his eyes tracked aimlessly across the room as if searching for something he could identify as real.

"I'm just a public defender," he mumbled, his hand shaking as he reached for his handkerchief and mopped at his sweaty forehead. "They don't pay me enough for this crap."

"At the risk of sounding stupid, what's a sifter demon?" I finally asked.

Enoch grunted, and Ezekiel watched him for a few seconds.

"Heinrich Agrippa, a lector of our Order from the fifteenth and sixteenth century, classified the lesser demons below the three major hierarchies," Ezekiel said. "Sifters are one of nine—"

"Say no more, Brother Lector," Brother Enoch said sternly, slapping his hand down on the table without raising his head.

Sarah and I gave each other sideways glances, and the ensuing silence was awkward.

Chapter 17

After Brother Enoch's slight outburst, no one wanted to say anything. To make matters worse, we waited for a solid hour before Dr. Dukes returned.

"Well, even though the injuries he sustained are severe, Taylon is going to be okay, and for the first time since we received him here, he's actually calm and resting, but he is heavily medicated," Dr. Dukes said. "Albeit it's the first time the medication has actually *worked*. Now, I must insist that you two explain yourselves." He fixed Brother Enoch and me with his attempt at a withering gaze.

I just sat back in my chair and put my hands behind my head. Brother Enoch made a lopsided facial expression that was probably meant to be a smile but was more of a grimace, revealing a few too many teeth on one side of his ruined mouth and disturbingly distorting the skin around his dead eye. The attorney and Dr. Dukes both jerked back slightly in reaction to the expression.

"To put it simply, Dr. Dukes, I did nothing more than exorcise Mr. Jones's demon, freeing his soul. Mr. Dore here was helping me make my case."

"I have been a forensic psychiatrist for several decades, Mr. Enoch, and I have never seen an inmate react like that," Dukes said. "Nor have I ever witnessed anyone pull free a chair bolted to the floor and then throw it through a pane of bulletproof safety glass, Mr. Dore."

"Well, that was some freaky stuff going on in there, and I got scared and thought Taylon might get free," I said, lying like a bad rug. "I panicked. You know, the adrenaline and all."

Sarah glared at me, her gray eyes the color of storm clouds. Cowen just shook his head, ready to be done with this whole mess.

"Agent Wright, I will be writing a report to your offices regarding what happened here today. You are lucky Mr. Jones will be okay," Dukes said, trying to sound threatening. "I should never have agreed to this in the first place. I'm sure you'll be hearing from Mr. Cowen's offices as well."

Cowen lowered his head farther, shrinking in stature a bit, and said nothing.

Sarah just sighed, shook her head, and pursed her lips.

"You would all be in much more serious trouble if the video cameras hadn't malfunctioned. And since no one is quite sure what they witnessed *before* Mr. Dore freaked out," Dukes said, throwing air quotes around the last part, "we will be chalking it up to a severely agitated state induced by an overly aggressive interaction, Mr. Enoch. Thankfully, no one besides Jones was hurt, and I think it's obvious his injuries came from his own thrashing and not directly from either of you two. I shudder to think what might have happened if we hadn't restrained the inmate first."

I snorted, and Sarah scowled again, scrunching up her nose at me.

"Mr. Jones should be much more cooperative and calm now," Brother Ezekiel said, "Though I doubt he will ever regain all of his sanity. I think it's fair to say his mind is permanently broken."

"I believe I am the only one qualified to make that assessment, Mr. Ezekiel. Now if you will all please leave. And be advised that if any of our footage is recoverable and I can identify what exactly you did to incite Mr. Jones, I will find a way to bring charges against you all for endangering a patient under my care," Dukes said, red faced, veins bulging in his neck and forehead.

"Not to mention violating Mr. Jones's rights... I think," Cowen said, croaking uncertainly.

Dukes shook his head. "If this hinders the state's case against him, so help me... Mr. Jones is a very dangerous man—both to himself and to others—and I will not have him released on a technicality," Dukes said mostly to Cowen, who was unable to focus at all.

Two security guards accompanied us through the security checkpoints and out the front gate. In the parking lot, Sarah glared at me in a way that made me stop in my tracks and recoil slightly.

I put up my hands in surrender. "Hey, I told you I wanted you nowhere near this thing and that *this* was only the beginning."

"I could lose my job over this"—she gestured wildly with her arm back toward the building we'd just come out of—"freakin' mess!"

"No, you won't. The Metis Foundation will help with that," I said confidently and slightly sarcastically.

"What did you learn?" Brother Enoch asked.

"Not really sure," I replied, leaning on the roof of the car, cautious about what I should tell him, given that his earlier outburst about demons had revealed he wasn't too keen on sharing. I decided to push him a bit. "What was he yelling at you?"

"The sifter was regaling me with threats of their great plan," Enoch replied.

"Yeah, well, I'm pretty sure he gave me nothing," I said, thinking maybe if I told him what I knew, Enoch would be more forthcoming with anything he learned. "The guy's mind is definitely broken. He indicated that this was done to him—and possibly others—somewhere near, well... Cocytus." It was so crazy to think a mortal could have gotten there that I almost hated repeating it. "Given that... piece of information, the only thing I have to go on is I believe a group called the Sons of Belial might have been involved," I said with a shrug.

"Wait..." Sarah said. "*The* Cocytus? The infamous underground S&M club in New York?"

My brain stopped for a second. "Uh, all I know is that he said *Cocytus.*" I shrugged again, shaking my head. "But if he meant some kind of club, it makes a bit more sense than him escaping from the Underworld. Wait... how do you..." I squinted at Sarah, confused.

Brother Ezekiel pulled a computer tablet out of his satchel and began poking furiously at the screen. Brother Enoch and I continued to stare at Sarah.

"Oh ho," Ezekiel said in a chipper tone. "According to the Order's records, it has been a continuing den of debauchery for over one hundred years in Manhattan, but we have no real information on it, nor any definite links to the Sons of Belial. But... apparently, it has had ties to various cults throughout its history."

"Well, it's difficult to track since their meeting places are known only to members," Sarah said.

"How did I never hear about this place? And what do you mean by that?" I asked Sarah.

"Well, its location changes on a regular basis," she said, her voice suddenly a little husky. "You have to be invited or be a member to find it and get in. Memberships are like a hundred grand a year or something." She cleared her throat a few times as we all stared at her.

"What do you guys have on the Sons of Belial?" I asked Ezekiel finally, after a very pregnant pause, trying not to think about why Sarah knew about a sex club.

"Not much recently," he said. "Most of our information comes from fifty or more years ago. As the surviving offspring of the Nephilim, the group is small, perhaps a few dozen actual members, but they organize rituals and conscript or recruit additional participants as needed. They are dedicated to freeing those they deemed to have brought all true knowledge to humankind."

"The Watchers," I said to no one in particular. "So it's true."

"We believe they may be responsible, yes," Brother Enoch replied.

"Responsible for what?" Sarah asked.

I got lost in the implications and stared off into space, thinking about the Axeman, until Brother Enoch's gravelly voice brought me back.

"It is possible that some ritual, maybe performed by the Sons of Belial—the Sons of the Most Worthless—actually succeeded in freeing one of the Watchers nearly a century ago. Possibly Ramiel himself. The very creature you, Diomedes, fought in New Orleans along with our brethren so many years ago," Brother Enoch said.

"But we have no conclusive proof of this," Brother Ezekiel interjected, "only supposition based on hearsay and random information, though it makes some sense. We have heard nothing definitive of either the Sons of Belial or Ramiel in decades."

"He would be biding his time, getting stronger, feeding off fear... and waiting," I said, still staring at nothing. "We need to find him and soon."

"You may well be right, Diomedes," Brother Enoch said. "Even the sifter alluded to the Thunder of God—which is what the name Ramiel translates to. But Brother Ezekiel's calling is different from mine. His pursuit and ultimate destruction would be a matter for the Brothers Justicar of our order."

I turned back to Sarah, perhaps a bit too quickly, startling her. "Do you know how to find this Cocytus place?" I asked her brusquely.

"I... I can check with local law enforcement and see what they have," she said, glancing down.

"Let's get going then," I said. "Brothers, it was a pleasure working with the Order again."

"If it is God's will, you will see us yet again, Diomedes. May he guide your path as well," Brother Enoch replied.

The instant Sarah closed her car door, I started in on her. "So... how do we know so much about an underground S&M club?"

"It's not what you think," she said, glancing at me sideways. "At the FBI Academy, one of the things we research is underground organizations, and that one was one of the more... interesting ones. We all dug into it a bit. There have been reports of everything from drugs and human trafficking to animal and possibly even human sacrifice associated with it for decades. Primarily, it's a sex club for the ultra-wealthy, where they can be as twisted as they want without prying eyes. It supposedly began as an offshoot of the Hellfire Club in England."

"I see." I had forgotten that she'd begun her career in the FBI before moving to the DHS in the hopes of a more stable life.

"Clubs like that one have become more and more common, especially out in LA. Cocytus is just the oldest in the U.S.," she said, trying to sound more professional about it.

"So just professional interest, then?" I replied, maybe a bit too cynically. "And just so you know, the Hellfire Club took its ideas from the Italian Ridotti clubs in the seventeenth century. They evolved into casinos for the wealthy classes of Europe, but they began with much more depraved and private intentions. Hence, the tradition of wearing masks at *Il Ridotto*. They liked to claim that the formal dress code, three-cornered hats and masks, kept the riffraff from betting at the tables, but..." I dragged my finger across my nose like the con men in the know did in that movie with Redford and Newman.

"And how do you know so much about *that*?" Sarah asked pointedly as she drove.

"Seriously?" I replied, feigning hurt. "How do you think? Anytime you have a place where they protect identities and there are any kind of morally questionable activities, some kind of nonhuman creature is going to be there, preying on primal human desires. Humans are suckers. Easy prey."

"Oh, I see..." she said, clearly not buying my explanation. "Just part of the job, then?"

"Of course. Why else would I go to *those* kinds of places?"

"Yeah, well, I'm going with you when we find Cocytus."

"Oh, no you're not," I said, aiming for an air of authority, but it came out sounding petty. "I told you what was at stake here. I will not expose you to demons, lesser or otherwise."

"You can't go into a place like that with guns or even swords drawn. You need to be subtle if you want information."

"No, *you* can't go in like that, but that's *my* specialty."

We didn't say much to each other for the remainder of the trip, partly because Sarah was on the phone almost the entire time, trying to find out anything she could about Cocytus, but call it intuition or sixth sense, I was sure she was upset with me, too. I was willing to live with that, because getting her killed—or lobotomized by a demon—was unacceptable.

Sarah managed to find out a few of the locations Cocytus had used recently but nothing about where it was going to be next. The place thrived on secrecy for good reason. Supposedly, its membership consisted of an international clientele that included a handful of billionaires, quite a few politicians, and more celebrities than an average Hollywood awards show. These people paid big bucks to make sure their freak flags didn't fly publicly.

By the time we arrived back in New York, I knew I had one option if I wanted to find the place, and *he* wasn't going to be happy about it. We pulled into the parking garage under the government building on Manhattan's Lower West Side.

"At the risk of making you angrier with me, I need you to give me a few minutes of privacy while I do something," I told Sarah, expecting the worst.

"Fine," she said, slamming her car door. "I'll be in the offices on the third floor." Then she headed to the elevators and glared at me as the doors closed.

I dug a small pouch out of my duffle. It held a special quill made from a roc feather and a roll of parchment made from reeds taken from along the river Styx. Then I pulled out my knife.

I wrote my message—basically "Call me ASAP"—then wrote down the full, true name of the individual I wanted it to go to. The last thing I had to do was cut my thumb and allow my blood to drip on a corner of the page. The energy from my blood combined with a simple enchantment created a connection allowing me to transmit what I had written as if it were a magical email. Once I was done, I burned the parchment. My blood and the name of the recipient were too valuable to leave around. By the time the parchment finished burning, my phone rang.

"Yeah, I'd like to order a large pizza," I answered the call.

"Then next time, send a message to a pizza parlor, not me, jackass," the voice on the other end said.

"Thanks, Duma. I'm sorry I had to contact you."

"Yeah, yeah, yeah, whatever. I'm still not fully recovered from Poveglia and rescuing that belligerent nutjob Belphoebe just to save your sorry ass," the Peri said, alluding to the last time we'd worked together.

"I know, I know. I still owe you—"

"Big time, buddy. You have no idea. Now what can I add to the tab *this* time?"

"Well, I'm making an assumption, but knowing you, it's a pretty safe one."

"And..." Duma said, clearly impatient.

"Do you know of an underground S&M club in New York City called Cocytus?" I asked.

I could hear him choke on something.

"Uh, yeah, sure. Of course I've heard of it," he said, trying to recover from the obvious surprise.

"Can you get me in or at least tell me where it will meet next?"

"Dude, are you serious?" he replied, practically screaming.

"Yes, it's important, or I wouldn't have asked."

"I don't care if it's life or death. If I introduce you—*you*—my membership status would be revoked almost instantly," he said.

Somehow, I knew he'd more than just know about the place.

"Fine, then just tell me when and where, and I'll handle it from there," I said sternly and a little hurt by the insinuation that I would wreck everything.

"No, you don't get it. The humans that go there—not to mention the nonhumans that also go there—are seriously heavy hitters in virtually every arena you can think of. You can't go charging around it like a bull in a china shop, D."

"I wouldn't do that," I said indignantly, pissed that he was the second one to tell me that in as many hours.

"Yes, you would, D. It's who you *are*. A blatant disregard for diplomacy is a fundamental part of your DNA."

"Whatever," I replied. "Like I said, I wouldn't have asked if it wasn't necessary, and you know that, Duma. I'm not asking you to get involved, but I have to do this. It's my only lead right now, and the stakes are potentially cataclysmic."

"Yeah, so what else is new?" After a long minute of silence, he exhaled heavily. "Damn, D, you are going to owe me big for this one. I mean B-I-G."

He told me what he knew and said he would get back to me with the next location, then I went upstairs to find Sarah.

THE FIELD OFFICE OF the Department of Homeland Security in Manhattan was located in a federal building that also housed government offices for the Department of Veterans Affairs, the United States Postal Service, and the Passport Agency. Taking the elevators up from the parking garage below saved me from having to make my way through the crowded first floor of the building, though I still had to ride up three floors in a packed elevator.

While the ride up had initially felt as though it would take forever, I found myself hesitant to get off, suddenly feeling as if the ride was all too quick. I wasn't going to be able to convince Sarah that the situation was far too dangerous for her. She'd survived the last creatures we'd gone up against, but demons were different—as different as a mushroom from a monkey—and I had no way to impress that on her.

I opened the nondescript unmarked wooden door across from the elevator and found a dimly lit cubicle farm buzzing with activity. Dozens of people talked into headsets or with others, clacked on keyboards, shuffled and shredded papers, and moved with purpose. High-definition monitors lined every inch of wall space, and others were suspended from the ceiling above the cubes. It was like the Metis Foundation, only more *institutional*. The whole tableau gave me the willies.

Across the sea of cubicles, in some sort of conference room with glass walls, Sarah was leaning on the end of a table, talking to three other people in suits. Pointing at a bank of massive screens displaying a dizzying array of images and colors, she had their rapt attention.

Against my better judgment, I waded into the maze of cubes to cross the room. I made it about halfway before a sudden fit of claustrophobia struck me and Sarah came to my rescue.

"Make your call?" she asked in a clipped tone.

"Huh?" I replied, which was about all I could manage in my fugue. "Is there someplace we could, uh..." I motioned to no place in particular, hoping she would psychically understand what I was try-ing to ask.

"Oh... yeah," she replied, pointing to a series of doors along one wall. "We can talk in there. They have me set up in a temporary office until I leave."

Everyone was watching me. I was way out of my element. Mur-derous fairies, acid-spewing dragons, and bloodthirsty demons didn't faze me, but this place and its frenetic energy freaked me out. Even more distressing, Sarah made no attempt at hiding the smirk across her face as we walked to her temporary office. Inside the white-washed room with light-brown pressboard furniture, I felt myself re-lax just a bit.

"Are all DHS offices this... chaotic?" I asked.

"Oh, no. Not at all. This is an intelligence unit, tasked with com-piling data on potential threats for Manhattan and the surrounding boroughs. This is a nerve center."

"Gotcha," I said, not really caring so much as trying to make con-versation. "Look... as far as going with me—"

"I get it, Steve, really. I do," she said, walking around the desk to her chair. "Demons are bad. Really bad. And so are the things they control. Maybe you're right, but I hate the fact that there's apparently nothing I can do about it. It makes me feel weak."

"That's just it. Compared to these things, you are. Well, not you so much as your mind. You cannot protect yourself from their abil-ities to invade your mind, and *I* can't protect you from that, either. And I definitely don't want to deal with the aftermath of that kind of attack. Not with you. I couldn't..." I stared down at my feet. I didn't even have the heart to bring up the separate issues I was currently having with the Strigoi blood feud.

She walked up next to me, then she took my hand. Our eyes met, and she stepped around to face me. Before I could say anything else, she kissed me—softly at first then more urgently, until her cell phone rang.

We quickly composed ourselves, then Sarah answered the phone. Clearly flustered, she tried to be nonchalant, and I found it amusing to watch her try to regain her poise and professionalism as she talked to a colleague. From what I gathered, she was needed back in DC.

When she finally hung up, she lowered her head and sighed deeply, hand on hip. "We can't seem to catch a break. I'm needed back in DC tonight. I'm pretty sure it's going to have something to do with our little trip to Connecticut. I'll be lucky if they let me out from behind a desk in the next decade."

"I wouldn't worry that much about it," I said with a smile. "Athena can be very persuasive. And recall, this was *her* deal. We did what needed to be done. She'll do right by you, I promise. But it's a shame you have to leave so soon. According to Duma, Cocytus meets again this weekend."

I decided to ride with Sarah to JFK if for no other reason than I had nothing better to do. She gathered her things, and we took the elevator down to the garage. I climbed into the back seat of a nondescript black sedan with my gear bag while Sarah got into the front passenger side next to some agent who was driving. We wound our way through the building's underground garage and stopped as a giant garage door rolled up out of the way.

I knew instantly that something was up, and my hand went toward the gun in my duffle.

As the door rolled up, a figure stood with his back to us, blocking our exit with complete indifference to our presence or the door growing open within feet of his backside. The figure wore black sunglasses and was dressed in a long black trench coat that covered him from neck to ankle. The only distinct characteristic was the mop of far-too-pale blond hair blowing in the wind. I knew who it was the moment I saw the defiant stance.

The driver leaned on the horn to get Duma to move, but all he did was slowly move to face us as if just realizing the situation, tip down his sunglasses with a single finger, then bend down slightly to peer in through the windshield. With an expression of mock surprise on his face, Duma waved politely without moving. Sarah started a bit, realizing who it was.

"Is that...?" she mumbled over her shoulder at me.

"Yeah, it's Duma," I said, opening the car door to get out.

Clearly not sure who it was or what exactly to do, the driver began to open his door as well, reaching for the gun holstered on his hip. I grabbed his shoulder before he could move much then patted it.

"No, you don't want to shoot him. You'll only make him mad." I could tell Sarah got my *Blazing Saddles* reference because she had to stifle a laugh. *I really do like her.* "I got this," I said, climbing out of the car, dragging my duffle bag behind me.

As I walked toward Duma, the driver's door closed with a solid *thunk* just as Sarah's door opened behind me. I couldn't help but smile at him as I approached. His shit-eating grin matched mine. We grabbed each other's hand then closed in to what amounted to a "manly" half hug that ended with Duma grabbing the nape of my neck. His attention shifted as Sarah approached.

"Well, well, well, if it isn't the fair maiden of the Raskovnik Fields herself!" he said, beaming at her and referring to their jaunt to find a rare herb that could unlock any lock.

Smiling, she gave a royal wave of her hand in response as she approached. "Hey, Duma, it's been a while."

They gave each other a friendly hug.

"I hate to hug and run, but I got a flight to catch, and I'm guessing you guys have other business to discuss." Her gaze shifted between us. "It was good to see you again, Duma."

She got back into the sedan, and Duma and I got out of their way. Ever the showman and pain in the ass, Duma bowed deeply as the car passed. Then he smiled at me.

"My car is right over here." He pointed to a massive black Land Rover with a host of aftermarket upgrades, including bumper guards and heavy-duty wheels and tires. He had parked half on the sidewalk in a no-parking zone next to a federal building.

I could tell by the steam coming from the exhaust that the car was running, and as I threw my duffle into the back then got in, I noticed that not only was it a comfortable seventy-two degrees in the cabin—a read-out on the dashboard said as much—but the seats were also heated. The massive SUV's interior was a mixture of red and black leather and black lacquered wood that bordered on gaudy, but it fit Duma's personality perfectly.

"Nice car," I said, looking around the rest of the vehicle.

"It's an SUV. A Land Rover," he said in a mock British accent.

"Gotcha. I bet it cost a hundred grand easy, too," I said, knowing Duma's penchant for exotic cars.

He just snorted derisively. "That's the base for this model. This one's loaded, then I added body armor and Lexan windows, among other things."

"Ah. Nice. You expecting to be attacked?"

"Always, D. You should do likewise—especially after Liuntika."

"No shit. I've been attacked every few days over the last few weeks. They after you too?"

"Hell no," Duma said laughing. "My relationship with them is, ah... a bit different than yours, D. And I did not wreck their caverns, my friend. However, they did offer me twenty mil to take your ass out."

"Oh, good to know. It'd be the toughest twenty mil you'd ever earn, buddy."

"But I'd get it." He flashed me a wolfish grin.

I had no doubt the Liuntika Strigoi had offered him money to kill me. They wouldn't be the first creatures to do so, but they clearly didn't understand our relationship.

"You could try. Might even cover your hospital bills. Where're we headed?" I asked as Duma wove his way haphazardly, though he would say expertly, through the crowded Lower Manhattan streets in the late afternoon.

"West 37th. I got a place."

Duma's place on West 37th Street was just down the street from the Javits Convention Center and right next to the Lincoln Tunnel. From the outside, it was an unassuming dilapidated bluish-gray, three-story brick bunker of a building sandwiched between an auto mechanic's shop and a drainage spillway. Windows lined the top two stories, but the first floor's only features were a massive garage door and some sort of other entryway covered by a sheet of heavy plastic cut into strips. Glowing sigils covered the outer walls, and I could feel the magical power within them. What it really was was a fortress.

As we pulled up to the garage door, Duma hit a button on the center console, and the large garage door began to slide sideways rather than rise. I could actually feel the rumble of the process from within the car.

"What the hell…" I asked, not expecting an answer.

"Door's made from multiple sheets of AerMet 340 with a tungsten alloy core. The rumbling is my garage door opener," he said, as if it was a simple aluminum door rather than a ballistic missile–proof door that probably weighed in excess of five tons.

We pulled in to a garage bay of some kind, and a series of lights flickered on automatically. The huge room, which was actually significantly smaller than the exterior dimensions suggested, housed at least ten other vehicles, including a few motorcycles. Once we were in the room's center, the rumbling began again, and the door, which was covered in some kind of leather on the inside, slid closed behind us, leaving us bathed in the unearthly light of dozens of fluorescent bulbs. I got out of the car and noticed the floor was shiny and spotless, as was the rest of the room. And it was cold. Damn cold, but not like it was just poorly insulated and winter outside. My breath hung in a mist in front of me.

Duma got out of the big SUV.

"Where do you keep the meat?" I asked as I walked to the back of the car to get my bag.

"Huh?" Duma seemed confused, then he waved his hand dismissively as he understood. "Oh, it's better for the cars and my server bank below. Come on, it's warmer upstairs."

He headed to the far corner and a tight spiral staircase that went down through the floor and up through the ceiling. As far as I could tell, it was the only means of egress apart from the massive metal door. Actually, the idea was brilliant from a tactical standpoint. I couldn't climb the narrow stairs without turning myself slightly, and it would be impossible to do so quickly. It created a nasty bottleneck for anyone trying to break in.

As I climbed, I noted the stairway was not metal but wood and so finely carved, it would be impossible by human standards. And no matter how hard I stared, I could not see a single seam or joint.

"Nice stairway," I said a little facetiously.

"Carved from the trunk of a single iwa by a tribe of kobolds we once helped."

Iwa was an archaic name for the common yew, but one big enough to carve a staircase from would've had to be ancient, and carving it must have taken years. It was one of the most magnificent pieces of art I had ever seen. The carvings along the risers, treads, balustrades, and railings depicted various Fae and other creatures as well as some epic battle scenes in intricately detailed miniature. The central post was carved with a host of sigils and symbols I only recognized in pieces, but I could see the magical power stored within them. I figured it had to be some sort of magical booby trap.

Once I got to the next level, I was instantly warmer. This floor was also a single giant room, again slightly smaller than the size of the building's exterior, covered from floor to ceiling in rich dark wood paneling reminiscent of an old boys' social club from days past. Then I noticed that while the second floor was ringed with windows from outside, there wasn't a single pane of glass in the room. The only light, a low warm glow, came from lamps and lighting fixtures along the ceiling and a large fireplace along the far wall. Overstuffed and opulent but comfortable-looking furniture covered in ornate fabrics filled the room. One wall even had a single massive tapestry hanging from it. The whole tableau was a mix between a medieval castle and a mansion in Newport.

"What? No mounted dragon's head?" I asked.

"What? Hell no, not here," he said, again no hint of humor in his voice. "It would clash with the décor, don't you think? Deer maybe, but not dragon."

"Why not? The place is clearly a fortress," I said, falling onto one of the couches.

"This isn't a fortress. It's a *hideout*."

I laughed, and he smiled his usual wolfish grin.

"Bedrooms are upstairs; computers are in the basement. Escape is via the roof and down into the sewers through the spillway next door. Stay as long as you need, but if you leave, don't try to get back in without Ab's or my help."

"Yeah, I couldn't miss the wards you have woven into the walls outside. And on the stairs, too. But that damn door... you expecting a frontal assault from the Marines?"

"Ha! I'm not worried about your race—even with your war toys. You of all humans know what's after me and Ab. This is all just my version of a security system so I can sleep at night."

He sat on a couch opposite the one I was on and put his feet up on the table between us in an inhumanly fluid and easy motion.

"Good to see Sarah again," he said, laying his head back and closing his eyes with a sigh. "Have you guys... you know?"

"How is that any of your business?" I asked, a little more forcefully than I'd intended.

"That's a no," he said, his head rolling from side to side on the back of the couch. "What are you waiting for?"

"I don't want to talk about it," I said defensively. "What I would like to talk about is Cocytus. Where are they meeting next?"

Duma just held up his hands in supplication. "I already told you, I'll get the location by messenger the morning of and not before. I told you everything else," he said, finally sitting up. "I don't know who organizes it, but I do know it's not human. It could be connected to the Sons of Belial or, for all I know, the Vatican. It's not a place I go to ask questions."

"Do people ever go missing during or after these, ah... gatherings?" I asked, trying to determine if Taylon Jones's story might be true.

"No clue. Since it's entirely anonymous inside, I wouldn't imagine it's impossible. Lots of stuff goes on in there. I mean *a lot*. If you can imagine it—hell, if *I* can imagine it, it's probably happening there."

"Can I assume, given your membership, that pretty much any and all races are welcome?"

"You can assume anything you want, and you'd probably be right about this place. I can tell you that you humans are far outnumbered by Fae of both Courts and any number of other creatures. I've never heard anything specific, but there is some sort of unspoken détente among those in attendance, because I have never seen or heard of any kind of, well, not *violence*, but rather *belligerence*—not even from those that recognize what *I* am. Some forms of violence are, shall we say, acceptable..." He rolled his hand in the air instead of finishing his sentence.

"Yeah, I get the picture."

"Hey, don't judge me," he said with a grin. "But that's exactly why *you* can't go in there shootin' up the place, Tex. You think this thing with the Strigoi is bad? You could bring all kinds of crap down on your head."

I couldn't argue with him there. I could start a political mess—or worse, a war—if I harassed or even treated some uppity Fae in a manner they deemed disrespectful. *And I just got my ass out of one of those slings.* This thing called for kid gloves, and Duma and Sarah were right. The only gloves I had were filled with lead shot for greater impact.

Chapter 18

The next morning, I woke up with a start and found a handwritten note from Duma taped to my chest. We'd spent the evening reminiscing until I fell asleep on the couch, and apparently, he had to leave and likely wouldn't be back for a few days. The note also included two warnings: first, a reminder not to reenter the warehouse without Duma or Ab's presence, and second, an admonition to tread lightly at Cocytus. He also said the courier would leave the address to the gathering in the mailbox before sundown.

I spent the rest of the day *carefully* exploring Duma's place. Frankly, I was half afraid to touch anything for fear it would explode, or worse. There was a full gym and dojo upstairs, and it was clearly set up to accommodate both Duma's knife-fighting preferences and Ab's much more physical form of hand-to-hand combat. Even the weight machines were custom made, with weights up to five thousand pounds, which I *had* to try. On the up side, I didn't give myself a hernia. On the down side, I clearly was not as strong as Ab.

Eventually, I decided to clean up and took a shower in a stall best described as a room within a room with glass and stone walls and water falling from the ceiling. I felt like a fish in a bowl. I couldn't find a TV and probably wouldn't have been able to work it if I had.

I poked around the cars in the garage but didn't recognize many of them beyond the emblems. Among them were a little red Ferrari race car of some sort with a big number "44" on the side and hood, a well-used old silver Mercedes racing car with open wheels and the number "12" on it, and some odd-looking silver open-wheeled racing car with four interlocked circles over "Auto Union" on the front of the hood. That one was familiar, but I couldn't recall why. Thinking about Ab trying to squeeze into any of them made me laugh.

Despite the frigid temperature emanating from below, I took the staircase down to the basement. Motion-activated lights came on instantly, and a bank of twelve large monitors flickered to life above a massive computer workstation in the corner opposite the staircase. Duma had filled the space with cars, as well, but an enormous lift to take them up to the garage above dominated the center of the room.

Two of the monitors above the desk showed images from security cameras around the building. The ones monitoring the outside tracked all movement, including animal and vehicle. Passing vehicles triggered a secondary response, making a small screen of code pop up then disappear. Each person passing by sent the computer into an absolute tizzy, initiating some sort of facial recognition program.

I supposed if I were more tech savvy, I might have been willing to plod around on the computers, but truth be told, the wall of monitors and computers was out of my wheelhouse. I couldn't find a keyboard or mouse anywhere, only a glass panel along the top of the desk. It was probably a good thing, because I had visions of me starting World War III with the push of a button. So in an effort to once again save the world, I went back upstairs and did something I hadn't done in a while: I took a nap.

My efforts to save the world were short lived, however. The sound of an alarm echoing throughout the building woke me abruptly. I bolted as fast as I could down the narrow and precarious staircase to find the alarm's source. By the time I got to the bottom of the goofy narrow staircase with the alarm shrieking incessantly, I was ticked at every one of the stupid carved faces along the banister.

Once I got to the basement, one of the computer monitors was focused on a nondescript guy in a dark suit getting back into the passenger side of a dark-colored sedan, which then drove off. *Mail-*

box kept flashing in large red letters across one monitor as a series of other codes ran in a small window underneath. I had no idea what I should or shouldn't do. I placed my hands on the glass desk top to lean in for a better view of the security feed, and the glass panel instantly became opaque, revealing a holographic keyboard and a smaller area next to it that I guessed was a mouse pad. Reflexively, I jerked back, and it all disappeared again. *Yeah, I'm not about to mess with this thing.* I checked the time then realized the guy on the screen was likely just the courier I had been waiting for.

Suddenly, the wailing alarm shut off, and the flashing *Mailbox* warning changed to green and stopped flashing. Again, a smaller screen popped up, only this time rather than nonsensical code, it simply said, "Object weight less than 1g. No threats detected. Deemed safe."

Holy crap, is Duma paranoid. In his defense, though, it was well founded. On the up side, that was my cue.

I went back up the stairs, grabbed my gear bag, and began suiting up. I pulled on my vest—a combination of my cuirass and a Blackhawk Omega Elite. As I began to put my Sig P226 Navy into the crossdraw holster, I thought about what Duma kept saying. After a few seconds of consideration, I threw the gun back in the bag and even left my swords. I did, however, feel it would be prudent at least to take both of my knives. I strapped them both to my vest, one upside down on my left shoulder and the other along my lower back. I checked my little LED flashlights, tucked them into pockets on my vest, pulled on my fleece, and headed to the roof. I left my bag sitting on one of the couches with a note on it telling Duma to keep it safe for me.

Up on the roof, the sun had almost completely set behind me as I peered over the side of the building and into the adjacent spillway. Lights from the buildings and passing cars reminded me just how big the city was. A cold wind cut across the roof, and I jumped.

I grabbed the note out of the mailbox and walked down to the convention center, where I caught a cab to the address on the card—89 Ludlow Street on the Lower East Side. On the fifteen-minute cab ride, I read and reread the instructions that accompanied the address: redbrick building, brown door, overhead light, enter only when flickering.

I got out at Sara D Roosevelt Park then walked the last few blocks. I stopped at the southwest corner of Delancey and Ludlow and glanced down the street toward where I figured the address would be. The nondescript redbrick-front building with the brown door lit up by an overhead light was about halfway down the block on the other side of the street. Some sort of delivery truck was parked on my side of the street near the doorway.

"Enter when flickering." I assumed that meant the light above the door, the only such fixture the building had, and not one of the two streetlights, especially since they were both currently out.

The building across the street from the doorway was a two-story gray stone structure with windows along the very top butted up against a taller redbrick building that vaguely resembled a tower. According to the sign above the rolling metal doors, the tower was some sort of Asian restaurant supply house. Number 89 Ludlow Street was about three stories high and had not a single window. Along the street, two simple doors flanked a large wooden double door inset with small windows. The top half of the building was uncolored cement. An ugly brown brick six-story apartment building in poor repair abutted it on the southeast corner of Delancey and Ludlow.

The street was dark. Not a single light showed in any of the buildings along the block except the one above the doorway, which was currently lit but not flickering. There were no sounds or movement along the street, so I quickly jumped onto the roof of the parked delivery truck then up to the roof of the building across from the doorway just to watch for a few minutes. If I was going to pull this off without causing issues, I figured I would probably be better off among the first to enter. The fewer beings inside, the fewer I could piss off. *Or kill.*

I didn't have to wait long. Minutes after I had situated myself on the roof, a long black limo pulled up just down from the doorway. Sure enough, the light above the door flickered, and a large figure dressed in a suit got out of the passenger side front of the limo and opened a door in the rear compartment. Someone got out wearing a long cloak with a hood pulled over its head. The massive garment covered its movements, but I would have sworn it moved just a little too easily to be human. Then three smaller figures got out, each dressed similarly to the first, though their cloaks were not as heavy. The figure that opened the door stood by as the four cloaked individuals entered the doorway, then the light again shone dully but consistently. The doorman climbed back into the limo, and the vehicle left. Within minutes, the light began flickering again.

I watched patiently as another two vehicles came and went before deciding I'd waited long enough. A silver Bentley pulled up, and I jumped down and crossed the street. The light was still solid, so I knew the passengers in the car would just sit and wait. I walked in front of the vehicle and waved as I passed, moving to stand in front of the brown door. Two men glared at me from the front seat. I smiled back and shrugged. When the light began flickering, I gave the two men in the car a mock salute, pulled the door open, and walked inside.

I was not expecting what I saw.

The door opened into a small, dim room with its walls covered in heavy red velvet draperies. A bed covered in red satin took up most of the available space. On the bed sat a strikingly attractive woman dressed in what I could only describe as red leather bondage gear, complete with dog collar. She was chained hand and foot—albeit loosely—to the bed. I saw no exit from the room other than the door

I'd come through. Undoubtedly, the draperies hid at least one other egress, so I began flipping through them to see what was behind.

"Ahem," said the woman chained to the bed.

"Well, how do I proceed?" I asked, continuing to search behind the heavy drapes.

"You're not a member," she asked, "are you?"

"No, I'm a... a guest," I replied.

"Then you'll have to wait for your sponsor to arrive," she said.

"Okay," I said, throwing my hands up then walking over to sit on the edge of the bed next to her.

"Outside..." she said in a mixture of exasperation and nervousness. "Please don't cause trouble here."

"It's cold out there. Why not just let me in?" I asked, continuing to take in the details of the room.

With a heavy sigh, she pulled on a chain, and the draperies fluttered just to the right of the bed along the back wall. A moment later, a hand parted the curtains, and three figures walked through.

The figures were all well built and exceedingly well dressed but wearing ornate Carnivale-type masks over black balaclavas. I could tell they were human by how they moved, but their movements also told me they were all highly trained. One of them moved a bit more lightly on his feet, suggesting he was likely a boxer or some other kind of fighter, while the other two had the bearing of former military. The smaller of the two soldiers carried a long metal rod in one hand. *Iron, for dealing with unruly Fae, no doubt.*

I stood up suddenly, mostly to see how they would react. The fighter shifted his weight onto his toes and clenched his fists. The rod wielder shifted the weapon so he could swing it if necessary, while the unarmed one relaxed a bit, leaving his arms down at his sides. This guy was a bit more than just a soldier or even former Special Forces. He probably had some sort of specialized hand-to-hand combat training. The fighter was the wild card of the trio and would likely be the first to throw a punch if things escalated. In these tight quarters, there wasn't enough room for them to come at me more than one at a time effectively. *And, I suppose, I really don't want to hurt these guys.*

"I just need to get inside," I said, trying to be honest and give the impression that I was not a threat.

"If you're a guest, then you need to wait outside for your sponsor, sir," the weaponless soldier replied just as calmly.

I took a few steps closer to them, and the soldier with the rod immediately put the tip of the cudgel into my chest to stop me from advancing farther. The fighter tensed and began to shift to his left, my right. I eyed the rod, clicked my tongue in reproach, then jerked the weapon away from the guy. I dropped it on the floor behind me, and they each took a step back in surprise, except the weaponless soldier. He stepped slightly forward.

"Let's keep this easy, guys. I just need to talk to whoever is in charge. I promise I won't cause trouble," I said raising my hands in acquiescence.

"He ain't no cop," the fighter said. "I say we kick him out the hard way."

The other two glanced at him, clearly suggesting that he shut up.

"Sir, we do not want trouble here. Please just leave," the lead soldier said.

"I don't want trouble, either," I replied. "Ten minutes with your boss is all I need, and then I'm gone."

"We have other patrons wishing to enter. If you don't leave immediately, you will force us to remove you."

The woman on the bed had shifted so that she was on the other side, stretching the chains to their full reach. I took another step closer, making eye contact with the lead soldier. His right eye twitched ever so slightly, and his right shoulder dropped as he shifted his body weight to throw a quick jab, probably intending to hit me in the chest and knock the wind from me. He was good but only human. Watching him move was like watching sports in slow motion—everything was predictable.

I caught his right hand in mine before he could fully extend his arm, then I dragged him back to my right so fast that it pulled him off balance. Then I shoved him hard with my left hand and sent him sprawling into his military buddy. They both fell back into the heavy drapery while the impacted soldier flailed at the material until he caught a handful. The combined weight of the two men pulled the drapery free along the wall they'd come through, revealing the door. The fighter was so stunned that he flinched as the drapery came down. I closed the distance to the remaining grunt faster than he could blink, causing him to suddenly jump back, tangling in the now-fallen drapery. He fell with a hollow thunk against the wall, hitting his head and knocking himself unconscious.

"This way, is it?" I asked the woman on the bed, pointing at the door. "No, no, don't get up. I can find my way." I stepped over the bouncers to the door.

"Who are you?" the chained woman asked.

"Would you believe me if I said I was the good guy?" I said over my shoulder.

She just stared at me, eyes wide, but not in fear as much as in disbelief.

The door had an electronic lock with both a fingerprint scanner and a number pad. If I'd had my swords with me, I would have just cut the lock, but my knives, sharp as they were, wouldn't cut through the case-hardened steel bolt.

"How do I open this?" I asked.

When I got no answer, I eyed the chained woman inquisitively. She shrugged in her bonds but said nothing. I glanced back down at the three bouncers, who were starting to regain their wits.

"How 'bout you geniuses? How do I get through here?" I asked, hooking a thumb back at the door. "I promise if you let me in, I'll be gone before you know it. Honest. I'll even pinky swear on it if it'll make you feel better. Otherwise, I'm just going to stay here and disrupt the evening's... festivities."

The lead soldier gave me the code, with a tone of acceptance in his voice, as he pulled himself to a seated position. I punched the code into the keypad, and the locking mechanism withdrew with a solid metallic clunk.

I opened the door, expecting to see a staircase or a hallway, but instead found myself staring into a wide-open room several stories tall and surrounded by catwalks two and three stories above. A forest of skinny metal columns on this level supported the catwalks. The walls were all lined with heavy maroon velvet curtains, and the courtyard was occupied with numerous massive sofas, chaise lounges, and even piles of pillows scattered about. The light came entirely from candles in sconces on the metal columns or from the three chandeliers hanging above.

A variety of humans and nonhumans—both male and female—lounged about in varying degrees of undress and complexity of costume. All of them wore masks of some kind. Despite the overall oddness, something else about the place was off, but I couldn't quite put my finger on it. Maybe a scent or a sound.

One thing was for sure: my presence brought everyone to life. Two human women slid from their seats and began to slink toward me. Both had bodies too perfect to be natural, and they moved as if under the influence of something. One of the women walked up and wrapped her arms around my right arm while the other pressed tightly against me. Even in the candlelight, I noticed their pupils were pinpoints rather than giant openings in the darkness. They were definitely on something, probably to keep them compliant. I went from uncomfortable to irritated in the blink of an eye. Duma had said whoever or *what*ever ran the place was not human, and if they were drugging humans to keep them here, then whatever it was, we were going to have a few problems.

"So, what's your thing?" the woman pressed against me purred.

"Where's your boss?" I replied flatly, still taking in the layout of the building.

"My boss?" she asked almost dejectedly. "Why do you want to see my boss?"

I began to step around her, and I could feel the other woman's grip on my arm tighten as she tried to keep me from moving. It didn't work, but she let go before she fell over. Both women stared at me in disbelief. One spun on her heel with an audible huff, and the other stood, staring, with her hands on her hips. Almost instantly, one of the men got up and began to walk toward me.

"Don't. Go sit back down," I said, pointing at him.

I walked to the nearest wall on my left and began rifling the curtains to see if I could find any other doorways. Short of jumping, there seemed to be no way to get up to the upper levels, but I knew there had to be some *normal* way up. I just had to find it.

I turned back to the people and beings lounging in the middle of the room. All eyes fixed on me eerily as I moved.

"I need to talk to your boss," I said in a loud voice made louder by the echo of the large open space.

No one said anything. I walked back toward the center of the room, assessing the catwalks, unable to get a good view of what was up there because of their height. I could hear movement from both floors above but saw nothing.

"Come on, people, just point me in the right direction, and I'll leave. Then you can get your freak on," I said, putting my hands on my hips.

Again, no one answered. I stared at the ground, shaking my head in growing irritation, then I noticed a woman on a chaise lounge across from me fiddle, ever so slightly, with her leather garter, which was just about all she was wearing. It was an absent-minded behavior—possibly one of distress under the circumstances. I looked at the feathered feline mask that hid her face and immediately noticed movement in her eyes. I could see the pale sclera flash and realized she was indicating above and behind me. When she realized I noticed, she immediately glanced away.

I stared up at the walkway above but again could see nothing from my position. I took a few steps to get closer then jumped, grabbed the railing, and pulled myself over. When I landed, I apparently startled a few people, because at least one person dropped something, which shattered, while another tripped and fell. *People* was the wrong description, though. The beings there were all decidedly *nonhuman* and included at least one Moroi vampire. Every creature tensed as I began moving around the catwalk.

The level was wide and circled the entire space below. Only the ambient light from the chandeliers in the atrium lighted it. More couches and chaise lounges filled the galley way, but I could identify only a single doorway in the corner to my left. Across from me was a large cage flanked by six big figures—three on each side—all wearing some sort of harness attached to machinery connected to the cage. I realized they were the lifting mechanism for a strange elevator. Shaking my head, I headed toward the door.

None of the creatures around me made a sound, but I could feel every eye following my movements. As I approached the door, numerous voices came from down below, and I realized security must be letting patrons in again.

I opened the door, releasing the smell of fresh paint and a sickly-sweet perfume but revealing nothing of the pitch-black space beyond. The odd sensation that had plagued me below became far more intense.

I unzipped my jacket and pulled a small flashlight from my vest. The narrow but intense beam revealed a long hallway reminiscent of an eighteenth-century brothel. Doorways lined the hall, which ran for about fifty feet before jogging to the right. None of the doors were marked, and I could hear nothing except the growing din from behind and below. Based on the layout, I assumed that I was in the multistory apartment building on the corner adjacent to the entrance of this place, and that multiplied the difficulty of my search tremendously.

I had a pretty good idea what was behind the doors, but I also had no way of knowing for sure unless I checked. And even if the lady down below was sending me into a trap, the being I sought had to be up here somewhere. Tentatively, I began opening doors, but the first few opened into unoccupied chambers. One actually had a bed in it. Another resembled something from Torquemada's brainstorm—hemp rope, wood, and leather everywhere. After opening the fifth door on the hallway, I sensed a presence behind me. Its strong, greasy, and unmistakable feeling was all too familiar to me.

"I'm not here for trouble, leech," I said through clenched teeth, addressing the figure behind me. I didn't want to face the Moroi vampire for several reasons, but mostly because I had no intention of showing it any sort of respect.

"Be that as it may, we can't just have you wandering around willy-nilly, possibly disturbing our guests," the creature said in a precise, languid feminine tone.

"I just need to speak with whatever runs this place, and then I'll leave, I so swear. But I'll take this place apart if I have to." Finally facing the parasite, I added, "Starting with you."

I'll admit I was a bit taken aback by her appearance. She was wearing a long, sheer pale robe, but at the moment, it was hanging open. *Wide open.* And she was drop-dead gorgeous, with dark hair and dark eyes in a face that might have been Asian, maybe Hispanic, or possibly some combination. Despite her appearance, it didn't take much for my hatred of their kind to reoccupy the thinking part of my brain, though.

"Now, now, Diomedes, don't be so rash," she said, her voice dripping with sexuality. "You wouldn't want to do anything that would upset our clientele, humans and nonhumans alike, would you?"

"I don't care about them, and I don't have the time to bandy about with the likes of you," I replied tersely before continuing my search.

"Oh, but you should care. Some of them would be devastated if it were revealed they were here—especially your precious humans."

I faced her again, reaching my free hand inside my jacket, and touched the knife on my shoulder without drawing it. *I don't like threats against innocents.*

"Did you know," she said, an evil grin forming at the corners of her mouth, "that the woman in the entryway is actually a DA. And that one of our guests that *just* arrived is a senator and potential presidential candidate. Another is the head of pediatric oncology for some big research hospital. And that doesn't include the nonhumans that would be less than thrilled to have you disturb their enjoyment."

I glared at her.

"Besides," she said with a smug expression, "*I* run this place."

"Fine," I growled.

I walked to her, grabbed her arm, pulled her toward the nearest door. She offered no resistance at all as I opened the door and threw her into the room, closing the door behind us. In fact, I got the impression she liked it.

Inside the room, lit by small sconces on each wall, a variety of manacles and restraints were bolted to the walls, ceiling, and floor. All kinds of leather and rubber things that only loosely resembled outfits hung from hooks along the wall next to the door. In the dimness, the place reminded me of a butcher shop. *Definitely not my world.*

"What do you know about the Sons of Belial?" I asked, a little off kilter because of my surroundings.

"I prefer the tough guy act, actually," she said, moving around the room, touching the various implements with relish.

"The Sons of Belial?" I asked again, wondering how much longer I would be able to tolerate the situation.

The vampire lingered over a tray of surgical tools and other instruments, touching a cat-o-nine-tails before grabbing a riding crop.

"One *last* time—Sons. Of. Belial." I reached up to pull one of the manacled chains loose from the wall behind me to demonstrate my increasing lack of patience.

"Who?" she replied without missing a beat, followed by the slap of the crop against her hand.

"I will gladly remove your head and use your skull as a planter, parasite," I said, wrapping the chain around my fist.

"All work and no play, Diomedes..." she said with a slight hitch in her voice.

I could tell she was trying to judge how serious I was. She knew who I was, so she had to know what I was capable of, but it was clear she wasn't sure how far she could push me. I pulled my knife from its sheath just so she knew I was done being toyed with.

"This is me not playing," I said, chain in one hand and knife in the other.

She tensed and lowered the crop to her side. "Fine. Such a shame, but if you insist—I know nothing about the Sons of Belial," she replied in a huff, flexing the crop between her hands.

"I have reason to believe that they either recruit or kidnap people from here from time to time. I suppose it's possible. Members try to stay anonymous, and everyone is free to leave with anyone they choose. How would I know if any of them are Sons of Belial?" she said, her tone indifferent.

Unfortunately, her rapid response and body language suggested she was being honest.

"Members may try to stay anonymous, but it sure sounds like you know all about them—DAs, presidential candidates, doctors, and all. And it also sounds like you're no stranger to the Sons of Belial. Just tell me what you know." I suddenly worried I'd hit a dead end.

"The quicker you tell me what I need to know, the faster I'll leave. *Peacefully*. Otherwise, you have about thirty seconds before I do something ridiculously violent that I guarantee you *won't* enjoy."

"You really are *no* fun." With a heavy sigh, she slapped the crop on her thigh.

"Not with human lives on the line."

"You're in the wrong place." Giving up on her seduction routine, she tossed the crop back down on the tray. "You should be looking at the Dungeon in San Fran."

"What? My lead told me Cocytus."

"I only *run* this place. I don't own it. The owners are at the Dungeon. *They* would probably know what you're talking about," she said, running her hand over the other instruments in the tray again.

"What do *you* know about the Sons of Belial?"

"Not much. I was told by the owners that they were sending someone particular a few months back. Rumor was they were Sons of Belial, but I had no idea who they were specifically or why they were even here. I only know that after the gathering's audit, two guests around that time used an administrative code to enter. I assumed it was them."

"Could they have kidnapped someone?" I asked.

"I suppose it's possible, but I wouldn't call it *kidnapping*. Guests leave with each other all the time. It's consensual."

"Where do you get your human hosts from?"

"Whenever we need new playthings, we place ads online and in certain lifestyle magazines. We aren't picky. As long as they're willing, we clean them up and set them loose. If they work out and they want, they can come back, but we have a pretty high turnover rate."

Playthings. The whole idea made my skin crawl.

"We don't pay them. It's all voluntary and because they *want* to do it. Some of them make some lucrative connections, but most are just here to escape, and they can't afford to be here otherwise. Many earn favors or even tips if they're worth it. You should try it, you might even like it..." She smiled seductively again.

"The Dungeon in San Francisco?" I ignored her last comment to make sure I'd heard her right.

She nodded. "But you should know that my bosses are a lot less friendly to uninvited guests than I am."

"If they're supporting the Sons of Belial, friendly will be all the way at the other end of the spectrum from what I'll be."

A sudden predatory glint in her eye suggested she would greatly enjoy it if I had to take her bosses apart. I replaced my knife in its sheath then stepped into the hall.

"Oh, Diomedes, I played your game. Now how about we play mine?" she said as I left.

Outside the door to the second-floor balcony, I almost ran into a guy—I was pretty sure it was a guy—on all fours, wearing a saddle on his back with a bit in his mouth and a bridle over his head. A smaller man was riding him like a horse. The smaller man was wearing only leather chaps, a leather vest, and a big black cowboy hat over his Lone Ranger–style mask. He was smacking the "horse" on the ass with a riding crop, screeching "giddyap" in a giddy voice that was way too squeaky for a man.

I steered clear, almost tripping over a table in the process, then contemplated jumping back down instead of using the elevator. The place was bustling with patrons and activities. I was afraid to look too closely at anything or anyone, so I chose to jump down into an open area below for the sake of expediency. Some things just couldn't be unseen, and I was afraid the little guy riding the "horse" was only the beginning.

Chapter 19

I stopped by Duma's place to leave a note in his mailbox, then I kicked the garage door to set off his alarms, just to make sure he got my message. *Damn massive door.* I nearly broke my foot in the process. Still, I needed the gear I had left at his place.

I traveled to San Francisco through the Ways. Unfortunately for me, the nearest path to San Fran opened onto a cliff at the northwestern end of a pleasant little place called Alcatraz Island. And after my detour past Duma's place, I didn't arrive until just past ten in the evening, after the island had closed to tourists for the day.

I stepped out from the Ways at a spot overlooking the Golden Gate Bridge, with the Marin Headlands and Angel Island to my left and Tiburon beyond to my right. Below me were the buildings where many of the former inmates used to work and the power plant. The iconic water tower and a cement paddock that used to be the foundation for another building stood right behind me. The ferry dock was also behind me—halfway around the island—but the next ferry off the rock wouldn't be for hours yet.

I really didn't think this through.

The place had always given off a creepy, aberrant sort of feeling. Even the earthquakes that ravaged San Francisco never upset a single stone on the island. The local Native Americans had always called it evil. Even though it didn't feel evil, per se, it certainly left one feeling depressed and somehow isolated—even with San Francisco and Oakland within sight and, on a calm night like tonight, within earshot. I always chalked it all up to the fact the island was a nexus point for the Telluric Pathways. Over the years, several psychics and more than a few shamans had told me that Alcatraz Island was one of a handful of anchor points linking our plane of existence to others. A lot of energy flowed to the island—good, bad, and indifferent. *Being a prisoner here had to be a special kind of hell.*

As cool as it had been in New York, the air was significantly colder in the middle of San Francisco Bay on the Rock. *I really did* not *think this through.*

I zipped up my fleece then made a couple of quick jumps down to the roadway below. The slog to the old guard house, where I could get out of the wind and wait to catch a ferry back to the mainland, took me past the ruins of the old officers' club.

The park rangers stationed on the island overnight rarely patrolled the grounds. While a few people had tried to *escape*, nobody tried to *break in*. I ducked into the sally port, found a darker corner, and curled up to rest.

I woke to foghorns blaring back and forth across the bay. My wet, cold clothes brought back memories of any number of campaigns that had all sucked. I stood, stretched, and realized a dense tule fog had socked in the island. I couldn't see twenty yards, but a cacophony of sounds came from the dock area. I checked my watch. It was 7:45, so the boat had to be the first of the day, bringing rangers, guides, and other volunteers to the island. That meant the first of the tourist ferries would be arriving shortly.

I arrived at Pier 33 on the mainland and pushed my way through the crowds gathered to await their spot on the next ferry out to the island. Just as I began contemplating buying another fleece jacket from a genius street vendor surrounded by frozen tourists, someone walked up to me. He was stiff—former or active military rigid—and carried a large duffle I recognized immediately as mine. He was definitely human, and his stoic face was oddly familiar.

"Mr. Dore?" he asked, with no tone in his voice at all. Despite the fog—or maybe because of it—his eyes darted around vigilantly, watching every passerby.

"Yes. Do I know you?"

"Not personally, but you do know my employer."

"Ah, is that mine, then?" I gestured to the duffle.

"Yes," he replied curtly.

He handed it over to me then turned, stopping briefly to say something over his shoulder. "Thank you for helping us on that train." Then he disappeared into the fog.

That's how I recognized him. He was one of the sacrificial mercs brought by that cambion sonofabitch to attack Kim Jong Il's train last month. Duma and Ab had hired them after all. The thought buoyed my spirits. I rarely got to see the personal impact of what I did or what I'd done over the past three thousand years.

My mood was quickly ruined by the fact that San Francisco was built on a cliff face. I was either going uphill or down, and it always seemed to be more up than down, no matter which way I went. I began walking south down the Embarcadero, figuring the flattest path would be along the waterfront. I took my time and stopped to grab food at a hole-in-the-wall Chinese restaurant that was so good it almost made up for the crappy weather—almost.

After only a few hours, I arrived in the Mission District and located the Dungeon. The establishment was in a massive tan warehouse at the corner of 16th and Folsom that covered half a city block. I walked around its perimeter to get a better feel for its layout.

Other than a series of garage doors, which clearly hadn't been used in ages, I found only one entrance. It struck me as completely out of place. About halfway down the block along Folsom was a recessed doorway tiled in black marble with a shiny gold-and-glass door at its center. There was nothing on the door—not even an address—but it was locked. Securely. The glass in the door was easily three quarters of an inch thick, and while the doorframe was gold plated, the metal was heavy and likely some sort of alloy. Even odder, I could see nothing through the glass. It presented a complete void. In a previous time, the building had likely been some sort of small-scale manufacturing facility.

After I poked around at ground level for a bit, I walked back to the door and jumped to the roof. I hung down over the edge to peek inside the windows along the rooftop, but they exhibited the same void-like darkness. Though they looked ancient from a distance, like the door, the windows and their frames were heavily reinforced and modern.

The only things on the roof were a single massive ventilation system and a series of old venting baffles, which had been welded shut. The ventilation system struck me as *significantly* oversized for the building, which meant the space below was probably bigger than the visible structure. That got me wondering about who ran the place. My first guess was more Moroi vampires, but there were none of the usual signs indicating it was part of the local Mateo Coven.

My options were limited. First, I could break in right away, while the number of potential bystanders was next to none, and poke around. On the down side, I would be walking into an unfamiliar environment, where everything focused directly on me. My next option was to wait until the place opened then head in to check things out. I wasn't thrilled with the idea of using bystanders as shields, but a mass of people did offer a bit of cover. The smartest choice was to combine the two: reconnoiter tonight then return the next day. That plan's only drawback was time—a luxury I wasn't sure I had.

I jumped down and walked to the back of the building, where several homeless people sat and rested, using the structure as a windbreak. I plopped down with them and waited. As dusk began to approach, a low thrumming started up inside the building, as if some sort of machinery began running within. At the same time, the dozen or so people gathered in the building's lee began to leave as a group—as if the vibration was their cue. I didn't move.

A grungy woman of indeterminate age—one of the last to leave—fixed me with sallow, watery eyes. "You gonna wanna leave before it gets dark. They don't allow no one to hang around once they open," she said in a husky, gravelly voice.

"I'm right behind you guys, thanks."

"They get nasty about it..." she said before shuffling off across the parking lot.

Goody. Belligerent guys wearing leather. Sounds like the Middle Ages all over again.

Once alone, I pulled my gear together and checked my Sig and Glock, verifying that I had a few fully loaded spare magazines. Then I placed them both back into my duffle, along with my swords and my vest. I tucked one knife into my boot, just in case. Despite the cold, I stuffed my fleece jacket into the duffle with my weapons. I was hoping that with everyone inside dressed in leather and rubber, I might be able to blend in wearing a black T-shirt, pants, and boots. The outfit was more fitting for a Goth club than a fetish club, but I didn't have a lot of options. I scanned the area to see if anyone was watching then jammed the duffle into a dumpster along the back wall of the warehouse.

I headed around the corner and toward the gold-and-glass door, only to find a roped-off line with several people already waiting. Surprisingly, only a few were dressed the way I'd expected, though they all wore varying amounts of leather or rubber. Walking toward the door, I recognized the droning vibration coming from inside as bass-heavy music. A massive figure easily half a foot taller than me and a good foot wider stood in front of the door, wearing a long leather duster. In the pale light of the streetlamps, the skin on the giant's bald head was ashen. Once the line moved closer to the door, I realized he—I was guessing its sex based on sheer size—had some sort of leather mask strapped over the lower half of his face, leaving his small eyes visible. The eyes weren't human. *Not even close.*

Once I was a few people back from entering, I was able to get a better view of the doorman. His eyes were an odd pale color that flashed like metal in the light, and he must have had a dozen piercings in each ear. When it was my turn, the gargantuan doorman gave me a once-over then waved me off dismissively, muttering something about "couples only." As the behemoth browsed past me to the next pair of people, I saw his pupils were cruciform—something I had never seen before. As big as this guy was, with those eyes, I honestly had no idea *what* he was or even what he might be. *That I do not like at all.*

"Hey, Gigantor, are those contacts?" I asked without getting out of line as he ushered a couple around me.

"Get lost," Gigantor said with a growl. "I told you, couples only tonight."

He spoke without any discernible accent, and I just didn't see any kind of aura of power from him. He didn't belong to any race of Fae I was familiar with, but he clearly was not human. Luckily, Gigantor had no idea who or what I was.

He directed another couple around me, but I didn't move. Frustrated, I grabbed the first person behind me—some androgynous figure dressed head to toe in a black Latex rubber suit with a matching leather harness and shorts over the top of it.

"How 'bout now, Gigantor?" I motioned to the rubberized person next to me. "See? Now we're a pair."

The person matching my absconded guest began to protest, but I just shot them a nasty and very serious glare, causing them to jerk back slightly and cease their protestations instantly.

Without looking at me, Gigantor shrugged and hooked a thumb toward the door. I dragged the rubber person with me through the door then let go. Inside the door, we had to pass through a heavy black curtain into a pitch-black space then through another heavy curtain. We were met by a virtual wall of bone-vibrating bass and ear-splitting noise that I guessed might have passed for music to some.

Another being similar to the doorman, only much slighter of build and just barely taller than me, stood behind a podium in front of us like some kind of maître d'. If Gigantor was male, then this one was female for sure. She was dressed in a red leather catsuit and, like Gigantor, wore a mask that covered her face below her freaky pale metallic eyes. Her head was almost completely bald, except for a single massive braid that started at the crown of her skull. Chains ran from her ears to her nose under the mask. Her severe eyebrows were also studded. The hostess desk she stood behind bore a sign that read $40 Per Couple.

The rubber person with me shrugged and pointed behind us. Rubber Person might have said something, but I doubt I could have understood it through the mask anyway. I got the message, though. I dug into my pocket, pulled out all the cash I had, and threw forty bucks on the desk, shaking my head in disgust.

Before I could move off into the crowd, the odd-eyed Amazon shot me a glance that made me uneasy, almost as if she knew why I was there. But that was nothing compared to how uneasy I became after I beheld the inside of the building.

Chapter 20

Unable to hear over the pounding electronic bass, I looked around the dark, cavernous space. The first thing that drew my eye was an area illuminated by bright lights about twenty yards in front of me. A flurry of activity centered around a stage, where two leather-clad assistants inserted hooks into the skin of the chest, shoulders, arms, and back of a skinny man in some sort of trancelike state, naked except for some kind of loincloth. The hooks were attached to wires that vanished into the darkness above. The scene reminded me of the Mandan *Okipa* ceremony—and frankly, watching them hoist the guy up off the stage made me queasy. As he rose into the air, I could hear cheers from the surrounding crowd, even over the music.

Spotlights highlighted additional figures, both male and female, suspended well above the floor—all bound and hung in various BDSM poses as well. As I gathered my thoughts and tried to refocus myself, I noticed the same sickly-sweet smell I'd encountered at Cocytus. In the Dungeon, however, the fragrance was almost overwhelming. I couldn't even smell the alcohol or sweat I'd expect to dominate a club like this.

I began to feel a bit less concerned for the suspended people, and I found it very hard to focus on why I had come, especially once I became acutely aware of all the women walking around in all manner of revealing outfits. In a single-minded haze, I followed a woman wearing only high heels and a leather mask.

An intense buzzing began in my head, stopping me in my tracks. I had to close my eyes and concentrate to remain upright—then all the fuzziness was gone. When I reopened my eyes, I suddenly remembered why I was there.

"Thank you, Athena," I whispered to myself. I shook my head to clear the cobwebs and again tried to gain a feeling for my surroundings.

More and more people crowded into the club. The mass of bodies combined with the intense thumping music and the strange lighting began to feel suffocating. As best I could tell, the club occupied the entire interior of the building and was open to the ceiling above. A bar ran nearly the length of the wall opposite the entrance and was lit by irritating and stark blue neon. Thousands of liquor bottles lined the wall behind the bar, and I counted at least ten bartenders. All of them were much closer in stature to normal humans, and none gave off an aura of any kind.

Three corners of the floor space were nearly pitch black, while the farthest corner to the left of the entrance was reasonably bright and manned by several extremely large figures. Occasionally, patrons would walk over to the giants in pairs or small groups then descend to a level below us.

The large stage at the end of the building was clearly the source of the music, but I could barely make out the DJ working there. In near blackness, a pair of lights somehow mounted to his head bobbed in time to the beat. Light reflected off glass above and behind the DJ. I guessed an office or some sort of private space was behind the glass. As I studied it, I began to make out a series of darkened windows that offered a view over the entire space. A narrow stairway ran along the wall to the right of the stage and up to the level of the office space.

The huge interior was divided into two distinct sections: the smaller part was a large dance floor closest to the stage and DJ, but the rest of it was dimly lit and randomly dotted with chaise lounges, couches, beds, and circular settees. Banks of TV screens hung from above or were mounted on the walls, and each flashed all manner of imagery, both erotic and just plain odd.

Maneuvering within the club became a test of concentration. The atmosphere was an assault on just about every sense simultaneously. Moving through the crowd, I noticed it was becoming increasingly difficult for me to maintain my composure. I had to stop myself from decking a guy with a three-foot-tall mohawk. He was dressed in leather suspenders, shorts, and old combat boots when he bounced into me while he was flailing about dancing. *Either that or he thought he was on fire.*

Out of irritation and perhaps to maintain some sense of order in this chaos, I kept checking my watch for time. After attempting to wander around for thirty minutes, I finally gave up and headed to a darkened corner. That was when I discovered why the corners were unlit. I honestly couldn't tell how many people were involved in what resembled a human version of maggots on a carcass. I left before I got sucked into the maelstrom.

I came across a young man dressed surprisingly conservatively in jeans and a T-shirt, sitting on a couch, a woman under each arm. He was kissing one of the women on the neck, but both women behaved as if they were well out of it. He was a Moroi vampire feeding.

I approached him deliberately, shoving people out of my way, and stood directly in front of him. He stopped his activities just long enough to flash me a wry smile. This punk was sloppy and feeding openly, which meant he had to be a young vampire. I could have left him to the Mateo Coven to discipline, but whether it was the atmosphere or my hatred of such vermin, I wasn't feeling magnanimous.

I kicked his leg to get his attention, and he lifted his hand off one woman's breast to shoo me without looking up. *Yeah. Fuck this.*

I grabbed a handful of his hair, pulled him up, and tried to throw him out into the crowd. I didn't get him very far before the handful of hair came loose from his scalp. The punk gave out a shriek loud enough that I could hear it over the music and crowd. I glanced at the wad of hair in my hand, grinned, then threw it down. The vampire became wild-eyed and tried to attack me, but the crowd was too thick for him to gain much momentum. By the time he pushed through the crowd back to me, I was ready and waiting. The second he was close enough, I planted my fist square into his nose as hard as I could, earning myself a very satisfying crunch of bone. The punk's head snapped back as he fell into the crowd behind him. Almost instantly, a cheer went up among the people around us, and some of them hoisted the semiconscious form over their heads and began to pass him around.

The parasite finally came to his senses about twenty feet into the crowd and began to thrash, causing the people supporting him to drop him. Pushing my way toward him, I noticed several more of the very large humanoid bouncers working their way toward us. I made it to the leech before the bouncers could make it to us. Completely out of control, the kid tried to rush me. Even in the tight confines, I easily avoided the punk's first haphazard swing then hit him with a right to his torso. Hammering my left forearm and elbow into the side of his head dropped him again.

I knelt over him, grabbed his chin in one hand, and began searching his neck for his coven's mark. Every coven marked its members, and unaffiliated vampires wouldn't dare tread on the territories of known covens. I couldn't find the mark that should have been under his ear, though.

I started to get up, dragging the dazed vampire with me by his jaw, when a pair of massive hands gripped me like vises and abruptly lifted me to my toes. Another figure grabbed the punk and pulled him out of my hands. As I tried to twist around, something caught my eye. The vaguest hint of a figure, or rather the odd brownish energy that enveloped it, hung in the shadows on the landing at the top of the stairs leading to the office space above the stage. The big hands that held me shoved me hard in that direction. The aura around the figure was intense and radiated *around* it rather than emanating *from* it. While the aura was similar, I could tell the creature was not a vampire.

So much for casual observations tonight.

The crowd parted in front of us as we headed toward the stairs. The giant pushing the punk vampire was a few steps in front of me. He had a strange empty holster on his left hip next to a canister of pepper spray and a telescoping stun baton in another holster on his right hip. At one point in our march, he lowered his left hand back to his side for a moment, gripping a Taser, a two-shot X2. I had to assume the giant behind me was similarly armed. Apparently, fetishists could get violent and unruly. *Who knew?*

My escort shoved me at one point, and I shrugged it off and began to turn to glare at him in defiance when the Taser's warning arc crackled behind me, followed by the unique smell of charged air.

"Keep moving," he said in a gruff voice over the din, "or you'll find out what fifty thousand volts feels like." I didn't have my cuirass on to insulate me from the shock, so I just kept moving.

Oddly, the crowd stared at us as if we were somehow stranger than they were. We made it to the base of the stairs, where the silhouetted figure reeking of power and energy stood. A long, skinny arm reached from the shadows and, with a bony hand, pointed at the vampire then hooked a thumb up to the office. Then he waved his skeletal hand dismissively toward the door, and a big paw closed on my shoulder, pulling me back toward the entrance. The other bouncer shoved the vampire up the stairs as I was thrown out into the street past a crowd of people waiting to enter.

I tried to act indignant, which wasn't very hard since I was. I quickly improvised being drunk and faked tripping over a crack in the sidewalk, landing sprawled out on the street. I picked myself up, confident that my ruse was convincing, then stumbled to the back of the building, where I'd left my gear. It was barely one in the morning, and I had no idea when the club would shut down.

I grabbed my duffle out of the dumpster then geared up, feeling normal again for the first time in days. I checked my sidearms out of habit then crouched next to the dumpster to wait. Less than an hour later, one of the giant bouncers came around the corner, heading right for me.

"Hey," he shouted, waving a hand at me as if I were some kind of animal in the trash pile. "Get out of here."

I stood to face him, checking my wrists to make sure the leather strips I wore over my hands were secure. "Make me, tough guy."

He pulled his stun baton from his belt and flicked it open as he stomped closer. "Damn homeless. I'm gonna enjoy this." He laughed, holding the baton low along his right side.

I had a brief conversation with myself, weighing the pros and cons of shooting him, cleaving him, or just beating him to a pulp. Reason won out: I could use him alive. Plus, gunfire would cause too much of a stir, cleaving was too messy, and having a meaningful conversation is tough when one of the participants is catatonic.

The giant took the last few steps in an ungainly jog, raising the baton over his head. If I'd been a normal human, the intended blow would have put me in a coma at the very least. I shot forward and met him in a tackle meant to stop, not drop him. I hit him in his rib cage with my right shoulder, cracking bones and halting his momentum instantly, then I rotated my body to bring my left elbow up to connect with his face with all my strength. I caught him squarely across the jaw, cheek, and nose. More bones broke.

The giant staggered back, dropped the baton, and reached for the ground with his left arm to steady himself as his legs gave out. I kicked his arm out from under him, and he fell forward in a heap, moaning. Standing over him, I rotated my sore right arm at the shoulder, lamenting the stiffness that persisted weeks after my last injury to it. The giant wasn't as strong or as fast as I'd expected, not much more than a human.

I picked up the baton he'd dropped and examined it as I returned to the giant's prone form. I crouched beside him, sitting on my heels.

"Wow, that was a spectacularly dumb move, junior." I grabbed the giant by his leather chest harness and pulled him to a sitting position. Whatever race he belonged to, he was as heavy as a damned elephant. "Now, when you're ready, you're going to tell me everything I want to know, right?" I waved the baton in front of him. His eyes began to focus again, following the moving tip of the baton, and he nodded.

"Ca—" He gurgled through the thick blood and broken teeth and bones, "Cam-ras." He pointed up along the roofline at the security cameras. He tried to smile, but it didn't work with his split lips. I did hear a few hoarse laughs in between coughs and moans, though.

Shaking my head at the sudden realization of my stupidity, I jumped up to the roofline, pulling myself up and over. Covering the camera lens with my hand, I redirected the cameras to provide a small blind spot below before jumping back down.

"That's better," I said, sitting down next to the injured bouncer. "And thanks for the warning, though I gotta admit it was dumb on my part not to think of it first. I just don't know where my head's been, ya know? Oh well…"

I held the baton so that I could zap him if I had to but also move it quickly to attack anybody who came to his defense. I figured someone would come out to help him, and if I played injured, as well, then they might come right to me. "Now you just relax. Someone will be along shortly to help you."

We didn't have to wait more than three minutes before another figure came around the corner, Taser in hand. In fact, I could see the red aiming dot on my chest. They were going to have to get a lot closer to use it, though, since the wires only reached fifteen feet.

"Hey..." said a husky female voice. "You okay? Az... you all right? Az..."

Az didn't answer. In fact, he didn't even move, which was odd because I was pretty sure he was wheezing. The female bouncer crept closer, keeping the dot on my chest. Once she was close enough, she kicked my foot, but I remained still. It was the catsuit-clad giantess who had collected the fee at the door. Once she got a better view of Az, she immediately changed her focus to helping him, forgetting me completely.

"Holy crap, Az! What happened?" She knelt next to him.

He tried to mumble something, then I decided it was my move.

"He underestimated me." I rammed the stun baton into her ribcage. I had to zap her several times and run the battery down, but she finally fell.

It took me a few seconds to get her into position next to Az, and I couldn't get over how deceptively heavy the beings were. They weighed far more than a serious weightlifter of similar stature. It was like their bones were made of lead or something.

"What the hell *are* you guys?" I asked offhandedly once I was done. "Actually, let's put a pin in that one for right now. I have more important questions for you. For starters, is your boss up in that office or downstairs somewhere?"

I tossed the used-up baton into the dumpster and grabbed the giantess's stun gun. Aiming it back and forth between them, I watched their eyes follow it rather than me. Az grumbled something unintelligible as his face and jaw swelled. The female bouncer still hadn't fully recovered, either.

"Oh, right, sorry. I forgot it might be hard to talk. Let's try this... blink once for upstairs and twice for down. How's that? And if you both don't agree, then you both get zapped again. Sound fair? Good. Now, upstairs or down?" I arced the Taser just for added effect.

They both blinked hard one time.

"Excellent," I replied. "Now, how many of you are there? Blink once for each of you."

They both began blinking, and I couldn't keep up with them at the same time.

"Whoa, whoa, whoa, hold on. One at a time. Same rules apply, though. You first." I pointed at Az.

They each blinked ten times.

"You're doing just fine. Now, are all ten of you here right now? Blink once for yes and twice for no."

They both blinked twice.

"Okay, how many are here now? You first," I said, again pointing at Az.

They both blinked six times.

"Six including you two?" I asked.

One blink from both.

"Anyone else in there tougher than you two?"

Neither blinked intentionally, and their eyes darted in every direction except mine.

"C'mon now. I don't want to zap you, but I will..." I wagged the Taser back and forth in front of them. "You should be able to talk by now, Catsuit, so spill."

Still, no response. Something inside the building scared them enough to risk the pain of stunning. The *boss* clearly wasn't the issue.

"Just one someone else?" I asked, arcing the Taser inches in front of their faces.

Their eyes locked on the bright-blue spark as it moved, but they still did not blink intentionally.

"Fine." I aimed the targeting dot at Catsuit's nose from about two feet away.

Her eyes crossed, and she cringed but still wouldn't blink. When I took my finger off the trigger, she sighed and fell backward. Even Az rolled his eyes in relief and exhaled heavily through his mouth.

"Wow, you guys are really scared of whoever it is inside there. Huh," I said, standing up and heading over to my duffle. "So, here's what's going to happen: we are going to sit here and wait until everyone leaves, and then I am going back in to talk with your *boss* and whoever it is you two are so afraid of. Sound like a plan?"

No response.

"Good," I said, pulling a skein of rope out of my bag.

Chapter 21

No one else came to follow up over the next few hours. Once the vibration of thumping music stopped, I peeked around the corner of the building, standing directly under one of the security cameras to avoid its view. I left the two bouncers trussed up. *Working in a place like this, they probably enjoy it anyway.*

The line of people at the door and the door attendant were gone. I watched for a good ten minutes without seeing anyone come or go—not even a car passed on the street—before I headed for the entrance. Halfway down the sidewalk, I pulled both my swords and prepared myself for a fight.

Despite my current combative attitude, I knew it was reasonable to check the door to see if it was open before going all ballistic on it. It was locked, but the prudent thing was to enter as quietly as possible, so I resisted the urge to kick it in and shoved my sword into the space between the door and its frame. After cutting through the locking bolts, I entered without setting off any kind of alarms that I could see or hear and used my sword to part the first curtain before peering through the second.

The inside of the warehouse was completely lit up from corner to corner, and two giants were mopping the floor. One was scrubbing very hard in the far corner near the stage area, while the other sloppily worked a mop near the bar. There was no sign of movement other than the sloshy mopping activity.

I walked through the curtain, swords in hand, and quietly started up the stairs to the office space. I made it about halfway up the steps before the two oversized janitors noticed me. Ignoring their shouting, I continued upward. Putting my shoulder and all my momentum into the metal door at the top, I hit it with sufficient force to rip it from its hinges and send it toppling into the room.

The office was small—less than a hundred square feet—with a plush white couch along the back wall and two deep white armchairs separated by a small bar across from it. In the far wall was a door. The windows behind the bar were incredibly thick one-way glass, probably made from bullet-resistant material.

At the foot of the couch, a vaguely humanoid shape lay wrapped up like a burrito in heavy plastic sheeting. The pale-pink stain oozing across the length of it matched the mess sprayed along the back wall and ceiling. There was no metallic scent of human blood, though.

My first guess was the remains of the unaffiliated Moroi interloper. Before I could make a move to check the contents of the burrito, the door on the other side of the room opened. What stepped through caught me off guard. *Gangly* was the first word that came to mind. The figure was just slightly taller than me but half the width. Its spindly arms and legs were grotesquely long while its torso was short. Conversely, the creature's head was large and round like a basketball, with two huge yellow eyes. Teeth stuck out at all angles from the gash-like mouth that split the head nearly in half. The figure was cloaked in an intense brown energy—the same energy I had seen earlier at the top of the stairs.

"An incubus..." I said aloud, but mostly to myself, wincing at the sight of the being's true form. "Makes perfect sense for a place like this."

Before it could respond, heavy pounding steps rang up the metal stairs behind me.

"Don't move!" a voice shouted from behind me.

The frightfully freakish figure in front of me didn't move or say anything. I began shifting slightly so I could get an eye on the attackers behind me while still keeping an eye on the incubus, but one of the two giants on the landing fired his Taser at me, hitting me just behind my left arm. The barbs only managed to snag the ballistic nylon of my vest and didn't penetrate, so my cuirass insulated me from the charge. I swatted the leads away with my left sword and faced the pair of giants.

"Let's not do that again," I said.

The giant shot me with his second charge, hitting me fully in the chest. I felt a tingle before I swiped the leads with my right sword. I made a sudden lunge without raising either sword, but it startled the first giant enough that he clumsily stepped backward into the one behind him, sending that one over the railing at the top of the steps. The giant hit the cement floor below with a meaty *thwap*.

I cringed, but it distracted the remaining giant long enough for me to move forward, sword raised. My sudden move drew his attention. The giant glanced rapidly back and forth from his fallen comrade to me. Screaming, he swatted at the blade with one hand then threw the spent Taser at me. Just as quickly, I batted the plastic yellow gun aside, shattering it, and brought my other sword up to meet the arm that had thrown the Taser, severing it cleanly just below the elbow. The bouncer howled, and I planted a heel in his broad chest, sending him tumbling backward down the stairs. The wailing stopped before the body reached the floor.

I returned to the office behind me, but by the time I spotted the incubus scrambling across the room's ceiling like some sort of insect on crack, it managed to flip down and kick me square in the chest with both of its spindly legs. The force sent me reeling backward into the doorframe. I narrowly missed smacking my head into the metal frame, but knocking it on the adjacent paneling was only slightly better. I managed to keep my footing, though I was dazed and momentarily without any idea where the incubus was. The next thing I knew, I was flying across the room in the other direction. I hit the far wall and fell to the floor in a heap of broken glass and wood. To make matters worse, I had no idea where my swords were, either.

I was picking myself up off the floor, trying to regain my bearings, when a tremendous blow hit my chest. It probably would have killed me if not for my cuirass. Instead, the attack knocked me back against the wall, and I instinctively threw my arms over my head. Luckily. I managed to block another blow aimed at the side of my head with my left arm and shoulder and reflexively struck out with my right in an arcing roundhouse punch that managed to connect solidly with something fleshy but firm.

The blow bought me a few seconds. I shook my head, regaining my wits but still not fully sure of my situation. The incubus had backed off and was favoring its left side. I pulled the Sig Sauer P226 Navy from the holster on my vest and aimed at the creature, which was hunkered low to the ground a few yards in front of me. An odd sensation began invading my mind, and I immediately blocked it out, shaking my head.

"That crap won't work on me, demon," I said in disgust. "No more than this gun will kill you."

The incubus was crawling across the floor, still favoring its left side, as it climbed over the rolled-up vampire, over the couch, then began to move up the back wall.

"We can be civilized about this, Guardian," the creature managed to say cleanly despite its tangled dentition. "I let you pass earlier when I could have had you killed like this wretch." It nodded briefly at the rolled-up corpse.

"I save civility for those that deserve it, demon," I replied. "For you, I prefer contempt."

The incubus hissed wildly then lunged. I pulled the trigger three times and ducked into a forward roll. Despite hitting the thing all three times, I knew the bullets wouldn't do much more than my punch had, but they did knock the incubus off trajectory just enough to get me out of the corner. The creature landed with a thud but quickly spun around to face me. We had traded places. I kept backing up slowly through the room, Sig still aimed at the incubus, until I noticed the thing suddenly become more agitated.

The muscles in its bony legs begin to tense as if preparing to leap, so I fired off a shot that hit it square in the forehead with a dull *whump*. The thing just recoiled slightly and shook its head like a cat that had just run into a screen door as the mushroomed bullet fell to the floor below it.

I continued to move back until I noticed one of my swords lying next to the remnants of the bar. The gun wouldn't hurt an incubus, but my swords surely would. Keeping my eye on the creature straddling the wall, I tried to close the distance to my sword. The incubus once again became incensed by my actions, probably aware that my swords presented a much more serious threat.

"Why do you come, Guardian?" the incubus asked, possibly as a delay tactic.

"Oh, you know…" I said, keeping my movements steady, "whips, chains, a little bondage. The usual."

"Don't be coy. Here, you are out of place. You are searching for someone, no? Tell me and perhaps I can help. There is no need for us to be enemies."

"No need beyond the fact that you view humans as objects to be used as you see fit," I replied.

"Not true. My kind requires your kind for our very survival. We are, in many ways, dependent upon you."

"Spoken like a true parasite."

I lowered my eyes just long enough to see how close the sword was, and the incubus leapt at me. I dropped to my knees, but instead of reaching for the sword, I let go of the Sig and caught the incubus, redirecting its momentum over my shoulder. It crashed into the re-inforced windows behind me then sprawled across the ruined bar. I grabbed the creature by its left arm and swung it back against the far wall, breaking through the paneling and knocking pictures from the wall. I followed and snagged the creature by its leg, swinging it back against the windows. It hit with a satisfying crunching sound, but the window remained undamaged.

Before it could even lift its head, I rammed its head into the window again. This time, the window cracked. I repeated the process twice more until the window frame began to separate from the reinforced sill. I dropped the limp creature over the bar and slammed the window with both hands one last time to break it completely free from its frame. The heavy composite glass crashed down on the stage below, where it spiderwebbed but stayed in one piece, held by its multiple layers of reinforcing films. Then I seized the incubus by the neck and tossed it through the open window space.

I picked up my gun, holstered it, then found my swords before strolling down the stairs. I stepped over the one-armed giant bouncer with the broken neck and past the other, whose limbs and head were twisted at odd angles in the middle of a spreading pile of dark liquid at the bottom. Swords in hand, I walked over to the edge of the stage and sat down. The incubus was less than a yard away, pulling itself across the stage in an attempt to get away. Despite the injuries, the demon would probably be just fine in a matter of hours if left to its own devices. But I had no interest in letting a creature like this remain free to run a place like this.

I gripped the demon by the neck again and dragged it across the floor to the bar. I slammed it down on the bar's marble top then jumped the bar. After finding a book of matches, I located a bottle of grain alcohol and doused the monster with the liquor.

"Now, here's what's going to happen: You're going to tell me what I need to know, or I flambé your ass." I struck a match.

The incubus's wet yellow eyes followed the match for a long second before it responded, its voice little more than a raspy croak. "I will answer... the best I can..."

"The Sons of Belial. Where can I find them?" I asked.

Its wet, phlegmy laugh stuck in its throat, but it didn't answer.

"What's so funny, pumpkin head?" I asked, a hair's breadth from burning the whole place down.

The creature's eyes travelled back toward the stairs up to its office. It took me a second to realize he wasn't eyeing the stairs but the two giants lying in a heap below them.

"Wait..." I said, the lightbulb finally going on. "You mean Tweedledee and Tweedledum there are Sons of Belial?"

The creature let out another phlegmy laugh. "For one so old, you are not very... intelligent."

Without blinking, I grabbed a sword off the bar and cut off its left arm above the elbow. The creature howled, thrashing on the bar so violently that I had to shove the sword through its chest and well into the bar to pin it down. Far from dead, it reached for the sword with its remaining arm but was too weak to pull it out. I put my hand on top of its hand on the sword's hilt, clamped down, and applied pressure. It wailed.

"Hey! Hey! Hey!" I said, screaming louder and louder. "Calm down, or I'll remove all your limbs, Stumpy. Besides, it'll grow back, won't it?"

The creature stared at me with death in its big yellow eyes.

"Back to the Tweedle brothers over there," I said motioning with my chin. "Those are Sons of Belial?"

"They all are." The creature coughed up a gobbet of something thick and yellow that just oozed down the side of its face. "They are... the offspring and descendants of the Nephilim. The last... of their kind."

"What do they want with Ramiel?"

"I know of no Ramiel," it said defiantly. "They only *work* for me."

I twisted the sword, cracking the marble below and eliciting a screech from the incubus.

"Don't lie to me, demon. I know they have a connection to Ramiel."

"I do not know this Ramiel..." It coughed.

Unfortunately, I believed him.

"Now who's the dumb one?" I said with a sneer. "Your boys seem to be in league with Ramiel the Watcher, late of Tartarus."

The yellow eyes widened.

"Yeah, scares me, too..." I said pointedly. "But your boys were also scared of someone or some*thing* else in here. Now what could that be?"

The silent fear in its eyes betrayed the fact that it knew exactly what they were afraid of.

"Oh ho, so you *do* have a boss," I said, allowing him to realize he had told me without saying a word. "So then, would this thing—I say *thing* because, well, I just can't imagine you being cowed by a human—still be here in this building?"

With that, the incubus began thrashing wildly again, kicking at me with its freakishly long legs. I grabbed my other sword and hacked off one of its legs, dropped the sword on the counter behind the bar, and picked up the severed limb. The leg continued to thrash a bit in my hand, a little like a snake with its head cut off, and it freaked me out a little. So I tossed it across the warehouse.

"Man, it's gonna take you all kinds of time to recover from this, Stumpy," I said, wiping my hand off on my vest. "But I'll take that as a yes..."

I pulled the sword from its chest and shoved the incubus onto the floor, where it began to pull itself away as if trying to escape. Frankly, it was doing a pretty good job, too, but the sight of it pushing and pulling itself with one arm and leg was bizarre. It moved unlike anything I'd expected from something so injured. *These things are tough.*

It was writhing toward the stairs that led down at the far side of the room, leaving a trail of yellowish ichor behind. I grabbed my swords, hopped over the bar, and caught up to it.

"Down there, huh?" I asked, pointing toward the stairs. "Think whatever it is will save you from me? Don't worry, Stumpy. I'm not going to kill you. Yet. I'm going to go check down here for your boss first if that's okay. You wait here, and I'll be right back."

Chapter 22

I probably should have stopped to think about what the hell might actually scare an incubus that badly. I also probably should have stopped for a second to figure out the best way to approach what was undoubtedly a blind alley and the perfect place to get myself ambushed. But there were only a few more of the quasi-Nephilim things around, and they really weren't that intimidating anymore. I was pretty sure that whatever was down there was *not* Ramiel. If it was, the entire block would have a hellish and vile feel to it—a feeling I could never forget. So I figured anything else would be a cinch by comparison.

I headed down the stairs without skulking, but I took great care not to present myself as an easy target, either. The air in the stairway was thick with the same sickly-sweet, almost intoxicating smell that I'd first noticed back at Cocytus then when I walked into this place. The aroma was much more concentrated and cloying—whatever created it was down there somewhere. The scent started to give me a headache. The hallway was dimly lit by electric fixtures but was not so dark that I couldn't see the full length of it. A dozen wooden doors lined both sides, and two more occupied the far end. The dark glass bubbles of remote-controlled surveillance cameras dotted the ceiling every few yards.

As I moved down the hall, swords down by my sides, I was struck by how quiet this area was. Not just a nobody-moving quiet, more like a sound-dampened hush that, along with the lighting, made everything more surreal. Thick red velvet covered the walls, and the dense carpet on the floor created a bizarre chaotic pattern.

I stopped at the first door on my right and threw it open. Seeing nothing in the darkness, I put away one sword and pulled out one of my LED flashlights. The beam revealed a rather large space that first struck me as some sort of torture chamber: all manner of racks and frameworks adorned with shackles and restraints of all kinds. Instantly, bile rose in my throat until I remembered what sort of place this *actually* was.

After regaining my composure, I went down the hallway, trying each door. Some rooms were all stainless steel and leather, while others featured raw wood and hemp ropes.

The closer I got to the end of the hallway, the more penetrating the odor became, and the bizarre sensation spreading through my mind became stronger. It was a disquieting mix of intense pain and pleasure. The ache in my head from my encounter with the incubus didn't help. When I reached the doors at the end of the hall, even in the dark I could tell without touching them that they were different from the others. While they had the outward appearance of the other doors, these were seriously reinforced, and each had its own dedicated security camera. I tried the knob on the door to the right, only to find it secure, as I expected. *What the hell? In for a penny and all...*

I shoved the blade of my sword between the door and its frame at the knob until the door shifted a bit, then I pushed downward, eliciting a soft sound like an aluminum can ripping. I opened the door and shined the light around. The large room was some sort of storage area for medical equipment. Another door stood in the center of the wall opposite.

I couldn't make heads or tails of why an S&M club would need IV regulators, heart rate monitors, and even several small glass-fronted refrigerators filled with IV bags of unmarked solutions. The moment I opened the refrigerator, however, the smell that permeated the entire building hit me like a truck. The scent overwhelmed me, and all at once, I found myself focusing on Sarah—*and undressing her*. I shook my head, concentrated on closing the door to the fridge, then stood up.

I went to the other door in the room and, surprisingly, found it unlocked. I threw it open only to find two very surprised men in full hazmat suits gawking at me.

"Oh, hi," I said, raising one sword slightly in a wave, more than a little concerned about their suits.

The light in the room came entirely from monitors they were watching, including some kind of a grainy black-and-white video feed of two patients on gurneys, with all kinds of tubes and wires coming out of them. The reflected lighting made the two hazmat-clad men appear wan and sickly behind their faceguards, and neither man—they were definitely human—moved.

"So... whatcha doin'?" I asked, making my way farther into the room.

The pair glanced at each other then back at me but did nothing. Both were seated at a desk that held all the screens they watched. It was some sort of monitoring station, but for what? The only other feature in the room was another door in the far wall.

"Um... you can't be in here," one of the men said in a soft, unsure voice.

"Sure I can," I replied, moving toward the other door. "I assume whoever *they* are, they're in here, right?" I pointed from the video screen to the door.

"No, you can't go in there. Stop..." the soft-spoken guy stammered before facing his companion. "Call her."

"But, she'll kill us if...if... she finds out we let him in..." he replied, his voice cracking with fear.

I stopped with my hand on the doorknob to the room beyond. "She who?"

"Please, mister, you got to get out of here. Leave now, or she'll kill you and then kill us," the first guy said.

"She who?" I asked again. "Tell me, and I promise I won't *let* her kill you."

"You can't protect us from her. You don't know *her*. She's so beautiful..." the soft-spoken guy said.

The other guy just started to cry softly, hanging his head. His shoulders shook ever so slightly. "It's too late... she's going to kill us," he mumbled as he cried.

Whoever *she* was, she had these two wound tighter than a clock spring, so they were useless. I opened the door to the next room and stepped into some sort of airlock formed from dense plastic sheeting. I put one sword through the side of the plastic compartment and created a slit to pass through. Inside the freezing space, that familiar cloying smell became so intense that I pressed my forearm to my nose and tried to breathe through my mouth, which didn't help. The odor, like rotting flowers, was so concentrated that it made me feel light-headed.

Just as I had seen on the monitor in the other room, two hospital gurneys sat side by side. On each was a humanoid form covered entirely by white sheets, made severely bright by the brilliant fluorescent lighting above. At the head of both was a complex series of wires, some tracing back to a machine that tracked what I could only guess were brain-wave patterns, while others went to a series of machines that resembled computers. A series of tubes connected to various IV bags, pumps, and ventilators hung from under the sheets. Tubes connected to bags like the ones in the glass-fronted refrigerators snaked under the sheets.

Cautiously, I walked over to the closest figure and carefully lifted the sheet.

A tinny voice spoke over some sort of speaker system. "Please, don't. You have no idea the ramifications your actions will bring."

Whatever.

I lifted the sheet enough to see the head and upper torso of a young man. The top of his skull was missing, dozens of wires stuck into his exposed brain, and tubes ran down his throat. My eyes went immediately to the device showing brain activity: there was a steady flat line with a regular massive peak every few seconds. The monitor for the other figure showed the same thing. I walked close enough to grab the sheet on the other body and threw it back, revealing a young woman with the top of her head removed as well. My stomach churned with disgust.

Still, something about the pair wasn't right. Their features were too symmetrical, too fine—too perfect. They were Fae of some kind. And they were being kept alive artificially—but why?

I pulled the sheet the rest of the way off the male figure. His abdomen was completely gone, and the empty space was filled with a pump of some sort that fed the many tubes protruding from the body. The large tube from the foot of the gurney snaked up between his legs and disappeared underneath the body. When I pulled the sheet off the female, she was in a similar state. I wasn't sure what to do or even how much time I had before *she* showed up, so I pulled out my cell phone and took a picture of each figure's face.

Whatever this place was and whatever these *things* were, they deserved better. Fueled by disgust at the lack of respect for these beings and a pounding headache, I began ripping the equipment apart and cutting all the wires and tubes. They at least deserved the dignity of finally dying.

I was on the far side of the gurneys when one of the two hazmat-suited men walked through the airlock with a Desert Eagle .50 pointed in my direction. He held the small cannon with both hands, shaking and unsteady. He actually managed to fire once before I could move, blowing a chunk of masonry from the wall about three feet to my right. The massive gun kicked wickedly in his hands, throwing him completely off balance. Before he could regain his composure and fire again, I shoved both gurneys hard, knocking them over, sending the limp bodies sliding to the floor before diving behind the metal tables for cover.

He fired once more, and chunks of cement and masonry rained down on me. I was going to have to hurt these guys to get out. Whoever *she* was, she was really pissing me off by using humans this way. *If I have to kill them to get out of here...*

Then the guy with the gun spoke in a panic. "What are you doing with that? You can't use that in here. You'll kill us all!" he screamed.

I remained behind the heavy steel gurneys but poked my head up just long enough to see that the second man in his hazmat suit was holding something small with both hands while the gunman, facing him, began to back farther into the room.

"We have to get rid of him... and all of the stuff in here, too, now that he's seen it. That's what she'd want, and you know it," the second man said in a strained voice laden with fear.

"But that'll kill us, too," the gunman stammered, holding one hand up, the heavy gun dangling at his side as he took another step back. "Put it down... I'll take care of this guy, and then we can clean it all up. I said put it down... or I'll shoot." He raised the gun with an unsteady arm while the second man stepped back into the other room and out of my view. *This has disaster written all over it, and I need to do something before we all got killed.*

"Guys," I shouted to get their attention.

Apparently, my shout startled the frightened gunman into shooting. I have no idea what, if anything, he hit, but the noise that followed sounded an awful lot like a grenade hitting the ground and rolling.

Shit.

Chapter 23

I pulled the steel table as close to me as I could, curled up underneath it, and braced myself. My mind raced, trying to remember if I'd seen oxygen anywhere, as the grenade detonated.

When I opened my eyes, the room was black, with sparks showering from several places. The shockwave knocked the breath from my lungs, but as I sucked in air, I tasted the cement dust and smelled the cordite from the grenade over the sickly-sweet rotting-flower smell that permeated the place. I could hear nothing except a high-pitched ringing, and my head felt like an overfilled balloon ready to explode. I moved my arms and legs in the dark then wiggled my toes and fingers to make sure everything was still attached and functional, then I pushed myself up. I pulled my flashlight out of a vest pocket and clicked it on.

Luckily, only about half the room—the half nearest the doorway—was wrecked. Most of the walls near the door and the ceiling above it were covered in gore. The two bodies lay mangled against the upturned gurneys, while most of the gunman fell near the remnants of the pulverized monitors and pumps. The bunker of a room, however, was still intact.

I grabbed my swords and fumbled through the debris back into the monitoring room, where nearly every surface was covered in blood and body parts from the would-be grenadier. Though the blast had ripped apart everything within it, the structure itself, like the other room, remained whole. Much of the masonry had been blown away from the interior wall, revealing a heavy "floating" steel structure underneath. The place literally *was* a bunker.

It took me forever to stumble back out into the hallway. My ringing ears combined with the intense smells and the smoke-and-dust-filled darkness kept me disoriented. In the hall, a pale female figure at the other end watched me through the haze before heading up the stairs. I wasn't sure if I was seeing things or not, but it occurred to me that the figure might be the *she* the two hazmat suits had mentioned before blowing themselves up. I tried to run after her, but I just couldn't coordinate my legs, so I staggered after her and up the stairs.

Just before the top of the stairs, I took a minute to gather myself so that I wouldn't just be inviting an ass kicking if I had to confront something. Carrying my swords, I loped into the open warehouse, where an intense but contained brilliant blue-white inferno burned near the bar. Broken glass from liquor bottles was scattered around the flames, and a mangled hand holding a lighter lay near the edge of the conflagration. The size of the flaming mound was too big to be just the lanky incubus.

Taking stock of the rest of the space, I noticed the two dead bouncers at the bottom of the office stairs were indeed gone. Thick wet trails on the cement floor led from the stairs to the bonfire. Across the floor, some twenty yards away, where I'd thrown it, the incubus's leg thrashed with rapidly decreasing intensity. I assumed the ruckus from behind the bar was its severed arm doing the same.

I was pretty sure an incubus could eventually heal completely from massive physical trauma—maybe even this. As tough as they were, I was also pretty sure that there was no way that a one-armed, one-legged, seriously injured incubus could have crawled back up behind the bar to grab a bottle of liquor then crossed back to the other side of the bar to set itself on fire, let alone drag two dead, weighty behemoths along with it into its pyre. Plus, I just couldn't see a demon of any ilk ending its own life.

Whoever *she* was, she was cleaning house. Then I remembered the two bound bouncers I'd left behind the building. Maybe she didn't know about them, and if they were Sons of Belial, then I needed them alive to question. I headed out to the back of the building, slamming into the entry door in such a hurry that I knocked it completely off its hinges, sending the glass-and-metal structure flying into the street. I rounded the corner and saw only one figure by the dumpster—the male, bent at several impossible angles in places that shouldn't bend. I stopped and immediately began searching the area for any trace of the female bouncer.

There was nothing on the ground around the dumpster—no drag marks or blood trails. In fact, I saw no signs of a struggle—except for a pile of wreckage that looked as though something had plowed through the parking lot less than fifty yards behind the building. Half a dozen cars were parked in the small lot. Something had run into three of them, pushing and twisting them relative to the others.

Swords at the ready, I made my way over to the parking lot. Two cars had been pushed into a third, forcing it over the sidewalk and into the street. The first car had been T-boned, with a humanoid figure embedded in the center of the impact. It was the female bouncer. Just as I was about to scream in frustration, she moaned, followed by a soft gurgling noise. She was still alive—for the moment.

"Hey," I said, "I'm going to try to help you. Just stay still." I had no illusions about actually saving her, but I hoped I might be able to keep her alive long enough to get some information out of her.

Once I was close enough, I became a little more pessimistic. In some places, it was hard to tell where the metal of the car stopped and her body began. Bones protruded through her arms and legs, and her torso was bent in two directions. I couldn't see her face because her head lolled on her chest, but I could see a dark fluid dripping from it. She'd hit the car so hard that she currently sat in what would have been the middle of the vehicle, and the force of her impact had shoved it at least fifteen feet. How she wasn't jelly was beyond me. I could do nothing at all to help, except, perhaps, ease her suffering. *Screw trying to get information from her.*

I knelt in front of her, ready to grab her head and twist. I could have shot or stabbed her, but that would have raised even more questions for the cops when they finally showed up. Just as I twisted her head, I got that odd feeling in my gut that usually meant I wasn't alone anymore. As I glanced over my shoulder, the remaining glass in the car's windows erupted in a hail of heavy automatic gunfire coming from the direction of the club. Dropping flat to the ground, I saw a large figure about thirty yards behind me.

I began crawling around the cars, swords in hand, trying to keep an eye on the legs of the gunman. A second pair of thick legs moved toward me from the street behind the car I was using for cover. I stopped, dropped the swords, and pulled the Glock from my hip. I didn't really have time to take aim, nor was I in a good firing position, but I tracked the legs of whoever was walking up from the street while the first gunman kept spraying the cars. I opened fire under the car, pulling the trigger as fast as I could, aiming at the legs. The right shin splintered as a bullet tore through the bone, but I continued firing until I emptied the magazine. I ejected it and inserted another as fast as I could, and from my prone position, I watched the bulky figure rolling on the ground, writhing in pain. I fired half a dozen more shots into the rolling form's torso, and the figure stopped moving.

Instantly, the barrage of automatic weapons fire shredding the car stopped, and a woman's honeyed voice broke the sudden silence. "Oh, Diomedes, what a mess you've made for yourself."

"This is nothing, lady," I shouted. "I'm just getting warmed up..." With that, the gunman sent another sustained barrage into the car then just abruptly stopped. I could feel the impacts down to my boots. Whatever she was using, it was big.

In the sudden silence, I could hear the woman talking to someone—presumably the gunman—but I couldn't make out what she was saying at first. "I shall be going, but I leave you in good hands, Diomedes," she said with a mirthful lilt. "And just to make sure you're *properly* warmed up, I've informed my sister of your current whereabouts. I would estimate her minions will be here momentarily." She laughed, then the clicking of her heels on the concrete slowly grew fainter. "Oh, and don't worry," she shouted, her voice now distant. "It will take the police at least thirty minutes to muster, so you'll have plenty of time to play. Enjoy..."

The click of her heels died in the cold stillness of the night air. I was stuck for something to say, confused by her comment about her sister's minions.

"Yeah?" I shouted, thinking furiously. "Well, fuck you!" Not my best comeback. If I survived this, I would correct it.

Once again, the gunman opened up and continued shredding the car. They had to have fired over well over a hundred rounds already, so I knew they were using a heavy SAW or something similar with a box or belt-fed ammunition. The prone attacker I'd shot hadn't moved, and blood continued to pool around the fallen body. I crawled closer to the back of the car, staying low enough to keep an eye on the active shooter's legs. I pulled myself under the rear of the car behind the tires in an attempt to get a better bead on the gunman.

Once in position, I could see that the gunman was likely one of the other giant Nephilim things. The guy wore full flak armor on his upper body that extended over his groin, and an odd featureless metal helmet covered his head. He carried a Russian RPD heavy machine gun—an odd cross between a Thompson submachine gun and an AK-47 that was capable of firing well over six hundred rounds per minute. At the moment, he was fumbling with inserting a new drum of ammo. *That's my cue.*

I rolled out from under the car. The second I got to my feet, I screamed at the top of my lungs and made a beeline for him. The war cry startled him badly enough that he dropped the ammunition. I fired the Glock as I ran, but the .45 caliber rounds just thudded against the heavy body armor with little more than a *thwack*. Still, the impacts occupied his attention long enough to let me close to within arm's length. I threw the gun at his head. It bounced off with a metallic clank, then I launched into a tackle, hitting his chest and sending us both sprawling on the ground.

I rolled out of it and got to my feet while the armored hulk slowly and deliberately pulled himself up. Because of his helmet, I didn't want to hit him in the head barehanded, and his body armor made hitting him in the torso almost as useless. My viable targets were limited to his knees and throat. Watching him regain his footing, I was betting that armor made him as slow as he was big. Now that he was unarmed, my best shot was to let him make the first move and bring him in close.

I stopped, let my arms hang relaxed at my sides, and stood straight up. I remained lightly on the balls of my feet, waiting. In the seconds that passed, time seemed almost to stop. In that moment, off to my left, I could see random movement in the glow of the streetlights along with shadows rapidly creeping along the façade of the buildings across the street as well. Once time began moving again, the hulk was charging, right arm swinging in a massive roundhouse that probably could crush bone if it connected. I sidestepped it, pushed the blow past, then kicked down on his right knee with all my strength. The leg buckled grotesquely, and the hulk let out a scream that echoed eerily through his helmet and the empty parking lot as he fell to the ground.

I pulled the knife from the rear of my vest and walked over to him as he staggered, trying to stand on one good leg. Once I got close enough, he tried to swing at me, but it was sloppy, and with a flick of the blade, I took three fingers off his hand. He fell onto his side, clutching his wounded hand, screaming.

I raced back over the piece of Swiss cheese that used to be a car, replaced my knife, and grabbed my swords. Once armed, I walked back out into a more-open spot in the parking lot to avoid surprise attacks from the shadows. I settled myself, the only sound coming from the whimpering gunman. As I considered my situation, I noticed at least half a dozen shadowy figures scrabbling across rooftops and along the street, staying just outside the lights. I knew I was surrounded, but I still had no idea by how many or even what.

A bloodcurdling screech, not loud so much as high pitched, split the air, and I knew they were Strigoi. *What a fucking day.*

Chapter 24

The first creature attacked from the top of the club to my right, and I put one sword through its upper chest and split its head while I cut it in half with the other. Its remains went in several directions across the parking lot.

The second and third creatures to attack weren't much different, and I barely had to move. Others came. I stopped counting, but after several minutes, the straightforward attacks stopped. I found myself standing amid a pile of stinking body parts.

I took advantage of the lull and moved to make sure I could keep the area around my feet clear just in case. Across the street, along the roofline, several more spectral figures stood more or less upright. Farther down the street was another, and I could feel more off to my left, though I couldn't see them. Again, the guttural screech that Strigoi made when communicating split the silent night, and two figures rushed me from either side. This time the figures came at me bipedally.

I held my position as long as I could then dove into a roll at the last moment. The creatures were able to stop themselves before they collided, but it allowed me enough time to return to my feet and attack. The first creature moved fast enough to duck my swing, but my slice caught the other vampire's right arm and severed it cleanly. I then stabbed my left sword into its face and violently wrenched the blade free. The leech hit the ground, flailing and screeching. The first vampire recovered and swung a bony, clawlike hand at my head.

I ducked most of the impact, but its razor-like nails raked across the side of my face and head.

I stepped sideways, forced my shoulder into the creature's exposed chest, and staggered it backward. I stabbed at it with my left sword, and the parasite batted the blade past, so I drew my right sword up and across its exposed flank, causing it to twist away in pain. Quickly reversing the motion, I drove the sword back down, jamming the blade through the creature from its neck to its abdomen, then yanked it free. The vampire's upper body split into two down to its waist.

Damaged as they were, the creatures I'd fought earlier were still a long way from dead. They weren't an immediate threat, but I still needed to destroy them.

"Damn tough bastards," I said with a heavy sigh.

As I surveyed the carnage around me, a blinding green flash caught my right eye, and my first reaction was to move to cover—*immediately*. The second I began to run, a bullet ripped past where I was standing and tore a chunk of concrete out of the parking lot just behind me. I ran for the dumpsters, and using them as a springboard, I jumped to the roof of the club, where I quickly dropped to my stomach. Two more shots whizzed past as I ran, but I never felt an impact.

Based on the angle of the green flash—undoubtedly a laser sight—I knew the shooter had to be on the roof of the buildings across the street. Given that the shooter was actually using a laser sight and had hit me in the eye, he wasn't that highly trained. No sniper worth their salt would use one.

I took cover below the roofline and crawled to the corner of the roof closest to where I guessed the shooter was holed up. I rolled over to peek over the side of the building, and the green beam of light passed through the fog overhead, sweeping across the rooftop. Based on the angle of origin, the shooter couldn't be much more than sixty or seventy yards away across the street.

I pulled the Sig out from my vest and racked a round into the chamber. At this range, in the dark, taking a snap shot was a low-percentage maneuver. I was banking on my assumption that the shooter was far from professional, and I hoped that me just getting close might spook him into exposing his position. I stuck the gun above the roofline and fired three times rapidly in the general direction of the shooter. Overhead, the green laser beam jiggled violently then moved out of sight off to my right. I closed my eyes, got to one knee, and steadied myself. I opened my eyes and waited for movement along the top of the buildings across from me.

Before long, a shadowy figure crouched next to the silhouette of some large object to take cover—only it was hunkered on the side that faced me.

From a kneeling position, I took careful aim at the figure, but I waited to see the green dot of the sight. That was my target, not the shooter. At this distance, with a nine-millimeter, I *might* kill a human, but I would just piss off a vampire. I *could* disable the scope or the gun—or both—and force the shooter into hand-to-hand, though. As soon as I identified the glow of the green dot at the origin of the beam, I fired three quick rounds, sparks flew, then the beam disappeared. I fired three more times into the same area just for good measure then holstered the gun, grabbed my swords, and jumped back down to the lot below.

"Well done," said a deep, guttural male voice, accompanied by clapping.

The voice was odd—soft, breathy, and slow. *Deliberate.* A figure emerged from around the building on the far side of the parking lot. It stopped clapping as it continued to walk toward me, its gait as off as its voice was. While the figure walked bipedally and almost like a human, it moved more like someone with a serious nerve disorder, only with more control. Once it passed into the puddle of light thrown by one of the streetlamps, I could see it more clearly. It was definitely a Strigoi, but in order to walk upright, it had to be an older and more powerful version. *I couldn't even imagine how it managed to talk.* It dawned on me that in all my time fighting them, I had never once heard one speak before. Screeching was one thing, but talking involved more than just forcing air over whatever passed for vocal cords in these things. What bothered me even more about the sounds they made was the fact that vampires didn't breathe.

"And who might you be?" I asked, spinning my swords for show. No response.

Even as it passed out of the street lamp's range, I could see its mouth split into what I can only guess was a grin—jagged, broken, and needle-like teeth jutted out in every direction. Suddenly, it jerked as if it might actually topple over from instability, but instead, it fell forward into a four-limbed lope that covered the remaining distance between us in a heartbeat.

The vampire launched itself at me—clawed feet and hands first—like some sort of demented cat pouncing on its prey. I rolled to my left, came out of my tuck, and swung back across at the creature. The instant it hit the ground where I'd been, it vaulted and twisted backward, contorting its limbs impossibly, and I missed completely. I followed up, swinging wide with the other sword, and began to press my attack with both weapons moving as fast as I could swing them, but the damned parasite just kept evading the blades as if I were moving in slow motion. Thankfully, my reach with the swords kept the creature from making another attack.

Finally, after pursuing the thing halfway across the parking lot without hitting it once, I managed to connect, severing its left hand just above the wrist as it tried to redirect the blow. With that, the vampire flipped backward about fifteen feet and crouched so low on its remaining limbs that it resembled an insect. It was hissing furiously as the severed hand wriggled on the ground. I stomped the flopping appendage as hard as I could and continued to press my attack, closing the distance between us slowly.

The creature sprang at me again, and I managed to impale it, but it kicked off my chest and threw itself back off the blade. Again, I pressed the attack, and again it dodged my swords as if I were a clumsy child. At one point, it finally twisted enough that it was able to kick me square in the chest. I was surprised by the lanky creature's strength, but the blow only knocked me back a step. *This is getting old.*

I threw the sword in my right hand down to stick in the concrete, and in the same motion, I pulled my Sig and fired five times as fast as I could squeeze the trigger. *I don't care how fast you are, you can't outrun a bullet moving over seven hundred and fifty miles an hour.*

I hit it at least four times, doing only minor physical damage even at close range. The impact of the rounds did stun the creature long enough for me to close the distance between us.

"Not so damn fast now, are you?" I emptied the remaining rounds in the magazine into its head from less than two feet away. While that wouldn't kill the thing, it would certainly put a damper on its plans for the next few days. But then I wasn't done yet.

I ejected the spent magazine, inserted another, and carefully watched for more movement, especially from where the sniper had been earlier. Nothing. I waited, watched, and listened for a few more minutes. Still nothing.

I beheld the extent of hacked-up vampires while I retrieved my nearly destroyed Glock from where it had landed after careening off the giant's helmet—suddenly, I remembered the injured giant with the heavy machine gun. *He was gone.* His gun and his fingers were still there, but there was no sign of him. I went to retrieve the severed fingers. When I bent over, blood and sweat fell from my face and landed on the ground.

Crap. I walked over to the nearest car to check my reflection in the mirror. The last thing I needed was something getting its hands on my blood. I spent a few minutes mopping the blood off my face and making sure the scratches on my head were finished oozing. Then I set about the task of using my swords to slash open the fuel tanks on the cars in the lot.

Once the entire parking area—especially the bodies of the injured vampires—was awash in gas, I made sure that the bodies of the bouncers were lying in the pooling fuel. Then I dragged my sword across the pavement to create enough of a spark to ignite the gasoline.

I grabbed my now-nasty, filth-covered duffle from the dumpster and watched the fire for a few minutes to make sure nothing crawled out. Before I left, I tossed the rags I'd used to clean the blood off my face into the flames.

As I walked up Folsom, I began to go over things in my head. Apparently, I'd managed to kill off every damn one of my best leads in the form of the Sons of Belial, except Three-Finger McGee, and I'd managed to let him limp away.

That wasn't even the worst of it, though.

When I finally made the connection to the Strigoi and the female in charge at the club, I got queasy. The only one strong enough to control Strigoi had to be their mother, Lilith. She had three sisters. I was pretty sure Agrat was dead. So that meant the sister at the club was either Eisheth, mother of the Moroi strain of vampires, or Na'amah, the first and most powerful of all the succubi.

All of the so-called sisters were lesser fallen angels associated with the Watchers, Samael in particular. According to the earliest texts I knew of, these four, along with dozens of others, were left to dwell on Earth as their punishment for rebelling. Given the nature of the Dungeon and Cocytus, I was leaning on it being Na'amah.

As I walked, sirens began to fill the early-morning air, and I could see the glow of fire in the sky behind me. I pulled the giant's severed fingers out of a pocket on my vest and contemplated them for a second.

Just as I was about to call out to Athena—which I never did—I felt her presence next to me.

"Yes," she said icily, clearly not happy to be summoned—or even *almost* summoned.

"Find the rest of this," I replied just as icily, handing her the fingers without stopping or even slowing my pace. "Please."

She took the fingers without saying a word.

"Oh, and can you ID these two things?" I dug my phone out of a pocket and pulled up the images of the two mutilated bodies from the Dungeon's lower level.

She took the phone and studied the images for a second, and in the literal blink of an eye, she was gone. *She actually took my damn phone.*

As I walked, the damp, cold night air began to seep back into my bones, fueling my darkening attitude. I pulled my stinky jacket out of my nasty-ass duffel and shrugged it on, gagging at the stench.

Why couldn't she have taken my mood with her?

Chapter 25

I made it to Pier 33, where the ferries left for Alcatraz, well before sunup. The fog had rolled back in, blanketing the docks in a thick, cold mist that did little to help my mood.

With everything closed to the public and the cover of the fog, sneaking into the area used for passenger loading was easy. While many of the piers in the area still housed working businesses, the ferry docks were strictly for tourists and currently devoid of life. Even the night watchman, coming up to the end of a shift, was undoubtedly more interested in staying warm and dry than keeping an eye out for someone trying to sneak into what was basically an empty lot. In the heavy mist, I followed the edge of the building on Pier 31 until I found a collection of machinery and construction equipment stored at the water's edge. I found a small spot and hunkered down to wait a few hours until the tourists began arriving. The constant moan of the fog horns was oddly comforting as I tried to nod off.

I woke abruptly but without a start. I sensed Athena's presence, then she walked out of the fog, bundled in a traditional trench coat. Even in the diffused light of dawn, I could see the intensity in her blue eyes.

"What brings you down to the docks so early?" I yawned.

"The fingers you gave me from the Bennephilim," she said as if I was supposed to know what the hell *that* meant, "gave us his current location."

"*Ben* what?" I replied. "You mean the hulk at the club? Oh... I get it. The incubus called them the descendants of the Nephilim—Bennephilim."

"Not bad for a goy," she said with the hint of a smile curling the corner of her mouth.

"Where is he?" I asked, standing and stretching.

"New Orleans." She handed me a folded piece of paper.

The address on the paper was in Faubourg Marigny. "Figures."

"Gather your gear and let's go," she said, heading back into the fog.

"Go? How? You want to swim, or do you have a boat in your pocket?" I asked, not intending to sound like such a smartass.

"It will be meeting us at the pier in three minutes."

I was impressed and a bit relieved I didn't have to wait any longer, but more than a bit dismayed the Bennephilim had made it to New Orleans. I had a love–hate relationship with the Crescent City. It was probably one of my favorite cities in the world, but every time I went there, bad crap happened. But my biggest problem with the city was that since I wasn't Fae, the nearest gate through the Ways was eighty miles away in Baton Rouge—in a swamp. I grabbed my duffle and followed Athena toward the floating docks where the ferries were berthed.

"Please stay downwind until you bathe," Athena said through the fog from just ahead of me.

"It ain't me, I swear," I said, jogging to catch up to her. "I stuffed my bag in a dumpster to hide it, and it got to my jacket."

Once I got close enough to see her again, I could see her fanning her gloved hand in front of her nose.

"Fine." I slowed down to let her stay in front of me.

The faint thrum of a powerful engine met us at the dock. Athena led the way down the gangway then aboard an antique wooden runabout that was so finely tuned, the engines purred softly even as the captain throttled up to head out into the bay in a pea-soup fog.

Before I could make any comments about the folly of such a trip without radar, I crossed the aft deck to stand behind the skipper, revealing a heads-up display glowing on the glass windscreen in front of him. He had full instrumentation, including depth, weather, GPS, and radar, holographically projected right in front of him.

"I gotta get me one of those," I said almost over his shoulder as we sped off across the bay.

The trip to Alcatraz took less than fifteen minutes, and I hopped off on a floating dock on the other side of the ferry landing without waiting to tie up. Athena got off behind me, her disembarkation so well timed that she seemed to be just taking another step along a street rather than off a bobbing boat. She nodded to the captain, who gunned the engines in reverse and headed back out into the fog.

She and I walked back up the island toward the gateway through the Telluric Ways I'd used before. Walking in the cold, dense fog provided the illusion of total isolation, which wasn't far from reality. Along the way, we talked about the current situation. I told her about my suspicions regarding Na'amah being involved as well and that the Bennephilim formed the Sons of Belial. Whether with Na'amah's help or simply under her orders, they'd managed to free Ramiel from Tartarus some years ago and were up to something again. Assuming Taylon Jones wasn't totally barking mad, why else would they be recruiting people as vessels for lesser demons to inhabit?

I could only speculate, but at this point, all I had were theories that covered everything from a simple jailbreak to free Samael all the way to tearing down the gates of Tartarus for good. None gave me warm fuzzies.

Unfortunately, every connection I'd run into so far was dead, except the Bennephilim in New Orleans and the female Moroi back at Cocytus—but I had no way to track her except *possibly* through Cocytus. I had no doubt Na'amah or whoever else was in charge of this mess would clean house, so I had to find this seven-fingered guy and fast.

After listening to my rambling without uttering a single syllable in response, Athena handed me back my phone then continued walking into the fog. She vanished the moment I lost sight of her in the dense mist. I worked my way over the uneven terrain, made worse by the increasing light of the morning diffused by the mist, and finally I got to the gateway to the Ways and headed for Baton Rouge.

There wasn't a single thing I was comfortable with at that moment. Least of all my smell.

Chapter 26

I passed through the Telluric Ways into a muddy, marshy field along a tight bend in the Mississippi River just west of Bayou Baton Rouge and slogged through the mire in a mental fog thicker than the real one I'd left behind in San Fran. After trekking a few miles over several hours, I finally made it to the parking lot of a stadium on the nearby university campus, where Athena had arranged to leave a car for me. In the trunk was a duffle with fresh clothes and a big can of spray disinfectant. She was *so close* to being a benevolent deity.

By the time I made it to the address on Marigny Street in New Orleans, it was early afternoon, and the air near the river was cool, humid, and still. Despite the apparent rebirth of the once-decrepit Marigny neighborhood, the long three-story redbrick warehouse-like building was derelict and apparently left out of the surrounding redevelopment. Blacked-out and wood-clad windows nearly the height of each floor covered the building's exterior, particularly at street level. A quick stroll around the structure revealed new locks on the substantial doors—distressed to fit in with the building's worn façade—and cleverly concealed video cameras placed regularly around the eaves. I'd seen this setup recently, and both times, I had tried to be subtle. I was done with tiptoeing around. I needed Seven Fingers alive, and I needed to find him immediately.

I contemplated kicking in one of the doors at street level but settled on jumping up to the rusted metal fire escape on the back side of the building across from an even more dilapidated warehouse. I climbed the corroding stairs up to the landing on the third floor and tried to peer through the crud-encrusted window—a massive portal made up of thirty panes of glass with the middle section flipped outward to allow access to the fire escape. It was like gazing into mud, so I broke out one of the panes with the butt of my Sig. Even with the window gone, I could still see only a short distance into the murky space beyond. The latch holding the swinging glass emergency access panel shut was either rusted or welded, so using one of my tanto knives, I quietly pried out enough panes of glass for me to fit then broke the metal framework to crawl through. Creeping over the narrow sill, I carefully lowered myself onto the floor inside.

The walls on either side of me were old plaster, but in the four-foot-square space across from me hung some sort of heavy blackout curtain. Pulling my Sig again, I drew one edge of the heavy drape back just enough to peek out. A short hallway stretched toward a metal railing overlooking a large open space beyond. There was a single door on either side of the hall, but I couldn't make out any specific details in the dim sunlight. I crept out from behind the curtain, where the faint scent of liquor mixed with a thick and pervasive musk that reminded me of an old gym assaulted my nose. A soft, low moan echoed through the cavernous space. Once at the railing, I got a sense of déjà vu. The place was set up similarly to Cocytus—a large, open central space circled by two higher-floor landings. While this place had a more permanent feel to it than the location for Cocytus, it was currently devoid of any furnishings. Down in the courtyard below, I could see something huddled just inside a shadow-line with an odd tawny-colored energy swirling around it.

Gun in hand, I hopped the railing and quickly dropped down to the railing below then to the cement floor of the central courtyard. The instant I hit the floor, I could tell the indistinguishable mass was actually two humanoid figures—one crouched over the other. The one on top, a heavily muscled figure, had *no* face, just a blank, featureless stump for a head. It reacted to my sudden intrusion, and the swirling aura of light-brown energy dissipated instantly. The rather substantial figure lying beneath it—likely Seven Fingers—twitched randomly but was otherwise rigid. The sight of the faceless thing took me by surprise when I hit the ground. It was one of the *rarer* vampiric creatures—an Alû—a beast that fed off the pain and terror inspired while their victim is in an induced dreamlike coma.

Every damn time I come to New Orleans...

I hadn't come across an Alû in centuries—and never during the day. While I had no actual proof, I speculated that the creatures were the offspring of either Lilith or Na'amah. Its method of absorbing energy was more similar to the way Na'amah and her succubi children fed, and given everything I'd found out over the last few days, it made even more sense. While just as hard to kill as their brethren, these monsters relied mostly on stealth rather than brutality and preferred to slink in and out of their victims' bedrooms while they slept. *But I was wide awake.*

Without much beyond strong hands and clawed fingers for armaments, the creature moved low to the ground on all fours like some sort of tailless lizard. Crawling off the prone form of Seven Fingers, it began to creep sideways to my left, farther into the shadows under the overhang from the floor above. Once it hit the wall, it began to crawl backward up it. The last thing I wanted was to chase this thing into the city. I emptied the Sig into the monster at less than thirty feet, harboring no illusions that the gun would do much more than piss it off. I needed it on the ground, where I could face it, though, not hanging off the walls.

Without a mouth or even a nose, the thing made no noise at all, even as the nine-millimeter rounds slammed into it—not that I could have heard anything over the echoing report of the gun in the enclosed space. Fifteen rounds didn't faze the beast, and it continued to crawl along the overhang. Desperate, I dropped my gun and pulled my swords, preparing to attack the creature as soon as it tried to crawl up onto the railing for the second floor. Instead, the creature leapt halfway across the open space, landing well behind me.

At least it's on the damn ground.

I charged the second it hit the ground, and it lunged forward simultaneously, hitting me square in the chest with its legs then using me for a springboard to flip itself fifteen feet to my right. The sudden impact spun me to the left, pirouetting like a drunken ballerina, until I fell to one knee with my back to the parasite. Before I could recover, it hit me from behind, sending me sprawling forward. I dropped both swords and slid on my cuirass with the thing riding me like a surfboard.

Trying to gather my wits, I felt something icy and painful creep into my mind, ripping into it as if searching haphazardly in the dark. Suddenly, images of Sarah helpless and tossed around like a ragdoll back in a cave on Mount Alvand flooded my mind, followed abruptly by visions of Duma's lifeless body smashing into a cavern wall and Abraxos smashed by a sphere of green energy from the same fight. The images kept replaying in my head, and pain began to well up and grow. I froze as my friends were battered repeatedly, and the images began to flow past quickly, drowning me.

Then anger rose, pushing aside the pain. *Defeat comes only when I give up.*

"No," I said, though I wasn't sure if it was aloud or just inside my head. I roared in utter defiance and twisted violently, throwing the Alû off my back and skidding across the cement floor. "Stay outta my head, monster. There's nothing there for you to feed on."

My head was still fuzzy, but as I faced the vampire thing, my growing anger sharpened my focus. My swords were too far away for me to grab without the creature blindly attacking me again, and my Glock was no help, but I still had my tanto knives. I pulled the Dvergar-made blades from their sheaths along my shoulder and left thigh and slowly closed the distance between us. I kept the blade in my left hand tucked along my wrist, prepared to sacrifice that arm as a shield if necessary, while I kept the blade in my right hand in a hammer grip. The monster kept scrabbling back and forth, as if trying to decide what the best move was as I cornered it.

Once I was within a body's length, I feigned an attack with my right hand, stomped my foot, and screamed. The creature shot forward and swung its right arm wide in a roundhouse-like swipe, attempting to rake its clawed hand across my head. It was the action I was hoping to elicit.

I stepped in, threw my left arm up to block the attack, and lunged across my body with the knife in my right hand, slicing back across the creature's abdomen. Then I stabbed the blade back at what should have been a neck, plunging the knife in to its guard before ripping it free. The Alû recoiled and crouched low to the ground. Nothing dripped from the gaping wound. I would have to all but dissect the thing to put it down, and even that was only temporary unless I burned its pieces.

I kept pressing in on it, forcing it farther into a corner until it leapt up and over me, twisting freakishly to land in the center of the room, facing me. *If I didn't know better, I'd swear these things have no bones.* Following the creature's maneuver, I saw my swords lying about twenty feet apart about halfway between us. I couldn't beat this thing with knives—even ones made by a Dvergar—so I had no choice but to try for one of them. In an attempt to bait the Alû into attacking on my terms, I made sure that it knew I was eyeing the sword to my left. Then I broke for it, knowing the vampire was faster. It jumped to the sword, and I lowered my shoulder and tackled the creature, ending up on top of it. I plunged both knives into its chest several times while it thrashed until it bucked me off. Dropping my knives, I scrambled back to the closest sword while the Alû silently twisted its body around to get its hands and feet underneath it.

Sword in hand, I began backing up toward the other sword with the creature tracking me at a safe distance.

Finally in possession of both swords, I spun them while the creature stood its ground. Since it was faster than I was and wary, my only real option was to get it to move first. I feinted right, hoping that the creature would move to intercept. It bought my ruse then realized its mistake too late while in midair, too late to change direction. I followed the bluff with a full attack just as the vampire landed where it assumed I would be. I brought both swords down on its left shoulder, destroying and completely severing its arm. Again, the creature twisted and contorted its body so fast—even with a limb missing—that I couldn't follow through with another attack, but I pursued, kicking the thrashing limb behind me. I would take it piece by piece if I had to.

Thinking I had the thing on the defensive, I began trying to formulate a plan to corner this jump-happy parasite and finish it. Its sudden attack caught me by surprise. I tried to twist and sidestep it, but the wide swipe was just too fast. Its claw caught me across my shoulder and neck and hung up on my cuirass under my vest. My sudden turn with its claw ensnared on my cuirass pulled it off balance, and I brought my left sword up to sever its remaining arm just above the elbow. While I managed to maintain my footing, I staggered from the intense burning across the left side of my neck. I could feel the warm blood running under my cuirass and down my shoulder. *Enough of this crap.*

I quickly moved toward the cornered and armless Alû, both swords held out to my sides. Since it was cornered, I expected the thing to jump up and over once I got close enough, so my plan was to hit it midair. I took two steps toward it, and it jumped. I followed, spearing its abdomen with my right sword, knocking it off balance. It hit the ground in a roll and kicked its legs wildly, struggling to right itself without arms. Before it could manage the maneuver, I hacked off both its legs then spent the next few minutes cutting its torso into small quivering pieces. Looking around for anything to set a fire with, I saw boxes full of liquor bottles just to the side of the bar along one wall. I grabbed the first two bottles I could reach, smashed one over the bulk of the still-writhing carcass, and began pouring the other on it, leaving a trail out into the center of the room. After I dragged Seven Fingers's rigid form well out of the way, I sparked a fire using one of my swords and stood back as the creature went up in flames.

The moment the flames roared to their fullest, a rising scream filled the empty space, finally reaching a high-pitched wavering screech. Despite being at a safe distance, Seven Fingers was desperately trying to wriggle away from the contained conflagration as if it were racing toward him like a train. His movements were uncoordinated and awkward, but his eyes were unbelievably wide, and his mouth was open, though no more sounds came out. He finally fell onto his back before rolling to his side and curling into a ball with his back to the fire. *At least he isn't in a coma.*

I cautiously walked over to him.

"Hey, buddy, you're okay," I said quietly, trying to sound soothing as I approached. "Seriously, that thing is dead. It's going to be all right."

Soft, muffled sobs came from the balled-up hulk. It was strange seeing someone so large reduced to little more than a puddle of tears. "Come on, man. It's over."

Seven Fingers shifted his head, turning an eye toward me. The second it focused on me, his brow and forehead furrowed. He tucked his head even tighter into his chest and began to scoot away from me and toward the fire. "No, no, no, no, no..." he screamed beneath his arms.

Dammit.

I grabbed his foot and began dragging his disproportionally weighty ass away from the flames. He halfheartedly resisted for a moment, kicking and squirming, then just went limp. I dropped him then crouched by his head. "Hey, I won't hurt you. This time," I said, wincing slightly at the memory of attacking him and cutting off a few of his fingers. "I swear." Though he wasn't watching, I made a show of slowly putting my sword down next to me then sliding it away a few feet. At the scraping metal sound, his head suddenly popped up from in between his gigantic arms.

His wide eyes travelled from me straight to my sword then back to me again. "No, no, no, no, no..." He shook his head ever so slightly before clutching at his ears and whimpering again, his eyes shut tightly.

"Come on, you're safe now," I said. "I just want to ask you a few questions, and then I'll take you anywhere you want to go." I kept my hands loose between my knees as I talked, trying to appear as non-threatening as possible. The Alû had clearly damaged his mind. "Was that Na'amah back at the Dungeon? Is she helping the Sons of Belial free another one of the Watchers?"

"Can't, can't, can't, can't..." He was sweating profusely, and I couldn't tell if the drops running down his cheek were tears or sweat.

"Sure you can," I replied. "I'll protect you from them."

"No," he said forcefully. "*You...* can't."

"I promise you I will—"

"You... *can't*... stop her—*Them*." His eyes suddenly opened, and his lips parted in a toothy, predatory grin that made me sit back on my heels. "It began with the Great Malefic, and now Judgment Day will come with the Transition of the Light Bringer."

The Great Malefic? Judgment Day? Transition of the Light Bringer? What the hell is he talking about?

"Well, no offense, buddy, but when the hell is that? And who's going to bring this Judgement Day? I'm pretty sure you guys managed to free Ramiel years ago, but who now? Samyaza? Maybe Samael?" Knowing the connection between him and the sisters, either of those other Watchers was a logical choice.

In a flash of movement, Seven Fingers slid over to my sword, grabbed it, and unsteadily scrambled to his feet. Instinctively, I drew my remaining sword, but I kept it low to my side.

"Come on, man. We don't have to do this. I will protect you from them," I said. "Just tell me about this whole Judgment Day thing, and then we're outta here to wherever you want to go." I held up my free hand, trying to calm him as I talked.

"Na'amah and my brethren will see to it that *they* will *all* be free, and there is nothing you can do about it." He grinned grotesquely, his eyes wild and in constant motion.

"They who?" I took a small step forward, preparing to rush him.

"The Iyrin." In one fluid motion, he raised the sword to his throat and cut before I could move. Arterial blood sprayed in every direction as his body fell to the ground. I jumped back as he thrashed for a moment then fell still, his head lying at an odd angle.

I stood staring in disbelief and disgust as I listened to the sound of the remaining air escaping his lungs. I stepped forward to grab my sword from his hand.

Holy hell. The force of his cut had nearly severed his own head. The gruesomeness of his self-inflicted injury paled in comparison to what he'd said. They were working to free *all* the fallen Watchers—all one hundred ninety-nine of the beings still imprisoned in Tartarus for their rebellion and corruption of humanity and kept in everlasting chains under darkness... until Judgment Day.

Chapter 27

On my way back to San Diego, I pieced together everything I knew—and it wasn't good. While I was pretty sure Na'amah was working with the Sons of Belial and I got the whole Judgment Day reference, I still had no idea what Seven Fingers had meant by the Great Malefic or the Transition of the Light Bringer. In my original tongue, Light Bringer translated to Lucifer, but that didn't make sense because *that* particular Old One wasn't among the Iyrin. *And what the hell would he be* transitioning *to anyway?* I drew a total blank about the *Great Malefic*—whatever that was. The only thing worse about what I knew and didn't know was the plan for my next move. It was a hellacious long shot. *Then again, long shots always were my specialty.*

Taylon Jones had suggested that the Sons of Belial were recruiting people from the clubs to secure hosts for possessing demons. I was betting that those possessions had to be somehow connected to Ramiel. The underground clubs were certainly connected to Na'amah. If the Sons of Belial could somehow recruit me at Cocytus or one of the other clubs, I could find out more from the inside. The sticking point was that any Old Ones or Parans involved would know *what* I was instantly even if they didn't recognize me first. Still, as my only real course of action, I went straight to the Metis Foundation and Athena with it when I got back into town.

By the time I arrived at the corner of 13th and Island in San Diego's East Village, the Metis Foundation doors were unlocked, but the office was deserted. Even the usually frenetic bullpen, which normally ran twenty-four hours a day, was empty and the monitors were off—except for Athena and Brey in the waiting area. Athena was leaning on the receptionist's desk, while Brey stood with her arms crossed over her chest. Both women wore solemn expressions as I entered. I understood the feeling. I wasn't even in the mood to harass Brey. I just explained what I'd found out then launched into my plan.

After a few minutes of soliloquy without the slightest twitch or change in expression on either of their faces, I hit them with my biggest concerns. "First, I have no idea of their time frame, started by whatever the Great Malefic was and supposedly culminating with the Transition of the Light Bringer, whoever that is. Second, whoever we send in has to be a *mortal human*. I could see if Frigate is available, maybe Geek," I said, offering the names of two of the three mortals to have recently survived working with me.

"Those terms are not familiar to me, either. Breygivila, would you please research them for me expeditiously?" Athena asked.

The elf nodded ever so slightly then silently disappeared up the stairs. Once Brey was gone, Athena continued with no discernable regard in her voice. "As for your second concern, I suggest Sarah."

I had specifically left Sarah out of the list, and my heart stopped when Athena said her name.

"What? *Hell no.* No way I'm getting her involved in this," I said, staring down at the ground with a single defiant wave of my hand.

"Why not? Her personnel jacket says she's done quite a bit of undercover work with the FBI before she joined the Fly Team. You know she's more than capable. And she obviously has much more experience at undercover work than either Kyle Sellers or William Elmsmore, who I will *not* permit to volunteer anyway. He is too valuable where he is at the moment." Her tone indicated that further discussion was moot.

Neither of us said anything while I paced, gazing at the ground. I rubbed at my hair and neck, trying to think of any reason Sarah *wouldn't* work. The only thing I could come up with was because I cared for her—and that wasn't rational.

"I—" I said, getting ready to make something up.

"Put your feelings aside, Diomedes," Athena said with a surprising tone of understanding. "You know she's the best qualified for something like this. You also know that I will do all I can to help her *and* you so that nothing happens to her. She is a valuable asset to the Metis Foundation."

She gazed at me as she said the part about being an asset, and I could see something playful in her eyes—not at all as cold as she portrayed. For some reason, her expression stopped me, and I glanced through the glass wall into the oddly darkened bullpen beyond. Everything I'd taught myself—all the things I'd learned and all the creatures I'd fought over thousands of years—served to underline one basic rule of combat: never be governed by emotions. *Three thousand years, and here I am, fucking up rule number one.*

I didn't even realize I was back in my truck until some dipdunk honked at me because I failed to move when the light finally changed. I made it to Point Loma on autopilot. I really needed to get my head back into the game, or I was gonna get myself—or worse, someone else—killed.

I spent the rest of the day and a very restless night trying to come up with *any* alternative plan for what needed to be done. I could not come up with a single idea for finding out where Ramiel, the Bennephilim, and Na'amah might be hiding short of waiting around for more deaths to occur. The only thing I knew was that the Bennephilim had recruited derelicts who'd volunteered to become vessels for possession. My grand assumption was that Ramiel would be wherever the black mass to induce possession took place. According to Seven Fingers, I had until the Transition of the Light Bringer—whenever the hell that was—to stop them from bringing about Judgment Day. As far as I was concerned, whatever the time-frame, I needed to move right away.

Based on what the female Moroi at Cocytus had told me, the club advertised for the hosts in certain underground newspapers. The *only* play I could come up with was to wait for those ads to come out then send in a human undercover. I couldn't ask Frigate. Though he and I had served together as SEALs in the DEVGRU, he wasn't trained for undercover work. In addition, he had a family. According to Athena, Geek was off limits. That left only Sarah. Objectively, she was perfect for this. But when it came to her, my objectivity was gone.

Sending someone in undercover was the best shot and the only *logical* move I had. But maybe I could convince Athena another random human would do. It would just have to be someone—*anyone*—other than Sarah. If I was really lucky, the Transition of the Light Bringer would occur too quickly to do anything beyond stage a frontal assault. *Because that would be better.*

Just past dawn, I decided I needed to make my case again to Athena, as shallow as it was, against sending Sarah. I showered, dressed, then headed down to the Metis Foundation. Predictably, the door was locked. Before I could even pull my security card out to open it, the heavy tumblers and deadbolts clicked, and lights came on inside. I yanked open the door and practically ran into Brey, who, by some odd coincidence, was expecting me.

"What the fuck, Brey?" I said, barely avoiding the collision.

"I'm sorry," she replied, remaining motionless and eyeing me the same way kids examine liver on a dinner plate. "I don't understand your line of inquiry. In fact, the question makes no grammatical sense whatsoever."

I just rolled my eyes. I didn't have time for her elf nonsense.

"I need to speak with Athena," I said, pushing past her and heading up the stairs to her office. "Now."

"That will be impossible."

"No, it won't. I'll speak, and she'll listen. That's how it works. I do it all the time."

"I am aware of the precepts of verbal intercourse. That is not the issue, Diomedes," she said, walking up to the base of the stairs. "She is not here."

"Well, where the hell is she?"

"You needn't get discordant with me, Diomedes. I have done nothing to draw your ire," she replied with an attitude that was as close to a huff as I'd ever seen in her.

"Look, Brey, I don't have time for this," I said, stomping back down the stairs. "I'm sorry for being... uptight. Do you know where she is?"

"Apology accepted. Of course I know. And so would you if you allowed yourself," she said like a mother scolding a child. "She is, in point of fact, in Washington, DC, to speak with the Department of Homeland Security and Agent Sarah Wright, with whom I believe you are acquainted."

"Shit!" I slammed through the door, running out to my truck.

Brey followed me outside. "By the way, I believe I have discovered what the Great Malefic and the Transition of the Light Bringer refer to, if you'd like to know," she said, her head tilted slightly and her hands clasped at her waist.

"Tell me quick, Brey. I don't have time," I said, half in the truck, talking to her around the door.

"I do believe the Great Malefic refers to the point in time when the planet Saturn is closest to Earth, or what is referred to as 'in opposition.' That would have been April fifteenth by the standard human calendar," she said matter-of-factly.

"And...? Come on, Brey, short on time here," I said, rolling my hand to move her along.

"Given that the Light Bringer can be several things, including the fallen angel Lucifer, I had a harder time identifying this event until I linked it to the Great Malefic. If my logic holds—and it should—then I do believe the Light Bringer, in this case, refers to the planet Venus, and therefore its 'transition' is the very rare astronomical event when it crosses in front of the Sun from our perspective here on Earth."

"And that would be when?" I asked, staring at her and desperately trying to get her to finish.

"The event will follow the eclipse of the full moon on the fourth, begin on the fifth, and terminate on the sixthof June."

"That's all I needed to know. Thanks, Brey." I slammed the door and started the car. That left me a little over a month before Judgment Day.

"Curiously, the last time these phenomena occurred in the same proximity was in 1874," I could hear her saying as I backed out and stomped the gas pedal to the floor.

I tried to call Sarah's cell phone and her office thirteen times on the way to my usual portal through the Ways just east of San Diego. Each time, the call went to voicemail, which meant she was probably in a meeting. If I was lucky, maybe she hadn't met with Athena yet.

The only way I knew through the Ways to DC brought me out near the Washington Monument on the Mall, and I just wasn't concerned about people seeing me at this point. When I came through, no one noticed, however. Fortunately, all the construction going on to repair the monument made it a somewhat less interesting place for people to gather.

It only took me ten minutes to jog to Sarah's office building. Once I reached the building, I calmed myself and tried to appear reasonable rather than deranged as I walked into the lobby and took the elevator up to her office on the fifth floor. The elevator was taking forever, and I was sweating profusely.

I had never been to her DC office before, and other than knowing where it was in general, I had no idea exactly where I was headed. On the fifth floor, the ancient linoleum floor and bright whitewashed walls lit by harsh fluorescent bulbs served to stoke my irritation even further as I stared at the endless line of nondescript brown wooden doors. Each door was numbered, but only a few had small placards next to them, explaining what lay behind them. After wandering the hall for a few minutes, I finally found a door marked "Federal Protective Services, DHS." I opened it and went inside. I found myself in a small reception area with the seal of the DHS on the wall over the receptionist's desk. In the glass wall, a doorway led into a large cubicle farm and communal work area.

"Can I help you?" the young man behind the desk asked courteously.

I fumbled in my pocket to pull out my Metis Foundation ID badge and handed it to him.

"I'm here for the meeting with Agent Sarah Wright," I said, lying, searching through the glass wall for any sign of her or Athena. I couldn't feel Athena, so maybe she hadn't arrived yet. I took a deep breath in relief.

"Um, Agent Wright's meeting with the Metis Foundation was at your offices, not ours," he said, then answered a call through his headset by tapping on his earpiece.

"Dammit," I said to myself. "Do you know when we were supposed to meet? Clearly, I've got everything mixed up," I asked, beginning to feel overwhelmed.

The receptionist just scowled at me as he spoke into his headset, making a point of letting me know where his current attention was. I shot him a look that should have withered his lower intestines but didn't, then I left before I popped his head off his shoulders. Again, I pulled out my phone and tried to dial Sarah's cell. Voicemail.

The freaking Metis Foundation's offices in DC were on First and C on the north side of the Mall by the damned Capitol building, almost another mile away as the crow flies. I exited the building like a shot, ran up Seventh to Maryland Avenue then across the Mall along Third. From there I turned on Constitution Avenue then up First to the Vincent Sombrotto Building. As much as I wanted to make the run a supernatural exercise in parkour, I kept my pace reasonable and limited my jumping to curbs and fire hydrants.

The entrance to the Sombrotto Building off First led into a massive and sterile white marble atrium open to the third floor. Simple marble staircases ran along both walls on either side of me, up and around to the mezzanine. Directly under the mezzanine was a glass wall with a room jammed with cubicles beyond—much like the bullpen at the office in San Diego, only larger and more sterile. A full half of the building was the Metis Foundation, and the activity on the other side of the glass included analysts, data miners, statisticians, techs, and all manner of other geeky types that all held multiple degrees from various top-notch schools around the world. Upstairs, off the mezzanine above, was a large auditorium, and above that were private offices and secure conference rooms. Athena's private office occupied the entire eighth floor. I expected that a meeting between Athena and the DHS would take place on either the third or fourth level in the conference rooms.

I took off up the marble staircase then accessed the stairwell off to the right of the auditorium by waving my Metis Foundation ID at it. I suppose I could have taken the elevator, but that would have required I enter through the work area on the first floor that everyone jokingly referred to as "the aquarium."

Once I hit the third-floor landing, I stopped for a second to see if I could feel Athena's presence. I didn't have to concentrate hard to feel her, although I could tell it wasn't on this floor. I shot up one more flight, waved my ID at the proximity card reader next to the door, then headed out of the stairwell into the hallway.

From previous meetings here, I knew there were four conference rooms on this floor, laid out with one in each corner of the level. I walked to the central hallway then to each door until I sensed Athena's presence the strongest. *Of course, it was the last door I checked.* I stopped outside, calmed myself, tucked in my long-sleeved T-shirt, then smoothed some wrinkles in it, grateful that it didn't have any fishing stains on it. I was sure I cut a dashing and professional figure in my jeans, boat shoes, and T-shirt.

I waved my ID at the card reader, it beeped, and the door opened. The room was quiet except for the noise of people shifting in their leather chairs to see who had entered.

Athena sat alone on one side of a thirty-seat glass-and-steel conference table. Across from her sat two men and a woman with a large gray spot in her hair. I recognized the woman as the Secretary of the Department of Homeland Security and one of the men as the Under Secretary of Homeland Security for National Protection and Programs. I had no idea who the third guy was, but I guessed it was probably Sarah's immediate supervisor. Sarah stood at the head of the table, leaning over a file folder full of papers and pictures. I stopped, feeling as conspicuous as a bad haircut, and cleared my throat.

"I... I'm ...sorry to barge in like this. Please forgive me, Madame Secretary, Mr. Under Secretary, sir." I faced Athena and Sarah. "Please continue, Agent Wright." I pulled out the chair nearest to me and sat down. Surprisingly, Athena wasn't the least bit perturbed—not even slightly miffed. That threw me. Still, there was no way I was going to launch into my protest in front of Sarah's bosses. Even I wasn't that big a jerk.

"Join us," Athena said in a tone that suggested nothing but cool professionalism, pointing to the chair next to her. "Madame Secretary, Mr. Under Secretary, Director Patterson, please allow me to introduce our finest investigator and troubleshooter, Steve Dore," she said, waving a hand at me as I got up and walked the length of the table. "He's the one mostly responsible for the information we've been reviewing."

Sarah gave me a subtle but terse glower. I nodded at Athena's acknowledgment, completely caught off guard by the fact I was somehow expected—at least by Athena and Sarah anyway. The other three didn't seem to care one way or the other. As I sat, I glanced over at Athena's ID badge lying on top of an open file folder. It read "Waters, T." under the picture of a large African American man with a heavy mustache. I rolled my eyes and sat down.

She was using a glamour that cast her as one of her public personas within the company: Director of Intelligence Terrance Waters. To be honest, I had no idea if the guy even existed or was just some concoction of Athena's. I also had no idea if Sarah knew, but I doubted it.

Sarah continued her presentation. To my great fears, it was about the organization running Cocytus and the Dungeon, their connection to abductions, and possible conspiracy to either suicide bomb or somehow attack a currently unknown target or targets.

Wait...What?

Once I caught on to the direction of her discussion, I became confused until it occurred to me there was no way to get DHS involved otherwise. Sarah detailed a plan—my plan—to infiltrate the organization with an undercover operative to discover the details of the plot.

I listened intently for a moment before I realized it really was all the information I'd given Athena, then I tuned out—trying to determine the best way of keeping Sarah out of this—until she asked if I had anything else to add. Hearing my name startled me, making me seem like an even bigger idiot. *So much for aspirations for a govern-*

ment job. Plus, I was pretty sure my defiant state of mind had become evident.

"Uh, I do have one question," I said. "Maybe I missed this part, but who, exactly, do you intend to insert into this group?" I knew the answer, but some sick part of me had to hear it.

"Agent Wright," came the response from Director Patterson. "She's one of our best, and she's the most knowledgeable about this situation, having brought it to our attention. With the Metis Foundation's, and your, help, of course."

I smiled somewhat impertinently. "With all due respect," I said, standing up. That earned me withering looks from Sarah, and I could feel anger rising in Athena. Frankly, I wasn't even sure just how much they knew about what had happened the night before last. I continued undaunted anyway. "I've only just begun to identify the key players in this group, and I'm pretty sure they have no issue with killing to clean up loose ends. Plus, it's an underground fetish club—"

"Duly noted, Mr. Dore. But given the events of the last few days, I think it is now necessary that we take this investigation out of the hands of a privately contracted investigator and begin examining things in a way that could lead us to a legitimate and legal conviction of those involved rather than incur a host of lawsuits for harassment and destruction of public and private property. Wouldn't you agree, Director Waters?" Patterson said, pointedly turning back to Athena's persona.

Athena nodded perfunctorily since it wasn't really a question. At least I knew they knew something about what had happened in San Francisco, but I doubted they knew anything about New Orleans.

"Maybe we should consider recruiting someone already involved," I said, trying desperately not to be ignored.

"Not enough time if what we've been told is true. We appreciate your concern, Mr. Dore, but Agent Wright is one of our most experienced agents, and she has an extensive background in long-term undercover work with the FBI. And we agree with her assessment, sexist as it may be, that as a woman, she will be ideally suited to infiltrate this type of club," Patterson said.

My heart sank, and my stomach began to churn. The muscles along Sarah's jaw tensed, and the determination in her eyes was unmistakable as she glowered at her notes. I knew right then that I would have a better chance of beating Ab at arm wrestling than changing her mind.

"May I at least request that Mr. Dore be added to your support-and-surveillance unit monitoring Agent Wright?" Athena asked, closing the files in front of her. "Strictly in an advisory capacity. He does have intimate knowledge of the group. More so than anyone else at this point."

Suddenly, it felt as if every eye in the room were burning a hole into my skull. I tried nonchalantly to study the backs of my hands on the table in front of me. After a long silence, mercifully, someone spoke.

"He could prove useful, wouldn't you agree?" the Secretary said, glancing over to the Director.

"Yes," he replied, "I would tend to agree. He could be helpful to Agent Wright. But only in an advisory capacity. He is a civilian, after all."

Everyone focused on me again. I just nodded and shrugged a bit. I certainly couldn't tell them the truth.

"Then we just need to make sure you stay completely out of sight and with our support team," the Director added, finishing his thought. "Safe and secure."

"Excellent," said the Secretary, closing her file folders as well.

It was a sentiment that everyone else shared. It was all I could do not to mock it like a petulant child.

I remained seated as everyone got up to leave. Athena stood, slid her file folder in front of me, then walked to a sideboard behind us as if to get a drink. Sarah gathered her things without saying a word or making eye contact, so I absentmindedly opened the folder. Clipped to the inside of the jacket were the two pictures I had taken of bodies in the basement of the Dungeon. Other pictures were loose inside the folder with a single piece of paper among them. The text on the page was simple: "Male subject appears to be Gancanagh, Unseelie, unknown individual. Female subject appears to be Samodiva, Unseelie, unknown individual." I was completely unfamiliar with both types of Fae. *More crap I don't know.* I really hated being in the dark. A handwritten note stuck to the piece of paper explained that Gancanagh had the ability to seduce human women and stimulate sexual desire, while the Samodiva had the same effect on human men. Once I read this, the hospital-like setup in the basement of the Dungeon made some sense. Those techs were probably harvesting whatever pheromone, hormone, or chemical these Fae produced and synthesizing it to use at the clubs to promote the proper atmosphere. I was also willing to bet the substance had been the source of the smell at Cocytus and the Dungeon. Maybe I wasn't in complete darkness.

I glanced over at Athena then at Sarah and decided in my moment of clarity that I probably should say something to Sarah before she left.

"Sarah," I said, desperately trying to keep my voice from cracking, "we need to talk."

"I have an undercover op to prep for and a team to assemble, Steve," she said icily.

"Perhaps I should give you two a moment," Athena said.

I glanced from Athena back to Sarah as she was walking out. I was ticked off at the whole situation. "Out of curiosity," I said, trying to direct my comment at Sarah as she passed, "Did you know that this was Athena?" I hooked a thumb over my shoulder at my benefactor. "I mean, I didn't realize she was in disguise until I saw her ID badge."

Sarah stopped, and I could see her eyes get bigger as she faced us.

"See my problem with sending you in undercover *now*?" I said, shifting so I could see them both. "At least *she's* on our side." I motioned at Athena, trying to emphasize my point. "Sarah, the creatures involved in this mess are vile, corrupt, and pure evil, and they can pull off this kind of trick as easily as she does. If you can't tell up from down, how on earth can you protect yourself in this situation?"

"Easy. Unlike most of my cases where I don't know who's innocent or involved up to their eyeballs, I'm just going to go into this one assuming everyone's flat-out malevolent," Sarah replied without missing a beat. "My goal is simply to find out where things are happening and when so that *you* can deal with them. I have no intention of trying to arrest anyone, and I *certainly* have *no* inclination to try to make any sort of legal case against a fucking demon. That crap was for them." She gestured toward the door through which the others left.

"These things are far worse than witches and ghouls, Sarah," I said, pleading. "They mess with your mind; they screw you up. Permanently."

"You keep telling me that," she replied, her eyes softening a bit. "That's exactly why we can't just send in some unaware agent. And these creeps know you, not me, and at least *I* know that there will be things other than humans in that place."

"She is our best option, Diomedes," Athena said. "And tactically, you know this."

I glared at Athena, and she matched my stare in intensity as her blue eyes blazed in response.

"Besides, apparently, you'll be right outside, just in case anything happens," Sarah said with a forced chuckle and half smile.

"Yeah, I know, in advisory capacity *only*..." I replied, making a stupid face. "I still don't like it. In fact, I freaking *hate* it, and I want to go on record as having said so." I pointed back and forth from

Athena to Sarah. "I swear, if Sarah even thinks about saying *ouch* in there, I'll rip the place and everyone in it apart. Then *you* can explain it to those goons," I said to Athena, pointing at the door Sarah's bosses had left through. "Oh, and if Brey is correct, we have until June fifth—that's the timing for the 'Transition of the Light Bringer.' Something to do with Venus and the sun."

Across from me, Sarah was actually blushing.

"Breygivila informed me of such as well. This leaves us just over a month. However, I do believe I should give you two a few moments alone," Athena said with a genuine hint of discomfort and embarrassment in her voice. She left another file folder on the desk in front of me as she walked out.

Once we were alone, I sheepishly fixated on my feet, not sure what to say.

"You know," Sarah said, "the main reason I'm okay doing this is because I knew *you'd* be right outside just in case—even if they didn't let you join my team."

"You'll have a whole freakin' TAC team standing by... just in case," I replied.

"Yeah, but like you said, you'd tear the place apart. And I know *you* can do it."

When I glanced back up from my shoes, she was standing just in front of me.

"For you, yeah, I would," I said, then she kissed me.

Chapter 28

I tried to gain my bearings as I stumbled around, taking in the chaos that probably used to be a neat and orderly little apartment. Somehow, I managed to find my boxers amid the rack and ruin and pulled them on. I could hear Sarah in the bathroom. The couch still felt solid enough, so I sat down trying to take stock of what had happened.

I didn't remember leaving the building or even driving anywhere. And I had absolutely no memory of arriving at her apartment. The events that had transpired after that were trapped in a hormonal haze. All I knew was that a day and a half later, Sarah's apartment was a total wreck. Somehow, her front door had been ripped from its hinges and sort of placed back into the jamb. Two chairs were also broken, along with a coffee table and a lamp, and the refrigerator was wide open. Orange juice, tea, and possibly mustard were all over the kitchen floor. Bread, cheese, and eggs were strewn across the kitchen counter.

Her bedroom was worse. The headboard was cracked, and the bedframe was bent so badly that at some point, we'd apparently moved the mattresses to the floor. Clothes were everywhere. Something had happened to her closet and an armoire, too.

I knew what had happened... but I needed to figure out what its implications were for us, or more specifically, for Sarah. Before I could get too deeply into depressing notions about living a thousand lifetimes as a chaste monk, Sarah tripped over some debris behind me. She was in a robe, drying her hair with a towel. She looked like every reason I ever fought to defend humanity and every thought that kept me going in the darkness. *Screw being alone.* Whatever else I was or wasn't, I was still human. I smiled at her as she tripped again over what was left of a chair.

"Found your boxers, I see," she said, sitting on the arm of the couch. "I wasn't sure they survived."

"Yeah, from the look of things, not much else did... Wow."

"Never took you for an impatient man," she said, taking in the entirety of the devastation of the room, finally landing on the door. "I really need to get that door fixed. There's no way that's safe."

"The whole door needs to be replaced." I grimaced. "Sorry. Keys were taking too long. I have no excuse for the rest of it."

"Well, if I recall," she said, moving to sit next to me on the couch, "I broke one of the chairs, that lamp, and that table, so it's not all on you."

I nodded toward the nook. "The kitchen was you, too."

"Only because you..." She poked me in the ribs, which then became a kiss.

"Okay, at this rate, we'll never clean this place up, much less get out of here," I said, stopping reluctantly. "And we have work to do."

That afternoon, a carpenter came to fix the door and its shattered jamb. Sarah and I spent the rest of the day going over a plan, until I'd almost managed to convince myself that it could work. Every ten or fifteen minutes, we kept hearing heavy sighs from the carpenter, and each glance in his direction was met with a glare of disapproval. I'm not sure what exactly the guy disapproved of—us in general, behavior that would have led to such damage, or the extensiveness of the damage.

Uncluttering the wrecked apartment aside, the more important dilemma at hand was making sure that Sarah's undercover persona would be picked as a hostess at Cocytus. To complicate things further, we had to also ensure she would be recruited by the Sons of Belial the same way Taylon Jones had been.

"Cocytus would more than likely prefer someone who was unattached and a loner but not a prostitute," Sarah said. "And somewhat healthy is better than strung out and emaciated, though some signs of drug use might prove worthwhile. It's been my experience, however, that the proper psychology of a fetishist is extremely tough to nail down."

"I agree," I replied, relieved not to have to discuss this aspect of her persona with her. "Probably best to let your team work on that. Fortunately, the Sons of Belial probably represent the easiest part of this whole thing. I would bet they are mostly concerned with finding someone who could virtually disappear and not be missed. I mean, why else would they have chosen Jones?"

"Okay, so what we have is a college-educated persona that recently moved to the city from somewhere south of New York and never stays in one place very long," Sarah said. "She will live in an SRO and struggle to meet weekly rent and bounce from job to job. She'll have very few real possessions, with the exception of a few very expensive outfits and the appropriate accessories to match. She's a recreational drug user but not an addict. She's lazy and slightly manipulative, would have grown up using her sexuality to get whatever she wanted or needed. That way, her willingness to use sex as a tool would make sense."

"Yeah, but she has to have a clean record," I replied. "Someone with a known criminal background might be seen as too much of a liability. The cover has to be deep and convincing. I fully expect Na'amah to employ investigators to vet thoroughly each potential candidate, and they'll utilize nonhuman means to check as well. An organization like this with an ultra-wealthy and secretive clientele will undoubtedly perform rigorous checks of everyone involved."

"Agreed." Sarah nodded. "We have to operate under the premise that if they smell anything fishy at all, they'll pass. If I can get into Cocytus as a hostess, then my unattached cover should make me attractive enough for the Sons of Belial. If we're lucky."

"Good or bad, it'll be some kind of luck for sure," I replied, thoroughly unhappy with the prospect of offering Sarah as bait. "Just remember that because of the likely nature of the background checks by the entities at Cocytus, we won't be able to use bugs, wires, or tracking devices of *any* kind. It will all have to be old-fashioned eyes-on surveillance and monitoring with maybe a few passive electronic devices." I really didn't like the idea of using electronic devices, though. They were too dangerous because they clearly indicated something was up if they were discovered.

"The one thing that is not optional," I said, "is that I will collect a small sample of your blood so that I can track your whereabouts anywhere on Earth." She had no response to my request as I watched the weight of our undertaking sink in. Of all things useful for tracking someone magically, blood was by far the most effective because it held the very physical essence of the being from which it came.

Sarah was intensely focused as we discussed the details. In fact, she became calmer and more in control, acting as if this were just another day on the job—all up until I started to talk about the non-human and supernatural elements that would be involved. At that point, her face went a little paler and her eyes got a little wider. She swallowed a bit harder, but the resolve in her face never suggested anything other than determination. She knew what was at stake, and she wasn't the type of person to back off when something needed to be done—even if it was daunting. That was the very essence of bravery—not an absence of fear, just the fortitude to do what needed to be done in spite of it. I had always believed Sarah would have given Penthesilea, the Queen of the Amazons, a run for her money, but watching her prepare for this infiltration, that feeling began to change. *Sarah would have kicked her ass.*

"I promise you three things," I said, taking her hand. "First, I will never be far away. Second, I will get Duma to attend the party at Cocytus; and lastly, if anyone or anything hurts you, I will destroy them." I was far from happy with the situation, but I'd managed to convince myself that I *could* keep her safe.

Sarah was resolute, at least on the surface, which was good, because every single aspect of the operation bothered me on an atomic level, none more than using Sarah as bait. I tried to hide my apprehension the best I could, but I could see the recognition of it in Sarah's face. Still she said nothing.

Chapter 29

Once the carpenter was finished repairing the apartment, I headed back to San Diego via the Ways. I needed to get my gear together, reschedule charters, and make sure Ned would watch over my boat for a while. I had a thousand things running through my mind. It was late, and I wasn't thinking straight as I exited the Ways into the scrub outside the casino parking lot just east of San Diego, where I always left my car.

Sudden movement in the darkness off to my left made me pause. Instinctively, I reached for a sword... that wasn't there, then the gun I hadn't brought and a knife that was still sitting in my duffle back home. I didn't even have a damned pocketknife. All I had was my Way Stone—a fucking rock.

A sudden rush of adrenaline brought my immediate situation into stark relief, and I found myself seriously pissed off. I was pissed at myself for being so brash and unprepared and pissed that I'd acquiesced to using Sarah as demon bait. I was furious that Sarah had even agreed. But right then, that anger was a good thing, and I fully intended to use whatever the hell was lurking out here for cathartic purposes.

I began walking away from my truck and the parking lot, farther into the scrub and away from prying eyes. Without any weapons, I pulled out my car keys and squeezed a couple of the keys between my fingers. Punching something that way would hurt my hand, but it would hurt the other guy worse. After watching shadows flit at the edges of my vision for a few moments, my patience finally gave way to my anger.

"Bring it," I said in a low growl.

The first shadow emerged from my right, loping in an awkward, jerky gait. I got a good glimpse of it as it jumped, covering at least twenty feet in the air. Strigoi. Again. *This feud is really getting old.*

I caught the attacker in midair with one hand and, in a single fluid motion, hammered it in the head with my key-filled fist, redirecting the creature over and past me. The second one struck from behind as I was stretched out, hitting me solidly in the back with both feet. I flew forward, tucked my head and right shoulder, and rolled back to my feet, quickly facing my assailant.

Rather than sit and wait, I screamed at the top of my lungs and charged. The bellow caught the bobbing creature flat-footed, allowing me to close the distance before it moved. With one hand, I grabbed the vampire at the junction between its bony shoulder and thin neck and began punching it in the face and head with the other. The second the rigid body went limp, another vampire hit me from the left side. The mindless rabble of the Strigoi didn't weigh much, but when combined with their preternatural speed, the impact was greater than I was prepared for. Something in my chest gave way at the collision, and a sharp pain shot through my upper body and shoulder as we hit the ground.

I brought my left elbow down on the creature's back with all my strength then grappled it around the neck in a reverse choke hold and began punching again with my right hand and the keys. The monster tried to scramble loose from my grasp, its clawlike nails shredding my pants and scrabbling at the ground in desperation as I held on, pummeling it. My skin burned everywhere the creature scratched me, and it hurt to breathe. I kept swinging, though, until the vampire's head was little more than a fleshy bag of broken bone and tissue.

I got to my feet, holding the mangled vampire's pulpy head still locked under my arm, and stared out into the surrounding darkness. I could still see movement in the shadows all around, but I couldn't tell how many creatures it represented.

The other vampire I'd beaten began to stir on the ground a few yards away. Breathing heavily, I dragged the pulpy-headed vampire over to the recovering leech and stomped its skull before it regained any more strength. Strigoi chittered like insects all around me, but nothing advanced.

The vampire I was dragging was starting to heal. I painfully managed to pry open my right hand and drop the keys, and then I dropped the creature, knelt on its chest, grabbed its mushy head with both hands, and pulled until the head came loose. I tossed it over my shoulder, earning myself a guttural howl from the darkness, and wearily got back to my feet.

The numbness in my right hand was starting to become a dull throb, and I kept my breathing shallow to avoid the pain of deeper breaths, but I stood my ground and roared back into the darkness as best I could.

With some unknown number of vampires still out in the darkness, I realized I needed to arm myself, so I did. I tore an arm loose from the Strigoi body on the ground and walked in the direction of the bray. I stood, waiting for the next onslaught, but it never came. Exhausted, I dropped heavily to the ground, landing hard on my butt. The jarring impact sent a shock of pain through my chest that stopped me from breathing and sent stars through my vision. Then I saw a figure I thought was Sarah standing over me.

The next thing I knew, I was waking up in my bed at my house in Roseville on Point Loma. I had an IV in my left arm and heavily bandaged ribs, and a cast on my right hand totally immobilized my wrist, hand, and fingers. Something slick and shiny covered my legs, and I could feel a persistent burning from the scratches, gouges, and welts underneath. There was pain, but not enough to bother me.

And then I tried to move. My vision blurred, and I immediately sat back, trying to assess the situation. The moment of contemplation also gave me time to catch my breath. That was when I noticed I was wearing an adult diaper. "What the hell? Why do people keep putting these things on me?"

"Would you prefer a catheter, mate?" came a response from a male voice with a heavy British accent from somewhere in the front of my house.

The voice was familiar, but I was still a bit too hazy and confused to place it.

"Who the fuck is there?" I said, shouting unnecessarily.

"Relax, Demo. It's me," he replied, clearly getting closer. "Or should I say Diomedes..."

Geek walked up to my bedroom doorway, tablet computer in one hand and some sort of earpiece along his jawline, wearing a stupid-looking pair of glasses with no lenses in them. I was surprised to see William Elmsmore—former Royal Marine and member of the Special Boat Service cum computer and technology uber-nerd. Apparently, he was also my nurse.

"You did this to me?" I said referencing my diaper.

"Oh, hell no. I'm just your nanny—oh, hang on a sec, mate." He touched his earpiece, changing his focus from me to somewhere else.

"Go..." he started talking again in a very uptight tone. "No, that's not what I said at all, you bleedin' prat. *I said* we needed to *in*crease the bloody effective data rate, not modulate it, you daft—"

I tuned out. After a few minutes of impressive drill-sergeant-like yelling, mostly using words I didn't understand, accompanied by numbers and a variety of expletives, Geek finally hung up and came back.

"Sorry 'bout that," he said, shaking his head. "Athena may be a being from another dimension, but most of the people she employs as computer techs are just bleedin' idiots. Good thing she found me."

"How long have I been here?" I asked through a very dry mouth.

"Oh, I just got here an hour ago, and the doc said you'd been sleeping since last night, so not more than ten or twelve hours. Took a good beating, I see, you mad bastard." He sounded almost excited. "What was it this time? Goblins? Revenants? Fairies? What?"

"Vampires," I said, smiling at his unabashed enthusiasm. "Some kind of blood feud I accidentally started a few months back."

"Awesome!"

"Knock it off, fanboy," I said a bit more harshly than I'd intended.

"Sorry, Demo," he said like a chided schoolboy. "Do you need anything?"

"Yeah, a few aspirin and then to get out of here and back to DC."

"You aren't going anywhere for at least a day. Doctor's and—more importantly—Athena's orders. You've got a few broken bones in your palm, mate. In your *palm*." He grimaced. "Not to mention a few busted ribs. You shoulda been wearin' your cuirass." He shook his head disapprovingly as he said the last part.

"Well, then bring me my damned phone," I said grumpily. "I gotta call Sarah."

He waggled his eyebrows. "Ooh, the lovely and capable Sarah."

I just glowered at him.

"Fine, be that way. Where'd you leave it?"

"It was in my pocket..." I said.

"Uh, no pants, except those hanging in your closet and in your dresser there—not that I snooped or anything."

"Dammit."

I reached up and removed the IV from my arm *carefully*. I knew better than to jerk it loose. I was man enough to admit that a needle in my vein kind of freaked me out. Once the thing was out, I got up a little too fast, sending a wave of pain through my chest that nearly caused me to black out and fall. Geek grabbed my arm with his free hand, and through sheer force of will, I managed to keep my feet under me.

"By 'busted,' you know I meant broken, right, mate?" he asked in a tone similar to one a teacher would use when asking a child a tough question.

I just glared at him since I really didn't feel like yelling at the moment. I pulled my arm free from his grasp, sending a whole new shock of pain through my chest. I expected it, though, and managed to stay upright on my own. I staggered to my dresser, pulled out clean underwear, then stumbled into my closet to grab a pair of jeans before going to the bathroom to get out of the freakin' diaper.

The more I moved, the better I felt—until I bent over to pull on my jeans. My vision faded to a single point of light, and my eyes watered. The pain from bending was so intense that the scratches on my legs didn't even register. Plus, my clubbed right hand was about as useful as an icemaker in Antarctica. Dammit if I didn't persevere, though.

"Can you get me a new phone?" I asked Geek, who was now back in my living room, as I struggled pulling on a T-shirt. The incessant clicking of his keyboard grated on my nerves.

"Sure thing," he replied. "What kind? iPhone, Android, Windows?"

"One that makes phone calls," I said in what sounded like a growl to me. I nearly pulled the sink from the wall in my irritation.

My old-fashioned push-button desktop phone came crashing down the hall as I exited the bathroom. It broke into pieces, and buttons went skittering everywhere.

Man, if that doesn't just sum up my life right now. I really needed to take a step back and gather myself before blindly charging forward.

Despite the pain, I bent to pick up the bulk of the phone's carcass then walked up the hall to my living room. Geek had set up some sort of mobile command station on my fly-tying desk with three laptops and a few other gadgets that I didn't recognize, all sporting squat antennas. He was typing furiously on two of the machines simultaneously. Clearly, caring for me wasn't his only priority at the moment. I sighed at the sudden realization that I wasn't the only one fighting and that mine wasn't the only fight around.

"Sorry," I said, dropping the phone into my wastebasket next to my tying desk, sending motes of discarded feather and fur from my fly-tying endeavors springing up from the basket.

"What the bloody hell..." Geek replied as he swatted feathers from in front of his monitors.

"I said I'm sorry."

"For what?" he replied without taking his eyes from his monitors.

"For being a pain in the ass and not treating you with the respect you deserve. Thanks for watching over me."

"No worries, mate," he said, barely regarding me before going back to typing furiously again.

"Can you get me a new cell phone?" I asked. "I don't care what kind, smart or dumb, fruity or robotic."

Barely missing a beat, he reached into a messenger bag on the floor next to him, dug around for a second, pulled out a phone in a heavy-duty case, and blindly tossed it to me.

With my clubbed right hand and my tentative movements, I missed, and the phone crashed to the floor with a thunk. Geek laughed. I bent over gingerly to pick it up, expecting to see the screen shattered into a million pieces, but it was fine.

"Shockproof and water-resistant, mate," Geek said. "I'm sure *you* can still find a way to break it, though."

Walking back to my bedroom, I quickly dialed Sarah's number. I got her voicemail, so I left her a long message about why I was running late. Then I realized I probably should have said something nice about the other day, too, so I called her back. I was leaving a rambling, semicoherent message that even I didn't understand, so I finally just hung up to save what was left of my dignity. *I was smooth, a walking chick magnet. Why wouldn't Sarah be all over me?*

Feeling totally out of sorts, I decided to go over my gear. I pulled open the heavily armored weapons locker I called my load-out room at the back of my closet and, with a wince and a pained sigh, grabbed my usual duffle off the floor where I'd left it.

I laid out my cuirass, my knives, swords, and guns then threw all the spare magazines into a pile on the bed. The tactical vest that normally covered my cuirass was destroyed, so I set about replacing it then took on the familiar and comforting tasks of refilling magazines and cleaning my weapons. *This is me breathing.*

The work might even have been relaxing if it hadn't been for my right hand. Instead, bullets went flying around the room and under the bed as I fumbled with trying to reload the spring-fed magazines. I sliced up my bedspread and sheets with my knives and swords then ripped apart the new vest I was trying to put over my cuirass when I tried to cut the webbing along its flank to fit properly. All in all, I accomplished nothing except frustrating myself even more.

Down the hall in my living room, Geek talked animatedly with someone again over his phone, speaking in what sounded like English but using words that could have been made up for all I knew. With a heavy sigh, I pulled the ruined cover off the bed and dropped it on the floor. Bullets scattered across the room like spilled marbles, and my knives, guns, swords, and cuirass clattered to the ground.

Maybe Athena was right, and I needed to rest, so I lay down to nap, more exhausted than I'd thought.

I awoke to stark silence and the sun shining through the lone window in my bedroom. For the briefest of moments, I was confused because it normally only did that in the morning. Then it dawned on me, literally. I shot upright in a flash of pain and squinted at the alarm clock on my nightstand through watery eyes. It read 8:15 in angry red numerals. I walked down the hall to my den, which was empty.

"Hello?" I called out to see if anyone was here.

Nobody answered.

I headed back down the hall and sensed Athena's presence at just about the same time I turned around and nearly ran into her. I was already wound so tightly that her sudden appearance startled me. I flailed for just a second before slipping and landing hard on my keister, which sent spasms of pain through my ribs. I did manage to keep my broken hand out of the way as I fell, though.

"For the sake of all that is good and decent in the world, for once, can't you just knock?" I rolled over to get back to my feet with as little pain as possible.

"I suppose, but this is far more expedient." She stepped past me as if avoiding gum on the ground. "I just wanted to check on you and give you some more information."

"And you couldn't help me up?" I said, getting to my feet. "I'm fine, by the way. Thanks for asking."

"You appear less so," she replied dryly without actually looking at me.

As usual, she was dressed in a severe pantsuit, a gray one, with a long jacket buttoned all the way up her neck. She wore her hair in a tight braid on the back of her head. Her blue eyes burned so brightly that they cast a cold hue through the darkened living room. I walked into the room behind her and sat down gingerly in my leather armchair.

"I believe I can help you with your pain," she said nonchalantly then walked past me back up the hall.

"Wait... What? Three thousand years of getting myself beat to a pulp, and *now* you tell me you have something to help with pain? Seriously?"

She returned a moment later and dropped a bottle of aspirin in my lap.

"You are human, Diomedes, and as such, you suffer as all humans do when injured. I can do nothing to stop that, short of giving you armor." She fixed me with a hard gaze that clearly underlined her point.

"It was a mistake I won't repeat," I snarled in return then pried open the bottle of aspirin and chewed a few.

"This feud with Lilith is intolerable," Athena said, not really addressing me so much as making the statement.

"Tell me about it." I snorted then winced.

"Once this thing with the Watcher is over, you should attempt to find a diplomatic resolution."

"Oh, I know the solution. If you have any suggestions on how to get Lilith to bare her neck to me, I'm all ears," I replied.

"You can ill afford a personal war with a being as powerful as Lilith, especially if you must now pursue her sister."

"Point. But in my defense, she and her brood were harboring a nasty piece of work. I didn't mean to kill any of them in the process."

"One," she replied without making eye contact.

"One what?"

"You only killed one of the Liuntika Strigoi when you collapsed the tunnel in their hive," she replied.

"What? Are you saying this whole bullshit war is the result of me killing one stinkin' parasite because they were providing refuge for a piece of trash I had to take out?" I asked, slapping the arm of my chair.

"Actually, no. The feud stems from your trespassing and the wanton destruction of a primary hive-structure."

"It was a tunnel... a single freakin' tunnel. Not the whole damned hive-thingy. Not even the *whole* damned tunnel. Just a small section of it." I held up my thumb and forefinger about an inch apart to drive my point home.

"To be honest," she said, shrugging, "I would prefer total destruction of her and her entire race, but it is not my place to make such decisions in your world, Diomedes. Unless that is your proximate goal, I suggest you find a way to arrive at an affable congruence. Or at least a tolerable one."

I nodded and shrugged noncommittally. I liked the idea of killing every last one of the bloodsuckers and all, but it sounded like a lot of work at the moment. And I had a busted hand and ribs. *Whatever.* I would worry about that crap later. I had more important things to worry about.

"In the meantime," she said, facing me, "we need to discuss the matter at hand."

"Sarah and I discussed it at length and came up with a pretty good strategy. I just need to make a few calls first, and then I'll meet up with her and her team," I said, trying to be cagey about contacting Duma.

Even trying to be evasive with Athena was stupid. While she actively avoided invading my mind, our connection was just too strong. Still, we'd had the conversation about my relationship with Duma and his brother more times than I cared to remember, and I wasn't in the mood to have it again. Athena just eyed me wearily, and I could see her debating whether or not to say anything. For once, she chose discretion. Then her expression changed to one of compassion.

"As always, I will trust to your perspicacity," she said, walking over to hand me a business card. "But before you head out, please make sure you meet with this person regarding your injuries. And, in the future, please remember to take full advantage of the implements I have given you for your protection and use. I would hate to have to find a new champion after so long."

I rolled my eyes, and she headed toward the front door but stopped just short of it. "While I am happy for your relationship with Sarah, I need not remind you that you have been down this road before, Diomedes. Several times. I will simply say that if you allow your feelings for her to become a distraction, it will become a weakness that can be exploited and may get you both killed."

"Understood, *Mom*," I said, being sardonic. "But for the first time in a long time, I feel human again, and she helps me remember what I'm fighting for."

I blinked, and she was gone. I stared at the phone number on the card. I pried myself loose from my chair and found the phone.

Chapter 30

Athena's doctor cut the heavy cast off my hand, took a few x-rays, then rewrapped it in a slightly lighter but equally rigid fiberglass material. The x-rays of my ribs showed one had been dislocated at the sternum and two others had been cracked. There was little to do but wrap my chest in bandages to stabilize them, which I cut off about three seconds after I left the office. The scratches on my legs were irritating at worst, but the doctor gave me ointment to put on them daily. He also gave me a prescription for painkillers, which I promptly ripped up and left in his office wastebasket. I could deal with pain. On the upside, my blood pressure and temperature all checked out normal.

By the time I had gotten my gear together and made sure my boat was taken care of, I received a message that Sarah and her team had already left for New York. The communication said that Sarah would arrive by train as part of her cover story, while the rest of her team would already be onsite, ready to begin their routine surveillance the moment she exited the station. I was supposed to meet up with the primary surveillance team in a building in the heart of Chinatown, on the corner of Hester and Bowery across the street from what would be Sarah's residence for the foreseeable future.

When I got to New York, I found the address. The white-stone building was old, with seven stories, smoked glass, and a wrap of ugly gray granite around the street level. A variety of small Asian markets and defunct shops occupied the ground floor. As I walked in through the only door leading upstairs, the penetrating smell of urine combined with the strong scent of Asian spices to assault my nose. Remnants of peeling and ripped linoleum covered some of the stairs, which, on the whole, appeared barely passable. Clearly, the upstairs hadn't been used in some time. Just before I began the climb, I glanced over my shoulder at Sarah's building—a ratty SRO called the Whole Earth Hotel across the street and a few buildings down. To call it a shithole would have been generous, and from what I could see, it made our building seem like the Ritz. *Yeesh.*

As I climbed the decaying stairs, I realized I was right about our building. It was a skeleton above the second level. At the fifth floor, I started to hear voices, so I continued cautiously upward but decided against drawing a weapon. By the time I reached the seventh floor, I had identified at least three distinct voices, including two women and a man. I stopped to survey the bright, open expanse ringed by windows on every side. The only thing that broke up the vast space was a series of metal studs extending from the floor to the exposed joists of the floor above in a pattern that made no sense whatsoever. The three people I'd heard, plus one other I hadn't, stopped what they were doing and glowered at me as a group.

"Steve Dore..." I said, painfully aware I was suddenly on stage. No one responded. "From the Metis Foundation..."

With that, they all went back to what they were doing as if I'd suddenly vanished. I stood slightly dumbfounded for a few seconds, trying to determine what to do next. I was familiar with the situation. I had experienced it several times when political geniuses tried to embed CIA operators into our SEAL Team. They wanted me to know I was unwanted but unavoidable. I figured I had several options: I could swagger in and be a big prick, I could just walk up and try to insert myself and be friendly, or I could be a church mouse and tiptoe around for a bit, playing submissive. Against every fiber in my body, I decided to try another tack altogether: open and honest. *Ish.*

"Again, my name is Steve," I said, walking over to the group gathered in the corner of the building closest to Sarah's hotel. "I realize my presence is a bit of an imposition, and for that, I apologize. I do, however, bring two important things to this group. First, I know the organization we are after better than anyone. I know who's in charge, what they look like, and what they are capable of. And I've seen their operation from the inside."

The last statement got their attention, especially the African-American woman in the group.

"So what's the second thing?" the woman asked, hand on hip. She wore a tan jacket and jeans, her short hair done in springy braids, and she had the air of someone in charge. I made a snap decision to trust her based solely on the fact that Sarah had chosen her.

"I picked Sarah for the job." I wasn't sure how they would take that or what they thought it meant, but I wanted them to know I was personally invested in her safety.

The woman nodded at me. "I'm Agent in Charge Graves. These are Agents Phillips, Mitchell, and Mendez."

She pointed out the other woman, followed by the man I'd identified, then the Hispanic man who was busy doing something with electronics. Wearing a massive set of headphones covering only one ear, he chewed a straw as he worked and completely ignored everything else going on around him.

I dropped my gear bag with a bit more of a thud than I'd expected, causing Mitchell's eyebrow to rise as he watched me out of the corner of his eye. Then the other eyebrow went up. Either he noticed my broken hand, or my fly was down.

"Oh, this," I said, holding up my casted hand. "Broke a few bones sparring the other day. No big deal. It won't slow me down. I'm good with either hand."

"You troubleshoot and investigate for the Metis Foundation," Mitchell said more as a statement than as a question. He was a balding man who had to be in his mid-forties and had the edgy appearance of someone who'd been on a few too many stakeouts.

"Yep," I replied.

"So just how are *you* qualified to be here with us?" he asked while everybody but the electronics guy stopped to listen to my response.

"I'm really good at poking my nose where it doesn't belong and shooting trouble," I said, walking over to see just what everyone was up to.

"Knock it off, Andy," Graves said in a short, clipped tone. "Wright wanted him here, so just deal with it." Then she faced me. "Bunks are one floor down. You can stow your gear there, and then I'll explain our setup and schedule. That goes for everyone. Sitrep in ten. Got it?" She made a point of making eye contact with everyone until she got an acknowledgment. She had to kick Mendez's makeshift milk-crate seat to get his attention.

I grabbed my duffle and headed back downstairs, found the five cots, each with a rolled-up sleeping bag on it, and dropped my duffle in front of the only unoccupied one. I spent a few minutes pulling out my vest and cuirass then checking my Sig Sauer before holstering it in the vest, along with three extra magazines. I fastened my drop holster around my left thigh and put my Glock in it. Then I remembered my right hand, so I set about pulling the cross-draw holster off the left side of the vest and changing places with the magazine pockets that normally went there, so I could draw it left-handed.

I pulled out my two tanto knives, put one in a sheath on the right shoulder of my vest and the other along its lower back, then began the painful process of pulling the cuirass and vest on over my broken ribs. The cuirass wasn't so snug that it hurt, but the moving and cajoling to get it on was no picnic. Once it was in place, however, I was good. The painful process distracted me enough that I hadn't noticed someone come up behind me.

"I'd say you broke more than your hand sparring," said the electronics guy, whose name I suddenly couldn't remember. He carried a small package in both hands and still wore the bulky headphones around his neck.

"Ah... yeah, rough bout, but I'm good. The brace under the vest will help," I lied, trying to cover the true nature of my cuirass.

"What? MMA, Muay Thai, boxing?" he asked.

"Oh, this?" I held up my casted hand. "Nah. This was from my knitting circle. Disagreement about what type of stitch to use. I said purl, she said knit, and the next thing you know, fists are flying."

He smiled at me and shook his head. The guy *had* been paying attention upstairs, after all.

"Oh, this is for you." He extended the brown-paper-wrapped package, suddenly acting sheepish as if unsure what to do with it. "Sarah left me specific directions to give it directly to you when you arrived."

"Thanks," I said, taking the small parcel from him. It wasn't big, maybe six inches square by four inches tall.

"Careful, it's really heavy," he said as he handed it over.

He was right. The thing weighed at least twenty pounds. *What the hell?*

"Thanks," I said with a grunt, shifting it a bit to get a better grip.

I walked with it back over to my bunk and sat down, thinking I'd better wait to unwrap it. Mendez walked over to a cot, pulled a heavy plastic storage case from under it, and snapped it open. After removing some sort of corded doodad, he headed back upstairs.

Once I was alone again, I unwrapped the package, revealing an ornately decorated black iron box. *That explains the weight.*

It had no lock, just a simple hasp, and the inside was lined with thick green velvet set with two shiny filigreed silver tubes about the size of a finger. Each tube was connected to a bright silver chain by its copper-colored cap. Recognition dawned quickly, and I grabbed one just to verify my hunch. The copper end where the chain attached simply pulled free from the silver sleeve. Inside the sleeve was a crystal vial with dark-red liquid inside, and it glowed the palest shade of pink from some sort of magical energy. *Sarah's blood.*

The workmanship of the delicate filigreed sleeves was impressive. They weighed almost nothing apart from the crystal and chain, and I guessed they were aluminum. It was clear that other-than-human hands had expertly worked each of the crystal containers, their copper lids, and the chains. Both containers were identical in every detail.

They were ideal tools for finding and tracking Sarah if I needed to. They were flawless creations that would allow energy to flow through them as efficiently as physically possible. In other words, they were tracking crystals that even *I* could use. I smiled. Sarah really didn't do anything halfway. I put one vial around my neck and under my cuirass then placed the other back in its wrought-iron box. Even that was smart. The raw iron would keep any but the most ardent Paran from getting hold of Sarah's very life essence.

I tucked the box into my duffle, rechecked my swords, then wrapped them securely in a microfiber towel. I closed the duffle, changed into my boots, and headed back upstairs to join the others.

Once back on the seventh floor, Graves began her group debrief. A lot of it was standard procedure for an undercover situation: maintaining audio and visual watch, keeping a safe distance, calling in and handing off tails, logging contacts, emergency meets, emergency signals, code words, and such. Graves gave us a very short list of people we could communicate with if necessary. It consisted of two people, one of whom had been at the meeting in DC. The other was a secure runner to communicate with DHS in person. The last thing Graves went over was Sarah's undercover ID.

"She chose the name Criseida Calchasidou," she said.

The name made me snort aloud. Everyone else giggled a bit, too, but for different reasons than mine. It was an odd name, after all. "Look, she chose it, so get over it," Graves said, trying to restore order to the group. "She said she'd go by 'Cris' for short."

I knew immediately that she'd chosen the name on purpose, knowing I would probably be the only one on Earth who would get it. I hoped that was true. The name was a variation on the name Cressida, the daughter of Calchasa, a turncoat Trojan priest who'd helped the Greeks during the Trojan War. In Shakespeare's play, *Troilus and Cressida*, Cressida was exchanged for a Trojan prisoner of war, where the story says she met *me*. The love affair was only a tiny part of the story itself, but I got her reference.

The next few days crawled by especially slowly since my entire contribution was limited to occasionally examining images of people Sarah interacted with to see if I recognized any of them. Unfortunately, still images, no matter how high the resolution, would never capture auras, glamours, or any magical energy. Infrared images could capture certain energy signatures, but the sudden bright flares were usually chalked up to errors or malfunctions and dismissed. As far as I could tell, every image was of a normal person I'd never seen before. There were only about eight million of those in the city. Throw in a few hundred thousand more beings who could pass for human, and I saw my days becoming long and tedious. I hated sitting on my hands.

After six days of mind-numbing inactivity and crappy take-out food, Mendez finally informed us that ads seeking hosts and hostesses for a private club had finally come out in the online versions of several underground and alternative newspapers. That morning, Sarah pulled open the curtain to her room and placed a small plant on the windowsill.

All at once, Agent Mitchell ran past me and upstairs in a blur of panic. That was Sarah's signal that she needed to make contact, and

Mitchell, dressed as a homeless person, was the one who would retrieve the information.

According to procedure, in twenty minutes, she would drop something in the garbage can down the street, where Mitchell would dig it out. Dressed in rags and ratty clothing, Mitchell bolted down the steps and around to the back entrance, leaving a rank cloud in his wake. He emerged onto the street through an alley, shambling along, checking out anything discarded on the sidewalk or street. He reached the designated garbage can and began digging. Within moments, Sarah left her SRO dressed in a short skirt and knee-high boots. The red streak in her shortened hair, which she had dyed blond, matched her bright lipstick. I disliked everything about the persona she had adopted.

On cue, she dropped a used coffee cup into the trashcan and continued off down the street. Mitchell grabbed the cup, stuffed it into his coat pocket, and kept moving. An hour later, the undercover agent made his way back to our roost, reeking of rotted food, stale coffee, and who knew what else. I made the mistake of rushing him to get the cup and felt like I'd been punched in the nose.

"Phew," I said, instantly recoiling and throwing an arm over my mouth and nose, suppressing a gag. "You take your job too seriously, man." I snatched the cup from him with my free hand then backed away as he continued upstairs.

"Yeah, yeah, yeah…" He waved me off. "I drew the short straw. What can I say?" He stomped up the rickety stairway, mercifully taking the rancid odor with him.

I popped the top off the cup, revealing the folded note within. Agent Graves walked up behind me, hands on hips, and glared. "Well?" she said, raising her eyebrows and waving an impatient hand.

"It says she replied to the ad in one of the alternative weeklies and has an interview at three p.m. tomorrow at a hotel near the 9/11 memorial. Here's the address," I said, handing her the note.

"Outstanding. Now we can really begin," she said, refocusing on the rest of the team. "Phillips, you and I will tail her at the hotel. I want you at this address by noon. I'll arrive shortly after. Mendez, get me feeds for traffic and street cameras, hotel security cameras, and a full layout of the hotel and the surrounding area as soon as possible. If you need a warrant, let me know. I want eyes on her at all times. Got me?"

Mendez and Phillips nodded.

"What can I do?" I asked, hopeful that I might be able to take a more active role.

"You watch the screens with Mendez," she said flatly. "If you see anyone you recognize, let us know. Mendez will be monitoring a lot of feeds. An extra pair of eyes will help."

Over three thousand years of kicking the shit out of creatures the world doesn't believe exist, and I'm relegated to watching TV because it's how they think I'd be most useful. Seriously?

Chapter 31

Through the hotel's security camera feed, I watched Sarah, dressed in another short skirt and a leather jacket over a blouse unbuttoned one button too many, walk across the hotel lobby and into the bar. She spoke briefly with the bartender, and he pointed at a woman sitting at a table alone. The other woman had her back to the camera with her head bowed as if studying a cell phone or tablet. She was wearing a long camel-hair coat and had very dark hair. As Sarah approached, the woman glanced up and reached out her hand. From the profile, I recognized her immediately as the Moroi who ran Cocytus. The two women shook hands, and the vampiress motioned for Sarah to take a seat across from her. Our view stank—the vampire blocked Sarah, and all we could see of the Moroi was the back of her head. Luckily, Agent Graves was sitting at the bar, while Agent Phillips was at a table by herself, eating and prodding the keys on a laptop. Both had a much better view of the meet than we did.

"The woman she's meeting with runs Cocytus," I said into a microphone. "My information suggests she's not thrilled with whoever she actually works for, but I know nothing about her beyond that."

Agent Phillips shifted in her seat, moved her laptop slightly, then hit a few buttons. A clear image of the woman's face just over Sarah's shoulder popped up on one of our screens. Seconds later, Mendez was running facial recognition on the picture.

"Damn, that woman is gorgeous," Mendez whispered over his shoulder at me. "You think she participates in the club's, uh, activities?"

"Possibly," I replied, trying to focus on Sarah.

He shook his head. "Wonder how much it costs to join."

They met for about thirty minutes before Sarah got up to leave. As they shook hands, the vampire handed her a card or small piece of paper, then Sarah left. The vampire stayed seated, and within a few minutes, another woman walked in and sat down across from her. Agent Phillips remained at her table by the window, but Graves got up, paid her tab, and left. The facial recognition software continued to run without so much as a beep.

"Whoever she is, she apparently doesn't have a driver's license, state or federal ID, or a passport, because she's not in any of our databases," Mendez said.

I followed the cameras until Sarah got into a cab headed back uptown. Then I took what seemed like my first breath in the last half hour, and I shook my head.

"Can you try a facial search on social media or anything?" I asked, trying to be helpful, but not really caring. I knew she was a Moroi, and I had no interest in who she was beyond that.

"Well, sort of, yeah, but it won't be as accurate, and it will take one hell of a lot longer," he replied. "It'd be so much easier if I had a name."

"I bet. So I guess you'll just have to sift through a lot of images of pretty brunettes," I said, smiling and prodding him in the shoulder. "Tough job." I got up, stretched, and walked toward the stairs with the intention of heading to my cot.

"Hey, wait," Mendez said excitedly. "Sarah just searched for directions to an address on her phone." He tapped rapidly on his keyboard for a moment. "Near as I can tell, it's some kind of small private medical clinic in the Village."

It made sense. They would want to make sure she was healthy before proceeding. Mendez did a quick background check and found the clinic itself was a dead end. It was legitimate, owned and run by a larger well-known healthcare company.

Sarah's visit was fully paid for, but getting access to her medical records to find out by whom was problematic. Laws prohibited even the DHS from legally getting the information, and forcing the issue could risk exposing Sarah's connection to law enforcement.

Mendez's facial-recognition search of the brunette Moroi produced a few matches that proved problematic for him. One image that came up as a seventy-five-percent match was a young woman in an old photo of a group of teenage native Hawaiian girls performing at a luau in honor of a visit by the Prince of Wales in the 1920s. The other was a higher-percentage match to an older but just as beautiful young woman at the Golden Gate International Exhibition on Treasure Island off San Francisco in 1940. Without question, both were the Moroi woman, and she hadn't aged since the later photo. Given the photos' ages, Mendez predictably tossed them out and considered the effort a failure. The only thing the pictures told me was that the vampire was close to a hundred years old.

Three days later, we were still no closer to identifying the vampire, but Sarah had delivered us a message through the garbage-can telegraph. I read the message over and over, hoping the information would somehow become less unsettling for me. The note said she had passed the physical and needed to meet with someone as part of a standard background check. They would come to collect her the next day during business hours. That was unusual, to say the very least. Each time I read it, my stomach flopped, and I could feel the perspiration break out on my forehead. I had to remind myself that she was a professional and had a solid team behind her, who expected that to happen.

At nine the next morning, I was glued to the monitors. An hour and fifteen minutes later, a sleek black Mercedes sedan pulled up right outside her hotel, and a man in a gray suit got out of the passenger side, carrying a briefcase. He straightened his tie and glanced around at the neighborhood. His brow wrinkled slightly as his gaze fell to the entrance to the SRO. Without thinking, I shot to the window to *look* at him. I had to know if he was human or not.

I watched as the man walked into the SRO. Nothing about him suggested he was anything other than human. My heart started beating again, and I suddenly realized Graves, Mendez, and Phillips were all frantically calling to me hoarsely to get me away from the windows.

"Damn, sorry. I wasn't thinking. My bad."

"All we need is for them to feel just the slightest bit off, and all of this work—all of Sarah's work—will be for nothing," Graves said, her voice raised and her tone stern. Phillips ran behind us and up the stairs, wearing a huge pair of headphones and holding a parabolic microphone. She was heading to the roof.

"License plate is registered to a law office here in Manhattan," Mendez said, drawing Graves's attention away from me. "That guy is one of the firm's investigators. I have all his info here. He's legit, and that law firm is one serious bunch of sharks. Sheesh."

That actually calmed me down even more. I knew of stories about a creature called a Luduan the Chinese used to detect lies in the royal courts, and all I needed was for Na'amah to somehow pull one of those things out of her ancient ass. Humans, even well-connected and powerful ones, didn't worry me.

Within a few minutes, a knock on Sarah's door was broadcast over speakers near Mendez's workstation, and everyone in the room became deathly silent. We listened intently to the conversation that followed, but it was, in fact, very professional and perfunctory. Sarah gave the details of her DHS-supplied identity. The investigator didn't ask anything rude or odd or even make a suggestive comment. Other than being run by inhuman beings, the club was probably a legitimate, albeit seedy, business. Part of me hoped the investigator would make some crude advance and that Sarah would coldcock him for his effort, but as soon as he was done asking his questions, he got back in the waiting Mercedes and drove off. Assuming all the details of Criseida Calchasidou's life held up to scrutiny, I could see no reason they wouldn't select her. Unfortunately.

Within twelve hours, Criseida Calchasidou was offered a hostess role at the next gathering of Cocytus. Sarah informed us, through our designated drop, that she would receive a call forty-eight hours in advance, then a limousine would pick her up outside her hotel at noon on the day of the event, and a liaison would be waiting in the car to brief her on specific club policies. She was told to expect to be out until at least five the next morning, but longer was possible and at her discretion. No specific date was provided. My skin crawled, and I shivered involuntarily.

Duma better be wide awake at this thing, or I'll kill him. But only if I don't freak out first.

Chapter 32

I found it impossible to hide my apprehension over the next few days. The entire team could tell I was on edge. Luckily, they all chalked it up to inexperience and rookie jitters. Mendez even tried to calm me down by explaining the surveillance procedures again and telling me a few stories about past surveillance ops that I'm sure he thought were humorous. *Funny stories. If he knew what I knew, he'd be throwing up and all but catatonic in a corner somewhere.*

We all expected the event to take place over a weekend, so it came as a surprise when a human messenger slid a note under her door at noon on the following Monday. That meant the event was that Wednesday. With events finally imminent, I had to fight to control my breathing and actively calm myself. I hated everything about what was happening, and I was dangerously close to needing to destroy something—partly from nerves and partly out of sheer boredom. However, the tension also increased notably among everyone else on the team, and they all became restless and antsy. *Long-term surveillance work sucks.*

That night, I took my gear bag and headed down one floor. In the dim, eerie light of a red-tinted lantern, I went over all my gear. Not because it needed it, but because the chore was familiar and calming. After cleaning my Glock and Sig and reloading the magazines for both twice, I decided I needed to remind Duma of his promise to me. I knew he hadn't and would never forget, but the idea made me feel like I was doing something productive nonetheless.

I couldn't text or email Duma without breaking security protocols for the operation, and sneaking out to make a phone call wasn't worth the consequences, either. Instead, I pulled the small chamois-wrapped leather sack out of my gear bag that contained a roll of thick parchment made from papyrus, a roc-feather quill, a bottle of traditional India ink, a small silver knife, and a flint and tinder. I wrote my message on a piece of the papyrus then wrote out Duma's full and true name. I used the knife to cut my thumb then said the short enchantment I was told was necessary before pressing my bloody thumb to the page.

As usual, I felt self-conscious because I understood so little about magic and how the enchantment worked. Part of me always assumed it was some kind of prank the Fae liked to pull on humans like me, like some kind of supernatural snipe hunt. I stared at the page for a second then bandaged my finger. Setting fire to the note, I made sure the flame destroyed my blood and Duma's full name.

I put everything away, gathered my weapons, and repacked my gear bag. After settling myself in a very dark corner of the abandoned floor, I switched off my lantern. In the stark silence of the night in the inky-black windowless room, I listened to the faint scraping noises and light, rapid pattering of rodent footfalls. Through holes in the floor, ceiling, and walls, I could hear the other members of my team moving about and talking quietly. Eventually, everything grew quiet, then I got that odd feeling in the base of my skull that told me I was no longer alone. My fists clenched involuntarily, and the hair on the back of my neck rose as I unsuccessfully scanned the blackness for movement, straining to listen.

"You call this place secure?" said a low, breathy voice from just to my right. The question was laden with sarcasm and an all-too-familiar smartass tone.

"Duma, what the holy hell are you doing *here*?" I whispered back, shifting slightly in the direction from which the voice emanated.

"Got your message," he said, and I could feel him sit down on the rickety floor next to me. "I'm all over it, D. I've been following you guys following Sarah on my free time. Your team is pretty good *for humans*. Course, they had no idea I was following them—"

"Shut up," I replied. "And thanks."

He didn't answer, and after a minute of silence, I began to wonder if he'd left.

"It's not just that it's *her*. Well... partly," I said, my voice growing hoarse and catching in my throat. I didn't even care if he'd left already. "I don't like putting others in harm's way or having them do my job while I sit on the sidelines and watch."

"I get it," Duma replied, sniffing. "I prefer to do my own wet work, too. Get in there close and personal. That way you know it's done right."

"Not what I meant, Duma." There really was something not right in his head. I knew he could be cold and merciless, but I couldn't tell if he was being serious or joking. Still, he said it so indifferently that I chose to believe it was an attempt at humor and couldn't help but smile.

"I know," he said, then he hit my arm. "Party is Wednesday night. I'll get there right off the bat and keep close to her."

"Keep close but don't look like you're trying to keep close, if you know what I mean. I want her safe, but she has to appear available so the Sons of Belial can approach her."

"Dude, I sure as hell know what I'm doing, and I'm pretty sure Sarah knows, too, D," he replied in the darkness, his voice coming from slightly higher than before. "And I'll keep you on speed dial, just in case."

"They allow phones inside?" I asked, confused by the idea that such a secretive group would allow them for fear of exposure of their members.

"Nope."

A sharp pain on the crown of my skull caused me to jerk my hand up and duck to the side.

"I'll use this."

"Ow," I said, just short of screaming. "What the *hell*?" I rubbed at the short hair just over my right ear. "Dammit. Did you need to jerk out so much hair?" I said, struggling to keep my voice low.

I got no answer. I climbed to my feet, stumbled into my gear bag, and stood there in the dark for a few minutes until I was sure he was gone. Then I grabbed my bag and headed to my cot to try to get some sleep. Knowing Duma was half a step behind—a potentially frightening scenario—was actually comforting. He was one of the few beings I trusted enough to allow him to take my hair or even my blood. The consequences of those bodily materials falling into the wrong hands could be catastrophic for me, and I could only imagine how much they would be worth on the black market. Duma and Ab's blood oath to me aside, I knew he would die before willingly giving up either. And I knew he would protect Sarah with the same commitment.

I managed to lie wide-eyed on my cot for less than ten minutes before I had to get up. Back upstairs, I sat next to Mendez in front of the monitors. Neither of us said anything, though after a moment, he held out his thermos toward me.

I waved my hand and shook my head to decline. "I'll take over if you want," I whispered to him. "I'll wake you if anything happens. I promise." He gave me a thumbs-up and walked off into the darkness. I could hear him settling down just outside the glow of the monitors, followed abruptly by light snoring.

I rubbed at the sore spot on my scalp and envied the tech's ability to disconnect. Then I sat and watched the grainy grayscale infrared images of the window to Sarah's room until the sun came up.

First thing that morning, Graves called us all together to go over our standard operating procedure for the day of the event. Since no one had a clue as to where the gathering would be until Wednesday at noon and Sarah wouldn't know until she was dropped off, our group would rely on a secondary unit to follow the car that picked her up. They would let us know the destination, and another group would take up position a few blocks away just in case Sarah needed help. Sarah would carry a special passive transmitter hidden in the pendant of a choker. She had to press it to send a signal. Duma would be there, too, but the DHS didn't know I had an inside man. If Duma pressed the panic button—some sort of hocus-pocus involving my hair—I would make a beeline for Cocytus, DHS be damned. Duma wouldn't concern himself with simple human problems, and neither would I.

The next day dragged on for us, especially me, but Sarah continued her life as Criseida without flinching. Wednesday at noon, a black Bentley Mulsanne pulled up in front of the hotel. The handful of people on the street stopped to stare or take surreptitious glances at the expensive vehicle in the dump of a neighborhood. A few nosy people came out of storefronts or peeked out of windows above. I didn't blame them. Even garbage trucks were rare in the area.

A driver dressed in a dark-gray vintage double-breasted chauffeur's jacket, breeches, tall boots, and hat left the car to fetch Sarah. The windows in the car were tinted so heavily that it was impossible to see inside it, but the IR camera showed one body, likely female and human based on stature and body temp, in the rear. Several moments later, Sarah, dressed in a black trench coat with her hair slicked back, followed the driver out of the SRO. The driver opened the rear passenger door, Sarah climbed in, and they left. A half hour later, we got word that she was being escorted into a three-story boarded-up bat-tleship-gray brick building that was under construction across town on the corner of Tenth Avenue and Thirteenth Street, in the Meat-packing District.

An agonizing eighteen hours later, a low-slung dark-colored vin-tage convertible sports car pulled onto Bowery, its massive engine revving and rumbling enough to vibrate everything that wasn't nailed down and a few things that were. The driver was making a spectacle as he slowly pulled in front of Sarah's SRO. Immediately upon stopping, the driver hopped out of the sleek vehicle without opening his door and smoothly strode around to the passenger side. His exit from the vehicle was too easy, too smooth, as was his gait. His thermal signature on the IR cameras showed he was the same temperature as his surroundings.

"Stupid camera glitch. I'll fix it in a minute, but get a load of this guy," Mendez said with a laugh. "I've never even *seen* a car like that before." His hands flew over his keyboard. "Holy crap, I think that's a 1966 Jaguar XJ13—the only one in the world. It's gotta be worth ten mill, easy."

Duma.

On the street below, the driver opened the passenger-side door with a low bow and took the hand of his passenger, who had to be Sarah. He helped her from the low-slung car then escorted her to the door of her room. Duma practically skipped down the steps to his car and gave a quick wave up in our direction before hopping over the driver's-side window and back into the car, where he roared off, nearly breaking every window on the block.

Subtle, he ain't.

Back in her room, Sarah passed the all-clear sign, and we breathed a collective sigh of relief. Then my mind began to wander. *What happened in there tonight? What kind of stuff did Sarah have to put up with, or even do?* The thoughts raced through my head. I felt sick and suddenly couldn't breathe again for entirely different reasons. I was frozen, but somehow time still passed.

A little after noon on the cloudy gray day, Sarah passed along a sitrep from the gathering of Cocytus. Unfortunately, she was unsure if she'd made contact with any of the suspected "terrorists," though she did report interacting with a number of celebrities, sports figures, and politicians—all of whom she left unnamed. She believed she'd made solid inroads for the next time.

Next time. No, that was it. I'm done.

"I need to check in with my boss at Metis," I told Graves. Without waiting for an answer, I added, "I'll be back in a few hours."

I bolted out the rear door and shot up several alleyways until I was well away from the SRO and the surveillance team. Rain began to pour down as I ran. I cut across town until I hit the Westside Highway then continued up to Thirty-Seventh Street as fast as I could go, unconcerned about mundanes noticing my speed—if they even would amid the downpour.

No matter what I did, I couldn't shake my thoughts and concerns about Sarah. It drove me crazy while I ran, and I ended up outside the bunker-like garage of Duma's urban fortress before I knew it. Without concern, I repeatedly kicked at the heavily reinforced steel door, hoping to set off every screaming alarm inside the place. After my tirade, I stood doubled over, hands on knees and panting as the rain soaked me and ran down my face. I felt a rumble in my feet and glanced up to see the massive door sliding aside.

It opened just enough for Duma to occupy the gap. He leaned his forearm against the metal bulkhead, legs crossed nonchalantly at the ankles, an empty glass in his other hand. He was still dressed in his tux minus his jacket, but his untied bow tie hung around his neck, and his suspenders dangled from his waist. *Of course he'd wear a hand-tied bow tie and suspenders.*

"You want to come in, or do you like standing in the rain?" He shook his head slowly.

After a few weeks of being cooped up, the run should have felt good, but the knots I was twisted in were not the physical kind, and no amount of running would help. Duma's expression told me that he could see it on my face as I glared at him. I walked past him into his garage and immediately recognized the dark-green Jaguar.

"Subtle move this morning," I said, walking over to the car to get a better view of it.

"Hey, don't drip on it." He raced over to me in the blink of an eye to grab my elbow. "Water stains. You know. Let's go upstairs. I'll get you a towel."

With an amused expression, he headed up the narrow spiral staircase in the corner. He was enjoying my agony a little too much. *I'm going to deck him.*

The moment I reached the top of the obnoxiously skinny stairs, mumbling to myself about how annoying they were, a towel hit me in the face.

"You are working yourself in the right direction for a proper ass kicking, Duma," I said, ripping the towel away before draping it around my neck. I slogged across the room, assessing which seat appeared to be most expensive, and flopped onto a long brown-leather couch without drying off even a bit. Duma cringed but said nothing. He just shook his head then finally laughed.

"You want a drink?" He held out his empty glass, shaking it.

"No," I said, slouching back onto the couch, clutching the ends of the towel around my neck.

"Just thought I'd ask. If we're about to have the conversation I think we are, then I'm having one. A double. Maybe two." He walked behind the bar at the far end of the room and poured himself a drink from a crystal decanter sitting out on the marble countertop. It contained a faintly pink liquid.

"What conversation?" I asked.

"The one about Sarah. Relax, D," he said, sitting down on the other end of the couch. "Nothing happened to her. She was barely out of my sight the entire night."

"What does that mean?"

"Look, I had to let her mingle, but I occupied as much of her time as I could without making it seem like she was *with* me. I took her into one of the rooms for a bit, just to make it seem like she was into the scene, and I even had another friend do the same. She was out of my realm of attention for maybe thirty minutes all night." He took a big pull on his drink.

"What do you mean 'friend'?" I asked, suddenly sitting up.

"Calm down, dude. Friend, you know—acquaintance, sometime exercise partner—if you know what I mean." He waggled his eyebrows. "She's a hulder."

"One of the Hidden Folk? That makes her Seelie. *You* trust her?" I asked.

"For something like this, sure." He shrugged. "Plus, she knows I'd do more than kill her if she betrayed me." He said the last part as if it were just another item on a to-do list.

"Did you see anybody there who appeared human, only significantly larger in all physical aspects? Man or woman."

He stared at the floor for a pensive moment. "Yeah, a male and a female. Serious bodybuilders. Big, but not as big as Ab, and definitely not the smartest pair. The woman was a sadistic beast. One little mousy masochist was all over her. I don't recall seeing this pair before, but there are always a few like them around." He snapped his fingers. "Now that you mention it, they both talked with Sarah at different times, but all out in the open and only for a few minutes, at most. Why?"

"They were likely Bennephilim, part of the Sons of Belial," I replied. "They are descendants of the Nephilim—human with some atavistic traits. Near as I can tell, they are working with Na'amah on this effort to free the Iyrin."

We sat and talked, and surprisingly Duma listened to me talk about Sarah without making many snide remarks in response. I explained to him what I knew of the Bennephilim so he could keep his eye out *next time*. Venting helped, but I still wasn't comfortable with the undercover op continuing.

After a few hours, I left Duma's place, caught a cab by the Javits Convention Center, got out a half dozen blocks from the SRO, and walked a circuitous route back to our building. Thankfully, it had stopped raining.

Graves met me at the third-floor landing, with her arms crossed over her chest and an expression on her face that suggested she was either upset or giving birth. I was pretty sure she wasn't pregnant. *This was why I work alone.*

"In case I didn't make it clear before, we have protocols, Mr. Dore." Staring daggers at me, she was blocking the stairs. "You feel the need to take off like that again, and I'll make sure you're off this detail by the time you reach the door. I don't care who you're connected to. You got me?"

I nodded.

"I'm sorry, did you say something? Because I didn't hear you, Mr. Dore." She held a hand up to her ear. "Do we understand each other?"

"Yes, we do." I wasn't about to apologize.

"I will not have some hotshot freelancer put one of our people in danger because they get the jitters or cabin fever or whatever. If you want off this detail, just say the word," she said, stepping aside so I could pass.

"Got it," I replied, walking past her and continuing up the stairs.

"Good. Sitrep in ten minutes. Make sure you're on time," she said, scowling.

I changed into fresh clothes then headed up to our main surveillance area for the meeting. Everyone showed signs of fatigue and boredom except Mendez, who would probably just be watching monitors and playing on the computer on his days off anyway.

At ten minutes on the dot, Graves began to explain a plan for allowing the surveillance team time off. Clearly, the op was taking longer than anyone had expected, and having everyone bouncing off the walls wouldn't make for an efficient team when things finally went down. Each of us would take a day off at a time until Sarah got notice of the next event. I didn't care about time off. If Sarah was in it full time, then I would be, too. I just needed to implement an exercise routine each day to knock the cobwebs loose.

Chapter 33

After another week in, everyone but me had already had a day off. To let off steam, I began exercising twice a day, just doing calisthenics and shadowboxing. Mitchell and Phillips began working out with me when they could. Graves was too focused, and Mendez was too... *something* to care. I kept it mundane when they worked out with me. Multiple sets of two hundred and fifty pushups would have freaked them out. After three more days, I cut the cast off my hand using my tanto knife and began rehabbing it myself.

I had settled in to the boredom of the routine and become somewhat numb to my previous concerns for Sarah, because nothing was happening. At the beginning of the fourth week, right at the end of May—less than a week from the Transition of the Light Bringer—Sarah got word again that Cocytus was set to meet again in two days. The setup was as before: a car would pick her up at noon, and she should expect to be out until at least five the following morning.

I began to get tense all over again—in fact, everyone did—but I didn't bother to contact Duma. Sarah didn't get chosen last time, and this would likely be our last chance before the astrological events occurred. It was now or never, and I was ready. I just hoped Graves and her DHS associates didn't get caught in the crossfire if the shit hit the fan. I kept trying to remind myself that innocent bystanders were innocent and not to be hurt, even if they got in my way. Sarah wouldn't want that. Part of me kept dismissing the idea of anything actually happening as utter folly.

The morning of the event, I pulled on my cuirass and vest then geared up, except for my swords, which I kept rolled up in a towel in my bag right at the base of the stairs on the second-floor landing. I checked my sidearms only once then glued myself to the monitors next to Mendez and Graves to await confirmation of the location from the tailing unit.

The meeting place was across the Hudson in Jersey City, in a large warehouse just outside the Holland Tunnel butted up against the interstate. The old factory building was six stories tall, with very few windows scattered along the lower floors. The only entrances were loading bays underneath access road overpasses with no clear line of sight from outside. The place was a virtual bunker with choke points for entrances. Because of the size of the building and its limited access, a secondary surveillance team was quickly positioned in a moving and storage company directly across the interstate from the facility, and a full TAC team took over one of the parking bays of the Port Authority building just down the street.

"Shouldn't we be over there with them?" I asked Graves, unable to think of any reason I could tell her why we should be but desperate to be closer.

"No, so just relax and let our people do their thing," she replied, her brow deeply furrowed as she eyed me.

I could feel every muscle in my body tighten, and the pain in my recently healed broken hand caused me to wince. I crossed my arms, watched, and listened intently as all supporting units checked in as ready over the next hour. The sun set, midnight came and went, and I hadn't moved. I wasn't even sure I had breathed.

Mendez held up a protein bar from his position hunkered in front of the monitors. "You want something to eat?"

Before I could answer, the reflection on his glasses caught my eye as a vehicle driving down the middle of the street came into view of the cameras outside our building. It was a military-style Humvee painted black or dark gray, with a canvas cover over its stubby bed. It screeched to a halt in front of the main door to our building, then something tumbled out of the back of the truck and flopped onto the street. Gracile arms and legs were splayed at odd angles from the lithe form, and my heart instantly stopped.

Without thinking, I bolted down the stairs, grabbing my wrapped swords as I passed my bunk, and slammed through the front door. It came loose from its rickety frame and tumbled onto the sidewalk as the Humvee suddenly shot off with a throaty roar. I ripped the Sig from my vest, but the truck rounded the corner and was out of sight before I could get a clean shot. I holstered the gun and ran to the naked form lying face down in the street. The pale skin was streaked with crusty and fresh oozing liquid I assumed to be blood and bore massive red and purple bruises up and down the back, legs, and arms. The long dark hair was matted and caked with more dark liquid. I realized that it wasn't Sarah at the very instant I noticed the woman's chest move faintly with the shallowest of breaths. Rapid and chaotic footfalls came from our building behind me as lights began to come on in the upper floors of the other buildings along the street.

"Call an ambulance and get me a blanket, now!" I screamed at whoever was approaching.

I gently turned the woman over to find a shiny metallic spike rammed into her chest amid vicious and deep cuts and bruises. Her face was only partly beaten, with her right cheek badly swollen and distended, but I recognized the face—the Moroi vampire who ran Cocytus. Her eyes fluttered slightly, and she moaned. I could see a trace of bluish energy leaking toward her from my arm as I cradled her head. I surprised myself by not jerking my arm away to stop her from feeding off me. As I stared down at her, I knew she was meant to be a message, and a burning sensation at the nape of my neck and skull began to grow. I rubbed at it until Phillips came down with a blanket and knelt next to me as we covered her up.

"Ambulance is on the way. Holy shit," Phillips said, seeing the injuries up close. "How is she even still alive?"

"I don't know," I lied. I stood and rubbed at the nape of my neck. The growing discomfort spread across my scalp, becoming a sudden shooting pain. And then it dawned on me—the pain was Duma's panic button. Sarah was in trouble.

I began running down the block toward Canal Street, but even moving as fast as I was, I knew it wasn't fast enough. As I approached the corner of Canal and Lafayette, a car was waiting for the traffic light to change. I pulled the Sig from its holster on my chest and shattered the driver's-side window with a quick backhand.

"Out. Now," I shouted at the driver. I didn't point the gun, but the young, well-dressed guy behind the wheel held up his hands, too scared to say or do anything but comply with my demand.

I jumped into the small sedan and floored it, heading for the Holland Tunnel as fast as the car could go. Thankfully, traffic late at night during the week was as light as it ever got in Manhattan, and I weaved through traffic on Canal Street and into the tunnel at ninety miles an hour. I blew through the tollbooth at the end of the tunnel, skidded through the intersection at Jersey Avenue, and bounced over a curb and into the parking lot adjacent to the giant bunker-like warehouse where Cocytus was meeting. I slammed the brake pedal to the floor, bringing the car to a rapid stop in the middle of the lot, shoved open the door, and jumped out without concerning myself with the car.

The only entrance into the building from this side was a boarded-up glass door flanked by a bank of boarded-up windows at the top of a covered landing a few steps up from the parking lot. I pulled my swords free from the towel I'd wrapped them in, slid them back into their scabbards on my back, then pulled my Sig as I ran. At nearly full speed, I slammed my shoulder into the plywood covering the doorway. The glass on the other side shattered, along with the wood, as the metal doorframe twisted then slid open awkwardly against its hinges. I didn't even slow down enough to think about the fact that the DHS TAC team was nowhere to be seen. Either they didn't know something was wrong or the situation was worse than I'd thought.

The door opened into what was likely a reception area at one time, but a pair of large metal birdcages were the only things in the space. One was occupied by a man and the other a woman. The walls were lined with a heavy velvet curtain from floor to ceiling. Light came from candles spread out on small tables and tall candelabras.

"Door," I screamed, pointing the gun first at the man then at the woman. "Now!"

Both of them began to freak out, and within seconds, two well-built men wearing carnival-type masks pushed their way through an opening in the curtain in front of me. Dressed in expensive suits, neither showed signs of being armed.

Stupid move.

"Let me pass, and I won't hurt you," I said.

"Funny," the one to my right said. "I was going to say, 'Leave, and we won't hurt *you.*'"

"I asked." I put two rounds into both of their legs, dropping them instantly.

As they writhed on the floor, I stepped past them, parted the curtain, and found the door. There was no knob on my side, so I heel-kicked the lock as hard as I could, rending the metal just enough to break it. The door swung partially open onto a long, dimly lit hallway. Instantly, a hail of bullets ripped across the hall from a single shooter twenty feet down, but I was able to duck behind the door without being hit. Kneeling, I slammed the door fully open, quickly put two rounds into the shooter's torso, then advanced with the Sig held in a combat high position. I knelt next to the shooter and grabbed his gun—a fully automatic Glock 18c with an extended magazine. I ejected the clip then smashed the composite frame into the concrete floor. The gunman was breathing, albeit raggedly, but I had no time to deal with him.

I continued to the metal door at the end of the hallway, which had a keycard entry panel next to the knob. Before trying to open the door, I quickly ejected the partially used magazine in my Sig and inserted a full one. Using one sword, I cut through the deadbolt as quietly as I could. Without the lock to hold it, the door swung open a few inches, and I returned my sword to its scabbard on my back then slowly pushed it completely open. Soft chamber music echoed below, along with occasional laughter and the sounds of indistinct conversations. I stood on a small metal landing at the top of stairs headed down, but they were blocked by another heavy curtain just a few steps down.

I cautiously pulled the curtain aside just enough to get a view of what was behind. In the diffusely lit cavernous space, several nearly nude women sat on an expansive red couch, flanking a man wearing a mask and a tuxedo. Stretched out above were six floors of catwalks and metal galley ways. The lack of other people unnerved me.

"Ah, Diomedes, I presume?" the man on the couch asked in a heavy French accent, removing his mask to reveal his face. He was very much human. "Go and get her, please, my dear," he said, leaning toward one of the women.

I pushed the curtain fully aside and began slowly walking down the steps, gun trained on him as I tried to take in my surroundings. He didn't worry me, but whoever "her" was did.

"Come, join us." The man stood and motioned to a broad and tall leather armchair across from the couch.

The space was half the size of a football field, and with all the metal around us, it reminded me of a giant cage. The only light came from thousands of candles spread randomly around the space, leaving large areas in utter darkness. Chains hung from industrial structures that had probably held machinery at one time, but other than a few random pieces of overly large furniture, the parts I could see were empty. I couldn't even see any stairways or lifts to the upper levels.

"No thanks, I think I'll stand," I said, continuing to examine my surroundings. "Who is she going to get?"

"Ah, well, the *new* management," he said with a dismissive wave of his hand. "I believe you knew the previous one, no? Please do sit down. Things are already tense enough, wouldn't you say?"

"Where is Criseida Calchasidou?" I asked, staring hard at the man. If he knew who I was, he wasn't concerned, which bothered me.

"You mean Department of Homeland Security Agent Sarah Wright, don't you?" He smiled a wide, very white grin that made me want to shoot him on principle.

I scowled at his response.

"Yes, we know. And we know that the *former* management of this organization gave you privileged information that led to Agent Wright's presence here." His smile widened further.

For the briefest of moments, I contemplated firing a round into the couch next to him just to scare him, but I didn't think it would help. This guy was a mouthpiece, not someone in charge. He knew what they wanted him to know and nothing more. He was worthless, not to mention smug, and he was beginning to annoy me. The way I saw it, he had chosen his lot and thrown in with monsters. So I shot him in the shoulder to shut him up. The gunshot reverberated in the empty shell of a building, but the spokesman's surprised scream mixed with the high-pitched wailing of the woman sitting next to him drowned out the echo.

"Shut up. You'll be fine if you remain quiet," I said, moving around the space to get a better feel for it. There were just too many dark recesses and places for attackers to hide in ambush.

"Now, now, Diomedes," said a deep, sultry woman's voice from somewhere overhead. "That was a little impetuous, don't you think?"

"It shut him up, didn't it?" I replied, trying to see if I could locate the source of the voice without placing myself in the open. "Besides, he'll live. He should have picked his associates better anyway." Out of the corner of my eye, I saw the remaining woman try to slink off the couch and run. "I suggest you stay put. You're much safer where I can see you," I said to her.

On the fifth-floor catwalk, someone stepped into the candlelight. It was the woman I'd encountered briefly in the hall in San Francisco, and it was very clear from the power and energy emanating from her that she was far from human. The energy formed some sort of grotesque and deformed bearing that kept blurring her physical form. One second, she was a beautiful dark-haired woman wearing a blood-red bustier and nothing else, and the next, she was a thick, hunched, apelike monster with long claws, massive uneven horns on its head and leathery wings.

"Na'amah, is that you?" I asked. "Forgive me, I have never seen one of the Sisters in person before. And can I add, ewww. Just ewww. Seriously."

"Such disrespect from a human, even one of the so-called Guardians." With a blurred and erratic flash, she instantly reappeared in the exact same position one floor lower. "Some Guardian. You cannot even protect those you care for. But that is of no consequence now."

"Hurt Sarah, and I will send you to your own personal hell, full of puppies and kittens and lots of soft, fluffy things," I said, trying not to growl while fighting every instinct to empty the magazine in my gun at her. It probably wouldn't hurt her anyway.

"Her, no, I have need of her. I meant him," she said with a grin that revealed lots of small, pointed teeth.

From the darkness, something came tumbling down in a deafening metallic rattle. It stopped with a jerk fifteen feet up. It was Duma, wrapped in chains and badly beaten. I couldn't tell if he was alive or dead. While I searched for some sign of life in my friend, an attractive blonde dressed in a white latex dress walked into a lighted area one floor up at the far side of the space. She was definitely not human. She had to be Fae of some kind.

"You think hurting those I care for will actually scare me off... or just make me more dangerous?" I asked in a low voice, trying to control my urge to start shooting everything and everyone. "And if you're the hulder *he* spoke of, I suggest you run. *Now*," I said, jerking my head at Duma dangling above me. "And pray it's me and not Abraxos that finds you."

"Scare you, Diomedes?" Na'amah asked, her voice dripping with pleasure. "No. I want your *pain*."

Screaming at the top of my lungs, I brought the Sig to bear on her position and pulled the trigger as fast as I could, but before the first bullet would have even reached her, she flashed again and vanished completely. It didn't stop me from emptying the magazine, though. Underneath the monstrous echo from the gun, I could hear sudden movement from every direction around me. I holstered the gun and pulled my swords.

"You two should leave. *Now*. If you remain, you will die here," I said to the wounded spokesman and his girl toy. She helped him to his feet, and they both headed up the stairs I'd come down.

Above me, a dozen men spread out over two levels, all dressed in black fatigues, helmets, and tactical vests, all pointing machine guns down at me. The letters DHS were stenciled in white on their vests. Every one of them had motes of blue-white energy dancing around their heads and faces. *Fairy magic.*

My eyes flashed to the hulder, who smiled and waved at me as she backed into the darkness above. *Oh yeah, she's definitely on the top tier of my shit list now.*

Half a dozen other figures emerged from the darkness on the floor around me. Among them were a male and female Bennephilim. He carried a four-foot-long cudgel, and she was lazily spinning a length of chain with a heavy spiked ball on the end. Sparks and chunks of cement flew every time it hit the floor. The rest were human—three men and one woman—all armed with pistols and dressed in suits. Unlike the DHS TAC team above, nothing about them suggested they were being manipulated.

"You four, leave," I said, addressing the mundanes in front of me while spinning the swords at my sides. "If you choose to stay and fight, I will kill you. I promise that whatever they are paying you, this isn't worth it."

A few scoffs and snickers met my offer, then I charged, roaring into the echo of the empty warehouse. My battle cry was nearly drowned out by the riot of automatic gunfire that rained down from the entranced TAC team above, but I moved too fast for them to follow accurately in their current state. I went for the four mundanes first, because they carried firearms, while the Bennephilim carried handheld weapons.

Despite my warning to them, I was still averse to killing mortals unless necessary. I hit the closest man of the group in the chest with my forearm at full sprint, sending him flying backward into one of the others, and the pair tumbled to the ground. I swung a backhand at the remaining male gunman, hitting him in the cheek. Bone cracked under the blow, and he spun as he fell, firing wildly into the air. I dropped and lunged, sweeping my leg out, catching the woman at her heels, knocking her onto her back with a thud as the air was forced from her lungs. Before I could stand and face the two giants, the male hit me in the chest with an underhand blow of his cudgel that sent me sprawling backward.

I landed hard on my back as the female's spiky ball barreled down at me from high overhead. I quickly rolled to my right to avoid the impact then rolled back, bringing my sword down on the chain just as the ball embedded itself in the cement floor next to me, severing it. I reversed direction and rolled to my right to get under cover of the catwalks to avoid a potential hail of gunfire from above.

The male chased me, and by the time I got to one knee, he brought the cudgel down at my head. I threw both swords up to catch the attack, and the force of the impact cut the weapon in half on my blades. The blow would have crushed a grizzly's skull if it connected, but the sudden destruction of his weapon tipped him off balance. As he stumbled toward me, I sprang forward to meet the behemoth, rammed one of my swords through his chest, and brought the other across his throat, nearly severing his head. Using our combined momentum, I directed him past me. Back on my feet, I squared off against the female Bennephilim, who was spinning her chain for an attack, until I dispatched her compatriot. The whipping end of the heavy chain fell to the ground with a metallic *chink* as the shock of what had happened sank in. I didn't have time for a staring contest—the others might gain their feet again any moment. I needed to move.

Before I could take a full breath, she began spinning the chain again. If she knew how to use the weapon, she would try to keep me at a distance, so I decided not to give her the opportunity. I spun, threw one of my swords at her, and drew the Glock off my hip. The blade hit her in the lower abdomen, inadvertently causing her to release the chain harmlessly past me. I dodged slightly just to make sure the chain missed and fired three times into her chest. To her credit, she took a full step before she fell to her knees. I walked closer and put a round into her head.

Of the four gunmen on the ground, only two were beginning to move with any purpose. I could have killed them easily, but Sarah's voice echoing in the back of my head told me not to. Finding her was my priority—and I could use Duma's help, but his motionless body still dangled from chains in the center of the giant room. I didn't even know if he was alive or dead, but either way, I couldn't leave him hanging there like a piece of meat.

I put the Glock back in the holster on my thigh, pulled the sword from the female Bennephilim's body, and took off running across the gaping space toward Duma's suspended body. Fifteen feet away, I jumped, swinging both swords at the chains holding him up, and his body crashed to the ground in a steely clatter that rang though the space like a bell. The Fae-influenced TAC team opened fire as I jumped, but once again, they failed to track me effectively in their stupor as I made it back underneath the cover of the catwalks.

Duma's body hit the ground just in front of the massive sofa then rolled as the chains he was wrapped in began to fall away and unwind a bit. And then his head moved jerkily left and right as if he were trying to look around.

He is *alive.*

"Shit," he mumbled through swollen and split lips. "*Ta rag dul a mharut.*"

I couldn't tell if the last part was slurred speech or just bizarre Fae dialect, but I was just glad he was still alive. *Tough bastard.* I moved around under the catwalk, trying to get as close to him as I could and remain under cover. The mesmerized TAC team ignored him, most likely because they had been told to fixate on me. If I could free Duma, I would be able to exploit that small tactical advantage. Two of the four-man team on the floor were beginning to get to their feet, completely ignoring the other, more seriously injured pair. *Mercenaries.*

"Duma," I said, trying to be quiet and not reveal my position to the team above. "Hey, Blondie ... are you okay?"

He spat a gobbet of yellowish goo onto the ground then groaned. "Will be... if I can get these fucking chains off me. Burn... like hell."

"Can you roll at all? I can't get to you for all the damn guns pointed down at you, and I got a pair of mercs down here about ready to regain their wits."

"They got Sarah," he said, trying to spit it out. "They got me first, but I tried... damn hulder bitch tipped them off."

"I'll get Sarah back. Right now, I gotta get you outta this mess. Just freakin' roll, would you?"

He grunted and rocked slightly a few times before he finally managed to roll once completely. More chains fell away as he stopped, still maybe ten feet away. *Good enough.*

I believed I could reach him and pull him back fast enough. I scrambled out from under the catwalk, grabbed him, and yanked, sliding him past me and under cover. As I ducked back, the hail of gunfire from above was too sloppy and slow to be a concern. The female merc and one of her partners, on the other hand, managed to open fire with trained accuracy. Four solid impacts pelted my back, followed by a burning jolt to the back of my right upper thigh below my butt. Another shot went wide and hit the cement floor next to me, sending debris flying into my face as I scurried low to the ground. The sandy grit blinded me momentarily, and I dived ahead blindly to avoid the random barrage from above.

Back under the cover of the catwalks, I scrambled behind one of the metal girder supports and rubbed at my watery eyes. I dropped my swords and pulled both my handguns as steady and focused suppression gunfire peppered the beam against which I leaned. Knowing I could move significantly faster than the all-too-human mercs, the second I got enough of my vision back, I steadied myself on one knee and took aim. Only the one gunman remained, taking cover behind the massive sofa in the middle of the space. The second he popped his head up to take a shot, I shot first, putting a bullet in his head. I scanned the darkness to find the remaining female merc. Unable to locate her, I holstered the Glock on my hip and scooted over to Duma, who was trying to wiggle out of the chains like some kind of freakish steampunk caterpillar.

Cautiously, I knelt beside him to help, keeping one eye out for the other merc while working as fast as I could. The crouched position put a lot of strain on the gunshot wound in my thigh, and I began to feel the intense burning sensation build through my leg and lower back. Finally unwrapped, Duma shuffled on his butt back against the wall to put as much distance as possible between himself and the metal restraints. The fingers on his right hand were twisted and broken, his hand was mangled, and the arm sat uselessly in his lap, though I couldn't see the exact injury that caused its lameness. His face was battered and puffy, with one eye completely swollen shut, and yellow blood oozed from a dozen cuts and abrasions I could see. His tux was shredded, and everywhere his skin was exposed, his normally pale skin looked frostbitten—the prolonged effects of iron on a Fae.

Breathing raggedly, he spat another glob of yellow blood onto the ground next to him, and the corner of his mouth rose slightly as if in a smile. "Ow," he said then coughed, suddenly grabbing his chest with his good hand at the spasm.

"You okay?" I slid closer to help him, ignoring my own pain.

"It's nothing." He glanced down at his twisted right hand then grasped his broken fingers with his left hand. Pulling and squeezing, he straightened them out. His howl of agony echoed through the building like a ghost's wail, and I couldn't help but cringe. "You think that's bad, wait 'til you help me fix my arm," he said, his breathing shallow and rapid as he leaned back and let his hand drop back into his lap. At least his hand and fingers looked somewhat normal again.

"Later. Right now, we gotta find Sarah and then get out of here," I said.

"I don't think she's still here," he said, shifting his position with a grimace.

"I need to make sure," I replied.

He tried to nod but stopped. Pain registered on his face as his misshapen lips tightened.

"Gimme a weapon," he said, reaching out his left hand.

I moved to pull the composite Glock from its holster on my hip, and he shook his head slightly. "No," he said, pointing at the tanto knife in its sheath on my shoulder.

"There's a woman down here somewhere and a dozen more guys scattered around the atrium on the floors above," I said. "All armed."

"Saw the guys staring down at me. Some sort of tactical response team or something, right? All under the control of that deceitful hulder bitch, right?"

"Yeah, and all human and *not* acting on their own," I replied.

"The chick ain't though, right?" he said with a nasty gleam in his swollen eyes.

"Only if necessary," I replied, pushing myself to one knee with some effort as my leg began to stiffen from the injury.

"You hit?" he asked, and I nodded in return. "Then it's necessary." He pushed himself to his feet, and for the first time I could remember, I actually heard him move as his joints popped and snapped. He winced at every sound his body made. "Only way to undo the glamour the TAC team is under is to *convince* the hulder, kill her, or for her to get far enough away."

I nodded my understanding.

"I really hope she's running, because I'm not feeling patient enough to convince her, and I'd really hate to have to kill that duplicitous bitch in a hurry just to get out of here," he said, lisping through his damaged lips. He limped off into the darkness under the catwalks, each step becoming easier and more fluid for him until he was no longer visible.

I rose painfully to my feet and tried to pull myself into a combat high position with my Sig, trying to locate the remaining mercenary. At first, my leg protested and almost gave out as it began to go a bit numb, but moving it, though painful, brought its usefulness back. As near as I could tell, the bullet was still in my thigh, and I was still alive, so it hadn't hit the femoral artery. It still hurt like hell.

I moved in the opposite direction from Duma around the warehouse, staying under cover but in the lit areas, hoping to draw out the remaining merc. I made it halfway around the warehouse before a single shot rang out and ricocheted off the metal catwalk above my head. I spun to face the shooter, and she staggered stiffly out of the shadows, blinking exaggeratedly, with her gun held loosely in front of her. Her hands fell to her sides after the first step, then she dropped the gun with a clatter. She stumbled forward a single step and collapsed, the hilt of my tanto knife sticking out from the base of her skull. Duma strode out behind her and bent over to remove the knife. He at least had the decency to grunt when he grabbed it.

The question was what to do with a dozen heavily armed, mind-controlled men. The expedient option would be to kill them. Even in my injured state, with Duma's less-than-healthy help, I was reasonably sure we could wipe them out in minutes. That was my last resort.

Unfortunately, I couldn't see a single option that didn't involve hurting at least some of them, possibly seriously. The mercenaries were acting of their own accord, and I'd given them fair warning, but these guys weren't in control of their actions.

I stepped out just long enough to get a good view of the situation above then ducked back under. No one had moved, but the haze encircling their heads was beginning to dissipate. While I tried to decide my next move, Duma walked up next to me and handed me my knife.

"Your swords are still over there." He hooked a thumb over his shoulder.

"You take them and get the hell out of here," I said. "I'll find you in the next couple of days. These guys are going to regain their wits soon, and you don't need to be here when they do."

"What about Sarah?"

I pulled the vial of blood from under my cuirass and let its fine chain dangle over my thumb.

"I'm sorry I couldn't stop them," he said, patting me on the shoulder.

"I'm just glad you aren't dead."

"This?" He laughed. "This is nothing. I've been through worse." He stepped soundlessly into the darkness.

Now alone, I could hear faint moans coming from the two injured and incapacitated mercs across from me, and I began to hear increasingly restless bootfalls on the metal catwalks overhead.

"What the...?" someone above said. "How the hell did we get here?"

"Where *are* we?" someone else asked.

"Hey, guys," I yelled, "is everyone up there okay?"

"All units report," one gruff voice said before it echoed through a number of microphones in the empty space.

I put my Sig back in its holster on my chest then walked out into the atrium, waving my hands so they wouldn't think I was an armed perpetrator. "What a freakin' mess," I said. I could hear voices reporting in, followed by slightly delayed mechanical echoes over their radios.

"Identify yourself," the gruff voice said.

"Steve Dore. I'm with the Metis Foundation as part of the surveillance team back at the Whole Earth Hotel with Agent Graves."

Within thirty minutes, twenty more DHS personnel were combing the place, trying to determine where Sarah had been taken and just what had happened, including why the entire TAC team couldn't explain how or when they arrived on scene. The two surviving mercenaries were carted off to a local hospital. One had broken ribs, a broken collarbone, a fractured hyoid, and a punctured lung. The other had a broken eye socket and jaw. They were lucky.

The forensic guys were flummoxed by the two dead giants and their injuries—especially since initial observations couldn't determine what exactly had caused some of the wounds. The rest of the building was completely empty, including all the rooms.

Graves showed up shortly after the forensic team, but she was the only member of our group to come, and she made a beeline straight for me. No one had asked me anything, so I hadn't volunteered any information, either. What I knew wouldn't help them anyway.

"Somehow, I knew I'd find you here," she said, eyeing me sternly as she approached. "You want to explain yourself? Because something about you just isn't right. In fact, this whole thing stinks."

"Nothing to explain," I said. "The fact that a couple of goons dumped a body outside our little hideout immediately set off alarms that Sarah... Agent Wright was in danger. That's why I'm here." I shifted to watch the pair of crime scene investigators examining the dead female merc, and I hobbled slightly more than I'd expected in the process. I shook my head at the pain, and Graves noticed the blood pooling around my foot.

"You were injured?" she asked, her eyes growing wide. "Were you here when this thing went down?"

"Barely," I lied. "I came in just as the TAC team was wrapping stuff up. One of these guys got me in the back of the leg." I stared at the ground for a second then let my eyes wander over the expansive space, now lit by dozens of halogen work lamps. I didn't have time for the red tape. I needed to find Sarah.

Graves moved around behind me and poked at the back of my vest. "Looks like you took a few rounds to the back as well. Good thing you were wearing that vest, I suppose." She walked around in front of me and glared, hands on her hips. "You and I need to have a conversation—a long one." Then she motioned toward some of the crime scene techs.

"We need to get this man some medical attention," she said in a loud voice that carried over the din of the forensic work that was going on. "And then you and me, we are going to talk." She pointed between us a few times for emphasis as she said the last part.

Yeah, I already had one, boss.

Within a few minutes, a pair of EMTs approached, wheeling a gurney with a large orange medical toolbox on it. I was not about to get a medical exam here. While I wanted to search the place for evidence the mundane forensic team would undoubtedly miss, being outside this building was one step closer to getting out of there. The downside was that I, or at least Steve Dore, was officially connected to the DHS via the Metis Foundation. No matter how much I wanted to, I couldn't just take off.

"Can we do this in an ambulance, or at least someplace more private?" I asked the EMTs. They just shrugged, and I hopped along after them, my thigh throbbing and numb at the same time.

Once they realized my injury was a gunshot wound, they immediately insisted I go to the hospital. I glowered at the young techs, but to their credit, they wouldn't relent.

"You know, it used to be all you'd do is pour some sulfur on the wound, I'd drink some whiskey for the pain, you'd give me a piece of wood or leather to bite down on, and then you'd dig the bullet out, junior," I said to a round-faced kid who barely appeared old enough to have a driver's license, let alone be an EMT.

"Yeah, and we used to chop off injured limbs, too," he replied without missing a beat. "You want I should do that instead?"

The ambulance ride to the hospital sucked but not as much as the hospital itself.

Spending the better part of a day trapped in the hospital, where I couldn't avoid the continuous stream of DHS agents that insisted on going over my story about what happened at Cocytus "just one more time," was far more painful than my injury. I nodded a lot and played very dumb and forgetful—which actually worked because the entire TAC team suffered from some sort of unexplainable amnesia as well.

When it wasn't the DHS, the medical staff told me repeatedly how lucky I was the bullet had missed my femoral artery and the femur and marveled at the mass of scar tissue and healed injuries that showed up on x-rays and scans.

Late that afternoon, Graves showed up with an expression on her face that suggested she had endured enough crap and wasn't about to accept any more. *She came to the wrong room.*

"What? No balloons or flowers?" I asked.

"Sorry, no. But you owe me an explanation," she replied, pulling a chair next to the bed and sitting down.

"I'll tell you like I told the others. I got there just in time to shoot the one gunman in the head and take a few shots in the back before the TAC team ended it. That's it. It all happened fast. It was dark, and I couldn't see much about what was going on upstairs or in the rooms." I shrugged.

"Mm-hm," she said, one corner of her mouth ticking up in a disapproving, mirthless smile. "Sounds good the way you tell it. How about the dead woman dumped on our doorstep? She was the one Agent Wright met with that day, but *you* clearly knew her. You want to regale me with some bullshit story about her, too?"

"Dead, huh? She ran Cocytus. She was my inside source," I replied. "When I recognized her, I knew Sarah, Agent Wright, was in trouble." I doubted the dumped woman was dead. She was Moroi, so even beat up pretty badly, she was a long way from being truly dead.

"She have a name?" Graves asked.

"Yeah, but I didn't know it," I said. "All I know is that she gave me information about Cocytus and told me to check out the Dungeon in San Francisco. That's it. Cross my heart."

"Well, we haven't been able to identify her, and now her body is missing from the morgue. Two attendants are also dead—both just fell over and died without a single mark on their bodies. Young guys, too."

"Really? That's crazy," I said, trying to feign surprise. "Who would want a dead body? She was pretty and all, but that's just twisted. Maybe whoever took her scared the techs to death."

"Yeah," she replied, peering at me sideways. "This whole thing reeks. I don't know what happened here, but one of my agents is missing, and you're involved somehow. I feel it as sure as I can feel the bile welling up in my throat. So rest assured, Mr. Dore, I will get to the bottom of this clusterfuck."

She left the room in silence.

I felt bad about being less than completely truthful with Graves, but the situation was way beyond her, and I didn't want any more mundanes involved. Still, whether as a result of professional courtesy for a fellow agent or out of friendship, she was clearly concerned about Sarah, and that made me like her despite the cranky, hyper-driven persona.

The only positive from the day was that just before I had to endure a hospital dinner, Athena managed to get me transferred to a "private facility."

Chapter 34

At my request, the ambulance supposedly transferring me dropped me off in front of Duma's bunker-like urban fortress with a canvas bag containing my gear. Bullet wound or no, I needed to get my swords from Duma, find Sarah, and stop an impending apocalypse. And I had just four more days to do it all. *No pressure.*

I hobbled to the door and pounded on it with my fist until the ground began to rumble and the door began to slide open. It opened halfway, and much to my surprise, Abraxos walked out, wearing nothing but shorts, his hands on his hips and his mouth drawn into a tight line. Mr. Universe contestants would have dropped out and changed professions at the sight of him. His forehead was heavily creased, and his white eyes were sunken into yellowish-brown sockets that stood out in the pale skin of the rest of his face.

"How is he?" I asked before he could say anything.

"He'll be fine," he replied, nodding a single time. "You okay? Duma said you got shot getting him loose."

"I'll live."

He nodded again, staring at the ground. "What about Sarah?"

"Not sure, but you can bet your ass I'm going to find her and get her back," I replied.

Because he towered over me, I could see his lips purse into a frown even though he was still staring at his feet. "Well, come on in."

I limped after him. Before we reached the narrow spiral staircase, I spotted my duffle bag from the surveillance roost sitting next to a workbench against the wall. "Is that my bag from the Bowery?"

"Yeah, I grabbed it last night. Duma had me put your swords in there, too." Ab pointed absently at it as he walked. He stopped after putting a foot on the stairs and fixed me hard with his sunken eyes. "Hey, D, I'm real sorry about Sarah. Maybe if I'd have been there, Duma and I could have stopped them."

"Ab, I doubt even your muscle would have mattered. You saw what they did to Duma." I grabbed my gear bag and hoisted it over my shoulder. "Besides, we were *hoping* the bastards would approach her. I just didn't expect them to find out who she was and *take* her."

He climbed up the carved treads with an ease that surprised me given his substantial size and the narrowness of the staircase. I, on the other hand, had the opposite experience trying to navigate the damned thing carrying two gear bags with an injured leg.

"That hulder bitch has no idea of the pain she's due," Ab said, mumbling just loud enough that I wasn't sure if he was addressing me or not.

The statement made me shudder. Knowing the brothers, I didn't even want to think about the reprisals. Calling the likely blowback "inhuman" would be an understatement, but then they *were* inhuman, and their world was different. I couldn't help but think about the misconception that the Fae are completely emotionless. I didn't know if Duma's and Ab's reactions to this betrayal was a simple blood debt or actual emotion that had rubbed off from time spent around humans for so long. Either way, it was scary and not for me to judge. If, on the very slim chance I crossed paths with this particular hulder before Duma and Ab found her, I would make her pay for her betrayal with her life, but it would be swift.

Once I reached the top of the stairs, I heaved my bags across the living space and into a corner, feeling like I had just emerged from a tar pit. Duma was lying on a sofa along the nearest wall, dressed in a thick red robe, with an actual ice pack on his head. I'd never even seen him need to take so much as an aspirin in all the years I'd known him.

The parts of his arms that I could see below the sleeves of his robe were now covered in alternating streaks of black, yellowish brown, and his normal pale white, and his hands, including the crushed one, were puffy. The lower parts of his legs resembled his arms. I knew the black discoloration was burns—or actually intensified frostbite—from where the iron chains had touched his skin.

"Man, you look like a thousand miles of bad road in the wintertime," I said, grimacing at the array of injuries.

"Thanks," he replied, sitting up with some effort. "Glad to see that bullet to your ass didn't damage your brain too badly." He was still lisping through his damaged lips, though it was evident from his movements that his badly broken arm had been properly set.

I grinned at him without showing teeth and rolled my eyes. "How's your hand and arm?"

"No worse than my ribs and face. Ab helped set my arm since you were too big a baby to help."

"It was broken in at least three places," I said. "It would have been like putting a jigsaw puzzle together, and I didn't have the time."

"Five," Ab shouted from another room.

"Five what?" I asked, slightly confused.

"My arm was broken in *five* places," Duma said with a subdued shrug. "It's all healing, though. I may not be full speed yet, but I can still help you get Sarah back. Clearly, she isn't dead yet, or they would have left you the body already."

"I'm ready to go whenever," Ab shouted, still in the other room.

"No," I said flatly. "Healthy or not, you aren't going with me. Either of you. Not this time."

"D, I'm the reason they took her," Duma said, tilting his head slightly.

"No, you're not. I am. I put her in that position. And you, for that matter," I said, pointing at him. "And look what happened."

"I bet Sarah would say she put *herself* in that position," Duma said, standing up, again with considerable effort. "But they *took* her because *I* trusted someone *I* shouldn't have. Which, incidentally, is also what got *me* thrashed."

I crossed my arms over my chest and just kept shaking my head.

"Don't be stupid, D."

"I'm *trying* to be smart," I replied.

"Well, quit it, because it looks painful," Duma said.

"Funny. But I'm not putting anyone else in danger on this one. Na'amah is far too devious. I stand a better chance of disrupting her plans and getting Sarah back alone. They are apparently dependent on a rare astronomical occurrence that happens in four days, and they *need* Sarah alive for it. I'll find them, grab Sarah, and distract them long enough for the event to pass. *Then* you guys can help me mop up afterward—when you're healthy."

"Sorry, but that sounds dumb," he said.

"Think of it as the big-picture view. Until I know where they're keeping her, I can't come up with the actual details. Speaking of which ..." I limped back to my bags and rummaged through the one containing the cuirass for the blood-filled crystal pendant. I tossed it to Duma, and his left hand shot out and grabbed it faster than I would have believed possible, given his injuries.

"Oh, yeah, this thingy," he said, smiling. "I take it you want *me* to scry for her, Mr. Wizard."

I nodded. "Better you than me, even with that." I pointed at the pendant.

"This, I can do," he said, limping off into a room at the other end of the space. "Gimme some time." He shut the door solidly behind him.

Without anything better to do, I did what I was most comfortable with—cleaned my weapons. Ab watched in the same cold, detached way people watch others mow grass. Nothing riled him. Even if he'd been about to storm the primordial succubus's lair, he would've appeared unaffected. His demeanor was always unnerving. I was starting to get a bit jumpy, dropping bullets as I tried to refill magazines.

Finally, Ab sniffed a few times then went downstairs. A few minutes later, he returned with a heavy canvas bag, which he dropped with a resounding thud right next to me.

"Case you want something heavier," he said, sitting down. "And more rounds for those." He pointed at my Sig and the Glock then went back to silently watching.

I opened the heavy bag, which contained an HK121 machine gun with several fifty-round belt drums, a bulky Striker automatic shotgun, an old M1918 BAR, a .357 Chiappa Rhino, and a Desert Eagle .50.

"What? No M214?" I asked, joking about the twelve-thousand-rounds-per-minute mini-gun usually mounted on helicopters.

"You want?" His eyebrows shot high on his forehead. "I got two downstairs, plus a few dozen thousand-round ammo cans. Those things eat up the ammo. Get hot, too. Didn't know if the eighty-five pounds would be too much for you or not." He smiled and nodded slightly as he said the last part.

"Smartass," I said, closing the bag back up. "I appreciate it, but I'm good with what I've got."

"Suit yourself." He shrugged. "I prefer to use guns that let you know you've fired them."

"Yeah, you and the *entire* battlefield," I said, putting my gear away.

"You sure you don't want me to come with you?" Ab asked, his blond eyebrows tented on his forehead.

"No," I replied. "Not this time. Besides, you need to make sure Duma is okay. They beat him pretty bad."

"I've seen him worse," he said, grabbing the bag of weapons he'd brought me. "He'll be okay. He thinks he let you down is all."

"It wasn't his fault, Ab, so make sure he knows that."

After a second of silence, Ab headed toward another doorway at the back of the room. He dropped the bag with a heavy thud at the door then came back with something small in his massive hand.

Once he was within a few yards, he tossed the object, and I caught it. The brown prescription bottle had a white lid and no labels. Inside were several small dark-colored pills, and I glanced at Ab.

"For pain," he said. "Won't help with the bleeding or infections, but it will dull the pain so you can move normally."

"I don't need—"

"I've seen you walk," he said, holding up a hand to stop me. "You think running and fighting are going to be easier? Besides, they are completely natural and safe. Well, they *should* be okay for a human."

Ab went upstairs to work out while I sat to rest my leg and wait for Duma. It took him almost three hours, which surprised me. His eyes were hooded, and he frowned deeply as he approached, smoothing back his pale-blond hair with his good hand. The pendant dangling from the other, he stared at the ground, rubbing his neck.

"Well?"

"I can't get her," he said in a voice just barely loud enough to hear.

I shot to my feet despite the pain. "What do you mean you 'can't get her'?"

He raised his head slightly. "Her position keeps bouncing around and won't settle. They're moving her. At least they have been for the past few hours."

"Is she in a general area? At least on this continent?" I asked, trying to contain my desperation.

He shook his head. "I'd guess they are using the Ways to move her, trying to throw off the possibility of a tail."

"There's no way they can shield her completely, is there?" After three thousand years, I was still unsure of how tracking magic and scrying worked.

"Theoretically, yes, but that's why she had these made." He held up the crystal. "They are as pure a link to her as can be made. Even if they ward her, we should still be able to track her *general* whereabouts. They just need to settle down first."

I rubbed my forehead and pinched the bridge of my nose with my thumb and forefinger. "Okay, if you still have the energy, keep scrying until you have a reliable position. Brey mentioned that this particular astronomical occurrence has happened before, about a century and a half ago—probably when they released Ramiel. I'm going to see if I can narrow down a potential location for their ritual based on what is known about *that* event."

He nodded and went back to the room he'd come out of, and I found my phone in my gear bag and called the Metis Foundation. I had to wait a few minutes while the receptionist tracked Brey down.

"Ah, Diomedes," she answered. "I hear you have been shot. I trust it is nothing life threatening."

"I'm fine, Brey," I said, trying not to be too brusque. "I need to know everything you found out about the last time Venus passed over the moon or whatever the hell it was you told me about."

"Venus passing the moon?" she asked in an exaggeratedly confused tone. "You mean the Great Malefic and the Transition of the Light Bringer?"

"Yeah, whatever. Just tell me what you know about the *last* time it occurred," I said. "You mentioned it happened in 18-something or other."

"I believe I said the last time these two rare astronomical events occurred in such proximity to each other was in 1874. The Great

Malefic on August seventeenth of that year and the Transition of Venus beginning on December ninth."

"Great, did you find anything that mentioned any kind of strange incidences or anomalies around the December ninth event? Disappearances, disasters, that kind of thing?"

"Actually, the most notable incident occurred in direct connection to the event," she said like a schoolmarm getting ready to lecture. "A supposed American scientific expedition went to the Desolation Islands to study the Transition of Venus at an observatory built on Pointe Molloy on the Courbet Peninsula, but all members of the team, save three, were found dead. One was never found, the leader returned safely to the US with questionable data, while the third showed up naked, terrified, and half crazed at a German expeditionary outpost—also present to document the same astronomical incident—on Anse Betsy twenty-five kilometers away. The crazed survivor succumbed to exposure several days later. The surviving expedition leader claimed all was well when he left to report the results and knew nothing of what might have happened at his observatory or the whereabouts of the missing team member. The Germans claimed the American observatory camp was littered with the bodies of the expedition members, most dead from exposure and all in the process of fleeing in panic."

"What was so special about this area of the Desolation Islands that they built observatories there?" I asked.

"I will do some additional research to find out, but apparently, five expeditions were organized to observe the Transit, and three of those were on Desolation Island. The British were also present," she said.

"Thanks, and if you do find a reason, can you please see if you can find any other locations with similar traits that might coincide with the upcoming Transit?"

"Excuse me, Diomedes, but *if* I find a reason?" she said. "I assume you meant *when*."

"Sorry. I meant *when*," I replied. "And if you can find anything else about the American expedition, that might be helpful, too. I have a bad feeling that was when Ramiel escaped Tartarus, and since Na'amah is bent on releasing the rest of his kindred, the more information I have, the better."

I sat heavily on one of the couches in the opulent room, suddenly feeling exhausted. All the information Brey had just given me, combined with what I knew and the fact that Duma still couldn't pinpoint Sarah's location, made me feel a bit like Sisyphus at the bottom of the damn hill. I rubbed at my eyes with the heels of my hands, trying not to focus on the fact that despite everything I knew, I still had no actionable intelligence. I leaned back and drifted off to a restless sleep.

I WAS JARRED AWAKE several hours later when my phone rang. It was Brey.

"I hope I did not disturb you too much, but I believe time is of the essence," she said the moment I picked up.

"As long as you found something useful," I replied through a yawn while scratching at my beard.

"I shall leave that determination to you," she said mirthlessly. "I can only present you the facts I have uncovered. Firstly, the only logical reason I can see that the Desolation Islands were chosen was for the location's remoteness and because it offered ideal viewing given the season. Geologically, it is unremarkable, and even the Telluric Pathways are entirely absent from its land mass. It is truly isolated. There are no places on earth that meet all of those criteria for *this* Transit. I would posit that the location in 1874 was simply one of isolation and opportunity."

"That's not at all helpful, Brey. Please tell me you have more."

"The sole survivor of the American team was a Dr. Gerald Porter Reed, an astronomer from the University of Chicago."

I squeezed my eyes shut in frustration. "Again, Brey, not helpful."

"Ah, but Dr. Reed had a hobby of sorts," she said with a tone that almost suggested excitement. "He revived the Most Ancient and Most Puissant Order of the Beggar's Benison and Merryland, Anstruther, better known as the Beggar's Benison."

"The Scottish gentlemen's *sex* club?" Despite my initial confusion, I suddenly made the connection. "Wait... that makes sense, and it has Na'amah written all over it. Were any others on the expedition team also members of the club?"

"All of them except one—a woman, the lone female of the group. Her body was never found."

"Yeah, well, I'm pretty sure I know where she is, and she's causing me all kinds of grief trying to free her old boyfriend and his cohorts from Tartarus."

Chapter 35

I tried, once again, to piece together everything I knew, but I was finding it harder to get past what Sarah might be going through. I sat on the couch, staring into space and working myself into a frenzy, until Duma walked out with a yawn that disfigured his already-distorted face. Without acknowledging me, he wandered into the kitchen.

He fumbled around with a glass for a few minutes, then, with some sort of dark-green sludgy drink in hand, he traipsed to the couch across from me and flopped down. I watched his every move intently. He sat for another few moments, drinking the thick gunk in the glass without saying a word. Finally, I couldn't take any more waiting.

"What the—" I said, ready to come off the couch at him.

"Relax, Sparky." He held up his battered hand. "I know where she is. And she's surprisingly close."

"How close?"

"Jersey," Duma replied. "Clifton. Like ten miles away."

I scowled at him, confused. "Are you sure? It's not just some stopping point?" I asked, ready to move since I had a location.

"All I can tell you is that I've checked a few times, and she hasn't moved in a while. I'll check one more time in a bit to make sure, but..." He shrugged. "I'll pull out a local street map once I make sure and get you as exact a location as I can."

Ab lumbered down the stairs like the albino version of the Hulk, rubbing at his short blond crew cut. As he trod past us toward the kitchen, he asked, "You find her?"

"Hopefully and nearby," I said, standing up.

"You know you should slow it down, D," Duma said, taking another drink of the glop in his glass. "I don't need to tell you that going to war to prevent the loss of something is a recipe for even greater loss."

"Saving Sarah disrupts Na'amah and Ramiel. That's my goal."

"You sure?" he said, eyeing me sideways.

"Just check to make sure Sarah's still in Clifton and let me handle the rest."

Duma stood, stared at me for a few seconds, then headed back to his room.

Maybe he was right, or maybe I just didn't care. As far as I was concerned, getting Sarah back would mean screwing up their plans, so doing one achieved the other. That was good enough.

I geared up, wishing I'd brought the Pelian Spear with me before quickly talking myself out of its usefulness. I headed downstairs to wait, because moving at least was doing something.

Before I put my foot on the cement floor of the garage, a sudden buzzing in the back of my head and down my spine told me Athena was nearby.

"While I may not approve of your company, Diomedes, in this case, I do agree with his advice," Athena said before she stepped from the shadows. "You should not be so rash. Ramiel is different than anything you have ever pursued. Powerful and ancient."

"Sounds to me like everything else I go after," I replied, finding her running her fingers down the side of one of Duma's cars. Her fiery-red hair was in a loose ponytail at her back, and she wore a severe black suit that made her skin even paler. Her normally electric-blue eyes were more the color of the sky before a storm—dull and flat.

"He has become far more powerful than the last time you faced him, or he would not be attempting to set his brethren free," she said. "Na'amah is a confounding factor as well. Who knows what they will have helping them or how many."

"I'll let you know once I count them," I said. "I don't plan on fighting them all. I just need to get Sarah back and harass them enough to make them miss their window of opportunity. Then I'll mop them up at my leisure."

"You don't even know where they are holding her."

"Pretty sure I do. Duma said Clifton. That would mean they are beneath the Gates of Hell. Why else would they be in Clifton?"

"Diomedes, I cannot affect your free will, or else, in this case, I would." Her forehead creased, and her brows pinched. "Rushing in blindly is a tactical mistake, and you know it. Do not let your feelings for her cloud your judgment."

"I disagree." I crossed my arms, glaring hard at her. "I think one insurgent with the element of surprise can cause them all kinds of grief. And they need her for whatever ritual they have cooked up. Na'amah said as much. So, I get her, I screw them up. It's that simple."

"You fail to see the obvious. It is clearly a trap to draw you in." She met my glare with equal intensity though her eyes stayed dull.

"No, I assumed it was a trap all along. I just don't care." I let my gaze fall to the floor. "I promised to keep her safe."

"Getting yourself killed will not aid her."

"Neither will me waiting around," I replied.

"Hey D, who you talking to down there?" Duma shouted from the top of the staircase.

Athena was gone. Given my bond with her, maybe she was never even there.

"No one," I replied. "Just waiting on you, sweetheart."

"Oh, well, she's still in Clifton, right behind—"

"She's at the Gates of Hell."

"Yeah, that place. Some two hundred feet below the surface," he replied. "The energy is strong, though, so I'm inclined to believe she is definitely still alive."

"Great. Can you give me a ride?"

"You mean right now?" he asked. "You're kidding, right? Do you even have anything actually approaching a real plan, Kemosabe, or are you expecting them to be awed into submission by your mere presence?"

"Something like that." I was becoming impatient and irritated with everyone telling me to wait and slow down, and I could feel the muscles in my jaw tighten.

"As your closest—and longest—surviving friend in the world, I gotta say that ain't smart. Sounds like a damn suicide mission to me."

"I didn't ask," I replied. "I just need a *damn* ride." Hands on hips, I let my head fall back in exasperation. Then I began to choose the order in which I would start destroying his car collection if he didn't get his fairy ass in gear.

"Don't get saucy with me, Béarnaise," he said, walking down the stairs. "You want to be like that, you can just walk."

"Hey, the faster I move, the less likely they are to expect me. And yes, I am well aware they are probably expecting me."

He shook his head slowly as he exhaled heavily through his nose. "Man, I ain't even in good enough shape to watch your back on this. I'm telling you I do not like it."

"I don't need you to like it, Duma. I don't like it, either, but—"

Duma pointed at the green Jag. "Just get in. And for cripes' sake, don't rip the leather with all your pointy crap. Oh, and you might need to help me steer. No power steering in this baby, and my arm is far from healed."

"Are you kidding me?" I hopped back out of the low-slung car, only to see him grinning at me while stifling a laugh.

Chapter 36

Forty-five silent minutes later, he dropped me off in the empty parking lot of a defunct storefront adjacent to the railroad tracks in Clifton, New Jersey. My stomach was twisted in knots. I hadn't felt so uneasy about going into a fight since I was a child. Almost on autopilot, I walked a half mile down the tracks to a dirt trail that led into the woods behind an old whiskey distillery. The largely overgrown trail led to a catch basin and underground drainage tunnels for Weasel Brook, the small creek that snaked through most of the town.

For the past several decades, the tunnels had earned a reputation for being haunted and frequented by demons, earning them the nickname the Gates of Hell. Kids took it as a challenge to explore them despite the fact that doing so was illegal. What they didn't know was that the main tunnel did have an entrance to a system of deeper catacombs that led to an underground nexus point along the Telluric Pathways. From time to time, locals would see one of the Fae or other creatures who used the Ways coming or going, giving rise to the tales and legends of demons, ghosts, and monsters that lived there. Its reputation and concentrated energy had made it a perfect meeting point for all kinds of ceremonial or ritual activities in the past, including Satanists, so it was of little surprise that Ramiel and Na'amah planned to tap into the energy source.

It was ten in the morning in the middle of the week, so I didn't expect to encounter anyone at the entrance to the drains. Shuffling down the dirt embankment toward the cement-walled basin that gave rise to the tunnel, I noticed someone sitting on the edge, bobbing from side to side to a beat I couldn't hear. A few feet closer, I began to hear the muted beat of bass and noticed the man's oversized headphones. From behind, I could tell he was a young African-American guy wearing a white tank top and a white ball cap rotated slightly to the left. The white headphones over the cap were accented with gold, and multiple gold chains hung around his neck. His shirt and cap were startlingly clean. Before I could say anything, he pulled the headphones down around his neck, turned off the music from his cell phone, and craned his neck around to eye me.

"Now ain't this interesting?" His tone was nonthreatening and almost friendly, so I didn't know what to make of him. I could tell he was human, but his mannerisms suggested there was something more to him.

"You know it's illegal to be down here." I remained a few cautious feet away, with my hands down at my sides. I hadn't decided if he was a threat or not, but I didn't want to evoke an unnecessary response by being too abrupt, either. For all I knew, he was just a neighborhood kid.

"No, it's illegal to be down *there*." He nodded toward the tunnel mouth heavily marked with graffiti, including *Gate to Hell* painted in large, sloppy red letters. "Sittin' right here is barely even trespassin'. Loiterin' at most. Besides, it's more pleasant down here than out on them tracks, even if this is the gate to hell." He smiled and chuckled a bit.

I couldn't see anything around him that resembled a weapon, and he had nothing on him except his headphones and cell phone that I could see. He wasn't surprised in the least by my presence or concerned that I was heavily armed. I frowned as I tried to figure him out.

"Relax," he said, climbing to his feet and dusting off his hands. He was smiling broadly. "I am a friend."

I eyed him sideways. "A friend of whom? I only have a few, and I don't recall you as one of them."

"My name is Simon," he said, holding out his hand. "Justicar Brother Simon, and I believe I am here to help you."

I almost took a step back. *This guy, a Justicar brother?* He was nothing like any of the other brothers of the Holy Order I had ever encountered before.

"I know I ain't an old white dude, but I am P-to-the-D fighting for G-O-D," he said, bobbing and throwing his arms around like a rapper as he said it.

He still had me at a loss for words. His movements revealed a large red-and-gold crucifix hanging from one of the chains around his neck. It was similar to others I'd seen adorning the armor or clothing of the Justicar brothers of Pugnus Dei, but given all that was going on, I was having a hard time buying the story he was here to help me, even if he was Pugnus Dei.

"How'd you know I'd be coming? I haven't talked to anyone in the Order in weeks." I kept my left hand low and loose by the Glock on my hip just in case.

"Didn't. Don't even know who you are, but I've been walking along the railroad tracks and praying all morning. Then I decided to take a rest and found *this* place." He motioned to the tunnel with a jerk of his head. "That's when you showed up dressed like some kinda slick-ass fly future ninja or something. Look like God's providence to me. Either that, or I misread the whole thing, and you an overdressed mugger who picked the wrong mark, cause I ain't got crap."

The kid was *nothing* like any of the other members of the Holy Order I'd ever encountered—especially the Justicar Brothers. He kept slipping in and out of being a gangster as he talked, and as he moved, I began noticing the dark tattoos over his arms and upper chest in the dappled light of the forest canopy. They gave off the slightest hint of power, almost like an unused battery, and they were more sigil than random images or words. He even had some scarification on his shoulders that resembled some sort of holy seals.

He noticed me studying his tattoos and scars and glanced down over his arms. "Reminders of who I serve," he said, holding out his arms. "I promise I ain't jerkin' your chain, man. We are here, together, at this place for a reason."

I noted a presence behind me just before another voice spoke. "Well, then why am I here?" a female voice asked.

I shifted my position slightly and backed up so that I could keep the kid in view and see the newcomer as well. This stranger was a tall woman with light-brown hair and the build of a serious athlete. She carried a large rucksack easily over one shoulder as she made her way down the dirt embankment toward us.

The kid smiled, clapped his hands together, and rubbed them with enthusiasm. "Well, I'll be. If it ain't the Sistah Justicar herself. Now I *know* we all here for a reason."

A sister *Justicar? That's new.* But then so was a young African-American. Apparently, the Holy Order was keeping up with the times.

"Who's this guy?" she asked, walking past me without concern and straight to Simon. They hugged briefly, then she dropped her bag down into the basin below with a solid metallic thump.

"No clue," Simon said. "He showed up just a few minutes ago dressed like he's headed off to some kinda high-tech Renaissance fair. And then there's that..." He pointed down at the entrance to the Gates of Hell.

"Seriously?" she said. "I read about this place but always assumed it was just an urban legend. My ride had to let me off up the street, and I heard voices down here and had *that* feeling that *this* is where I should head, you know?"

Simon nodded exaggeratedly.

"A Sister Justicar of Pugnus Dei?" I said, mostly to myself, back to being unsure about these people again. I was after beings that were, by their very nature, deceivers.

"This ain't the Dark Ages anymore, mister," the woman said. "I'm *Sister* Justicar John, but they all call me Joanie. Who might you be?"

"The guy about to head down that tunnel," I said, pointing to the Gates of Hell. Whoever they were and whatever they were doing, they could do without me.

Joanie rolled her eyes. "Seriously? You're going to play mysterious stranger with two Justicars of Pugnus Dei? You know who we are, so you must know what it means that there are now two of us present, right?"

Her statement stopped me in my tracks, but before I could offer a flippant answer, I got the feeling someone else was approaching again.

"Three," said another voice from out in the woods farther up the path.

"Oh, shit," Simon said. "Three Justicars together in one place? Damn."

Silhouetted by the light through the trees, the newest addition to the group was a tall, well-built man with someone equally as tall right behind him, carrying a large, broad bag on his back and what resembled a long walking stick in one hand.

It's becoming a regular freakin' party down here. I sighed heavily, becoming impatient, and watched as they made their way through the trees toward us.

The lead man of the pair, dressed in well-worn tiger-striped fatigues, was in his thirties, bald with a reddish Van Dyke beard, and he had the lithe build of a long-distance runner. The blond kid following him was lankier and probably half the other man's age. He was sweating and slightly winded in comparison to his companion. Assuming the first was yet another Brother Justicar, then the other man would probably be his Coadjutor Novice.

The three Justicars greeted one another like the oldest of friends, while the novice remained aloof, dropping the heavy bag at his feet with a surprising *clank*. He leaned on the long, cloth-wrapped staff he carried as he breathed and wiped at his forehead with his sleeve. I was drawn to the staff as if it called to me. I took a few tentative steps toward the younger man, trying to figure out why. The closer I got, the more familiar the feeling became. It was the Pelian Spear—*my* spear, the one I took from Achilles at his funerary games back at Troy. It was supposed to be stored in my vault-like weapons locker at my house.

"Where did you get that?" I asked the kid, pointing, immediately incensed and about ready to start swinging, Pugnus Dei or not. The kid took a few steps back, but to his credit, he drew what he believed was just a simple staff under his arm outward and squared his shoulders and feet for an attack.

"Whoa, boss," the newcomer Justicar said. "Just relax, man. We got the walking stick from an old lady down the road. She was taking out some garbage and asked if we could take a few things to someone for her. Said we'd find him if we took a shortcut through these woods."

"Well, *that* belongs to me," I replied.

"You sure?" He eyed me suspiciously. "The old lady did say the owner of the stick was a little uptight, so that fits." The kid holding the spear laughed a bit, as did Simon.

"It's not a staff. It's the Pelian Spear," I said, backing off a bit.

None of the Justicars were riled in the least, but I was ready to throw down. While I didn't agree with everything Pugnus Dei did or even the way they did things, I had always respected them. And they were never quick to anger or fight. I, on the other hand, tended to lead with my fists. Some called it a character flaw, but I always thought of it as prudence.

"A spear?" the bald Justicar asked. "Unwrap that thing, Jonesy. Let's see what's inside."

The kid relaxed and began to unwrap it, revealing the dull, tarnished yellow metal of the long leaflike bladed head and a few feet of the shaft. In his hands, it didn't resemble anything close to special and looked more like a cheap reproduction.

"Wow, that thing looks old... and kinda crappy," Simon said. "But it is a spear like the man said."

"So does the shield belong to you, too?" the novice asked with a slight accent I couldn't place.

"Shield?" I replied. "Only if it has a boar on it."

"Boar?" he asked, glancing past me to his master.

"Yeah, a big pig," the bald Justicar replied. "Yep, indeed it does, my friend," he said with a lopsided smile and a quick tilt of his head.

The kid spun the spear deftly and offered me the butt of the weapon. The instant I touched it, the dull metal blazed as if highly polished, and the blade's finish shone brilliantly, reflecting what little light penetrated the forest canopy. A collective gasp spread around the small group. After a moment, the novice knelt to dig into his bag and produced the shield given to me by Athena over three thousand years ago.

I stood staring at them. As far as I knew, both had been safely locked behind ten inches of reinforced steel inside my loadout room back in my house in San Diego. *Athena.*

"What did this old lady look like?" I asked the novice.

The kid's eyes travelled past me to his master, and I followed his gaze. The bald Justicar spoke instead. "She was a gray-haired old woman, but she clearly would have been a knockout in her youth, you know? She had a way about her."

"Blue eyes," the novice added quietly. "Bright-blue eyes."

The bald Justicar pointed and nodded at the novice's addition to his description.

My eyes travelled the length of the spear and settled on the shield. I hadn't used my shield in centuries. It just wasn't practical on a modern battlefield anymore. *What did Athena foresee about this battle that I didn't?* Being honest with myself, I realized the answer was probably *everything*. I had more skin in this game than usual, but there was no way I could back down. I sighed heavily and closed my eyes.

"Who are you?" the bald Justicar asked.

I did not respond or even raise my head. I couldn't. I wasn't behaving like myself at all.

"His name is Diomedes, the Son of Tydeus and the oldest of the Guardians," came a new, strong, resonant voice. "And he fought the Ancient Gods on the battlefield of Troy over three thousand years ago. And won, I might add."

The statement sparked something inside me, and I searched to find the source of the new voice.

"Brother Peter," the bald Justicar said in a near-jubilant shout. "I haven't seen you in months."

Across the cement draining basin from us stood an older man with a full white beard and thick white hair dressed in an old button-front shirt and khaki pants. His exact age was hard to determine because he was powerfully built. The age of the clean-shaven Asian man with him was also hard to determine, though he had to be over fifty. Both men carried heavy packs and stout walking sticks.

"Four of us?" Joanie said. "When's the last time that happened?"

"Never in my lifetime," Brother Peter replied. "And the last time three of us gathered, this man fought alongside them, my predecessor included." He pointed at me with his staff. "He is an unlikely ally, but honorable and worthy of respect."

"When was that?" Joanie asked.

"1919," I replied. "New Orleans." I'd had no idea what exactly I was facing then, and I wasn't much better off now.

Brother Peter and his novice walked through the woods and around the drainage basin to join us.

"Who brought food?" the bald Justicar asked, rubbing his hands together.

"Cool it, Bart," Joanie said. "Clearly, there's a reason we are all together in *this* place."

I could feel all eyes focus on me.

"Same reason as New Orleans," I said after a moment. "Only worse."

"You mean the Iyrin Ramiel?" Brother Peter asked.

"Yes, and he's working with Na'amah, the Sons of Belial, and who knows what else. They are working to free the rest of the Fallen from Tartarus. I don't know how exactly, but I know it will happen in two nights' time, down there." I pointed toward the opening to the tunnel that led to the Gates of Hell. "And they have taken my friend to use as a vessel."

"Oh, this is all related to that stuff Brother Easy and Brother Frankenpuss did up at that hospital earlier this year," Bart said.

"Be respectful, Justicar Brother Bartholomew," Brother Peter said.

"Guy looks like a thousand miles of bad road—potholes and all. Just sayin'," Bart replied, shrugging. "Plus, he scares me."

Simon and Joanie nodded their agreement vigorously.

"But yes, I believe it is related," Peter continued. "Perhaps we should settle for a bit to gather our wits and prepare for what awaits."

"You guys settle. I've got a friend to save." I picked up my shield and spear before hopping down into the drainage basin.

"Diomedes, wait," Peter said, standing on the edge of the basin. "We are all here together for a reason. We can aid each other in this fight. I implore you, do not go this alone. You were not meant to."

"She doesn't have time to wait," I replied.

"Well, then tell us what she looks like so we can find her after we step over your dead body," Joanie said, walking up next to Peter and crossing her arms over her chest as she glared down at me. "'Cause if what you're saying is waiting down there, then I don't care who you are, going alone is suicide, plain and simple. And that's just a waste."

"Sister Justicar John, that is uncalled for," Peter said, glaring at her. "But, Diomedes, I would have to agree. Wait. You said it happens two nights from now. Wait, and we will all go with you. And it is written that when two or more are gathered together in God's name—"

"He will accompany and bless us," the group said in unison, though Bart rolled his eyes as he said it.

They were right about going in alone. I knew what these guys were capable of, and having them with me dramatically increased the odds of not only surviving but actually stopping them. I wasn't happy about it, but it was the smart choice. Eyeing the tunnel, I threw the spear at the graffiti marking it as the Gates of Hell as hard as I could. The ancient weapon pierced the hardened concrete half its length into the wall with barely any sound at all beyond a slight metallic ringing. I hung my shield from the protruding end and glowered up at Peter and Joanie. "You win. I'll wait."

Peter smiled broadly and hopped down into the basin with me with the ease of a practiced gymnast, and the others followed.

Over the next few hours and into the early evening, I sat and watched as the assembled members of Pugnus Dei *settled* into their routines. Given my experiences with them, I was more than a little surprised to see that each of them was preparing in their own way. Only Justicar Brother Peter and his novice sat in quiet, reflective prayer. Simon listened to his music, Joanie doodled and drew on a sketchpad, and Bartholomew did yoga while his novice boiled water for tea over a small camp stove.

In the past, I'd known the Justicars of Pugnus Dei as highly disciplined warrior monks, but this group was like a high school class, and I began to feel uneasy with my decision to work with them.

The relative inaction and lack of urgency really began to grate on my nerves. I understood slowing down to come up with a plan of attack, but we weren't doing that. We had already waited several hours longer than I wanted, and nothing suggested we would get moving any time soon.

Sighing heavily, I slapped my thighs then got up with the intention of heading into the tunnels. Before I could grab the shield, a deep, resonant voice carried through the forest from the direction of the railroad tracks above. Someone said something incoherent, followed by two distinct laughs. Instantly, all activity in the drainage basin stopped, and all eyes focused on the ridge above. Through the indistinct shadows and darkness, a large figure emerged from the trees on the ridge above the tunnel's mouth, flanked a moment later by two significantly smaller forms. All three carried heavy bags with them, but the giant carried two—one in each hand—down at his sides rather than over his shoulders like the others.

"I can hear that hip-hop crap from here, so that must be Brother Simon," said a deep voice with a heavy Caribbean accent.

"Justicar Brother Paul," Peter said, climbing easily to his feet even after sitting for so long.

Paul set his bags down and jumped down the ten feet to the basin floor near me. In the waning ambient light, I could only tell that Paul had very dark skin and was built like a defensive lineman with the height of a basketball player. He was a little over a foot taller than me, which made him just taller than Ab, though not nearly as well built. He immediately reminded me of Ajax the Greater on the battlefield of Troy.

"You, I don't know," he said while taking a few aggressive steps toward me.

"We've never met, so why would you?" I replied, squaring myself to his stance, unwilling to give an inch.

"Brother Paul, meet Diomedes Tydides, the oldest of the Guardians," Peter said, walking up beside us, his voice ever calm and even. "It seems God has brought us all to this place for a reason." Peter shined a small but powerful LED flashlight at the cement wall and the graffiti.

Bart, Simon, and Joanie joined us, but the novices all remained aloof.

"Five," Paul said with a whistle. "Plus this one." He motioned at me with the wave of a hand as if I were an unwanted annoyance.

"Do you see why we were waiting?" Peter said, clapping me on the shoulder. "*His* plan for us is always perfect."

Paul motioned for his two companions—still above—to join us. They dropped his bags down to him one at a time, and it took considerable effort on both parts, suggesting the bags were incredibly heavy. The massive bags also jangled—though only slightly—suggesting some sort of armor or weapons were within. Then the two companions tossed down their own bags, which were much lighter, then jumped.

Paul's cohorts were smaller than me, with one easily a foot shorter than I was. Both were stocky and well built, and their landings on the cement floor of the basin were easy, though not as effortless as Paul's had been.

Paul put his things down next to Peter and sat down gracefully. The two men leaned in close and began to speak in hushed voices as Paul's friends began digging through their bags.

I'd had it with waiting. These weren't the knights of Pugnus Dei that I remembered. Waiting for them wouldn't help me or Sarah. I began pacing. On the one hand, I knew what these people were *supposedly* capable of. I also knew that they rarely fought in anything greater than pairs of Justicars. To see five Justicars together suggested the situation was grave. On the other hand, several of them were kids, and there was no way they had that much combat experience—God with them or not. They simply didn't come off as being anywhere close to ready for what lay down those tunnels. I was ready to move, and my plan was simple—kill anything that got in my way and get Sarah back. If I didn't make it, then this motley group could come mop up my mess. And I wouldn't care because I would be dead.

I gazed at my spear and shield hanging from the wall outside the tunnel. Before I could make a move, a hand clapped my shoulder.

"I can see the doubt in your eyes, even in the dark," Peter said. "Though they may seem young, they are all experienced and skillful fighters. Brother John—Joanie—has faced more demons than I have in her short calling, if you can believe it. Brother Simon is the most skilled swordsman I have ever witnessed, and Brother Bartholomew single-handedly destroyed the demon Count Furfur as a novice after his master was killed during the fight."

"What about him?" I asked, motioning at Paul with a curt nod of my head.

Peter said nothing for several long minutes as we watched him unpack his gear while his companions went for food. To my surprise, the large bags contained pieces of plate mail armor that glistened like glass in the scant moonlight. As he reverently handled the parts, he chanted something under his breath.

"Contend, Lord, with those who contend with us; fight against those who fight against us. Take up shield and armor; arise and come to our aid. Brandish spear and javelin against those who pursue us. Say to us, 'I am your salvation...,'" Paul said quietly as he worked. Dozens of angelic sigils across the armor began to glow softly with a pale blue-white light.

I hadn't seen full plate armor used for over five hundred years, and then only on horseback. And I had never seen any, including my own cuirass, infused with such power. I could feel my jaw drop open a bit.

Peter chuckled, clapping my shoulder again. "He is our juggernaut. He is the first of our order to wear that armor in over two hundred years, and with it he wields *Vayichar Af Hashem*."

"God's Wrath?" I replied as I watched, enraptured by the power the metal emanated.

"God's *Fiery* Wrath."

Once Paul had placed the armor in order on the ground, he began removing pieces of what could only be a weapon—a pair of heavy, wide, almost circular blades and several pieces of a handle. Glowing markings similar to those on the armor covered the parts. He continued the chanting, almost as if in prayer, as he assembled the object.

"Therefore, put on the full armor of God, so that when the day of evil comes, you may be able to stand your ground, and after you have done everything, to stand. Stand firm then, with the belt of truth buckled around your waist..." Paul's hands moved deftly, efficiently, and with reverence.

Within a few moments, he had assembled a massive double-bladed axe that had to weigh over a hundred pounds. Paul completed the construction and finished his prayer simultaneously. The coursing blue-white energy flared and engulfed the entire weapon in a blinding glow, and a surge of energy washed over me, making every hair on my body stand on end. Paul stood and spun the heavy weapon in his hands like a baton, forming a broad, glowing shield in front of him, and I had to block my eyes with my arm to keep from being blinded. I realized only I could see the energy, because as bright as I perceived the emanation to be, nothing in the drainage channel was illuminated. Peter did not flinch or even squint as he watched.

"You can see it, no?" Peter asked. "The scribes of our Order tell us that armor and axe were wielded by the Archangel Uriel himself when he destroyed the Sennacherib. We will need him to face the Thunder of God, don't you think?"

Paul stopped spinning the axe, its glow died down to a night-light-like intensity, and I dropped my arm.

"What was he saying?" I asked, curious about the chanting that I only caught in parts.

"He was reciting the Rites of Preparation," Peter replied. "As he dons the armor, he will recite the Litany of Defense, as will I. He and I are the last of our order that do so. They are traditional prayers for our Order as we prepare for battle, but the world has changed. The younger generation prefers to pray and prepare themselves in their own ways. Simon has his music, and Bartholomew has his yoga," he said, waving his hand nonchalantly toward them as he spoke. "As much as I prefer to remain traditional, God created us all to be different. But when the time comes, we will all pray the Litany of Battle together."

"I'll admit Paul and his armor are impressive," I said, "But how much longer until you guys are ready to go? Putting on plate mail takes almost an hour—"

"Our timing is not His timing," Peter replied like a pastor consoling one of his disappointed flock. "It will be *soon*, I am sure."

"What does that even mean?" I asked. "Two hours? Five? What?"

Peter shrugged, patted my shoulder again, then walked over to Paul.

Holy Bladed Glow Stick of God or not, I'd had enough.

Chapter 37

I grabbed my shield, pulled the Pelian Spear from the wall, and walked off into the pitch-black tunnel. The smell of decaying leaves in the cool, humid passage filled my nose as I splashed through puddles of stagnant water. I didn't stop to see if anyone was behind me, and I wouldn't have stopped if there had been. After the ambient light completely failed a few yards into the passageway, I pulled a flashlight from my vest and continued undaunted down into the catacombs. Alone.

I walked down the drainage tunnel for a few hundred yards, the small beam of my flashlight playing across the cement tunnel walls and their continuous coating of graffiti, until I felt and saw the wavy energy that formed the heavy glamour shielding the entrance to the actual catacombs that stretched for miles below. The light from my flashlight couldn't penetrate the glamour, so I could see only blackness beyond.

Despite the fact I hadn't used them much in recent years, the shield on my arm and the spear in my hand felt familiar and comforting, and I barely noticed their weight as I gripped them. I had faced death hundreds of times before. *It is who I am. Better me than someone else.*

Besides, I don't feel like dying today.

I dug into a pouch on my vest for the little brown bottle Ab had given me. I took two of the pills then walked through the glamour. On the other side of the barrier, the air was hot and fetid, and I was instantly aware of a discordance of soft noises, like the dull droning of a thousand conversations occurring at once. The sound was punctuated by everything from water drips to wind and random echoes, and once by a train rattling past a hundred feet overhead. The smell was strong and earthy, with just enough sulfur to sting my nose and make my eyes water slightly. The catacombs were natural formations, but thousands of years of use by all manner of creatures and beings had left the main passage worn and obvious. That was my path.

I secured my flashlight to the spear just in front of my hand with a short length of paracord. I choked up on the lengthy weapon to use it more efficiently to stab within the confines of the tunnels. It was decidedly not a weapon for close quarters, but on open ground, it would allow me to create a space around myself as I fought, and though I could use it against Ramiel only once, it would be a much more efficient projectile than any bullet. I would just have to pick my one shot wisely. At some point, I would probably abandon the spear, forgo the extra protection my shield afforded me, and instead use my swords while relying on the protection of my cuirass. And I still had my Glock and Sig if I needed them. Things would certainly get messy. I was counting on it.

Moving as quickly as I could while remaining quiet, I followed the path for less than ten minutes before finding the small cavern that contained the nexus point for the Telluric Energy that crisscrossed the Earth and formed a pathway of sorts. The energy within the space shimmered and glowed like the filament of a dying light bulb, but I was the only thing in the space. I'd expected sentries or guards at the least, but it was unprotected. And something about the nexus point was off. It was dying—*or being drained.*

I retraced my steps back to the first branch in the tunnel and saw two more within a few yards. There were dozens of passageways, and I had no way of knowing which to take. I walked to the first fork, knelt, and remained very still as I strained to listen for anything that might indicate activity. Hearing nothing, I moved to the next and repeated the process until I came to an opening where the conversation-like sounds were louder and more distinctive. I examined the ground for footprints or signs of recent activity, but the rocky surface revealed nothing. Heading down the shaft, I began to notice the temperature increase and the smell change from earthy to acrid.

The sulfurous odor that stung my eyes and nose began to take on a sour taste, like spoiled meat. The temperature continued to increase, and before long, I began to sweat. I passed several forking tunnels, but each offshoot was cooler and smelled less foul. Choosing my path based on the smell and temperature, I continued on for the better part of an hour before the conversation-like sound began to increase in volume and change to a throbbing vibration. The hum continued to increase in intensity the farther I travelled, and I began to hear random high-pitched shrieks mixed in. The sounds were bestial and guttural, and they made my skin crawl with each occurrence. The cries were so feral that they might have been ripped from the creatures making them, and my thoughts instantly shifted to Sarah. I began moving faster despite the possibility of bad air the deeper I travelled.

The passage jogged left, right, rose, and fell any number of times and seemed to go on forever. Then it straightened out and climbed steadily as light flooded in from ahead. Within the incessant humming, I could now distinguish grunts and groans while the screeches bored into my skull like a high-speed drill, simultaneously setting my teeth on edge and freaking me out. I had never heard sounds like that before.

The closer I got to the end of the passageway, the more apprehensive I became. It was a sensation I wasn't used to, and I didn't like it.

Maybe I rushed into this. The last time I had faced Ramiel, he had nearly killed me. Now, besides him, I didn't even know what else I was facing. *Fuck it. There's no way I'm leaving Sarah to face whatever is in there alone. She trusted me to protect her.* I pulled the flashlight loose from the spear's shaft, rolled my shoulders, and walked to the end of the tunnel.

Intense heat hit me like a speeding truck, and I instinctively raised my shield to cover my face for a moment. The tunnel let me out onto a narrow rock ledge that overlooked a massive domed cavern. A spike of blinding-white energy extended straight down from the center of the dome like a bolt of lightning. It had to be energy siphoned from the nexus point from the caverns above us.

The ledge encircled the cavern part of the way around then gave way to carved steps that descended to the floor some thirty feet below. In the center of the cavern floor was an enormous pit of blue-white fire nearly twenty feet across, encircled by a glowing pentagram and sigils carved into the floor. The cavern was easily a few thousand feet across, and from my vantage point, I saw no other entrances or exits.

Hundreds of living things writhed and moved below me, some on legs while others crawled, pulled, or pushed themselves along with various appendages or moved using a disturbing combination of their limbs. None were similar in form, and all were hideous and grotesque mockeries of human beings. Among the misshapen creatures, eight normal but giant humanoids that I guessed to be Bennephilim stood head and shoulders taller than everything else, including twenty other seemingly mundane figures, who were likely humans dressed in hooded black robes.

Off to the far side of the firepit, at the apex of one point of the pentagram, were two gracile and striking naked female forms—one blond and one with red hair. I recognized the blonde from her sanguine aura as Na'amah. She stood, rope in hand, at the head of a line of twelve bound humans, six male and six female—all naked and connected to each other by the rope around their waists. Their hands were tied behind them, but their feet were free. They all stared at the ground, unmoving. I didn't recognize the redhead with Na'amah, but she projected a greasy blue-gray aura that played off every living thing around her. I may not have known who she was, but she was a Moroi. Given her proximity to the primal succubus, she had to be Eisheth, their progenitor.

Around them stood twelve beings, six of whom emanated the same brownish aura as Na'amah, only less intense. The six had humanoid form, but they were thin with lanky arms and legs, a short body and large round heads with gaping toothy mouths. They were succubi and incubi in their true form. The other six resembled humans in every way except for the same parasitic aura as the redhead. *I interrupted a freakin' demonic family reunion of some kind.*

Almost every creature capable of standing was facing the being at the next point of the pentagram to Na'amah and Eisheth's right. What I saw there caused my stomach to churn and my skin to grow cold.

It was the embodiment of fear—the same unctuous, black, cold mass of energy I'd encountered in New Orleans nearly a hundred years before, only more coalesced and far larger in magnitude. At the center of the nebulous writhing mass, which spread over nearly a quarter of the space below, was the ghostly shape of a giant of a humanoid at least three times the height of the humans, his human-like features utterly handsome and inhumanly perfect. His extremities were lost in the miasma surrounding him, but his upper body was muscular.

He stood with his face upturned as if basking in the reverence of his followers. The conflict between the comely countenance and the horrific murk disturbed me to my very core. I couldn't tear my eyes away from his visage until something next to him drew my attention to a laser-like focus.

There, to his right, on some sort of rock altar, was Sarah—naked and tied tightly hand and foot. She was also unconscious. My heart pounded, my breathing became shallow, and for a moment, I couldn't think or even move. I was witnessing everything I had been terrified would happen to her.

Suddenly, a high-pitched, piercing wail erupted from one of the misshapen forms below me, snapping me back to attention. The creatures emitted the humming noise, which sounded like a vast hive of bees. Though I had never encountered one before, they had to be limbo demons, the low-level, barely sentient minions most often summoned and controlled by stronger ones. Not necessarily evil or particularly strong, they took on the personality and strengths of whatever controlled them. And they needed a human host as a conduit for entering our realm. I was staring out over the result of hundreds of human sacrifices. My blood ran cold.

The only sources of significant power other than the bolt of energy from the Nexus came from Na'amah, Eisheth, their minions, and the monstrosity that had to be Ramiel. The limbo demons produced almost no auras at all, and every being in the cavern focused on or reached for the towering figure of Ramiel.

I had no idea what exactly was happening, but I had to act before they sacrificed another one of the humans. Throwing my arms out wide, I howled with all the pent-up fear and building rage inside me. The bellow echoed into a thunderous cry that drowned out every other sound within the cavern. My reputation as the Lord of the War Cry was well founded. Every eye—even Ramiel's—focused on me, and the incessant humming stopped abruptly.

"Sorry to interrupt the party, but the only way out of this rathole is *through* me," I said, my voice thundering, as I gazed across the myriad of misshapen and human faces staring up at me.

"My my, Diomedes," Na'amah said. "You aren't even going to give us an ultimatum for the healthy release of Agent Wright?"

"You think Sarah being alive or dead will change my intentions for you? Any of you?" I replied at the top of my lungs. "But you make a point. I tell you what. Let all the humans go—especially

Sarah—alive and well. If you harm any of them at all, so much as a single stubbed toe, I swear to you that I will devote the rest of my immortal life hunting down and killing every last wretched offspring in your vile lineages."

"How dramatic," she said. "Your ego is indeed impressive. Either that, or you're too stupid to realize your immortal life is almost over."

"How many times do you think I've heard that in the past three thousand years?" I asked.

"And how many times do you think I have been threatened in my existence, boy?"

"First time by me." I jumped down into the mass of misshapen demons below.

I landed hard on several demons, crushing one and ramming my spear through the chest of another. Withdrawing the spear from the body, I raised my shield and began pushing straight into the horde between me and Ramiel as fast as I could move, stabbing and bashing anything that got into my way.

Within seconds, I could feel a slight buzzing in my head. I continued fighting forward through the throng of demons as the buzzing increased and began to become comprehensible as speech.

"It has been some time, has it not?" the voice in my head asked. I didn't hear it as much as feel it resonate inside my skull. I didn't respond, because conversations with demons rarely ended well.

I spun the Pelian Spear's blade in a wide arc, slashing several creatures with each pass while creating as much space for myself as I could. I used my momentum, driving the edge of my shield into any demons that skittered close enough, severing limbs and cracking bones.

"You and the so-called messiah's knights could not defeat me on our last encounter," the voice boomed in my head. "And you are too late to stop me this time, for it has already begun. I will release my brethren as the Light Bringer finishes its journey, and your world will once again be *our* world. Cease your futile efforts and exult in our re-birth."

I glanced up to see how far I had made it, and a second wave of limbo demons swarmed over me. I was still not even halfway to Ramiel, and I was starting to feel my efforts. I could feel the sharp rake of claws or fangs bite into the flesh around my calves, thighs, and arms, but I kept stabbing and swinging the spear, hacking and smashing anything close enough to hit with my shield, but I was quickly becoming overwhelmed.

Rather than advancing, I was focused on merely trying to hold my ground. The limbo demons began attacking in such heavy numbers that I couldn't keep up even as fast as I was. They weren't particularly tough or strong, but there were far too many of them. Several of them hammered me from behind, knocking me momentarily to one knee, and a demon raked my hand, almost causing me to drop the spear. My eyes travelled up to the inky-black pall that surrounded Ramiel, and he seemed a thousand miles away. *I'll never make it.*

Then I began to feel an upwelling of energy building in my chest and limbs. Several of the demons around me collapsed, and a growing chant echoed through the chamber.

"He shields all who take refuge in him," said a voice that began to increase in intensity within the cavern.

"Protect us, O God," a host of voices answered in unison.

"With your help, I can advance against a troop."

"We will not fear."

"You have armed me with strength for battle."

"We fight in your holy name."

"So great is your power that your enemies cringe before you."

"Your enemies will fall before us in your name."

My eyes rose to the entrance above, and the activity around me ceased almost instantly as the terrified limbo demons backed off. I pushed myself back to my feet, using the spear as a crutch, and watched as a plate-mail-clad figure emerged carrying a massive axe. Immense glowing, gossamer-like wings spread to his sides, radiant as the energy from the nexus in the center of the room, and his voice carried clearly over the din around me. Brother Justicar Paul stood at the edge of the pathway as the other Justicars and novices filed in around him, and their singular chant continued undaunted and increased in volume. Paul led, and the rest responded.

"We will pursue your enemies and destroy them."

"They will fall beneath our feet."

"As smoke is blown away by the wind, may you blow them away."

"We will be your wind."

"As wax melts before the fire, may the wicked perish before God."

"We will be your fire. He trains my hands for battle."

"We are your weapons. You will crush the heads of your enemies."

"We are your mailed fist."

"Amen!" Justicar Brother Paul slammed the pommel of his giant axe, *Vayichar Af Hashem,* on the ground.

For the briefest of moments, a towering white-winged figure stood where Paul had been. Its enormous wings beat a single time, and a wave of pure white flame erupted and washed over the space. I slammed the Pelian Spear into the rock floor and held fast as the conflagration washed past me, leaving me unharmed. Dozens of limbo demons around me fell where they stood. The flame instantly obliterated many others, while untold scores of them tumbled across the chamber like dry leaves on a windy day.

But hundreds remained standing, along with Na'amah, Eisheth, their followers, the Bennephilim, and every human minion and prisoner. At the center of it all, Ramiel began to gather his dark energy around himself like armor.

Justicar Brothers Simon, John, Bartholomew, and Peter began running down the pathway to join the fray. They were all dressed like knights of the First Crusade: chainmail hauberks, skirts, and coifs covered by a white tunic with a red cross emblazoned across the chest. Bart and Peter wore great helms and plate coverings over their arms. Simon had chosen to forego head coverings completely, and Joanie wore her coif pushed back. Peter and Bart both wielded bardiches, while Simon used a claymore. Joanie carried a pair of single-handed axes. The four novices remained on the ledge above. Wearing armor similar to the knights', they were armed with two longbows and two modern crossbows.

Paul, bringing up the rear, charged down the inclined path far more nimbly than I would have expected for someone wearing something like full jousting armor that had to weigh over a hundred pounds. At the bottom of the path, the limbo demons scrambled and scattered like cockroaches in the light as the Justicars waded into them. From the far side of the space, the giant Bennephilim charged toward the Justicars, followed by the robed humans. The vampires and succubi remained on the far side of the fiery pit from me, along with Na'amah and Eisheth.

I debated for a moment about attacking them—until I remembered Sarah. I spun around, trying to locate her on the altar next to Ramiel, who was stamping, albeit quickly, through the crowd of cowering and retreating demons, parting them and brushing them violently aside using the darkness that surrounded him like a snowplow. *This is my chance.*

I began to run toward the last place I'd seen Sarah. Before I made it more than a few yards, four figures rushed at me from either side of the blazing pit—two Moroi and two succubi. Building speed, I shifted my grasp on the spear from a stabbing grip to a throwing one and launched it at the farthest of the parasitic quartet, impaling the Moroi in the upper chest as the spear passed straight through. The creature stumbled and fell, but I knew it was far from dead. As the spear left my hand, I spun and threw the shield like a discus at the closest of the group in a move that would have made Captain America jealous. It hit a succubus in her torso and nearly cut the creature in half as it shattered her chest. In the next step, I drew both swords and continued my charge.

The remaining Moroi and incubus split up, and I targeted the Moroi, a male. We closed at frightening speed, and just as I readied my attack, the incubus tackled me from my right, sending us both careening off into a crowd of retreating demons. The incubus screeched as two arrows hit it solidly in the flank, and it reared up, flailing its lanky arms. I drove both swords through its stunted ribcage then used them like a pair of scissors to cut the incubus in half. The legs fell away, writhing and twitching, and I shoved the upper body away as I got to my feet. Far from dead, the upper body kept clawing and grasping at me. I kicked at its face with my heel then severed one of its arms above the elbow and rammed the other sword through the top of its head, causing its giant yellow eyes to roll over to black as it started to gurgle. I jerked the sword free and searched the crowd for the Moroi. I was under no illusion that the incubus at my feet was dead, but severely injured would have to do.

Behind me, the five Justicars of the Holy Order went toe to toe with an ancient and primordial demon of immense power—light against dark. Seeing Ramiel's spectral black veil spread into dozens of tendrils and attack the knights brought back the memories of that night in the small park in New Orleans all those years ago. Visions of Francis's face frozen in fear and dread caused me to rage as I watched the tendrils hammer at the knights, lighting up the cavern with showers of white sparks as they met the barrage. To a knight, everyone attacked ceaselessly, refusing to give up even an inch of ground, but failing to gain any momentum, either.

For now, it was their fight, though. I had to find Sarah. I began running, hacking and slashing my way through the limbo demons, back in the direction of the altar.

One of the Bennephilim pushed her way through the demons to face me. Carrying a slightly-larger-than-normal buckler in one hand, she began whipping a two-headed flail around with the other. Both of the spiked heads attached to the baseball-bat-like handle were the size of cantaloupes on chains nearly a yard long. With that weapon, her reach was nearly twice mine.

Dirty pool or not, I quickly threw one sword down to stick into the stone floor, pulled the Glock from my hip, and fired off five quick rounds into her center mass. Each round struck with a dull thwap, hitting some sort of ballistic armor, but even given her size and protection, at close range, five rounds to the chest from a forty-five was devastating. She staggered as the impact drove the air from her lungs. As her arms went limp at her sides, the heavy flail smashed into several limbo demons, which, in turn, jerked the weapon from her flaccid hand. The massive woman rocked slightly and blinked heavily as she tried to catch her breath. I fired three more times into her head, and she fell to her knees then slumped to one side. The report of the weapon echoed through the chamber, drawing all attention to me. At least they knew I was a threat at a distance, too. I holstered the weapon, grabbed my sword, and continued working my way toward the altar.

I could now tell exactly where the altar was because, unfortunately, four Moroi surrounded it while a fifth one stood on it, holding Sarah's limp body with a gun to her head. One of the leeches had a gaping wound in its chest from the Pelian Spear, though it didn't act much the worse for wear. The parasite holding Sarah was a young man who probably had been in his early twenties when turned, and his sneer suggested he liked causing pain. *I wonder how much he likes being on the receiving end.*

Because there was no way I was fast enough to reach him before he pulled the trigger, my only option was to get as close as possible by faking acquiescence. I put away my swords, held up my hands, and slowly walked toward them.

"Not a chance, Boy Scout," the sadistic leech said. "Guns down on the ground and then swords. Slowly, or your girl dies, and we have to find a new vessel." He made an overly dramatic pouty face then wiggled his gun at me to prompt my divestment of weapons.

No way was I giving up my weapons. I kept moving forward as I made a show of slowly reaching for the Sig in the cross-draw holster in my vest. I kept the other hand raised, but only slightly. I was waiting for a momentary lapse on his part—anything that might allow me to act quickly enough to separate him from Sarah. He began to shake his head, then a screaming whistle split the air behind me, travelling just over my head, causing me to flinch slightly as an arrow hit the stone altar a few inches to the left of the hostage taker then ricocheted off harmlessly. The sound and the arrow caused the sadist to jerk to one side and drop Sarah enough to expose his chest and lower his gun. I drew the Sig, put three rounds into his upper chest, then put two more into the face of the closest vampire before the wounded one hit me with a roundhouse punch to the head.

In slow motion, I reeled and watched the sadist lurch back, let go of Sarah, then fall off the altar backward, while the other vampire I'd shot fell straight to the ground. The force of the blow to my head knocked me off balance, and I doubled over but managed to keep my feet under me. Holey Chest raised both hands together high overhead in an attempt to bring them down in a crushing blow, but I managed to fire the gun in a snap shot from under my left arm—fortunately hitting him at least twice before he could connect. The impacts knocked him backward and gave me enough time to regain my stance and empty the magazine into his upper body and head from a few feet away.

I ejected the spent mag, slammed in a new one, and turned my attention to the two vampires who were still left. To my surprise, one of them was wrestling with an arrow protruding from his face just under his left eye, while the other was gone. The vampire I'd shot in the face was clumsily getting back to his feet with half of his face still a yawning bloody ruin, so I put three more rounds into his head from less than a yard away then three more into his chest before kicking him away. I jumped up onto the altar next to Sarah. She was lying in a limp heap right where she'd fallen. Horrified by the thought of what I would see, I bent down to check on her. Something grabbed my ankles and jerked my feet out from under me.

My gun went skittering off, and I twisted over, trying to see my attacker. It was the sadist. I wrestled and kicked my legs, freeing one from his grip, then began to kick at his already-damaged head. I scrambled to pull one sword free, sat up, and thrust it at his head, stabbing him through the nose. His body instantly went rigid. I jerked my leg free, pulled my other sword as I got to one knee, and brought the blade down on his head with a satisfying blow that cut his head apart from his temple to his jaw. I pulled the sword from his face, and the body fell to the ground.

Sarah was still breathing but completely unresponsive. There was no residue of magic causing her syncope, so it could have been caused by trauma or even drugs, both of which worried me. They'd said they needed her body, but I didn't know if that included her mind as well. I put down my swords and began to lift her, but there was no safe place to put her within the cavern, and I couldn't leave the knights to fight on their own. Contemplating my limited options, I realized only four knights were still fighting Ramiel, and they had lost ground. Bart was nowhere to be seen, and Simon's and Joan's attacks were slowing considerably. Only Peter and Paul continued to attack with any force, though each of Paul's blows had a noticeable effect on the fallen one. Still, they needed my help and fast.

Three novices on the ledge above were still firing arrows around the chamber at random targets, but sudden movement on the rocky path down to the other knights caught my eye. Nearing the bottom, Jonesy was running at full speed to join the fight, broadsword in hand, and again, I had flashes of Francis staring blankly up at me, his clawlike hands rigid near his chest.

Instantly, a black tendril shot out from Ramiel's flank, crossed the expanse between us in the blink of an eye, and hit me square in the chest like a freight train, sending me flying backward through the air.

I didn't feel myself hit the ground. Instead, I was back in the park in the Lower Ninth Ward, watching Francis become trapped in his horror as Ramiel the Axeman killed a Knight of the Order. I felt cold and alone, helpless, useless, and weak all at once. *I was afraid.* Not for myself but that I would fail to protect those who counted on me—whether they knew I existed or not. I saw Francis's face and the faces of a thousand comrades in arms as they died. I watched in horror as the faces melted and warped into twisted masks of pain and dread. Each one's anguish and torment washed over me like an icy river.

Then I saw Sarah's face. "It's not your fault," she said as plainly as if she were standing in front of me anywhere else in the world. I shook my head and squeezed my eyes shut.

When I opened them again, I was back in the cavern. Peter landed a savage blow with his bardiche, throwing white sparks as high as the cavern's ceiling several hundred feet overhead, and Ramiel fell back ever so slightly. Just as Paul reared back to press the attack further, a winglike appendage made from the void that surrounded Ramiel coalesced and swung down on the heavily armored knight like a Mack truck falling from the sky. Paul caught the impact on the giant axe, which flashed so brightly that I had to shield my eyes for a second, but it forced him down to one knee. Jonesy waded in behind them, deftly ducking and parrying the attacks of several large extensions of Ramiel's void before I lost sight of him along the demon's other flank.

I got up, smashed into and through several limbo demons while running to the altar, grabbed my swords from where they lay next to Sarah, and charged at Ramiel's flank. I closed in from the rear, where I saw Jonesy standing over Bart, protecting the fallen knight as a mass of black energy pounded at him. To my surprise, he parried every blow with an inhuman speed and dexterity, but he was clearly on the defensive and could not mount an attack. Bart was scooting away slowly on his butt, dragging a twisted leg and cradling an injured arm across his chest. I headed right for them and arrived just in time to deflect a flanking blow that Jonesy didn't see coming.

"Jonesy!" I screamed over the din of battle. "Get Bart to safety and then get the other novices down here and get any people the hell out of here. *Now!*"

Sweating profusely, Jonesy's face was fixed with determination. Clearly exhausted, he was far from willing to give up. He took a deep breath and nodded as I took his place in the fray, and I blocked another attack directed at him as he moved to help his fallen master.

I began to attack as fast as I could swing, trying to move and change directions, hoping to push Ramiel off balance. It made no difference, though. The entity had no issues defending itself and attacking on all fronts simultaneously. For the moment, however, my erratic movements did keep Ramiel on the defensive. After a few more moments, I began to notice that my blades were not doing any serious damage. I was simply expending energy—rapidly. Somehow, we had to get through his void-armor and attack *him* directly.

I fought through a forest of striking limb-like bolts of energy around the Watcher, making my way toward the remaining knights. Flashes of black and white lit the cavern, and I wondered if the clash of energies was visible to all or just an artefact of Athena's gifts to me. I could only imagine how frightening the image of a demon fighting the power of God would be. Rolling under a wave of blackness, I came to my feet just in time to see another thick appendage of void bear down on Joanie as she dragged the listless body of Simon away from the melee. I charged forward to hit the limb with my forearms braced across my head in an effort to redirect it enough to allow her to escape. It was like hitting an icy wall, but I refused to go down. I kept my feet churning, and it began to move. I loosed one arm and began hacking wildly at the appendage until it simply resorbed back into the miasma surrounding Ramiel.

"Help the novices clear the place of any remaining people," I shouted over my shoulder to Joanie as I blocked another attack from a tendril of energy the size of a telephone pole.

An epic explosion of black energy flooded the space, sending us into darkness for a second before the burning-white energy of the remaining two knights pushed it back. In the blink of an eye, numerous tendrils shot out at Peter from all directions. Paul landed a vicious blow to a briefly undefended spot with his glowing axe, causing Ramiel to screech so loudly that the pain in my head doubled me over as I pressed my fists to my ears to dampen it. Ramiel staggered back, and the attacks ceased just long enough for me to glance over and see Peter skidding like a ragdoll across the stone cavern floor until he came to a rest in a heap. Paul stopped to watch, distracted just enough for Ramiel to hammer the heavily armored knight with a wave of black energy the size of a truck. The glowing white energy was gone from the room—all of it—as the void swallowed Paul. His giant axe flew up and back then embedded itself in the cavern wall halfway up the stairway to the exit above.

I stopped thinking—stunned by what I was witnessing—but my body refused to stop moving. When my brain kicked back in, I found myself weaponless and running up the pathway toward the embedded axe. I could feel a buzzing inside my head as I ran. By the time I reached the weapon and pulled it free from the wall, the buzzing was intelligible as speech.

"The Savior's knights are defeated, child," Ramiel's voice said, causing every nerve ending in my body to fire at once. "If they could not best me, what makes you think you alone can do so? Rest and bear witness to the rulers that humanity truly desires. When your race was young, we were the ones that showed you how to harness this world's energy." As he spoke, the void around him began to fade, revealing the beautiful manlike creature within. "My brethren and I taught you the signs of the earth, how to read the skies, and about the celestial bodies above. *We* loved your race, and we were punished for it, but we will once again be among you. And you will love us once more. Come. Lay down your arms, child. Fighting me is useless. After all, *we* revealed to you your belligerent spirit. We showed you how to make weapons and how to war. *We* are responsible for who *you* are, Diomedes. Join us. We have so much more to teach you. All we ask is your fealty. Offer yourself as host for one of my brethren, and you will know real power."

"What about free will?" I asked, trying to catch my breath and regain some semblance of control. "What if I don't want to? What if others don't want to?"

"Free will is an illusion, child," Ramiel replied. "Your kind are most secure when you are *told* what to do. It is your nature to submit. It gives your short lives purpose and meaning."

"Well, then consider this me being insecure." I jumped off the staircase at Ramiel, stretching the axe high over my head.

Time slowed to a standstill. Ramiel roared and threw his arms wide as the cloak of darkness enveloped him once again, and I began to fall. I fell into a void. It was cold and dark, and I was alone, suspended. The cold penetrated to my very core, and a sensation like thousands of blades cutting me apart from the inside ripped through my body. Something was attacking me, but not physically. Something was ripping my mind open. Thoughts and memories flooded out, some of which I had long forgotten or repressed. Battles, loves, friends, tragedies, lies, betrayals—everything all at once.

"I see your life in all its misery, but I do not see fear, child." Ramiel's voice split my psyche like a cleaver. "Oh, but wait—"

The cold became more intense, and the pain in my head became more acute. I could focus on nothing but the images of my life that flowed from my mind unchecked—everything all at once. It felt like I was a thousand feet underwater and running out of air. I began to panic.

"Ah, there is fear in you. An exquisite dread. It is not like the mortals you try to protect, though, is it? They fear everything, don't they? But your fear is focused: failure."

Pain shot through my entire being as if someone had twisted a hot knife in my skull.

"You fear it so completely that you drive yourself beyond limits to avoid it. It consumes you and forms your very core. Oh, to have everything focused to the point of a needle—when the needle pricks, its wound is annihilating. And I will show it to you."

Ramiel laughed. It was deep and resonant, and I could feel it through every nerve in my body. I saw a vivid image of Sarah's limp body, and it gave way to thousands of broken and mangled bodies scattered across fields and streets under a deep-purple sky. People smashed and hacked at each other, and blood soaked the ground under them. I tried to scream in protest, but I had no air in my lungs to expel. Ramiel's laugh became more resonant through my body. I was unable to gather myself or focus my thoughts. All I could do was feel the despair and horror of thousands of people magnified through the lens of my own hopelessness. I wanted to give up.

I *wanted* to give up. But I couldn't. Something even more primal and primitive inside me refused to give in. The laughing stopped abruptly, the cold began to abate, and I gasped for breath as if I'd just reached the surface of the water. I filled my lungs and screamed. I began to feel a tightness in my hands and realized I was still gripping *Vayichar Af Hashem.* Suddenly, I could see into the void as the giant axe began to glow in my hands.

"Why fight *for* them, Diomedes Tydides?" Ramiel asked. "They don't even know your name. Those who do know you from an ancient storybook. You were a king. You were meant to be a ruler *over* them. Join us. Help us, and you shall take your rightful place *above* them. They will love and honor you as you deserve."

Ramiel's voice had changed. It was more urgent, maybe desperate. I could feel my grip strengthen around the axe, and I began to see the vague outlines of a humanoid shape take form at the edges of the void.

"No. I do what I do *for* them." I wasn't sure if I'd said it or just formed the words in my mind, but I began to regain the focus of my feelings. "I belong among them, *with* them. I fight for them so that they can live. That is who I am."

"You would die protecting them?" Ramiel asked, confusion and a lack of understanding evident in his question.

"Yeah," I said, hearing my voice loud and clear within the void. "But to be honest, I'd prefer to kick the shit out of any threat to them instead."

I found myself falling for a moment until my feet struck something solid. Then I stood face to face with Ramiel. He was beautiful, perfect in every way—and nearly twice my height. Enormous, striking black feathered wings stretched out from both shoulders. He had piercing blue eyes and long black hair, and he held no weapons, wore no armor.

Vayichar Af Hashem weighed nothing in my hands and glowed the way it had when Paul carried it. Ramiel eyed the weapon and me then took the slightest step back. I had become a threat to him and his plan.

"Now who's afraid?" I asked, sneering.

Ramiel laughed, only it was hollow and almost human in its contempt. In the blink of an eye, the two coal-black wings lashed out at me, each black feather like the blade of a sword. I rolled to my right and blocked one feathered appendage with the pommel of the axe, eliciting a howl as it met the glowing weapon. The other wing grazed my chest, hip, and thigh. My cuirass protected my chest, but the feathers sliced deep into my hip and leg, dropping me to one knee. The cuts were so clean that they hadn't begun to bleed yet, but I knew that the moment I moved, the wounds would open.

Again, the wings came at me—one as if to spear while the other slashed toward my legs. I spun on one knee so that the one wing would catch me mostly in my cuirass while I brought the axe down on the slashing wing. The axe connected and cut through the limb as if it was made of tissue paper, but the impact of the other wing on my cuirass sent me reeling and skidding. Along with the blow, I felt several sharp jabs under my left arm and along my shoulder, but I managed to hang on to the axe. An ear-shattering howl split the air, and I pushed myself up to see Ramiel hunched over, protecting his left flank and the injured wing.

Even with one wing gone, the reach of the remaining limb could easily keep me far enough away that I could never attack Ramiel unless I was close. I had to get inside the wing's range. While Ramiel recovered, I pushed to my feet and ran at him, keeping the axe low, intending to deliver an uppercut. I moved slowly at first, but I picked up momentum quickly. Ramiel moved to block the blow with his remaining wing, catching the blade between feathers. For a moment, we were locked in a stalemate, but the longer we stayed connected, the brighter the axe glowed. Ramiel finally screeched and spun away. I pursued, keeping the axe ready for any opportunity to swing it. At first, Ramiel was reluctant to attack, but he moved and dodged so quickly that he left me virtually no openings for a solid attack.

With each feint or swing of the big axe, the wounds in my shoulder and side began to ache more and more, and I could feel a burning sting in my leg from the cuts as the blood began to flow freely. I was injured and tiring fast, and the fallen angel knew it. He was biding his time.

The wing slammed down on me, and I had just enough time to block it with the axe. I was on the defensive, struggling to move fast enough with my waning strength to parry the wing. Each time the black-feathered wing touched the axe, however, it glowed brightly and Ramiel jerked back. After a few moments, his attacks stopped as he eyed me.

With no other options, I went back on the offensive while I still could, desperate to find an opening. My attacks quickly became slower and weaker. Ramiel sensed my failing strength. He lashed out at me with his remaining wing, and I managed to dodge the blow, but my injured leg buckled beneath me. Ramiel grabbed my vest with both hands and lifted me off the ground. Blood flowed down my arm, making my hand and its leather coverings slick, and it took all my strength to hold on to the giant axe, but I couldn't have swung it if I'd wanted. I was spent and bleeding badly. If he didn't kill me right away, I would bleed out before long anyway. Barring a miracle, I was done. *But there has to be a way to take the bastard with me. Or at least piss him off before I go.*

Ramiel drew me close to his face. Once beautiful, it was twisted with rage and pain, transforming into the true monster the fallen angel was. His icy-blue eyes burned with hatred and anger, and in my periphery, I could see his remaining wing stretch out beside him, ready to run me through. Just as I contemplated kicking him in the groin in hopes that the move *might* be effective on an angel, he went rigid, and his face changed. His eyes tracked erratically upward, and he stared off beyond me, his brow knitted. His jaw fell slack, and he glanced around as if searching for something before glaring at me blankly for a moment. Then he lowered me slightly as he staggered. A brilliant blue-white light began glowing in his chest just in front of me as the heavy curved blade of a bardiche erupted through it.

Ramiel let me go, and I managed to catch myself on my good leg to avoid falling. Instantly, the cold, shadowy void around us evaporated, revealing the entirety of the cavern once again. Ramiel threw his head back and roared loudly enough to shake the entire cavern as his arms weakly fell to his sides. I raised the giant axe with all my remaining strength and buried it in the Watcher's neck as he began to sag. The explosion that followed threw me across the cavern, but I was too weak to try to control my landing or to even care. I saw a blinding light then hit a wall.

Chapter 38

I sensed vague recollections of hazy faces, bright lights, occasional jostling, then nothing. Then I felt like I was awake but alone, enveloped in Ramiel's void again. I couldn't move or view my surroundings, but there was no way to see in the darkness anyway. The only difference from before was the temperature—I wasn't cold. Weary but unable to move or do anything with my body, I tried to just give in and rest, but I couldn't. The instant I closed my eyes, I began to hear voices. Indistinct and more whispers than full speech, it sounded at first like dozens of people speaking over each other, but it began to change. As the number of speakers decreased, the volume and clarity increased.

"Diomedes," said a distinct and audible female voice. *Sarah.*

I tried to answer but couldn't. I didn't know if I didn't have air in my lungs or just couldn't move my mouth, but I began to panic. I wanted to struggle, but there was no way even to fight what was holding me still. I couldn't take a breath, but I didn't need to.

"The battle is over, soldier," Sarah said. "Time to rest now."

What does she mean? Am I dead? Does that mean she's dead, too?

Then I took a deep breath, and suddenly, I could feel my arms and legs move, though it took effort, as if they were being restrained. And it *hurt.* Everything *hurt.* A lot. I forced my eyes open to see painfully bright lights and the shadowy images of people rushing around me. I could hear an incessant beeping noise and excited, uptight voices from all directions.

And then fingers snapped in front of me.

"Mister? Hey, mister, are you with me?" a woman's voice said as I tried to focus my eyes past the bright lights to a shadowy face in front of me. "We need you to relax, okay? You're badly hurt, and you've already hurt a lot of people who are just trying to help you. Just relax."

"Diomedes, calm down," said a familiar male voice from somewhere to my right.

I tried to move my head, but something was stopping me.

"You're in a hospital, my friend."

"Peter?" I asked, finally able to focus a bit. "Get that fucking light out of my face." I tried to sit up, but the pain in my arms, back, and legs stopped me short. Pain was good. It meant I was alive and not paralyzed.

"Get him to calm down, now, Brother Justicar, please," the woman said. "We can't control him."

"Yes, I'm here, Diomedes," Peter said. "These people are just trying to help you. No one means you any harm."

I relaxed, and I could hear everyone around me exhale heavily. Someone moved the light above my head so it wasn't directly in my eyes. A moment later, I could see a bit better, and I could feel people let go of me.

"You are at a facility that the Order uses, so you are safe, Diomedes. Trust me," Peter said.

I was definitely in some sort of hospital room—stark white walls and light-brown wood furniture set up to be more functional than aesthetic. And it stank like a cross between vomit, diarrhea, and industrial cleaning supplies. I discovered that I had a neck brace on, and with a considerable effort and not a small amount of pain, I was able to roll to my right to see Peter. He was laid up in the bed next to me with his leg in traction.

"Where's Sarah?" I rolled back to a more comfortable position.

It took him a few minutes to respond. "She is alive and being cared for. Get some rest, and I will tell you more later."

Before I could say anything in response, Jonesy walked into the room. Slightly battered and bruised around the face, he was all smiles. For some reason, I found his attitude infectious and was glad to see the kid had survived largely unscathed.

"Ah, and to what do we owe the pleasure of your company, Jonas?" Peter asked.

"I just wanted to check on you guys and let you know that Brother Justicar Paul is finally awake and that Joanie's surgery to mend her broken jaw went well and that she is fine, as well," the kid said. His accent sounded thicker, and it made me smile.

"What about Bart and Simon?" I asked, expecting the worst.

Jonesy just shook his head and averted his eyes. Then he crossed himself.

"I expect that means you'll be Justicar in no time," I said, trying to lighten the mood a bit.

"After the heroics he pulled with Ramiel, he'll likely take over my position as Grand Master," Peter said with a chuckle.

"Heroics?" I asked.

"After he and the other novices fought their way through the limbo demons to gather the intended sacrifices and get them to safety, he came back and helped Justicar John with Simon and Bartholomew and then came back again for Paul and then me," Peter said like a proud father. "Then he went back again to help you."

"God's will," Jonesy said, staring at the ground. "He should get the glory, not me. We lost two friends and good men taking that creature out. I was just glad I was there to help. Thankfully, God brought us Diomedes to bolster our ranks."

"Wait—Jonesy—the bardiche through Ramiel's back—that was you? Holy..." Both of them averted their eyes as I said it. "Sorry. Okay, yeah, *you*, I get, but I'm not sure *I* was part of God's plan," I said, trying hard not to roll my eyes as I said it. I was impressed with the kid. What he'd done had taken the kind of guts men win the Medal of Honor for, and he'd gone back for more.

The room got very quiet for a second—so quiet it was audible.

"Even after that, you still don't believe?" Peter asked.

"What? In Jonesy or God?" I replied, trying not to offend them. "Oh no, I have no doubt he's real. I've seen what he does through you guys, and I once witnessed the power of your Christ."

"But knowing and believing are two different things, Diomedes," Peter replied. "You *know* he exists—just as you *know* humanity is not alone on this planet. Believing is an act of faith, done with your heart despite what your head says."

"Maybe, but I have been around long enough to see many different gods come and go, and I know what they truly are—otherworldly beings of far greater power than us. Most of them like to screw with us, but fortunately, your God is benevolent. Others of his kind have not been as nice."

Peter laughed. "There are no others of his kind. And do you really *not* think you do his good work just like we do?"

"I work with the Protogenoi who once called herself Athena. Not God."

They both laughed.

"Has it ever occurred to you that your Athena is simply the aspect of God that he believed you'd be most comfortable with—the one you'd identify with most—a being of honor, intelligence, diligence, faithfulness?" Peter said, his tone soft but serious. "Believe me when I say he is capable of showing himself exactly as he wishes to inspire the best in each of us if we will only see it. At the very least, he is powerful enough to use anyone he wants to achieve his will." Peter chuckled again.

"From what I witnessed," Jonesy said, "it is clear that even if you don't believe in him, he believes in you."

"You do his work, Diomedes, whether you know it or not," Peter said. "If you would like more proof, then recount our battle with Ramiel. The only way to defeat a demon—truly defeat it—is through grace, truth, and service. You show grace through your service and devotion to humanity. You reveal the truth in the very nature of the creatures and monsters you battle. You can see them for what they truly are, can you not? And you never fail to respond to a threat and do not fear death in doing so. *That* is God working through you."

"You guys are giving me a headache," I replied, exhaling and trying to relax. "You're overthinking it. I do what I do because it's the right thing to do and because I can—better me than someone else. But in the end, just because I fight against monsters, it doesn't mean I'm not one."

"I disagree," Jonesy said, his face stoic and serious.

"Where's Sarah?" I asked again, desperate to change the subject.

"She's at a... different facility," Peter said.

"Where?"

Peter and Jonesy gave each other sideways glances for a few moments, but no one responded.

"I'll ask again—"

"Hart Island," Jonesy replied.

"That derelict prison out near Long Island Sound?" I asked. "Why is she there?"

"It only gives the impression of being abandoned, but that's the point," Peter said. "It's a unique facility for the Holy Order. Kind of a specialized hospital."

"Specialized? What do you mean? And where exactly are *we*?"

"*We* are in Pennsylvania. At the Sacred Heart Hospital in Allentown." He sighed. "Hart Island is for people damaged by an encounter with the demonic."

I didn't know what to say. I vividly remembered Francis Derringer's face frozen in horror and then Peter telling me they would take care of him and give him peace. I'd assumed that meant last rites, not locked up in a mental asylum and heavily medicated until he died of old age. I became furious.

"You mean to tell me you have her locked up in some sort of looney bin just because she's catatonic?" I said, practically spitting.

"No, not at all, Diomedes. That is not what we do at Hart Island," Peter replied. "It has medical capabilities, but it also houses our exorcists, demonologists, and archivists. Something happened to Sarah, but we don't know what. She's unresponsive, but we can find no medical reason for it. She doesn't exhibit any of the characteristics we normally associate with unprotected exposure to a demonic entity, but then we've only dealt with the effects of one of the Grigori once before. We are trying to help her as best we can. But it will take time, Diomedes."

"Once before," I replied. "You mean Francis Derringer."

"Yes," Peter said softly.

"Your namesake promised me they would send him on in peace," I said. "That's what they did, right? Tell me right now, they didn't make that kid live on, trapped in a mental prison, did they? I swear to you—"

"Absolutely not," Peter replied in a stern voice, holding up a hand to calm me down. "They brought him there and tried everything they could to mend his mind—his shattered psyche—but it became clear that the damage was beyond our understanding. He was given his last rites and sent on. But from what I understand, Sarah does not exhibit Francis's tetanized state or lack of brain activity, so our people are hopeful with modern technology, and no small measure of prayer, that we can help her recover."

I felt hollow. I didn't know what to say. *I failed to protect her. I promised her I would keep her safe, and I didn't.* I'd promised I would tear apart anyone or anything that hurt her. Then I thought about Na'amah, Eisheth, and Ramiel.

"What about Ramiel?" I asked, fighting back the rising bile in my throat. "Na'amah and Eisheth and their whole ritual to free the remaining Fallen from Tartarus?"

"As best we can tell, Ramiel is no more," Peter replied with a hint of something in his voice that might have been pride or perhaps relief. Maybe both. "The other two must have escaped us. We incinerated the succubi, incubi, and vampires we found that you had injured and chased down most of the limbo demons, though a few may have escaped us for now. We killed the Bennephilim that were present—not that they gave us much choice. All human souls were left alive, repentant or not. We do not act against humanity, no matter the circumstance."

"Yeah, well, that's where we're different," I said, pushing back into my pillow and staring at the fluorescent light overhead. "If they willingly stood against us, I would have ripped them apart without a second thought."

I began to think about my promise to Sarah, and something inside me broke. "I want to see her."

"Once you are healed, I promise we will take you," Peter said. "But for now, rest. I promise you she is getting the best care possible."

Chapter 39

Two weeks later, I was waiting for the nurse to bring the stupid wheelchair so I could leave. While I waited, the familiar buzzing in the back of my head and the hair standing on end on the back of my neck let me know Athena was close by. I'd had similar sensations several times since waking up, but she hadn't shown herself.

"Do not go down this road, Diomedes," she said in a friendly but parental tone as she emerged from the shadows of the darkened bathroom. She was dressed like I remembered her depicted in my youth—a shocking white toga, with her fiery hair up in a braid, held in place by a golden tiara, with an equally brilliant sash around her waist.

"What road? I'm in fucking Pennsylvania. I don't know any roads here."

"You know what I mean," she said. "Revenge, retribution, whatever you wish to call it. For Sarah."

Fortunately, the nurse came in pushing the wheelchair, and Athena vanished into the darkness.

Outside the hospital, the air was warm, and I had to shield my eyes from the bright early-summer sun as I sat and waited for a taxi. Just as a cab pulled up, a strange sensation overtook me and immediately made me push out of the wheelchair, sending it skidding into a bush behind me. The feeling was old but weak energy, unmistakably that of a Protogenoi. The sight of the wings on her back caused my heart to race, and my first instinct was to reach back and grab the wheelchair as a weapon, but before I could, she spoke.

"I am not what you think I am, Diomedes," she said in a soft, lilting voice. Like most Old Ones, she was beautiful, with high cheekbones, a slightly aquiline nose, jet-black hair, and eyes that matched. Her wings were dirty brown, and she was dressed just as Athena had been a few moments ago. Around her waist, she wore a long, thin dagger nearly the length of a short sword. "I am no angel, fallen or otherwise."

"Then who are you?" I asked, suddenly feeling more annoyed than concerned.

"I am Adrestia, but you might know me as Nemesis," she said seductively. She stepped closer and opened the car door. "And I was just wondering if we could share the cab."

Dear Reader,

We hope you enjoyed *Rebellion Reborn*, by Brian S. Leon. Please consider leaving a review on your favorite book site.

Visit our website (https://RedAdeptPublishing.com) to subscribe to the Red Adept Publishing Newsletter to be notified of future releases.

Also by Brian S. Leon

The Metis Files
Havoc Rising
Chaos Unbound
Rebellion Reborn

About the Author

Brian S. Leon is truly a jack-of-all-trades and a master of none. He began writing in order to do something with all the useless degrees, knowledge and skills--most of which have no practical application in civilized society--he accumulated over the years.

His varied interests include, most notably, mythology of all kinds and fishing, and he has spent time in jungles and museums all over the world studying and oceans and seas across the globe chasing fish, sometimes even catching them. He has also spent time in various locations around the world doing other things that may or may not have ever happened.

Inspired by stories of classical masters like Homer and Jules Verne, as well as modern writers like J.R.R. Tolkien, David Morrell, and Jim Butcher, combined with an inordinate amount of free time, Mr. Leon finally decided to come up with tales of his own.

Brian currently resides in San Diego, California. You can visit his Web site at www.BrianSLeon.com.

www.ingramcontent.com/pod-product-compliance
Lightning Source LLC
Chambersburg PA
CBHW030555170726
48283CB00002B/336